Pattie !
to get to ~~~~
you
Thanks !

PATTIE'S BEST DEAL

Dawn Dittmar

DAWN DITTMAR

I dedicate this book to my late husband Walter Dittmar, a dear, wonderful man who inspired me to be the best person I could be and who encouraged me to pursue my dreams.

ACKNOWLEDGMENTS

Writing a novel is an amazing experience. It is often a lonely endeavor, yet at the same time, it is such a huge project that no one can do it alone. I absolutely adore my special friends who encouraged me and generously gave me the gift of their unlimited help and support. Unfortunately, not everyone who started out with me on this journey is still here. Although those who have passed away may not be able to read this acknowledgment, here it is, memorialized in print, sealed with a kiss and blown across the veil with love and sincerity.

First and foremost, I want to thank my Higher Power, without whom nothing would ever have happened. May I ever be mindful of the fact that You have my back and that everything really does work out in the end.

To my late husband, Walter Dittmar, you were the heart and soul of this book since its very inception. Your constant love and support spurred my self confidence. May God his rest your soul.

To John Salvi, thank you for being an extremely important part of Pattie's Best Deal. Your amazing insights during my revision, your beautiful artwork "Leland's Door" which graces the cover, your support at the Round Table and above all, your friendship all mean a lot to me.

To Jackie Smith, you have been incredibly generous with your time, practical advice and talent as an editor and with your support at the Round Table. I have gained so much insight from you.

To William Duff, for your inspiration with the character of Ryan Pilgrim, your help with my computers and with your support at the Round Table.

To Laura Leonard, thank you for your sensitivity, constant encouragement and selfless emotional support. Your practical wisdom and insights served to make my life a lot easier and so did your efficient tips on many subjects, ranging from health to beauty and everything in between. Your presence during times of "overwhelm" saw me through many weeks of stormy post production.

To my feline children who kept me company during this endeavor, your patience, devotion, companionship and unconditional love while I wrote, revised and edited have meant more to me than anything!

To Denise Alfano Gspann, you gave me varieties of support, comfort, companionship wisdom and coffee during the post production of this book. Thank you.

To Bob Miller, you turned "Leland's Door" into a proper book cover. They say "we can't judge a book by its cover", but you and I know otherwise. Right?

To Jack Jupp, who like Walter, didn't live to see this book come to fruition, I am grateful for your encouragement and special insight with rats.

To Photographer Irene M. Zagorski, who captured my personality on the back-cover photo. Thank you! I absolutely love it.

To Leo De Faria, thank you for educating me on the difference between pellet guns, stun guns and tasers.

To Tara Curtis, thank you for your insight into the secret life of the South Street Seaport.

To Gilda Healy for your sympathy, good advice and support at the Round Table.

To Ariana Borges, who proved that it is possible to escape from a headlock.

To my special friends who took the time to come to Camp Sunshine and sit at my Round Table, Jackie Smith, John Salvi, William Duff and Gilda Healy, thank you for your direction, feedback and encouragement. You helped me to polish Pattie's Best Deal until it was a shiny apple.

Many others have provided me with information, inspiration, guidance, time and support. In the event that I have inadvertently omitted your name from these pages, please forgive me and accept my thanks now. I appreciate you all.

"That which does not kill us just makes us stronger"
—Friedrich Nietzsche

PART ONE

PLANTING TIME

CHAPTER ONE

A DAY IN THE LIFE

Pattie Anwald's breathing was shallow and her skin was the color of parchment. Her heart pounded and her palms glistened with sweat. She looked up from her file in an effort to distract herself from her anxiety. The countless coats of pea green flat paint that covered the walls and their overlay of random smudges belied the fact that this gothic horror had at one time been a beautiful, new, state of the art courthouse. Most of the bulbs in the overhead chandelier were burned out and the sun's rays could barely shine through the layers of grime that covered the windowpanes. Pattie dodged a white paint chip that dislodged from the cathedral ceiling. It wafted down toward her, like a deranged piece of dandruff.

"We have saved the case ending in Docket Number 1213, People v. Roy and Penny Edwards for last, because the victim is a minor. The courtroom must be cleared before we can proceed," the clerk intoned.

Court officers shuttled everyone out of the courtroom, leaving only those parties and attorneys who were directly involved with the case. Pattie approached the counsel table and stood there on wobbly ankles. She tried to steady her shaky hands by clutching the oversized velvet tote bag that served as her briefcase. It was as black as her glossy, long hair. She glanced up at the judge and squinted in order to read his nameplate.

"The Honorable Frederick J. Benchley" peered scornfully over the rim of his Benjamin Franklin style reading glasses and squinted right back at her. He looked like a middle-aged curmudgeon, with his pursed lips and steely gray eyes. His mouse brown hair was swept around his cranium in a probable attempt to make it look "full". He sat between a faded New York State flag and a dingy American flag with a gold fringe border. The judge and the flags looked like a worn out, but as yet undefeated trio who had all seen better days.

"Who are you?" Judge Benchley asked.

Pattie looked at him like a deer stunned by headlights. Her hands continued to shake. She gripped the edge of the counsel table and tried to clear her throat, but only a squeak came out.

"Um, God. No. I mean good," she somehow managed to bleat.

She couldn't understand why her quivering voice sounded almost an octave higher than usual.

"You're good? How reassuring."

"No, your Honor. I meant to say good afternoon. That's all."

"Well, good afternoon, but you still haven't answered my question."

"Oh. For the record, my name is Pattie Anwald."

"Pattie?"

"Yes?"

"No. I'm not calling you. I'm asking you if that's your name."

"Yes."

"Not Patricia, Patrice or some other such thing?"

She shook her head.

"No."

"Well, Pattie's a tad too informal for court in my opinion. Anyway, Pattie, what brings you before me today?"

"Well Your Honor, I represent The Defendants' twelve-year-old son, Justin, in a companion case at the Family Court."

The judge squinted again, cupped his ear and pointed at the Court Reporter.

"Do you see her Ms. Anwald?"

"Yes, Your Honor."

"Great, because you have to speak up. You see, no one can hear any of your utterances and that poor soul is forced to take them all down."

Pattie tried to clear her throat again, this time with some success.

"I'm sorry, Your Honor. Anyhow, since both cases involve the same set of facts, I'm concerned that if either of these cases goes to trial, my client will be forced to testify about how his parents abused him," Pattie said, as loudly as she could manage.

An attorney behind her jumped to his feet and shook his head. His face looked like the mask of tragedy.

"Your Honor, Attorney Elliot Glutz, representing Roy and Penny Edwards. I object!"

His flat, nasal voice filled the courtroom. Pattie turned to look at him. His baby blue polyester suit screamed "Bargain Basement."

My God! I wonder if that thing's washable, Pattie thought.

An attractive woman in her mid-thirties stood next to Attorney Glutz. Her long blonde hair hung straight and sleek like a super model's. Her royal blue silk dress, which ended in the middle of her well-toned thighs, matched her vertiginous four-inch spike pumps. Her smoky gray eye shadow made her piercing blue eyes sparkle like sapphires.

A tall man with strawberry blond hair and a beard stood on her other side. His hooded eyes were half closed, in an unsuccessful attempt to conceal a basilisk stare. He wore a plain black suit with a white linen tunic and no tie. The crown jewel in the ensemble, was the diamond stud earring in his left ear. He glanced up in time to join Penny and Attorney Glutz as they glared at Pattie. Their joint and collective expressions revealed such a degree of malice that the little hairs on the back of Pattie's neck stood on end. She shuddered and turned away.

"Your Honor, I thought that the courtroom was supposed to be cleared, yet I see people with Attorney Glutz," she said.

"These so-called people aren't just anybody! They're my clients, Roy and Penny Edwards! Doesn't she even realize that as actual parties to this case they have a right to be here?" Elliott Glutz bellowed.

"OK, OK, but I still don't understand the basis for Mr. Glutz's objection," Pattie said.

"Your Honor, the basis for my objection should be clear, even to an idiot!"

"Your Honor, please tell me that Attorney Glutz didn't just call me an idiot."

"Just spell out the basis of your objection, Attorney Glutz," Judge Benchley said.

"I'm objecting to her audacity! How dare she drag us all into court and force us to watch her prance around and misuse the word abuse, when there's never been proof of any abuse at this point?"

"Objection sustained," Judge Benchley said.

Pattie cleared her throat once again.

"OK, OK, I think I get it. I'm sorry that I said abuse instead of alleged abuse. I'd also like to add that I've never pranced around this or any other courtroom."

Judge Benchley sighed. His expression looked like he had just gulped down an entire glass of milk, before realizing that it was sour.

"Ms. Anwald, I don't know what goes on over at the Family Court, nor do I care, but this is the no-nonsense Criminal Court, where the adults practice law. So, next time you speak, stick to the facts and keep the decibels up. I've had a long day and I'm worn out!"

He picked up his gavel, but before he could dismiss Pattie's motion, she spoke up again.

"I'm sorry your Honor," she said in a louder voice, "but The Defendants allegedly belong to a Satanic coven whose rituals allegedly include routinely abusing Justin."

Judge Benchley frowned and let the gavel go limp.

"I know that, but what I don't know is why you're over here instead of back at The Family Court, where you belong."

"Well, I said it before, Your Honor. I'm here because, if this case goes to trial, I'm not even sure that Justin can testify."

"Well, why not? What's the problem? Is he a mute or something?"

"No, Your Honor, but if he testifies about the alleged abuse, it might be the same for him as if he actually relived it. I need an expert to psychologically evaluate him in order to determine whether testifying will end up destroying him."

Another middle-aged man, who had been sitting not far from Pattie, lumbered to his feet. He had gray hair, brown eyes and his tight fitting plain beige suit did little to conceal his weight problem.

"Your Honor, I'm Toby Barnett for the People. May I be heard?"

"By all means," Judge Benchley answered.

"Attorney Anwald's representations accurately reflect the information in our files. At the time of the arrest, the police lawfully seized several home videos of Roy Edwards and others abusing his twelve-year-old son Justin, all in the name of Satan. Penny Edwards tried to obstruct justice by grabbing the tapes and screaming it wasn't Roy's fault because 'The Devil' made him do it."

"Objection! I intend to file a Motion to Suppress those videos along with Mrs. Edward's alleged statement," Elliot Glutz shouted.

"Objection sustained. All references to any videos or admissions are hereby stricken from the record, pending the outcome of said motion, but Mr. Glutz, I'm warning you not to wait until the last minute to file it."

"Your Honor, may I receive a copy of that motion, along with any other motions that have already been filed?" Pattie asked.

"The People have no problem with that," Toby Barnett said.

"Well, Mr. and Mrs. Edwards do have a problem with it! They've had just about enough of this Anwald character inflicting her presence on them. Just who does she think she is coming in here and making demands on us when she never even bothered to send me a copy of her motion?" Elliot Glutz shouted.

"Your Honor, our file reflects that no Guardian Ad Litem has been appointed in these proceedings to protect Justin's rights. Under the circumstances, Ms. Anwald is the most logical candidate for the position," Toby Barnett said.

"Your Honor, I'd be happy to accept the appointment," Pattie said.

"So ordered," Judge Benchley said.

"Your Honor, as Guardian Ad Litem, Attorney Anwald is entitled to copies of every motion filed in this case, along with the original police report," Toby Barnett said.

"So ordered. Compliance by all parties is to take place within one week from today."

"Thank you, Your Honor," Pattie said.

"You're welcome. Mr. Barnett, I see nothing from your office, which either supports or opposes Attorney Anwald's Motion for a Psychological Evaluation of the victim. What is The Peoples' position?" Judge Benchley asked.

"Your Honor, since Mr. and Mrs. Edwards cannot be compelled to testify against themselves nor against each other, if Justin is kept from testifying, our case goes right out the window."

Judge Benchley frowned at the Edwards.

"Yes, Your Honor, but if testifying destroys Justin, that doesn't serve Justice either," Pattie chimed in.

"Well, Attorney Anwald, if I were to grant your motion, just whom do you expect would bear the costs of the evaluation?" Judge Benchley asked.

"I'll object if she thinks my clients should have to," Elliot Glutz yelled.

Pattie cleared her throat.

"Your Honor I'm requesting that The People pay for it. Justin certainly doesn't have the means," Pattie said.

"Attorney Glutz, what is The Defendants' position?"

"I'll go along with the motion as long as The People bear the costs of it, along with the costs of a second evaluation in the event that my clients don't like the first one," Elliot Glutz said.

Both Toby Barnett and Judge Benchley glared at him. Pattie's mouth hung open in shock.

"Mr. Glutz, if The Defendants don't like the first evaluation, I'll grant them the right to seek an independent one at their own expense, however, they must request it within one week of receiving the original evaluation and they must share its results with The People and Ms. Anwald. Do you have an expert in mind, Ms. Anwald?" Judge Benchley asked.

"Yes, your Honor. Professor Henry Keith at Omnia University, who specializes in Adolescent and Juvenile Psychology," Pattie said.

Pattie heaved a sigh of relief when Judge Benchley granted her motion and banged down the gavel.

"Thank you, Your Honor," she said, but Judge Benchley didn't hear her. He was already on his way back to his chambers. His black robe billowed behind him like a cape.

The Court Officer announced that court was in recess until Monday morning at ten o'clock. Elliot Glutz stormed out, with both of his clients in tow. Pattie walked over to Toby Barnett and introduced herself.

"I hope you don't mind if I ask, but are there other members of the coven, besides Roy and Penny Edwards?"

Toby Barnett nodded.

"Yes, but Roy and Penny are the only ones the police have been able to locate so far. Of course, if anything changes, I promise to keep you in the loop."

Pattie thanked him, returned to her table and slid Justin's file into her tote bag. She hurried out of the courtroom and when she reached the ground floor, she spun through the exit. Once outside, she stood motionless and glanced up at the manmade mountains of glass and steel that soared toward the sun like steeples. She smiled as the first spring breeze of 2003 caressed her face and neck. She glanced at her watch. It was four thirty. She ran down the steps and waited for the traffic light to change, while a myriad of cars, trucks, busses, motorcycles, bicycles, skateboards, roller blades, pedestrians, scooters and taxis honked, clanged and rattled past her. Only after the light had changed in her favor, did she realize that Roy and Penny Edwards had appeared out of nowhere to flank her. Roy hooked his arms around hers, bore a hole through her with his stare and locked her in place on the curb.

"Well, well, well, if it isn't our son's lawyer. Hey, you must not be very good at your job. After all, the entire court proceedings made you more nervous than a whore in church," Roy said.

His voice was almost a hiss.

Pattie cleared her throat and maneuvered out of his grasp.

"First of all, don't put your hands on me again. I happen to know Judo and second of all, Attorney Glutz represents both of you, which means I'm not supposed to communicate with you directly. So, if you have something to say to me, do it through him."

Roy hunched his shoulders, tilted his head to the right and stared straight through Pattie.

"Listen carefully. As long as this case is pending, you will never enjoy a minute's peace," he said.

His malefic scowl informed Pattie that he was dead serious. Pattie felt chills identical to the ones she had experienced in the courtroom earlier.

"I don't know who you think you are or what you think you can get away with, but I don't like being touched or threatened," she said.

Roy nodded.

"I know you don't, but should I care? Besides, I'm not threatening you. I'm merely making a promise."

Before Pattie could respond, he and Penny vanished.

Oh great, she thought, as she watched the traffic light change back to red. She stepped back up onto the curb. As more rush hour traffic rumbled past her, she reached into her tote bag, pulled out her cell phone and speed dialed her best friend Ryan Pilgrim. He answered the call halfway through the first ring.

"Hey Ryan, I won!"

"Good. I had a feeling you would. Where are you now?"

"I'm on my way to the drug store across the street from the Courthouse."

"Great. I'll meet you there in five minutes."

CHAPTER TWO
RAIN

Nancy Speck, Clerk of the Family Court, removed a gray trench coat from an antique iron coat rack that looked like a carry over from World War Two. The coat's red faux fox collar matched her hair.

"I'm worried about you, kiddo," she told Pattie.

"Well, I'm worried about me too. After all, tomorrow is Justin's in court review and I still haven't been able to reach Dr. Keith."

"I think it was very unprofessional of him not to have called you back."

"I agree and it's out of character for him as well."

"So, why don't you use Dr. Alt like I told you?"

"Because, all he ever does is talk about the day when he can finally retire and go fishing. Besides, his evaluations are outdated."

"Now, wait just a minute, he"—but before Nancy could finish, Pattie's cell phone rang.

"Hey! It's me Ryan! Bad news."

Pattie frowned.

"Why? What's up?"

"I'm over here at Dr. Keith's office. It's all locked up and the light is out."

"Well, I guess I have no choice but to go over there and try to track him down myself."

"Well, be careful driving. It's like winter all over again."

"Well, I won't exactly be driving. I'll be taking the subway."

"Why?"

"Because, my car is back at the dealership."

"Oh God. Again? What's wrong with it this time?"

"The horn doesn't work."

"Ouch. Not having a horn in this city can be murder. Anyhow, do you want me to meet you over at the Psych Building?"

"No. That's OK. I'm heading straight for the Dojo after that."

"Well then, let's meet when your Judo class lets out."

"Great. I'll drop in at Cosmo's around nine thirty."

"Perfect. In the meantime, call me if you need anything."

"I will."

"I'll keep my phone on vibrate."

"Ooh la la!" Pattie said.

They chuckled. Nancy tapped Pattie on the shoulder and pointed at herself.

"Nancy Speck says 'hi'."

"Tell her I said 'hi' back."

"Ryan says 'hi back'."

Nancy beamed.

"Actually, now that I think of it, there is something you could do for me, if you don't mind. I was supposed to have dinner at my parents' house tonight. Could you call my mother and tell her that between having to go to Omnia and Judo class, there's no way I'll be able to make it?"

"You're kidding. Right?"

Pattie didn't respond.

"OK, but now you owe me," Ryan said, in a perfect imitation of Marlon Brando's Don Corleone.

Pattie laughed.

"OK," she said and hung up before Ryan had a chance to change his mind.

"So, when are youse two gonna get married?" Nancy asked.

Pattie's jaw dropped.

"Married? We're not even dating. We're just platonic friends."

"Well, if you let a great kid like that slip through your finger tips you're crazy. Besides, two can live as cheaply as one in this city. If nothing else, you should at least move in with him."

"Well, he's got a big family over there that he lives with. It's an unusual arrangement but it seems to work for them."

"Listen kiddo, I know all about it. That could have been me living in that palace. Didn't I ever tell you that I used to date his father?"

Pattie glanced at her watch.

Only a million times, she thought to herself.

"Hey, if I don't leave for Omnia right this second I probably won't be able to find Professor Keith."

Nancy nodded, stepped outside and waited for Pattie to follow her so that she could lock up the courthouse. Nancy fought with her umbrella, while the rain pelted Pattie's face.

"You know, you scare me sometimes," Nancy said.

Pattie frowned, as the wind whipped through her lightweight black trench coat.

"I do? Why?"

Nancy rubbed Pattie's coat between her thumb and forefinger.

"Well, take a look at yourself. You have all the education in the world and yet you don't even know how to protect yourself from the elements. You claim that your body temperature is lower than everybody else's and that you're always cold but it's no wonder, when you don't own an umbrella and you run around in such a flimsy little coat."

"Well, the weather was nice when I left for work this morning. It only got lousy after the day wore on," Pattie said.

"Well, good night and good luck and for God's sake try to stay warm," Nancy said, as she walked up the street to the bus stop.

Pattie braced herself and ran the other way toward the subway station. Even though she held her tote bag over her head, the wind and rain battered her face. Each drop felt like Novocain, as it first stung, then numbed her.

CHAPTER THREE

PHOTOGRAPH

Edie Anwald slammed the receiver down on the old fashioned, red, dial-telephone that hung on her kitchen wall. She was "fifty something", of average height and at least thirty pounds overweight. Her fuchsia spandex tube top clung to every one of her bulges and highlighted what she believed to be her magnificent cleavage. Unfortunately, it also revealed her equally large pot belly. Her brassy shade of dyed black hair, was fluffed and teased into the style of a helmet head. A plastic bow from the Dollar Store, whose color almost matched the color of her tube top, was fastened at the crown of her head, where it jiggled like a peanut every time she moved. Her thick, black eye liner eclipsed what could have been her best feature, her turquoise eyes and her overdone mascara lay on the ends of her eyelashes in clumps.

She shuffled across the faded linoleum floor in slippers so old and dirty, that it was hard to figure out their original color. When she reached the white metal cabinet over the sink, she pulled on the handle. When the cabinet door didn't budge, she punched the dent in the lower left hand corner that matched the outline of her fist and like magic, it popped open. She reached inside, grabbed a prescription bottle and shook two pills into her hand. Not bothering to close the door, she padded over to her old, gray and white "faux marble" Formica table and flounced into the red Naugahyde chair that was wedged between her son Lou and his mousy girlfriend, Cheryl. She picked up her jumbo-sized margarita glass, popped the pills into her mouth and gulped them down. Still clutching her glass, she flicked her tongue and swooped up some salt from around its rim.

"And people wonder why I drink," she said, through clenched teeth, in a voice that was so harsh it could have cut diamonds.

Although Lou was in better shape than his mother was, he too was overweight. Unlike Edie, who was flabby, Lou was solid and beefy. His hair was almost as black as Edie's and he sported one of those paramilitary buzz cuts that were suddenly becoming popular in law enforcement circles, even though the style didn't particularly suit his face. His eyes were gray and their expression revealed a basic cynicism.

"What's going on?" Lou asked.

Edie jerked her head toward the telephone.

"Pattie strikes again!"

Lou scratched his head.

"Why? What did she do this time?"

"She bagged out of coming here for dinner. She didn't even have the decency to call me herself. She got Ryan Pilgrim to do it for her," she brayed.

Lou shrugged.

"Oh well, maybe she had some kind of an emergency with one of her clients. You know how it is with those child advocates. They're totally overworked and like the rest of us public servants, they don't have the privilege of turning clients away."

Edie waved, as if to dismiss such a notion.

"Well, the least she could have done is call me herself. After all, if she found the time to call Ryan, she could have found the time to call me!"

"Well, you know what she's like."

"Uch!" Edie let out a groan.

"Now what?"

"Another hot flash just kicked in!"

Lou looked out of the window at the Nor'easter.

"In this weather?"

"Trust me, Louie. A hot flash knows no season."

Edie picked up her glass, gulped her margarita and reached for her pack of cigarettes. She pulled out a cigarette, lit one with a cheap plastic lighter that read, "As Long as You Have Your Wealth" and dragged on it as if it were the elixir of life. She held the smoke deep down inside of her for several seconds and then slowly released it through her nostrils. In the meantime, Cheryl scrutinized the kitchen and mentally remodeled it, right down to the last nook and cranny. Only when Edie slapped a photo album open in front of her and jabbed her in the ribs, did Cheryl snap out of her reverie. Edie took another greedy swig of her margarita and pursed her lips.

"You may as well know now that all of Louie's ancestors on his father's side were Hessians who fought on the wrong side of the Revolutionary War."

Cheryl shrugged.

"Oh well, we can't all be winners," she said, not really knowing or caring about what a Hessian was.

Edie sighed and stubbed out her cigarette with a vengeance.

"You got that right."

Lou pointed at the page.

"Look Cheryl. That's the original tintype of this very house. It was made the day my great, great, great, great, great grandfather finished building it."

"Yeah and there's been a not so great, great, great, great, great Anwald living in it ever since. Sure, we could get a bundle for it in today's housing market, but my husband Chet won't hear of it. He insists on keeping it," Edie chimed in.

"Well, that's because it's my inheritance," Lou said.

Cheryl pored over every detail of the tintype and then looked up at Lou.

"How do you know that you're the heir apparent?"

Edie punched the table.

"Because I say he is," she yelled.

Cheryl smiled at Lou. Edie stood, picked up her glass with one hand and dragged Cheryl into the dining room with her other. Instead of following them, Lou went over to the refrigerator, pulled out a bottle of beer and twisted the cap off. He flung the cap into his mother's ashtray, sat back down and guzzled.

The mahogany dining room table was set for five people with an olive-green tablecloth and orange place mats. A huge gilt framed mirror, with an American eagle, hung over the matching sideboard. One of the eagle's claws clenched a small wreath. Edie admired her reflection, as she wound her tongue around yet another wad of salt from the rim of her glass.

"Are the things in here antiques?" Cheryl asked.

Edie nodded.

"Yeah. They all belonged to the same dysfunctional bastard who built the place," she said.

She gazed at Cheryl warily and sized her up from the top of her mouse brown pixie haircut all the way down to her beige vinyl sneakers. When she was done, she once again tugged on Cheryl's sleeve and led her back into the kitchen. When she passed behind Lou, she put her hand on his shoulder.

"I'd better get your laundry into the dryer. While I do that why don't you wake your father up so that we can eat?"

Lou nodded. When he went upstairs to wake his father, Edie drained her glass.

CHAPTER FOUR

DOWNTOWN TRAIN

Since it was rush hour, all of the passengers were packed into the subway car like sardines. It smelled like a combination of feces, urine, broccoli and some other ingredient that Pattie couldn't identify. She tried not to inhale too deeply. Since she had no chance of getting a seat, she walked to the nearest pole and hung on gingerly. A few minutes later, a man came up behind her and body slammed her into the pole. She let out a groan and tried to distract herself by watching the man next to her, as he drooled and stared into space. She slid her foot back in order to ensure that his DNA never got chance to splatter onto her instep.

"Hey! Watch it! You just kicked me!" The body slammer screamed.

When she turned around to apologize, she noticed that he only had one eye. He wore no eye patch or prosthetic device to cover the gaping hole where his eye should have been. He hooked his index and middle fingers into a claw and gestured at her, as if he were going to scratch her eyes out. She turned back toward the pole and accidentally made eye contact with a derelict who stood across from her. He leered, winked at her and stuck his tongue out. Then he licked the pole several times with long, slow strokes. In the meantime, the one-eyed man behind her kept digging into her heel with the tip of his work boot. The train careened and screeched to a halt, causing everybody to lean into everybody.

How do these subway workers avoid going deaf? Pattie wondered.

The doors opened and the crowd inside thinned out for a few seconds. Since Pattie's stop was next, she decided to position herself as close to the door as she could. She walked past another pole whose lone occupant performed a pole dancing routine. The pole dancer's hips swayed back and forth as if she were dancing the hula. She shimmied up the pole, kicked one leg out and then the other. Then she pointed her toes, tilted her head back and arched her back. Then she hooked both of her legs around the pole and corkscrewed her way to the floor. Pattie lost sight of her once the train swelled with the new, incoming crowd. A few minutes later, the train screeched to a halt again and Pattie was the first passenger out.

CHAPTER FIVE
A DEAL GOES DOWN

Thank God that's over with, Pattie thought, as she dodged a sea of litter. She made her way across the subway platform and ran up the stairs, where a man was sleeping in a cardboard box. She did her best to ignore the white slime that oozed in slow motion down one step at a time, like a deranged slinky.

By the time she emerged from the city's underbelly, it was dark. The wind blew more rain into her face. A Rastafarian with sunglasses and a white cane greeted her as she surfaced and shoved a paper cup under her nose.

"Change for the blind?" He asked, in a sing song accent.

Pattie rummaged through her tote bag, found her last dollar bill and stuck it in his cup.

He gasped.

"One fucking dollar is all you can spare? You cheap bitch!"

"Oh my God! You're not even blind!" Pattie said.

She reached into the cup, but before she could retrieve her her dollar, he snatched it away, slapped her on the back of her hand and zig zagged down the street. She sighed and glanced at her watch. It was already ten after six. She hurried across the street toward the Omnia University Student Center. When she opened the door, the security guard sat up straighter, tilted his head to the side as if to impress her and flashed the special grin he reserved for only the youngest, prettiest girls.

Pattie cleared her throat.

"Can you please tell me the shortest way to the Psychology Department?"

He stretched his arms above his head, folded his hands and arched his back.

"You got ID?" He asked in a bored tone of voice.

She looked surprised.

"Why? Do I need it in order to ask for directions?"

He stared her down.

"Ain't you heard of 9/11? Where the hell'uv you been?" By now his tone was abrasive.

Pattie pulled out her driver's license and handed it to him. He inspected it, jotted something in a ledger and returned it to her. He pointed to the doorway behind her.

"That leads to a tunnel that will take you all the way over to the Psychology Department on the other side."

"Thank you," Pattie said, grateful that she didn't have to go back out into the storm.

"Don't mention it," he said, yawning.

I won't, Pattie thought, as she hurried toward the doorway.

The tunnel was dark and narrow and the ceiling was low. Old paint chips crackled beneath her feet as she walked. The exposed pipes a few inches above her head sizzled and belched forth random bursts of steam. As she ran her hands along the unpainted cinder block in order to keep herself steady, she wondered why no one had ever bothered to replace any of the burned out light bulbs. Her trip through the tunnel wore on and she wondered why she never remembered it from her time as a student here.

What if this idiot deliberately misled me?

She was almost ready to turn back, when she saw the sign that read "Psychology Department". She heaved a sigh of relief, stepped into the hallway and blinked, as her pupils adjusted to the increased light. Ignoring her discomfort, she ran up the stairs and hurried over to Dr. Keith's office.

The door was ajar. She hovered in the doorway and peered inside at the lavish furniture. She overheard a man talking with a British accent over a speakerphone.

"Call me a commitment-phobe if you like, but all I know is that I can't handle another disappointment. Lingering memories still haunt me. So, even if Love personified walked through my door and Cupid himself shot a hole through me, I'd do my utmost to remain oblivious," he said.

"Well, I hear you and although I'm probably way too sentimental for my own good, I still believe that everybody is looking for the same thing. To love and be loved," a man with a southern accent responded.

"Not everyone, my friend. Only incurable romantics such as yourself, but in any event, it sounds as if congratulations are in order."

"Indeed, they are. It's not every day I get engaged, although we haven't set a date yet."

Pattie wondered whether it was more impolite to continue to stand there and eavesdrop or to simply barge in. Finally, the man glanced up and beckoned her into his office. She nodded and inched her way through the door, trying hard not to gawk at him. Instead, she gazed around the neat, cozy little office and focused on the diplomas which hung on the wall behind him.

"May I phone you later? I believe I've got a visitor," he said.

"Sure, no problem."

After they said good bye and hung up, the man stood. He was tall, slender and well dressed. His dark brown hair was tousled but not unkempt. Pattie thought he was handsome and she noticed that he was not wearing a wedding band.

"Hello, I'm Jordan Armstrong. May I help you?"

Pattie cleared her throat.

"Hi, I'm Pattie Anwald. I'm sorry that I interrupted your call. I'm looking for Dr. Henry Keith."

Drip, drop, drip, drop. She stared in horror as her coat dripped all over his Persian rug.

"Well, this used to be his office, but since he's a commissioned officer in the military reserves and a war in Iraq may be imminent, he was called into active duty and deployed overseas. I've taken over his classes."

Pattie nodded vaguely as she processed the information.

"Well, that explains why he didn't return any of my calls."

"I would have returned your calls and let you know all of this, but I haven't been able to unlock his voicemail. In fact, I can't even get it off of speakerphone."

Pattie smiled, revealing her dimples.

"Yes, I noticed. You might want to call the Communications Center."

"Well, I have called them. Several times. Maybe they can't unlock their voicemails either."

Pattie giggled.

"Stranger things have happened, I guess."

"You poor thing. You must be drenched. Here, let me help you out of your Mac."

Pattie stared at him with a blank expression.

"My what?"

"Your raincoat?"

She nodded.

"Oh," she said.

He stepped out from behind his desk and helped her out of her soggy trench coat. He placed it on a hanger and hung it over a hook on the back of his door.

"Thank you."

"My pleasure. Please have a seat," he said, pointing at a soft, white, leather armchair.

She nodded and sat. She could still hear her coat dripping. He reached over and handed her a dial.

"What is this?"

"The chair has a heater. Flick the switch and turn it up as high as you like. It will help to remove the chill from your bones," he said.

"That's great because I'm freezing."

She cranked the heat, touched a wet strand of her hair and glanced down at the tops of her black leather boots. They were ruined.

"I'm so sorry that I don't have a towel to offer you."

"Oh, don't worry about it. I don't think most professors keep linen closets in their offices. Can I ask you a personal question?"

He nodded.

"Sure."

"Are you from England?"

"Actually, I'm from Scotland."

"Well you have a beautiful accent. You could probably read the phone book and it would sound great."

"Thank you. What a lovely thing to say. Your accent is nice as well."

She shook her head and smiled.

"But I don't have any accent. I grew up right here in New York City, so I just talk like everyone else."

He smiled back at her.

"Well then, that means that you have a New York accent."

"Wow. I never thought of it that way."

"May I ask why you came here to see Dr. Keith?"

She nodded. As she explained Justin's situation, she felt the chair melt the cold from her bones. She looked down and realized that she had been wringing her hands the entire time she spoke. She silently commanded them to stop.

"Well, perhaps I could help you. I'm a psychologist and I specialize in the Psychology of At Risk Youths."

"Well, have you ever been an expert witness in any New York Family Court proceedings?"

He shook his head.

"No. I haven't been here long enough."

"OK, well then have you at least testified in any court proceeding? Anywhere?"

He shook his head again.

"I can't say that I've done that either."

Pattie reached inside her wet tote bag, pulled out a file, which had miraculously managed to stay dry and placed it on his desk.

"Well, at this point I guess it doesn't matter. It looks like we've got a deal. You're hired."

He tried to conceal a smile.

"I see. So now what happens?"

She reached into her tote bag and handed him her card.

"Here's my card. Call me as soon as you've read the file and familiarized yourself with the case. That way we can schedule a time for you to meet my client, Justin."

Jordan nodded and handed her his card.

"Great. Here's my card as well."

Pattie tossed his card into her tote bag.

"Thanks. Do your best to get caught up sooner rather than later and don't worry. The District Attorney's Office will pay you."

He chuckled nervously.

"All right. So now let's seal the deal with a cup of tea. I was about to brew some for myself and I hate to drink alone."

She smiled.

"That would be great."

He spooned some loose tea into an infuser and plugged in an electric kettle.

"Milk? Lemon? Sugar?"

"None of the above, thanks. I'll just take it straight."

Before long, the water reached a boiling point, but it took a few minutes for the tea to brew. When it was done, he poured it into a porcelain teacup, placed it on a matching saucer and handed it to her. She traced the rim of the cup lightly with her index finger and blew on the tea. When it was finally cool enough for her to drink, she lifted it to her lips.

"This is the most delicious tea I've ever tasted," she said, as she reunited the cup with its saucer.

"I have some lemon biscuits to go with it."

She shook her head.

"Uh, no thanks. I just ate," she lied.

She drained the cup, carefully placed the cup and saucer on his desk and stood. He followed her lead and stood as well. She shook his hand.

"Well, I hate to drink and run but I have to go."

"I'm delighted that you stopped by."

She nodded.

"Me too. Thank you for agreeing to help my client and also for thawing me out. Two miracles for the price of one."

He chuckled.

"I hate to see you go back out into that rain again," he said, as he came from behind his desk.

Pattie shrugged.

"Oh well. C'est La Vie. Right?"

He helped her back into her trench coat and walked her to the door. Once she left, he returned to his desk and telephoned his friend.

"Well Clint, my visitor turned out to be a lovely, young, raven haired attorney."

Clint chuckled.

"Raven haired?"

"Yes. Her hair was as black as a raven's wing."

"Well, too bad you don't believe in love at first sight."

"You're so right. It's a pity."

He leaned back in his chair and gazed out of the window, while he listened to Clint discuss his fiancee. A few minutes later, he caught sight of Pattie walking on the street below. He watched her until she receded into the pitch-black night.

CHAPTER SIX
SAVOY TRUFFLE

Cosmo's Astral Plane Café, a coffeehouse near the Village on West 14th Street, was deserted except for Ryan Pilgrim, a nice looking young man with dark brown hair and brown eyes. Like Pattie, he was slender. He wore jeans and a black T-shirt that said "Mind Closed Until Further Notice." He sat in a fluffy armchair in front of a brick wall that was covered with a huge black tapestry of a beige Zodiac wheel and he had positioned himself as far away from the entrance as he could get. Pattie rushed in and waved at him, just as he was about to take the first sip of his coffee.

"I finally made it," she said, as she started to drag an arm chair toward him.

"Here, let me do that," he said, as he got up to help her.

She backed away from the chair so that he could move it into position for her.

"Hey, it's good to know that chivalry isn't dead, but after having just come out of a Judo class, the least I could do is pretend to be indestructible," she said, as she flopped into the chair.

"Well I was raised to be chivalrous, but these days I never know whether I'm being mannerly or whether I'm insulting a woman."

She smiled.

"Well you never insult me. I love chivalry."

He smiled back at her.

"Well, that's good to know. FYI, I took the liberty of ordering a Raspberry Latte for you! It should be here any minute."

"Why thank you, Kind Sir."

"Ah, but don't thank me yet. I also got you this in case you worked up a thirst in judo class," he said and handed her a bottle of spring water.

She read the label.

"Hey it's even the real deal from some natural spring upstate."

He nodded.

"Whenever I see drinking water from upstate, I think of your Mother, because she's convinced that the only thing of any value once you get outside of New York City, is the drinking water."

Pattie shook her head and chuckled.

"I know. Right?"

The barista arrived with Pattie's Latte, so Pattie tossed the unopened water bottle into her tote bag and sipped the Latte instead.

"So, enlighten me. Did you ever find Dr. Keith?"

She took another sip of her Latte and went on to explain how Dr. Keith had been deployed to Iraq.

"Wow. It's disturbs me to think that someone who is smart enough to get a Ph.D. can't even figure out a way to keep from being sent off to war," Ryan said.

Pattie nodded absentmindedly.

"Well, if this turns out to be another Desert Storm or Grenada, he'll be back before we know it," she said.

"True, but in the meantime what are you going to do?"

"His replacement has agreed to be my expert witness."

"Is he any good?"

"Who knows at this point? One can only hope. In any event, he's attractive enough to make some lucky girl very happy outside of the courtroom."

Ryan frowned.

"Oh really? Well, that's not going to help your case any."

She nodded.

"I know."

He handed her a paper bag.

"What's this?"

"Oh, just a little something I thought you might like," he said.

She reached inside and pulled out a bumper sticker that read "Honk if your horn is broken".

She smiled.

"Thank you! I love it! You are too funny."

"I know, but let's not forget that I'm serious too sometimes. In fact, I have some serious news that might well prove to be a call to adventure for you!"

Pattie's eyes lit up.

"Really? What is it?"

"Legal Aid has an opening for a Staff Attorney right where I work."

"Well, I don't know. I was pretty intimidated when I was over there for Justin."

"Yeah, but in the end, you got everything you asked for."

Pattie nodded.

"I know, but it was at a great cost to my nervous system."

"But the position pays better than your current job and it has better benefits too."

She smiled.

"See that? Who ever said 'crime doesn't pay'?

Ryan chuckled.

"Probably a Legal Aid Attorney."

Pattie nodded.

"Very funny, but seriously, I'm very happy over at the Family Court."

He sipped his coffee and pondered.

"Yeah, but I think you should apply for the job and check it out, even if you end up not taking it. I could pick up the application for you and bring it to you tomorrow night, if you wanted me to."

"OK. I'll order Chinese food for us, so plan on staying for dinner."

Ryan smiled and lifted his cup to toast her.

"Great!"

"Speaking of dinner, did you call my mother?"

Ryan nodded.

"Oh, yeah. I called her all right."

"And? What did she say?"

"She went into a tirade and slammed the phone down on me."

"Ouch."

Ryan chuckled and clutched his left ear.

"Yeah. I know. Now I know how Vincent Van Gogh must have felt."

CHAPTER SEVEN
FAMILY PLOT

Later that night, Lou's girlfriend Cheryl, sat across from her mother at a kitchen table in Jersey City that was almost identical to Edie's. Her mother wore a faded, rose colored, chenille bathrobe. Her gray hair was pressed against her scalp into tiny pin curls. She had a beer can in her left hand and she used her right hand to remove the unfiltered cigarette from one of the grooves in her black, plastic ashtray. She took a long drag, stared at the ceiling and let the smoke go.

"So, what's this one like?"

Cheryl shrugged.

"I don't know. A typical cop, I guess. Not too bright, but at least he's down to earth."

Her mother looked up at the ceiling and rolled her eyes.

"Jesus Christ, you sure do know how to pick 'em. Can't you find anything better?"

"How? I'm a dispatcher at a police station. Cops and criminals are the only people I ever get to meet."

"Yeah well, is this one at least smart enough to be on the take?"

"I doubt it. He may not need to be though. He's got a real sweetheart of a deal."

The mother's eyes lit up.

"Really?"

"Yeah. His mother's a real barracuda but she and her husband own this big old brownstone in the West Village. Apparently, George Washington slept there or something."

The mother squinted and took another drag on her cigarette.

"That's nice for the parents, but so what? It doesn't sound like it benefits him any. Does he live with them?"

"He has his own separate apartment there. It's what his mother refers to as a pied a terre."

The mother nodded.

"Uh huh. Whatever that means. Anyhow, is he at least an only child?"

"Well, he's got this sister, but the mother insists that he's the heir apparent, not her. Anyhow, the whole place has the potential to be breathtakingly beautiful."

The mother took another drag on her cigarette and admired the dazzling skyline across the river. It sparkled like a Christmas tree against the dark backdrop of the night sky.

"All I've ever wanted in my whole life was to get the hell outta here and cross that river over to The Big Time. Just look at that Skyline! The Big Apple is only four miles away, but it might as well be four million for all the good it does me."

"You know, if you had my job you wouldn't love that city so much."

The mother shrugged, lifted her beer can and took a good-sized gulp.

"Well, if you play your cards right, you won't have to work there for long. So, does this sister live there with all of them?"

"No. She's a lawyer of some sort."

Cheryl's mother slammed her beer can down and shook her head vehemently.

"Well, if that's the case, then there's no way this guy's the heir apparent. The minute those parents bite the big one, that lawyer will pull the rug right out from under him. You'll see."

Cheryl frowned.

"Really?"

Her mother nodded.

"Of course! Being a lawyer is like having a license to steal!"

"So, now what do I do?"

The mother stubbed her cigarette out with a vengeance. With each stub, she repeated the word "bastards." When she was done, she flicked the butt into the ashtray and gazed out at the skyline. She twirled the lone stray hair on her chin and pondered the dilemma.

"You need to cement the relationship."

"How?"

"By getting yourself knocked up as soon as possible."

The timer on the microwave beeped. The mother got up, removed a plastic tray of macaroni and cheese and dumped its hot, steamy contents into an old plastic bowl. She brought it back to the table, stabbed it with a fork and blew on it.

"So, what did you have for dinner? On second thought, don't tell me," she said, as she shoveled a heaping forkful of macaroni into her mouth.

Cheryl stood.

"I'd better get to bed. I have an early commute back to Fun City in the morning."

The mother nodded, waved good night absently and pushed some more food into her mouth.

CHAPTER EIGHT
LOOKING FOR LOVE

Early the next morning, looking sharp in his court officer's uniform, Ryan sauntered past the secretary in the Legal Aid Office and headed straight for the door that read "Brad Curatolo, Supervising Legal Aid Attorney".

Brad was tall and lanky, with watery blue eyes, thinning blonde hair and a bushy, unkempt mustache. Even though it was spring, he wore a wool blend maroon jacket and shiny gray pants, both of which had seen better days. His brown shoes were scuffed and run down at the heels.

His office looked like someone had stolen the furniture from the set of an old Sam Spade movie. Countless files, scraps of paper and note covered napkins were strewn across the blotter on his desk. A coffee cup was permanently stuck to one of the scraps and one of the corners of the desk housed a pile of loose change. He got up to retrieve a file, when Ryan appeared in his doorway.

"Hi Ryan. Come on in," he said. His voice sounded nasal, with a "flat affect".

"Hey, I never realized that you have a window in here. Good for you. They're a rare commodity in this building."

"Don't I know it! It took me eight long years to get this window seat. Anyhow, what's up?"

"I heard that you have an opening for a Staff Attorney and I came to pick up an application."

"Well, sorry Cholly. You'd need a Law Degree first. Plus, you'd have to pass the bar."

"I know."

"Yeah? So? Do you even have your Bachelor's?"

"Not yet. Eventually though."

"Well, what's your major?"

"I'm studying to be a rodeo clown."

"That will probably come in handy over at that arraignment court."

Ryan chuckled.

"You're right. It does. Seriously though, my major is Drama."

"Impressive" Brad said, sarcastically.

"Listen, the application isn't for me. It's for a friend."

"Here's the thing, Ryan. I'd like to help your friend, but we're almost at the deadline and I already have a potential candidate in mind. So, do me a favor and tell your friend better luck next time."

"Well Brad, since the deadline hasn't actually expired yet, I'm going to insist that you give me the application, as requested."

Brad sighed, shuffled out of his office and walked over to the secretary's desk, while Ryan dogged his every step.

"Ceil, you know Court Officer Pilgrim. Don't you? He was just getting ready to leave."

Ryan and Ceil nodded at one another.

"Yeah. I will. Once I get what I came for," Ryan said.

Ceil smiled at him.

"And what's that Ryan? Coffee, tea or me?"

"Ceil, Ryan wants an application for the Staff Attorney's position."

Ceil reached into her bottom drawer, pulled out an application and handed it to Ryan.

"There you go," she said.

"Thanks," Ryan said.

She winked at him.

"You got it."

"You know, you would be doing your friend a favor if you just took the application and threw it in the garbage. This place ages people fast," Brad said.

Yeah and you ought to know, Ryan thought, as he waved good bye and left.

CHAPTER NINE
RESCUE ME

Jordan Armstrong's telephone rang the second he stepped into his office. He leapt at it in order to prevent the call from switching over to voice mail.

"Dr. Armstrong? This is Pattie Anwald. Do you remember me?"

Her voice sounded tentative.

"Of course, I do. How are you?"

"I'm fine, thanks. Actually, I'm calling you about Justin. He's over here at the Family Court and he's just had a huge meltdown."

"Do you know what triggered it?"

"No. He was OK when he arrived here this morning."

"Well, can you keep him there?"

"Sure."

"Good, I'll head over there right now."

"That would be great. Thanks."

After they hung up, Pattie convinced Justin's Foster Mother to remain in the courthouse with Justin. She waited in her tiny, windowless office, whose furniture looked identical to Brad Curatolo's. She poured herself a cup of coffee, brought it over to her desk and reviewed Justin's file. She was so engrossed in it, that she jumped when Jordan knocked on the door.

"Hi," she said.

She noticed that he was as impeccably dressed, just as he was the last time they met and she waved him into her office.

"Come on in and make yourself at home while I run and get Justin," she said.

She slipped out and returned a few minutes later with Justin. When she struggled to close her door all the way, Jordan came over to help her.

"Why does your door stick like that?" Jordan asked.

"The wood is warped, so it no longer fits into the door frame," she said.

When she returned to her desk and sat, Jordan returned to his seat, but Justin hovered by the door.

He was short for his age. With his honey-blonde curls and angelic face, he could have easily passed for an altar boy. Only his clothes belied that image. He wore the male, preteen uniform of the day, a gigantic discount house Tee shirt and a pair of oversized jeans with their obligatory low slung waistband. His baseball cap faced backwards. His socks and sneakers were new and clean though. He had piercing blue eyes like both of his parents and like his father, he wore a large diamond in his left ear.

"Justin, this is Dr. Armstrong. You remember me telling you about him. Right?"

Justin stood silently and used the same basilisk stare on Jordan that his father had used on Pattie at the Criminal Court.

"Well, aren't you going to at least say something?" Pattie prodded.

"Why should I? Did it ever occur to any one that I'm tired of being in court all the time and constantly having to talk to doctors and lawyers?"

He worked the door open and left and Pattie glanced at Jordan sheepishly.

"Wow. That didn't go too well. I feel really guilty for dragging you over here for nothing," she said.

"It's all right. I didn't expect him to say very much at this point anyway. At least his meltdown appears to have subsided."

Pattie nodded.

"That's true."

"What triggered it?"

"I don't know."

"Well, what brought him into court today?"

"Just a routine review of his case."

"Well, did anything extraordinary happen during the review?"

"No. Not really. In spite of his foster mother's special qualifications to work with at risk children, she testified that she can no longer handle Justin and she went on to request that the Administration for Children's Services find another placement for him as soon as possible."

"Did he overhear her saying all of this?"

Pattie nodded.

"Sure. He was standing right next to her at the time."

"Well, that explains it then. If his foster mother has such special qualifications, she should have known better than to make a statement like that in his presence," Jordan said.

Pattie nodded.

"I agree, but since he was required to be in court and she was required to say it on the record, I guess she had no choice. Anyhow, since you're evaluating Justin for the Criminal Case, our judge wants you to evaluate him for our case as well and that evaluation would include determining the best placement for him."

"I'd be happy to do so. Of course, I'll be in a better position once I've had a chance to speak to him at greater length. One possibility does spring to mind already, though."

"Oh really? What?"

"There's a Juvenile Residential Center up on Riverside Drive called Beau Rivage. It's run by a husband and wife team, April and Kyle Higgins. They're both licensed psychologists."

"Well, I was hoping that he could stay in a more homelike setting."

"I can understand that, but if a specially qualified foster mother testified that she is having trouble handling him, foster placement doesn't sound feasible for him right now. April and Kyle provide a therapeutic, but yet warm environment for at risk teenagers."

"All right. Let me look into it and discuss it with Justin's Social Worker," Pattie said.

A young, freckle faced court officer knocked on the door.

"Judge Bender is ready to return to the bench," he said.

Pattie nodded, stood and collected her files.

"Well, I guess that's my cue," she said.

Jordan followed her out of her office and they walked down the hall together. They said their good byes and parted ways, when Pattie entered hearing room. Judge Bender and Nancy Speck were already waiting for her.

CHAPTER TEN

HOT CHILD IN THE CITY

Judge Bender was a middle-aged man with a kind face and a receding hairline. He peered over his reading glasses, just as a teenage girl entered the hearing room, accompanied by her overweight, middle-aged Social Worker, whose waist length gray hair, earth shoes and outfit made her look as if she had just stepped out of Woodstock. The teenager wore a black Naugahyde micro mini dress with a white faux fur vest. Her makeup detracted from what could have been her pretty features. Her long hair was bleached to the point of being fried. She winked at the court officer, causing him to blush.

"Your Honor this is the case of Bonnie Louden, aged thirteen," Nancy Speck said.

"Good afternoon, Your Honor. Pattie Anwald appearing for Bonnie Louden. May the record reflect that Bonnie is present in court with her social worker, Geraldine Latham.

Judge Bender nodded.

"So noted," he answered, in a soft, gentle voice.

Bonnie smiled at him.

"Good morning," she said, sweetly.

Judge Bender smiled back at her and returned her greeting.

"Your Honor, according to the police report, Bonnie is one of twenty-three foster children who were part of a juvenile prostitution ring. Six foster mothers allegedly ran this ring and rented the girls out to high-end patrons. Sadly, this has been going on for more than two years," Pattie said.

Judge Bender scowled.

"Ms. Latham, don't you even bother to screen these foster homes before you send children to live in them?"

Geraldine Latham stood. Her blouse buttons bulged open, revealing her lack of a bra.

"Well, Your Honor, I don't run the agency and it's not my job to do the screening and whether you believe it or not we are doing our best," she said.

Judge Bender leaned forward.

"All right. I can understand that you weren't the one who did the initial screening, but didn't you even visit the foster home in the past two years?"

"Of course."

"Well, apparently, you weren't paying attention. Next time keep your eyes and ears open and your blouse closed, because your best just isn't good enough."

Geraldine Latham glanced down at her blouse, fumbled with it for a few seconds and sat. Her face was beet red.

"Your Honor, one of these so called high end patrons is alleged to be Judge Julian DeVittorio, a New York Family Court Judge over in Queens," Pattie said.

Judge Bender shook his head.

"Shocking," he said.

"I agree, Your Honor. I can certainly continue to represent Bonnie, but as Bonnie's counsel, it's a conflict of interest for me to represent any of the other victims in this matter," Pattie said.

Judge Bender nodded.

"Of course it is. Your job is to focus solely on Bonnie's interests. Therefore, I hereby order the Clerk to appoint twenty-two outside attorneys from our panel to represent each of the other victims as special counsel," Judge Bender said.

"I don't even know if we have that many attorneys on our panel," Nancy Speck answered.

"Well, with all of the starving lawyers in this city you shouldn't have a problem rustling up a few," Judge Bender answered.

Nancy nodded.

"I'll do my best," she said.

"Your Honor, I think these circumstances warrant a psychological evaluation, so that we can ascertain the impact that these alleged experiences have had on Bonnie," Pattie said.

"I hereby order the Clerk of this court to arrange for Ms. Louden to meet with Dr. Alt," Judge Bender said.

"Your Honor, Dr. Jordan Armstrong from Omnia University is a specialist in Children and Adolescent Psychology. Judge Benchley appointed him to evaluate one of my other clients, who also has a matter pending in this court. I'm requesting that he conduct Bonnie's evaluation instead of Dr. Alt."

"So ordered."

"Thank you, Your Honor."

"Is there anything else, Attorney Anwald?"

"Yes, Your Honor. By the time I get out of court at night it's often too late to visit my clients. Since this court does not normally convene on Fridays, I'm requesting that I be able to use Fridays for that purpose," Pattie said.

"So ordered. Will that be all Attorney Anwald?"

"No, Your Honor. For obvious reasons, in view of what happened to Bonnie and the other victims, I'm hereby requesting that Bonnie be placed in another foster home immediately."

Geraldine Latham stood.

"That's already been taken care of, Your Honor. Bonnie has been temporarily relocated to another foster home," she said.

Judge Bender nodded.

"Great. Will that be all?" Judge Bender asked.

"Yes, Your Honor."

"So, that concludes this matter for today. Ms. Speck, let's adjourn until four weeks from today."

"Yes, Your Honor," Nancy Speck said.

The judge rapped the gavel.

"All rise please," the court officer said and every one stood, except for the judge.

"I'll come and see you on Friday," Pattie whispered to Bonnie.

"Cool," Bonnie said.

She turned around in the doorway and waved good bye as if she were leaving a nightclub full of paparazzi and adoring fans.

"How many more child protection matters do we have to-day?" Judge Bender asked.

"None, Your Honor. That's it," Nancy Speck answered.

"Fine. Then let's take a fifteen-minute recess so that we can commence with the delinquency docket," Judge Bender ordered.

"All rise please," the court officer said.

Judge Bender stood and left and everyone else followed suit.

CHAPTER ELEVEN

BAD TO THE BONE

Fifteen minutes later, Judge Bender, Nancy Speck, Pattie and Assistant Corporation Counsel, Frank Bernard, assumed their respective places in the hearing room.

"Ms. Speck, please call the first delinquency matter," Judge Bender ordered.

"The People v. Thomas Amissah, age fifteen," Nancy called out.

The Court Officer left and returned with a young teenager, who was accompanied by his parents. His father was from Nigeria and his mother was from England. Although both of his parents were well dressed, Thomas' clothes were remarkably similar to Justin's, except for the absence of a baseball cap. His medium brown hair was braided and the tip of each braid looked as if someone had dipped it in a pot of sepia paint.

Frank Bernard stood.

"Your Honor, Frank Bernard for the People. Thomas Amissah was arrested because he shot a classmate with a stun gun during lunch period at his school cafeteria."

Pattie stood.

"Your Honor, Pattie Anwald representing Thomas Amissah. There's evidence to show that the fracas began when the alleged victim, stun gun in hand, tackled Thomas. Thomas only grabbed the stun gun after the alleged victim dropped it," Pattie said.

Frank sneered.

"Yeah, right and I suppose it went off accidentally too," he said.

Pattie nodded.

"Yes. That's exactly what happened," she said.

Judge Bender frowned at Thomas.

"Mr. Amissah, weren't you recently before me on vandalism charges?"

Thomas stared down at the floor.

"That's right Your Honor. It wasn't all that long ago when our young hero appeared before you for having slopped paint remover all over his math teacher's car. I gave him a get out of jail free card that day, but I did it only out of sentiment," Frank Bernard said.

Judge Bender squinted.

"Sentiment?"

"Yes, Your Honor. I hated Math too. Once in a while I get my kicks by living vicariously."

Thomas chuckled. Judge Bender shot him a venomous look, which sobered him up immediately.

"I'd like to see both counsel in chambers," Judge Bender said.

"All rise," the court Officer said.

Pattie and Frank followed Judge Bender into his chambers, which was an oasis in an otherwise decaying building. It was huge, with pale blue walls and an ivory satin trim. Judge Bender slid out of his robe and eased into his plush leather chair. Pattie and Frank sat in the two visitors' chairs on the other side of the massive mahogany desk. Frank turned toward Judge Bender, in a deliberate effort to exclude Pattie.

"Seeing that Amissah kid back here on such a serious charge so soon after his last caper truly disturbs me, Judge. Every dog gets one free bite and he already got his," Frank said.

"I have to agree with Frank here, Pattie. I'm letting you know right now that if you insist on taking this case to trial, I won't be lenient with him. I'm sick of his face as well as those God damn sepia braids."

"Well, maybe we need some psychological input," Pattie said.

Frank frowned.

"Why are you asking for so much psychological input these days?" Judge Bender asked.

"Because she finally figured out that's it's a really great stall tactic," Frank answered.

"Your Honor, since you posed the question to me, don't I at least get to answer it for myself?" Pattie asked.

"Sure, so just jump in anytime and answer it," Judge Bender said.

"Well, if someone is accused of shooting off a stun gun in a school cafeteria, let's face it, we need to look into his mental state."

"OK. File an oral motion when we go back on the record and follow it up in writing as soon as you can," Judge Bender said.

"Thanks Judge. No problem," Pattie said.

"In the meantime, I don't think this kid should live at home pending the evaluation. Maybe some residential placement that's not a detention center would be a good idea. After all, he is innocent until proven guilty," Judge Bender said."

Both Pattie and Frank agreed.

Judge Bender picked up his phone and pressed a button.

"Yeah?" Nancy Speck squawked over the intercom.

"We're returning to the courtroom now," Judge Bender said.

He hung up, stood and reached for his robe and Pattie and Frank followed him back into the hearing room.

CHAPTER TWELVE
MAKING PLANS

After court, Pattie returned to her office, poured herself a cup of coffee and carried it over to her desk. Sipping it, she sat, logged onto her computer and drafted the Motion and a supporting Brief for Thomas. She printed out copies for all parties and delivered them to Nancy Speck.

"I'll get it onto the docket as soon as I can," Nancy promised.

"Thanks," Pattie said.

She returned to her office, poured herself another cup of coffee and called Jordan.

"Hi, Dr. Armstrong?"

"Guilty as charged."

"It's Pattie Anwald calling again. I hope you don't mind, but I've recommended that you conduct two more evaluations. Our Chief Clerk Nancy Speck will send you the relevant information."

"Great. By the way, I was going to phone you."

Pattie smiled.

"Really?"

"Yes. I wanted to arrange to take you on a tour of Beau Rivage. I think it would be an ideal place for Justin."

"Fine. The problem is that I'm not available until Friday."

"Friday would work. Could you make it at nine in the morning?"

"Sure. I could even pick you up. I've got a car."

"In this city? You must be mad."

"Hey, it beats the subway. Anyway, where should I pick you up?"

"How about right in front of the Psych building?"

"Perfect. Look for a little black car. My license plate reads 'ILLSUEU2'."

"Oh my, that's priceless."

She chuckled.

"Yeah. I think so too. Now, if my horn works that day I'll honk when I see you," Pattie said.

"If it works?"

"Yes. It never seems to work no matter how many times I take it into the shop to get it fixed. It's like a glitch in the system or something."

"And if it doesn't work? What then?"

"I'll just wave and holler 'yoo hoo'!"

"Sounds like a plan!"

CHAPTER THIRTEEN
BEAU RIVAGE

On Friday morning, the sky looked as if the sun had punched a bright yellow hole through it and without even the hint of a cloud in sight, the people of New York City were graced with an abundance of unexpected spring warmth. Right at nine o'clock Pattie pulled up in front of the Psychology Building, where Jordan was waiting for her. Once inside the car, he told her to head North on the West Side Drive. Although traffic was still heavy with residual morning commuters, it moved steadily, so it took them less than thirty minutes to arrive at Beau Rivage.

When Pattie pulled into the driveway, a scowling janitor in his late thirties intercepted her car. He wore a forest green jumpsuit that had been tailored and nipped in order to showcase his enormous biceps and enviable V shaped torso. The name "Willie" was boldly emblazoned across his left breast pocket with heavy gold thread. He wore a United States Marine Corp ring on his right hand. He rapped it against Pattie's window so hard, that she thought he was going to crack it. When she opened the window, she got the full force his stale beer and onion breath, which he deliberately exhaled into her face, before ordering her to park in the farthest space from the brownstone. He watched her park, with his arms across his chest and he tapped his toe and shook his head until she and Jordan got out of the car. When they walked up to him he glared at them and spat on the ground.

"Follow me," he ordered, as he led them up the path toward the house.

Once they were inside, he walked them down a long hall. Pattie noticed that the dining room on the left and the living room on the right both looked like typical rooms in any private home. When they reached the last door on the left, Willie ushered them into an attractive outer office. He tapped his ring against the French doors that led to the inner office and left when a blonde woman in her late thirties came out. She looked every bit the professional in her crisp navy and white pinstriped pants suit. She smiled and greeted Jordan and Jordan introduced her to Pattie. Her voice was rich and warm. She led them into her office and offered them coffee, which they both declined.

"So, April, where's Kyle this morning?" Jordan asked, once they were all seated.

"Unfortunately, he got called away on an emergency. In any case, I'll do my best to answer all of your questions."

"How many beds do you have?" Pattie asked.

"Twenty licensed beds in all," April answered.

"Do you accept delinquents?" Pattie asked.

"Yes. We are even licensed to accept high risk offenders."

"Well, doesn't that put the non-delinquent juveniles at risk?" Pattie asked.

"No. They live in a separate area."

"Are you a coed facility?" Pattie asked.

April nodded.

"Oh yes."

"What are the ages of your residents?" Pattie asked.

"They range in age from twelve to eighteen. All of them attend local public schools. Kyle and I work closely with their guidance counselors in order to maximize their educational opportunities."

Pattie smiled.

"I can think of three clients who might do well here, but right now my main concern is a client named Justin Edwards, who is in need of immediate placement."

April nodded.

"Yes. Dr. Armstrong spoke to me about him. Why don't we talk about what we can do for him, while I show you two around?

An hour later, Pattie and Jordan were back in the car.

"Should we stop for a mid-morning breakfast?" Jordan asked.

Pattie smiled and nodded.

"Why not?"

CHAPTER FOURTEEN
ANOTHER DEAL GOES DOWN

Three weeks later, while Pattie pored over one of her files, Frank Bernard appeared in the doorway to her office, waving a set of papers and grinning from ear to ear.

"Hey Pattie! I don't want to burst your bubble or anything, but I got the Psychological Evaluation on Amissah. After reading it, all I can say is 'I told you so'!"

"Well, I just started reading it myself," she said.

"Great. Let me save you some time. Flip to the last page and read the part where this Armstrong guy wrote and I quote, 'apparently young Thomas is of perfectly sound mind and therefore competent to stand trial'."

"OK then, make me an offer I can't refuse, before I end up moving to Plan B."

"Which is?"

"Self-defense."

"Why are you doing this to me?"

"Hey! It's a legitimate affirmative defense. Remember, not only do I have the right to assert it, I'm obligated to do so."

"OK, smarty pants. Here's my offer. How about he does some time cooling his heels in Detention?"

"In view of what Judge Bender said the last time we were in his chambers on this matter, I'm sure you can come up with a better deal than that."

"Actually, I can't. He's escalating."

"Well, if you insist on making him do time, I'll won't plead him out. I'll just take my chances at trial," she said.

"Now you're the one who's forgetting what Judge Bender said. He's not going to go easy on him and while we're at it, you should thank your lucky stars I didn't transfer the case over to the adult court, because the next time this kid gets arrested that's exactly what I'm going to do."

The court officer knocked on the door.

"Judge Bender wants you both in chambers. Now."

Pattie and Frank glanced at each other and followed him down the hall. Once in chambers, Judge Bender picked up his copy of the evaluation.

"Hey this new Psychologist is great!"

Pattie nodded and smiled.

"What have I been saying? He even pulled strings to get Justin Edwards a bed at Beau Rivage," she said.

"That's wonderful. How's he making out up there?"

"He's adjusting well. Dr. Armstrong called the DA's Office the other day requesting more time to complete the evaluation for the Criminal Case though. Justin simply hasn't opened up to him yet."

Frank cleared his throat.

"I hate to interrupt, but I thought we were here to discuss Amissah."

"Sorry Frank. Sure. So, what's the plan?" Judge Bender asked.

"There is no plan. We can't come up with an agreement," Frank said.

Judge Bender frowned.

"I don't like the sounds of that. What's the story?"

"Frank refuses to offer me probation. All Thomas needs is balance, restoration and above all, to get away from the bully who went after him with the stun gun in the first place," Pattie answered quickly.

"I offered her detention. That's away from the so-called bully," Frank said.

"I already told you, it's too harsh at this point," Judge Bender said.

"For a stun gun, Judge?"

"In self-defense?" Pattie said, mimicking Frank's incredulous tone.

"What's wrong with scaring this kid straight? If you don't like the idea of detention then let's start off by sending him to boot camp. Afterwards, we could follow it up with a period of probation. Discipline never hurt anyone and the good news is that he'd be off the streets AND away from the bully," Frank said.

"Your Honor, studies have shown that boot camps don't always have promising outcomes," Pattie said.

Frank gasped and pointed at Pattie. His mouth hung open in shock.

"Oh my God Judge! I don't believe it! Wasn't it only yesterday when she sat in that very chair extolling the virtue of boot camps?"

"Well, maybe she hadn't read the studies at that point," Judge Bender said, as he and Frank laughed together.

Pattie cleared her throat.

"Excuse me Your Honor, but in yesterday's case juvenile boot camp was the most ideal solution. However, as I recall, Attorney Bernard was arguing for military school. No matter what, he never gets it right."

"OK, well, I think we can all agree that this kid needs to be away from the bully. Is that right?" Judge Bender asked.

Pattie and Frank both nodded.

"OK then. I think the answer is long term, intensive Probation and I do mean intensive and while he's on probation he can go live in some residential placement facility with professionals who can help him, instead his parents who are nothing more than enablers. So, Pattie plead him out and while you're at it, impress upon him that he's making out like a bandit," Judge Bender said.

Pattie stood.

"He and his parents are already in the building. I'll talk to them right now and recommend this, but in the end, I can't force them to agree," she said.

"Why not? It's the deal of the century," Judge Bender said.

"Judge, I already told Pattie this, but I think it bears repeating before she swans out of here, that if Thomas comes back here again I won't play around with him. I'll just send him over to the adult court."

Pattie nodded.

"Fine. By the way, I have a question," she said.

"What?" Judge Bender asked.

"How come Thomas is the only one who got arrested? Why didn't the police charge the bully with anything?"

"That's no concern of hers, Judge."

"Why not? The Sixth Amendment gives my client the right to confront his accusers."

"Yeah, but only if we go to trial," Frank said.

"Pattie, why don't you just forget about the bully and concentrate on what's best for Thomas," Judge Bender said.

"I am! That's why I asked the question," Pattie said.

CHAPTER FIFTEEN

THE TIMES THEY ARE A CHANGIN'

Later that afternoon, Brad Curatolo rifled through a stack of papers on his desk. When he zeroed in on Pattie's application, he picked up the phone and telephoned the Family Court. He reviewed the application while he waited for Nancy Speck to put him through to Judge Bender.

"Hello Brad. How are you?" Judge Bender asked.

"Fine thanks, Judge. I hate to bother you, but I'm calling to inquire about someone named Pattie Anwald, who applied for a job in my office."

"Oh. That's terrible news."

"Why?"

"Because I hate the idea of Pattie leaving us. We like her over here. She's an extremely conscientious and competent worker."

"Well then, tell me something awful about her that will deter me from having to hire her."

"I can't. There isn't anything. She's highly qualified."

Brad sighed.

"Wow. That wasn't what I was hoping to hear."

"Knowing you these past twenty years, I have no problem believing that. You've never once hired a woman for anything other than Admin, but the times they are a changin' and the time for finally breaking past that proverbial glass ceiling is long overdue. So just do it, Brad."

"Thanks," Brad said.

He waited for Judge Bender to hang up before he slammed down the phone.

"Shit."

He flung Pattie's application into the air and watched it pirouette to the floor. He sighed again and slid another application out from under his blotter. He reviewed it, picked up the phone and dialed.

"Hello, Millard? It's Brad."

"Hi. How are you?"

"I've been better. Look, I might as well cut to the chase here. I'm sorry to have to tell you this, but I can't hire you, even though you were my first choice."

Millard groaned.

"Why? What happened?"

"Internal Politics is forcing me to choose a female over you. I'll have a problem on my hands if I don't pick her. She's got better qualifications."

"I'm disappointed, but I appreciate you letting me know."

"Listen, I have a consolation prize for you. I hear there's going to be an opening for a Children's Advocate over at the Family Court. If I were you I'd apply right now before it goes public. Oh and when you do, be sure to tell Judge Bender that I sent you, because he owes me a favor."

"Great. Thanks.

"And another thing. Come back and reapply with me in six months' time, because by then I'll be sure to have an opening for you."

After they hung up, Brad slid Millard's application back under his blotter for safekeeping.

CHAPTER SIXTEEN

THEY SAY IT'S YOUR BIRTHDAY

The following Saturday night, Jordan Armstrong stood in his bedroom deciding what to wear to Frank Bernard's birthday party. He knew that the only reason he even accepted the invitation was so that he could "accidentally" run into Pattie.

By the time he arrived at Frank's townhouse, the party was well under way. The rooms were filled with guests, but he did not find Pattie among them. What made matters worse for him was that he didn't recognize anyone, until Nancy Speck rushed over to him, grabbed him by the arm and dragged him over to the Baby Grand Piano, where a petite red haired woman dominated the room with tales of war stories about her career. Her pixie haircut, pallid complexion and watery red rimmed eyes made her look like an albino town mouse. Her off white linen pants suit and lime green silk scarf were her most attractive assets.

"Come on over here and sit down between me and my husband," Nancy told Jordan.

Her voice carried, drowning out the red-haired woman, whose nose was so out of joint at the interruption, that she shot Nancy a dirty look. However, the minute she laid eyes on Jordan she smiled and batted her eye lashes at him. He smiled back at her politely.

She waited until he and Nancy were settled in on the piano seat before she continued to speak. Her voice was high pitched and intense. She projected it as if she were playing a part in a high school play. Every time she spoke, she gesticulated and waved her arms. When she stopped talking long enough to take a breath, she kept her hands still, which enabled Jordan to notice that her fingernails were bitten right down to the quick. Her cuticles were so picked at and ravaged that they were almost as red as her hair.

"I heard what you were saying Annie and I agree with you all the way. It's exasperating the way the Constitution caters to all of the criminals and thugs, by preventing us good guys from cracking down on them," Frank Bernard said.

Annie leaned over and clasped both of Frank's hands. Frank leaned over too, in order to inspect Annie's non-existent cleavage.

"Well, I'll be the first one to admit that I don't know a thing about Juvenile Justice, but it sounds like you at least understand what I'm talking about. Whether we're prosecuting adults or kids, let's never lose sight of the fact that we're in the right," Annie said.

Jordan quietly asked Nancy Speck whether she had seen Attorney Anwald that night.

"Good question Dr. A, but no I haven't. Hey Frank! Ain't Pattie Anwald comin' to this shindig?" Nancy asked.

"I invited her, but she had a prior commitment and couldn't attend," Frank said.

"Hmmm, Anwald. Now that name rings a bell," Toby Barnett said.

"She's my opponent at the Family Court," Frank said.

Toby nodded.

"Oh yeah. I know who she is."

Annie waved her ravaged hand in dismissal.

"Your opponent? My God, you mean you'd let a defense attorney in here?" Annie asked.

Frank nodded.

"Why not? She's harmless enough," he said.

Jordan turned around and played a soft tune as a way of distracting himself. As soon as he did, Annie bolted.

"Now where did she run off to?" Nancy asked.

Toby chuckled.

"Who cares?"

A few seconds later, Annie returned, carrying sheet music.

Toby stood up.

"That did it! If she's gonna sing, I'm outta here," he muttered, as he walked into the other room.

Annie ignored him and handed Jordan the sheet music.

"This is the sheet music to my favorite song. It's called 'It's All About Me'. Are you familiar with it?"

Jordan shook his head.

"No."

She frowned.

"Well, can you at least read music?"

"Yes. I'm a bit rusty, but I'll do my best," he said.

She smiled.

"Great."

She banged down hard on the lowest piano keys and pressed her foot down on the sustaining pedal until she succeeded in silencing the room. Once she was sure she had everybody's undivided attention she addressed the group.

"OK everybody. I'm going to need you all to remain quiet while I sing the theme song from the Broadway Musical, 'It's All about Me'."

She pointed at Jordan and asked him his name. Jordan blushed and answered her.

"For those of you who don't know me, I'm Anne Carey and this here is Jordan Armstrong. Jordan has graciously offered to accompany me. Jordan, I sing in the key of D."

Jordan looked nonplused.

"That's a bit high. Isn't it?"

She stamped her foot.

"Just do it!"

Jordan shrugged and played the introductory bars in the requested key and Annie came in right on cue. She sounded like a fourth grader as she painstakingly plowed through the song. At one point, she sounded flat. A few seconds later, she sounded sharp. Right at the high note her voice cracked, but no matter how badly she butchered the song, Jordan played flawlessly. At the end, everyone dutifully applauded while she bowed and grinned from ear to ear.

Still blushing, Jordan rose, said his good byes to Nancy Speck and her husband and worked his way across the living room. When Judge and Mrs. Bender entered, he greeted them, paid his respects to Frank and his wife and walked toward the foyer. Annie tried to follow him, but he managed to slip out the door before she could catch up to him.

CHAPTER SEVENTEEN
IRREPLACEABLE

Pattie and Nancy Speck were the first to arrive in the hearing room on Monday morning.

"I went to Frank's birthday party the other night and you'll never guess who I saw," Nancy said.

"Who? Frank?"

"Very funny, but actually, I was referring to that nice Dr. Armstrong. I think he was there looking for you, because once he realized you weren't coming, he vamoosed."

Pattie smiled.

"Oh really? That's nice to hear," she said.

"Why weren't you there anyway?"

"I got promoted to a green belt and the Dojo had a celebration."

"Congratulations. I'll tell you something. Back in my day girls didn't go in for Martial Arts."

The court officer appeared in the doorway and knocked. Judge Bender stood behind him.

"All rise please," the court officer said.

Pattie and Nancy stood, but Judge Bender smiled, shook his head and waved his hand.

"Oh, don't even bother with that, Mike. There's nobody here but us chickens."

Once he was seated, Nancy Speck addressed him.

"You know Judge, since Dr. Alt is planning to retire, maybe we should hire Dr. Armstrong to do all of our evaluations," Nancy said.

Pattie smiled and nodded.

"I agree. It would be a great idea," she said.

"The only fly in the ointment is that he's a full-time professor over at Omnia. I mean, what if he doesn't have the time to testify?" Judge Bender asked.

"Well, academics get a lot more time off than we Legal Eagles do," Pattie said.

Judge Bender chuckled.

"Well, who doesn't? OK, look into it for us Nancy and find out if he's even available," Judge Bender said.

Chapter Eighteen

YOU BELONG WITH ME

Several weeks later, Pattie entered the hearing room where Judge Bender and Nancy Speck were already waiting for her. She greeted them and a few seconds later, Mike, the Court Officer, entered.

"Sorry for the delay Your Honor. Bonnie Louden and her social worker are at the metal detector. They should be here in a few minutes."

"Why is everything taking so long today, Mike?" Judge Bender asked.

"Well, first of all, we don't usually have hearings on Fridays, so we're understaffed to begin with and then when you factor in the twenty-two companion cases to this case, it's like a mob scene out there," Mike said.

"Oh well. We didn't have a choice. We had to squeeze everything that Pattie could possibly wrap up on her last day here," Judge Bender said.

The door opened and Bonnie Louden and Geraldine Latham came into the hearing room and sat down next to Pattie. Bonnie looked more respectable than she did on her last court date.

"Now that the cast is all assembled, bring me up to date on this case, please, Attorney Anwald," Judge Bender said.

Pattie stood.

"Dr. Jordan Armstrong filed his psychological evaluation, along with his recommendations for Bonnie. He and Mrs. Latham were able to get Bonnie temporarily placed at Beau Rivage on an emergency basis, so at least she's safe. I'm asking your Honor to order that the placement become permanent."

"Attorney Anwald have you run this past your client?"

"Yes, Your Honor, in detail and Bonnie is in full agreement."

"Ms. Latham, what is the Agency's position?"

Geraldine Latham stood.

"We also agree that it would be in Bonnie's best interests for her to remain at Beau Rivage," she said.

"Do we have any information about Former Judge DeVittorio's pending criminal matter?"

"My understanding is that he pled not guilty and is out on bail. Dr. Armstrong also recommended that Bonnie undergo pregnancy and HIV testing as well," Pattie said.

"What is your position?"

"Bonnie and I agree."

"The agency does not object," Geraldine Latham added.

"Dr. Armstrong has also recommended that Beau Rivage look into an alternative high school for Bonnie when she reaches the ninth grade this coming September and we're in agreement with that as well," Pattie added.

"So is the agency," Geraldine Latham said.

"All of the recommendations are hereby incorporated as court orders," Judge Bender said.

"Thank you, Your Honor," Pattie, Bonnie and Geraldine said, almost in unison.

"All right then. Now Bonnie, today is the start of a new life for you. Do your best to make the most out of every opportunity that comes your way."

Bonnie stood.

"I will, Your Honor," she said.

"I'm ordering you and your Social Worker back here in six months for an in-court review," Judge Bender said and then Mike escorted Pattie, Bonnie and her Social Worker out into the hall.

Bonnie hugged Pattie.

"Thank you for everything," she said.

"My pleasure. I'll visit you later today," Pattie said.

They said good bye and when Bonnie and Geraldine were gone, Pattie returned to her office, where she managed to dodge the half-filled cardboard boxes that were strewen around her office and she poured herself a cup of coffee. She sat down and was about to take her first sip, when the telephone rang.

"Pattie Anwald here."

"Hi, it's Toby Barnett. I'm calling to let you know that Judge Benchley granted Elliott Glutz's Motion to Suppress the videos, along with Penny Edwards' admission."

"Oh, my God! That's everything!"

"I know, but don't worry. I'll appeal it."

"Can't you just offer them a deal? That way you can still get a conviction and poor Justin won't have to testify."

"I doubt it. They don't want to plead out to anything that entails jail time and I won't offer them anything that doesn't include jail time."

"I don't blame you."

"By the way, Judge Benchley questioned your absence."

"I never got a Notice of the Hearing! As a matter of fact, I never even got a copy of the Motion," Pattie said.

"Well, that's typical of Elliot. He just refuses to send out notices to people he doesn't like, even if it violates a court order."

Pattie chuckled nervously.

"Wow. Well then, I guess that tells you where I stand. But, isn't that unethical?"

Toby chuckled along with her.

"Oh, so now you expect him to become ethical? Anyway, don't worry about it. I'll fax all future notices to you, just to make sure you get them."

"Thanks. As of Monday, keeping me in the loop shouldn't be too difficult though, since I'm transferring over to your neck of the woods."

"Really? That sounds like an interesting turn of events."

"I know, except I'll be playing for the other team."

"Well, at least we can glare at each other in the hallway."

Pattie chuckled again.

"That's actually funny, but even if we find ourselves against each other ninety nine percent of the time, I'll always be on your side as long as you have Justin's back. That's the one thing that will never change," she said.

"Glad to hear it."

Just as they hung up, Pattie glanced up to see Jordan Armstrong standing in her doorway.

"Good morning," he said.

She smiled.

"Good morning to you. How nice to see you. Come on into what's left of my world."

He walked into her office and stood in front of her desk.

"I happened to be in the building delivering evaluations and I'm delighted that it gave me an excuse to drop in on you."

"Thank you. I was going to call you anyway and thank you for the recommendations you made on Bonnie Louden's case. They were very helpful."

Jordan smiled.

"You're welcome."

He pointed at the boxes.

"Are you going somewhere?"

"Yes. I'm transferring to what we Family Court Attorneys jokingly refer to as 'the adult court'."

"May I shut your door for a moment?"

She chuckled.

"You can always try."

She watched him close her door as far as he could. Then he approached her desk.

"May I sit down?"

She pointed at the visitor's chair.

"Sure."

He took a seat.

"Ever since the first night we met, I found you to be attractive. Then, the more I got to know you, the more I grew to like you."

Pattie blushed.

"Why, thank you Jordan. What an incredibly nice thing to say."

"Well, I've been waiting to say it for a long time, but since we both worked on the same cases, I never felt right about saying it or asking you to go out with me. However, now I'm doing both. So, would you like to go out to dinner with me a week from tomorrow?"

She cleared her throat and nodded.

"Well, first of all I'm flattered."

Jordan smiled.

"Well, that's a relief. Does that mean the answer is yes?"

She smiled.

"Before I answer that, I do have to remind you that we'll both still be working on Justin's case. I'll still be his Guardian ad Litem and if that case goes to trial I guess we'll have to disclose it to all parties concerned."

"I see."

"So as long you understand that, I'd love to go out to dinner with you."

He nodded.

"Great. So how do I get a hold of you after today?"

She tore a piece of paper from a small pad on her desk and scrawled her number on it.

"This is my cell phone number. I don't have a landline. If you happen to lose this, you can also call me at the Legal Aid Office, because that's where I'll be working."

He folded the piece of paper up, stuck it in his wallet and smiled.

"Oh, don't worry. I won't lose it. I'll guard it with my life."

He stood, walked over to the door and pried it open. He said good bye and once he was gone, Pattie broke into a smile. She reached into her tote bag, pulled out her cell phone and speed dialed Ryan.

"Hey those boxes you gave me are coming in handy for my move."

"Good."

"Guess what happened? Dr. Keith's replacement dropped in and asked me out on a date."

"Of all the nerve!"

"No. It's not like that at all. Once I recovered from the shock I was actually flattered."

"You're kidding."

"Why? I already told you he's cute."

"So does tht mean you're planning on going?"

"Why not?"

"Look. I've got to go. Recess is over," he said.

He hung up before she had a chance to respond. She stared at her phone for a few seconds and shook her head.

CHAPTER NINETEEN
SURPRISE, SURPRISE, SURPRISE

A few minutes later, Mike knocked on Pattie's door.

"Judge Bender wants you to report to the Hearing Room right away."

"Why?"

He shrugged.

"I can't say."

She picked up her tote bag and accompanied Mike, the Court Officer to the hearing room where Judge Bender, Nancy Speck and Frank Bernard were waiting for her.

"So, young lady, what are your lunch plans?" Judge Bender asked Pattie.

"I don't have any."

"Yes, you do, because we're all surprising you with a farewell luncheon at Voltaire's," he said.

"We even ordered a stretch limo!" Nancy chimed in.

Pattie's eyes lit up.

"Really?"

"Yeah and it's black! I wanted a white one, but this is your day and we all know how much you love the color black," Nancy said.

"Yes, I do. Thanks! Wow!" Pattie said.

"I wonder whether we'll run into some celebrities", Frank said.

Nancy nodded.

"Hey, you never know. Right?"

"By the way, did you know that Voltaire's used to be a speak easy back in the Roaring Twenties?" Judge Bender asked.

Pattie shook her head.

"No."

"Well it was."

Nancy lifted a large gift box from the seat next to her and handed it to Pattie. It was wrapped in shiny black paper and tied with a huge red velvet bow.

"This is from all of us. It's our going away present to you," she said.

"Thank you. Can I open it now?" Pattie asked.

"Sure. Why not?" Judge Bender said.

Pattie gently slid the ribbon off of the box and carefully unwrapped the paper. She removed the box top, pulled back the tissue paper and saw a red leather designer briefcase. She removed it from the box, ran her fingers over it and opened it.

"Oh, my God! Thank you so much. It's beautiful and soft."

"I know, right? It's designed with the woman executive in mind," Nancy said.

"Think of us when you use it, because we'll all be thinking of you," Judge Bender said.

"And missing you, kiddo," Nancy said, as Pattie gently returned the briefcase to its box.

Frank nodded.

"Yeah. Even me," he said.

Pattie smiled wistfully. Her eyes filled with tears.

"I feel the same way about all of you too. You're all great. Even you, Frank."

Frank chuckled and smiled at her, along with everyone else.

"I pray that you'll be happy. Quite frankly, I never particularly liked that Courthouse. I found it to be way too dog eat dog," Judge Bender said.

There was a knock on the door.

"That must be your other surprise," Nancy said.

Judge Bender nodded and Mike opened the door. Pattie looked up and let out a mild gasp, as Mike led Jordan into the hearing room.

"Aha! Now the truth comes out as to why you just so happened to be in the building," Pattie said.

Jordan nodded.

"Guilty as charged," he said.

"Hey, you'd better be careful when you go around saying things like that in this place," Frank said.

"Well, we might as well get going," Judge Bender said.

"All rise," Mike said, when Judge Bender stood.

Judge Bender chuckled.

"Now, now, there's no need for that at this point, Mike," he said, as he slid out of his robe.

Pattie stood and took a long, last look around at the place where she learned how to become a lawyer.

CHAPTER TWENTY
THE VISIT

Later that afternoon, Bonnie and Thomas sat next to each other on a rose colored Victorian Couch in the warm, well furnished living room at Beau Rivage. Thomas was holding his portable disc player high overhead. Bonnie tried to take it from him several times, but Thomas kept it just out of her reach. She slapped him playfully. He retaliated by gently nudging her with the toe of his sneaker.

"Oh, come on! Let me borrow it for a few minutes," she whined.

He closed his eyes and shook his head.

"No way."

"Why not?"

"Because it's mine and I'm using it."

She rested her foot against his calf and pressed lightly. He jabbed her once again with the toe of his sneaker, just as Pattie walked in. She pointed at two matching Queen Anne chairs, which had been embroidered in crewel work.

"Why don't you sit in that chair, Thomas? Bonnie, you can sit over there in that one."

Thomas and Bonnie stood, gave each other dirty looks and sat in their newly appointed seats. Thomas stuck his tongue out at Bonnie and Pattie sat on the couch.

"What are we? Seat warmers?" Thomas asked.

Pattie ignored the question and posed one of her own.

"Where's Justin?"

Bonnie shrugged.

"He left," she said.

Pattie frowned.

"Why?"

"Maybe because you never showed up. I can't believe it took you this long to get up here. It's almost dinner time," Thomas said.

Pattie cleared her throat.

"Bonnie, didn't you give Thomas and Justin the message that I wouldn't be able to get here until now?"

Bonnie shook her head.

"I forgot," she said.

"Nice," Thomas said.

Justin showed up and gingerly planted himself on the arm of the couch. He waved at Pattie and ignored the other two. The whites of his eyes were red. Pattie squinted, stood and went over to him. She peered into his eyes.

"What's wrong with your eyes?"

"The doctor said I have pink eye."

"Well, I hope he gave you something for it."

Justin nodded.

"Yeah. Drops."

"Good. Make sure you use them. Anyway, I'm glad you're all here because there is something I need to discuss with you," Pattie said.

"What's up?" Thomas asked.

"Well, since there's no easy way to break it to you, I'll just come right out with it. Today was my last day working at The Family Court."

"Oh God. Did you get fired or something?" Thomas asked.

Pattie shook her head.

"No. It's nothing like that. I decided to leave for a better paying position."

Justin looked down at his sneakers.

"You mean you sold out?" He asked.

"So, what's going to happen to us now?" Bonnie asked.

"We're gonna get thrown to the wolves just so that she can make more money," Thomas said.

"Oh, that's just great," Justin said.

"There's no need for any of you to worry. You all have my cell phone number and you can still call me any time you need me."

Justin shook his head.

"That's nice. Thanks, but what about the case where you're my guardian?"

"I'll still continue to be your guardian ad litem both at the Criminal Division, where I'll be working and also at the Family Court."

"Well, that's great for him, but what about Bonnie and me?" Thomas asked.

"They hired someone named Millard to be my replacement. He'll be covering my cases as of Monday."

"Yeah, but will he help us like you did?" Bonnie asked.

"He'd better or else he'll hear about it from me!" Pattie reassured her.

"Did you mean it when you said that we could still call you at any time?" Bonnie asked.

"Of course, she didn't mean it," Thomas said.

A young man burst into the room and Bonnie got up and ran over to him. He was big and stocky and he wore a gray sweat suit.

"Attorney Anwald this is my boyfriend, Kenny. He's the captain of the football team," Bonnie said.

Pattie knit her brow.

"Boyfriend? But you're only thirteen. Aren't you too young to be dating?"

"Thirteen may sound young to you, but remember, I'll be turning fourteen in six weeks."

Kenny walked over to Pattie, grabbed her hand and pumped it like a well.

"It's nice to meet you," he said.

Pattie nodded.

"Thank you. It's nice to meet you too."

Pattie stood, walked over to the doorway and beckoned for Bonnie to join her out in the hall.

"Bonnie, I need to speak with you for a minute, please."

Bonnie turned to Kenny.

"Hang on a minute. OK, Kenny?"

Kenny nodded and sat down on the couch. Justin got up and followed Pattie and Bonnie into the hall. He gave Pattie a quick kiss on the cheek and ran down the hall. Once he was out of sight, Pattie stared at Bonnie and frowned.

"Exactly how old is Kenny?"

"Seventeen."

"Wow. That's way too old for you."

"Oh yeah? He's only one third as old as Judge De Vittorio. Besides, he's nice and I like him."

"Does he live here at Beau Rivage?"

"No. He lives with his parents."

"Still. I'm not so sure I approve. What do April and Kyle think about all of this?"

"April doesn't see any problem with it. She says that age is irrelevant in relationships."

CHAPTER TWENTY ONE
BAPTISM BY FIRE

Monday morning's Arraignment Court was packed. Ryan Pilgrim stood in the doorway by the judge's entrance and other court officers were dispersed in various locations throughout the courtroom. Pattie's brand new emerald green velvet dress was the brightest item in view. Pattie made her way through the sea of people and walked over to Ryan. As soon as he saw her, he smiled.

"Hey Pattie! Welcome aboard!"

Pattie smiled back at him.

"Thanks!"

"Don't tell me that Brad actually assigned you to this courtroom on your very first day here. Sheesh! Talk about a baptism by fire," Ryan said.

She nodded.

"I know, but it's OK. I've done a million arraignments in Family Court, so I kind of know what to expect. Due Process is Due Process is Due Process if you know what I mean."

He smiled and nodded.

"Now that's the attitude to take. Confidence. I'm glad to hear you're not nervous."

She chuckled.

"Well now, I wouldn't go quite that far."

She pointed at the huge French windows, which were practically opaque from years of never being washed.

"Can't somebody open one of those windows and at least let some sunshine and fresh air into this place?"

"I don't think they even open any more. Maybe they never did, so it looks like you're the only ray of sunshine or breath of fresh air that this place is ever going to see."

"Wow. Anyway, thanks for the compliment."

"Don't mention it. By the way, I'm treating you to lunch today at my favorite deli."

"Lunch should be on me. After all, you got me the job."

Ryan smiled.

"Lunch can be on you when pay day rolls around. Deal?"

Pattie nodded and smiled.

"Deal."

A rotund figure in a black robe walked up to the doorway and stood behind Ryan. He knocked three times on the old oak door. Even though it was only ten o'clock in the morning, he looked as if he had already worked a full day. A middle-aged woman stood behind him, holding a stack of files.

"All rise please," Ryan called out, as he moved out of the way to let the judge pass.

All chatter in the courtroom ceased and everyone stood. Pattie scurried across the room to find a vacant seat in the attorneys' section. There was dead silence, except for the sound of the grit that crackled under the soles of her boots. When Pattie reached the attorney's section, she realized that all of the seats had been taken. When she looked up, she also realized that Judge Fanshaw was standing at the bench, glaring at her. She blushed, cleared her throat and stood against the wall.

"Hear ye, hear ye, hear ye," Ryan said, announcing that court was now open and in session and that the Honorable Judge Cuthbert Fanshaw was presiding.

Judge Fanshaw nodded at Ryan, thanked him and quickly read every one their rights in a monotone. When he was finished, he glared once again at Pattie and then at Assistant District Attorney Annie Carey whose black patent leather designer pumps clicked against the floor as she entered the courtroom late.

"Call the first case Attorney Carey," Judge Fanshaw ordered. His words punctured the air like bullets.

"Your Honor, for the record, I'm Assistant District Attorney, Anne Carey representing The People this morning. The first case is People v. Scott Lee, docket number ending in zero seven one six."

When no one appeared, Ryan called out "no response, your Honor," and Judge Fanshaw glanced up.

"Is Scott Lee here?" He called out into the sea of faces.

"No response, Your Honor," Ryan said again.

Annie could barely conceal her glee at the hopes of having this defendant's bail revoked.

Judge Fanshaw glanced at the clerk.

"Has Mr. Lee retained an attorney?"

"Not yet, Your Honor," the clerk answered.

"Attorney Carey, why don't you call the cases involving defendants who are already present with their high-priced defense attorneys? That way we can save them beaucoup bucks, while at the same time giving latecomers like Mr. Lee a reasonable opportunity to show up."

"Your Honor, the People are not bounty hunters. Since Mr. Lee is not present in court, we request that his bail be forfeited and that a rearrest warrant be issued."

Judge Fanshaw shook his head.

"I guess you didn't hear what I just said. Call some other case. Now," he snapped.

"The next case is People v. Melissa Carmen."

"Great. Where's Legal Aid?" Judge Fanshaw called out.

Pattie approached the counsel table and cleared her throat.

"Right here, Your Honor," she answered.

She turned around and watched, as an attractive woman came from the back of the courtroom and stood next to her.

"State your name for the record," Judge Fanshaw said.

Pattie cleared her throat.

"Pattie Anwald, Your Honor."

"Just Pattie?"

Pattie sighed.

"Yes."

"All right. I take it then, that Ms. Carmen is the woman standing next to you?"

"Yes."

"Great. Proceed Ms. Carey."

"Your Honor, according to the police report, The Defendant placed several harassing telephone calls to a police officer, both at the Fifth Precinct where he works and at his home. The calls continued in spite of his repeated warnings to stop," Annie said.

"Can he even prove that it was her?" Pattie interrupted.

Annie gave Pattie a dirty look, but directed her answer to Judge Fanshaw.

"Your Honor, both the precinct and the officer have caller ID, just like everyone else in this city."

Judge Fanshaw glared at Annie and held up his hand as if he were stopping traffic.

"Excuse me, Ms. Carey, but are you chewing gum in my court room?"

Ryan shook his head, while Annie blushed and gulped.

"Your Honor, I can honestly say that I'm not. Anyhow, as if the telephone calls weren't enough, The Defendant also sent the officer several harassing emails," she continued.

"Show me the printouts," Judge Fanshaw ordered.

"They're not in the file, Your Honor."

Judge Fanshaw scowled.

"Well, where are they?"

"I don't know."

"Well, why don't you know?"

"Because I didn't do the filing. I thought that they were there. In any event, Your Honor, The People are requesting an Order of Protection prohibiting the Defendant from contacting the officer again, so that in the event she violates it, she can be charged with contempt of court and go to jail," Annie added, attempting to conceal a smirk.

"Your Honor, I object. First of all, we have no proof that any of this ever even happened," Pattie said.

"Well, wait a minute. What I want to know, exactly, is this. Who in their right mind would call a law enforcement officer and harass him?" Judge Fanshaw asked.

"Your Honor, The People failed to disclose a material fact. It's not as if the parties are random strangers and Ms. Carmen is some kind of stalker or something. Ms. Carmen and the complainant, Officer Ralph Carmen are married."

Judge Fanshaw frowned.

"What?"

"Yes, Your Honor. Their divorce is currently pending over at The Family Court. They have a five-year-old son, who resides with Ms. Carmen. The calls that the People are characterizing as 'harassment' were merely routine calls which Ms. Carmen placed to her future ex-husband, to discuss child visitation and support issues."

Judge Fanshaw picked up the file. While he read it, an expensively dressed defense attorney leaned over to Elliot Glutz. His elegant Armani suit formed a great contrast to Elliott's shiny gray polyester attire.

"Who's the new kid on the block? I think the least that Annie Carey could have done was to share her bubble gum with her," he whispered.

Elliott chuckled.

"Agreed Reginald. I always love a good cat fight first thing in the morning," Elliott answered, in an uncharacteristic whisper.

Reginald grinned.

"I find it endearing whenever anyone attempts to take Annie down and it's also refreshing to see that Brad's new neophyte isn't yet another clone of himself. God that was getting old," Reginald whispered.

Elliott nodded, just as Judge Fanshaw put the file down.

"All right, Attorney Anwald. Have you anything further to add?" Judge Fanshaw asked. His eyes bore holes through Pattie.

"No," Pattie said.

"Thank you. Now, Attorney Carey, just when were you planning to inform me that the complainant and the Defendant were married? Or weren't you?"

"Your Honor"—

"Save it. Your antics are bordering on prosecutorial misconduct. This case is dismissed!"

"Thank you, Your Honor," Pattie said.

Melissa Carmen turned around and left without saying a word.

"Call the next case, Attorney Carey," Judge Fanshaw ordered.

"Your Honor, this is the case of Christopher Foreman, docket number ending in zero eight nine seven, but the People have decided not to go forward with the prosecution."

A light haired blue eyed man in his late twenties approached the defense table and stood next to Pattie.

"Well, that is certainly out of character for you, Ms. Carey. What's the scam?" Judge Fanshaw asked.

"There is no scam, Your Honor. It's just that the Defendant is charged with rape and the only witness is the victim, Cara Forrester, who's got serious credibility issues. There is nothing to corroborate her allegations and as we all know, the Defendant is not required to testify against himself."

"What are these credibility issues you're referring to?"

"Well, Your Honor, the victim has a criminal record."

"So what? Is it for perjury or something?" Judge Fanshaw asked.

"No. Prostitution."

Judge Fanshaw banged the gavel.

"Case dismissed. You're free to go, Mr. Foreman."

"Thank you, Your Honor," Pattie and Robert Foreman said at the same time.

As Robert Foreman turned to leave, an attractive, African American woman stood. Her lilac silk dress suit showed off her shapely hourglass figure and it made a swishing sound as she made her way into the aisle.

"Good afternoon. My name is Cara Forrester and I am the victim in this case. I don't understand why this case was just dismissed." Her voice sounded rich and velvety.

"The case was dismissed because the People have declined to prosecute. It's out of my hands and that's all I can say on the matter," Judge Fanshaw answered.

"But, Your Honor, this man raped me! I can't tell you how horrible I feel, hearing that the case against him is being dismissed. In fact, it makes me feel like I'm being raped all over again."

"I understand what you're saying, but my hands are tied. If the People don't want to prosecute someone I can't force them to do so. That's the way the law works," Judge Fanshaw said.

"Well, I thought the victim's background isn't supposed to come into play in a rape case, so I'm beginning to wonder whether this is a black thing," Cara Forrester said.

Judge Fanshaw scowled at Annie.

"Ms. Carey?"

"Of course, it isn't!" Annie said.

Judge Fanshaw banged the gavel again, motioned for Ryan to call a recess and raced out of the courtroom.

"All rise please," Ryan announced.

Ryan followed Judge Fanshaw into his chambers and watched him flounce into a comfortable leather chair.

"Why, oh why did that lame ass Anne Carey have to set me up like this?" Judge Fanshaw lamented.

Ryan shrugged.

"I have no idea. Her mind has always been like a labyrinth to me."

"What mind? Does she think just because the victim is a prostitute that the People won't be able to get a conviction?"

"Well, it would be hard for her to get a conviction even if the victim was Mother Theresa," Ryan said.

Judge Fanshaw chuckled.

"The victim was right when she said that her background shouldn't even be an issue. After all, this is the Twenty First Century."

"Well, why didn't you just sanction Annie when you had the chance on that Carmen case? She's getting more and more out of control each day."

"You're right. Listen, do me a favor and make sure you rail-road that Forrester woman out of this building. I don't care how many of you guys it takes"

"How? After all, it's a public building."

"Who cares? Just do it. Get her outta here and make sure that she doesn't get back in."

CHAPTER TWENTY TWO
THE FICKLE FINGER OF FATE

Pattie and Ryan stood in the hallway and waited for the elevator.

"I am so proud of you! You totally kicked Annie's ass this morning. You rule, girl," Ryan said with a grin.

Just then, the door to the stairwell squeaked open. Annie stepped into the corridor and power walked over to Pattie and Ryan.

"What's your name again?" She asked, squinting at Pattie.

Pattie frowned.

"Again? Why? Have we met?"

"No, but you stated your name earlier in court. You know. On the record."

"Oh yeah. Pattie Anwald."

"Uh huh. Well anyway, I hope you won't go around saying that I never gave you anything."

Pattie shook her head.

"What?"

"Sometimes, we angels have been known to throw you devils a bone or two. You know. Like the one I threw you this morning."

"I'm drawing a blank here," Pattie said.

"I'm talking about Robert Foreman. Have you forgotten so soon that I practically threw that dismissal in your lap? Sheesh, talk about your ungrateful people."

"Oh yeah. Thanks," Pattie said.

Annie shook her head in disgust, turned on her heel and power walked back toward the stairwell. She opened the door, raised her right arm and flipped her middle finger at Pattie and Ryan before disappearing. Pattie's mouth flew open and she let out a gasp, as the hinges on the door squeaked shut.

"Oh, my God! Did you see that?"

Ryan nodded.

"Yup. She's an asshole with a personality disorder, so you might as well get used to her," he said, as the elevator door opened.

CHAPTER TWENTY-THREE
THE DELI

Pattie and Ryan squeezed into a small table at an overcrowded deli not far from the courthouse. A few minutes later, a harried waitress brought an iced tea for Pattie and a steaming cup of black coffee for Ryan. She turned around and returned a few minutes later with a hot Pastrami on Rye for Ryan and a small plate of six grape leaves for Pattie. Ryan attacked his sandwich, while Pattie picked up her fork and toyed with her grape leaves. A few seconds later, Elliot Glutz walked past their table.

"Oh hi, Officer Pilgrim! How are you today?"

"Good, thanks and you?"

"Well, apart from having been stuck in court all morning, I guess I'm OK. At least I got to sit next to Reginald Reese. Did you see me?"

Ryan nodded.

"Yeah. Maybe it will be the start of a brand-new friendship, just as long as you're never against each other in any cases. I hear he tends to take his cases personally," Ryan said.

"As nice as a friendship between us might be, it's unlikely to ever happen. We don't have very much in common. He's the best criminal defense attorney in this city and he's got a silk stocking clientele, while I've got more of a meat and potatoes kind of practice."

Ryan nodded.

"I hear you. You're both good lawyers though. By the way, Attorney Pattie Anwald this is Attorney Elliott Glutz."

Pattie and Elliott nodded coolly at one another.

"Actually, we've met," they said in unison.

Ryan looked surprised.

"Oh really?"

"See you later," Elliot said, as he left to eat alone at the counter.

Pattie chuckled.

"Oh, my God! 'What a nice man', said no one ever!"

"Actually, he's not too much worse than any of the other sharks around here. The only difference is that he's louder."

"Great. All these not so nice characters and a freezing cold courtroom. Who could ask for anything more?"

"How could you have felt cold with all of those people packed around you?"

She stabbed her grape leaf.

"I don't know. All I can tell you is that I was actually shivering in there."

"Wow. By the way, the protocol is for you to be in your place, before the Judge comes into the courtroom."

Pattie twisted the grape leaf back and forth with her fork until it was in shreds.

"Why? What is this? Grade school?"

CHAPTER TWENTY-FOUR
A MORE RAREFIED AIR

Meanwhile, Judges Fanshaw and Benchley spent their lunch recess occupying a rosewood booth in an obscure corner of Mata Hari's, a dimly lit, upscale, urban steak house. Judge Fanshaw dabbed his mouth with the white linen napkin that matched the tablecloth and shook his head.

"Oh pal. Just wait until you catch a glimpse of that new Legal Aid Attorney," he said, as he returned the napkin to his lap.

"Really? What's his name?"

"It's not a he this time. It's some girl named Pattie somebody or other. Anwald maybe?"

"Anwald! Oh God! I've had her in front of me, before."

"Poor you. She's a real pain in the ass and she created a lot of hell for me first thing this morning when she got into a cat fight with that Carey broad."

Judge Benchley smirked.

"You mean the overzealous Squeaky Fromme clone?"

Judge Fanshaw chuckled and tore into his black and blue steak with a vengeance.

"Yes. I really hate to see my courtroom being invaded by these droves of girl attorneys. They've watered down the profession to no end."

Judge Benchley nodded.

"I hear you. It's sickening."

Judge Fanshaw drained his Martini glass and held it up until the waiter noticed it.

"Refill!"

After the waiter disappeared with the empty glass, he continued with his rant.

"Yeah, I mean it was bad enough when I only had Annie to deal with, but now I've got two of them prancing around in stereo."

"That Carey broad prances? What the hell is she prancing for? She's got nothing to prance with."

Judge Fanshaw chuckled.

"Tell me about it. She's coyote ugly and on top of it, both she and that other broad have these noisy shoes that clickety clack every time they walk. They think they're a pair of Imelda Marcos' or something."

"Oh, now that would just drive me to drink," Judge Benchley said.

The waiter returned with Judge Fanshaw's martini and Judge Fanshaw raised his glass in a toast.

"Tell me about it."

"Yeah and that reminds me. You can't keep doing this in public. Remember the old saying?"

Judge Fanshaw shook his head.

"No. What old saying?"

"Sober as a Judge?"

"I don't smoke and I don't gamble, so I need something to get me through the day."

"Well, what about the deaf game?"

"What's that?"

"I found out one day, quite by accident, that it really rattles these female attorneys when you pretend that you can't hear them."

Judge Fanshaw nodded.

"I could probably pull that off. It sounds like fun."

"It is, but I don't recommend doing it too often. After all, no one wants to wind up with a courtroom full of Elliott Glutzes."

They both laughed.

CHAPTER TWENTY-FIVE
UNFINISHED SYMPATHY

At the end of the day, Pattie put her files down and took a good, hard look at her new office. It was even dustier and dingier than the one she occupied over at the Family Court and the furniture was even older. She wanted to do something to spruce it up, but didn't know how. She glanced at her watch, picked up her briefcase and opened her door. Just as she was leaving, Ryan almost collided with her.

"So, how did you like your first day?" Ryan asked, as they walked down the hall together.

Pattie groaned.

"If that damn judge barked at me to speak up once this afternoon, he must have done it a hundred times. What the hell is wrong with the judges in this courthouse? Are they all hard of hearing or something?"

The elevator door opened and they stepped into the crowd. No one spoke until the elevator reached the main lobby. Ryan stepped aside and let Pattie out first. Once they were out on the street, Ryan stopped in his tracks and squinted at Cara Forrester.

"Oh no! What the hell is she still doing here?" Ryan asked, as Pattie ran up to her and tapped her on the shoulder.

"Excuse me Ms. Forrester. I shouldn't even be saying this, because I represented the accused in the case that got dismissed this morning, but I wanted to let you know how sorry I am."

"Well, I'm sorry too, but thank you for your sentiments."

Ryan ran up to them and pulled Pattie away from her. Once they were out of earshot he laced into her.

"Are you nuts? You just made a statement against your own client's interests. You can't go around doing that, unless you want to find your ass in a sling one of these days!"

"Oh, for God's sake! Why must you be so melodramatic? That poor soul was a victim who went through a soul-destroying experience."

He frowned, shook his head and led her down the street.

CHAPTER TWENTY SIX

FIRST DATE

On the following Saturday night, a taxi stopped around the corner from Pattie's apartment on Peck Slip. Jordan picked up the white porcelain flowerpot that was lodged on the floor, between his feet. It contained a miniature tea rose in full bloom. Its pale white blossoms were so delicate, that he could almost see through them. He paid and tipped the driver, but he requested that the driver wait for him.

"I will, but my waiting time is still on the clock," the driver said.

Jordan nodded. He held the flowerpot carefully as he stepped out of the taxi and closed the door behind him. It was a humid night. Even though the fish market was closed for the day, the unmistakable odor of raw seafood hovered in the air. The wind from The East River was strong and it tousled his wavy hair.

He hurried past a group of tourists who had stopped to window shop. When he turned the corner onto Peck Slip, he walked alongside Pattie's building, right below an antiquated fire escape. He slid on a patch of slimy fish scales and his legs flew out from under him, but he somehow managed to regain his footing before either he or the flowerpot crashed onto the cobblestones.

He glanced up. The number on the building matched the one that Pattie had given to him when he called her to finalize their plans. He pushed the outer door. It wheezed open and it didn't close properly behind him. It was hotter in the vestibule than it was outside. The fish odor from outside merged with the smell of dust, mold and cabbage. The walls had been painted a depressing shade of maroon many moons ago. He grabbed the black lacquered handrail. The raw gouge where someone had carved the word "fuck" revealed that it was oak underneath. It wiggled and creaked under the weight of his hand and each stair squeaked in response to every one of his footsteps. The ceiling at the first landing was made from an engraved tin whose artistry had been smothered with coat after coat of now graying, white lead paint. When he finally reached Pattie's apartment on the third-floor landing, he noticed that her door was warped and rickety, just like her door at the Family Court. He knocked and the wood was so thin and parched, that his fist almost went through it.

Pattie opened the door, smiled at Jordan and breezed out into the hallway. Then she slammed the door behind her. She was made up to the hilt and her hair cascaded down her back. She wore a jade green, Chinese style, silk dress and her black velvet Mary Jane style shoes were embroidered with dragons whose color matched it. She carried her black velvet tote bag in one hand and her key ring in the other.

"You look lovely," he said.

"Thanks. You don't look so bad yourself. I especially love your hair," she answered.

He looked surprised.

"Surely you must be joking."

"But I'm not, though. It's great."

"It's always a bad hair day when you're me. Anyway, this is for you," he said, as he handed her the tea rose.

She held it up to her nose and bathed her nostrils in its scent.

"How beautiful. Thank you. Wait here, OK?"

She opened the door wide enough to slide back inside with the plant. She returned a few seconds later and once again slammed the door behind her.

"I've got a taxi for us," he said.

"That seems crazy when my car is right downstairs. I'd be happy to drive, if you want me to."

"There's no need for that. He's already waiting."

He walked down the staircase ahead of her. Once they reached the bottom landing, he gently led her around the corner and helped her into the taxi. She looked at him and smiled as he slid in next to her.

CHAPTER TWENTY-SEVEN
THE BISTRO

Jordan sat across from Pattie at the French Bistro in Soho. The light from the sconces on the wall behind her formed a halo around her head and the light from the votive candle on the table danced across the white lace tablecloth. He picked a rose from the vase in the centerpiece and placed it in her hair and she smiled.

"Up until the time I picked you up, I had no idea how close you were to the South Street Sea Port."

Pattie giggled.

"Really? Didn't the word 'Slip' give you a clue that I might live near water?"

"No, but I suppose it should have. In any case, it's good to finally see you again and to be spending time with you. I've missed you."

Before she could respond, the waiter arrived to take their beverage order.

"Shall I order a bottle of wine for us?" Jordan asked.

"Count me out. I hate alcohol."

"Oh? What do you drink then?"

"Iced tea."

Jordan ordered a half bottle of Bordeaux for himself and an iced tea for Pattie.

"So how did you like your first week at your new job?"

"I guess it's OK for the most part. It's too soon to tell."

"What do you like to do in your spare time? Perhaps a better question might be, as a lawyer, do you ever have any spare time?"

"Not much, however I do manage to squeeze in some Judo and Performance Poetry whenever I can."

"Judo. Now that sounds interesting. How did you get involved in that?"

"I originally took it up for self-defense. After all, you really don't have anything if you don't feel safe."

"True that," he said, just as the waiter returned with the drinks.

He poured a small amount of wine into a glass for Jordan. Jordan sipped it, smiled and nodded. Then the waiter filled his glass. When the waiter left, Jordan lifted his glass in a toast.

"Anyhow, here's to you always being safe," he said.

Pattie smiled, clicked her glass against his and sipped her iced tea. A few minutes later, the waiter returned with a platter of chilled crudités and hummus.

Pattie ordered a California Platter from the list of appetizers and Jordan stared at her in amazement.

"My God! Is that all you want?"

She nodded.

"Believe me, it's plenty. I had a very late lunch."

He glanced at her with a jaundiced eye and ordered Boeuf Bourguignon over mashed potatoes with Green Beans Haricot.

"I know this next question is rude, but I'm curious to know your age," Jordan said.

Pattie cleared her throat.

"Well, you're right. It is rude, but since I'm not yet old enough to feel offended by it yet, I don't mind answering it. I'm twenty-five."

"Aren't you going to ask me my age?"

"No. I figure if you want me to know, you'll tell me."

"I'm thirty-seven. I hope that's not a problem."

"It's not a problem for me if it's not a problem for you. I recently heard that age is irrelevant in relationships," she said.

Jordan smiled and nodded.

"Well, that's good to know."

Pattie dipped a celery stick into the hummus, chewed off the tip and placed the remainer on her plate. They sipped their drinks and chatted until the waiter arrived with their meals. After they finished their dinner, a Blues band took the stage in the next room.

"Shall we order some dessert?" Jordan asked.

She shook her head.

"Not unless you want some."

"Well then, why don't we take a walk around Soho? It's such a lovely evening," he said.

Chapter Twenty-Eight
DOWNTOWN

Pattie and Jordan walked hand in hand through the boutiques and galleries that stayed open in Soho on Saturday nights. When they reached a New Age store, they went inside. Pattie perused aisles and aisles of cauldrons, smudge sticks, incense, candles and clothes. When she reached the book aisle, she spent several minutes looking at a book of Spells. Jordan watched her and when she returned the book to its shelf, he smiled.

"Let me guess. You were looking for a love potion to attract me."

Pattie cleared her throat.

"That would be a nice idea, but actually I was trying to found out whether it's possible to put curses on people."

Jordan looked shocked.

"Why? Is there someone that you really hate or something?"

Pattie shook her head.

"No. It's just that Justin's parents are in some kind of a coven and they once told me that I would never know a minute's peace as long as their case was pending against them. So now, I'm trying to figure out whether they put some kind of a whammy on me or whether something like that is even possible."

"Well, I truly don't know whether it's possible or not."

"Well, this book seems to imply that it is."

"Millions of people believe in it. I'll tell you what. The next time I talk to Justin I will try to find out if his parents claim to have those kinds of powers."

"Thanks."

"Well, don't thank me yet. So far, he's been extremely closed mouthed with me. I haven't been able to make much progress with him at all."

By the time they left the store, it was dark. Jordan hailed a cab and took Pattie home. When they reached the landing outside of her apartment, she unlocked her door, clenched her hand around the doorknob and smiled at him.

"Well, thanks for a lovely evening. I had a wonderful time," she said.

He smiled back at her.

"So did I. Would you like to do it again?"

Still smiling, she nodded.

"Sure."

"How does next Saturday sound?"

"Perfect."

"Shall I pick you up in the afternoon at around one o'clock? That way we can spend more time together."

She nodded.

"I'd like that."

"Dress casually. I'll plan something sporty and athletic."

"It sounds intriguing. Anyway, good night," she said.

She opened the door as narrowly as she could and slipped into her apartment. She stood by her door in the dark until she heard him descend the staircase. Once he was gone, she pulled the string on the fluorescent light above the old card table that served as her combination dining table and work station. It flickered several times before it went all the way on. She smiled at herself in the full-length mirror that hung on the back of her door. She hugged herself and twirled around. When she came full circle, she blew a kiss at her reflection and twirled around some more.

CHAPTER TWENTY-NINE
I FOUGHT THE LAW

Judge Fanshaw frowned. It was late on Monday afternoon and there were still too many cases to plow through.

"People v. Amissah," Annie called out.

He familiarized himself with the file, while two correctional officers escorted Thomas Amissah into the courtroom. Thomas' hands were cuffed behind his back. April Higgins walked up to the counsel table and nodded at Pattie. Thomas stood between April and Pattie and the correctional officers stood behind him. He leaned over and whispered in Pattie's ear.

"Hi Attorney Anwald! I can't believe you're here!"

Pattie frowned at him.

"Yeah, well, I can't believe you're here either," she whispered back.

Annie walked over to Pattie and handed her a piece of paper. Pattie read it and returned it to Annie, who handed it to Ryan. Without looking at it, Ryan walked it up to the Judge.

"This notice states that Assistant Corporate Counsel, Frank Bernard, has transferred this case over from the Family Court, so that the defendant may be treated as an adult," Judge Fanshaw said.

"That's correct Your Honor," Annie said.

"Your Honor, Dr. April Higgins is present in court as Thomas Amissah's Guardian," Pattie said.

Judge Fanshaw glanced at April.

"Well, where are his parents?"

"Your Honor, April Higgins and her husband Kyle are psychologists who run Beau Rivage, the group home where Thomas Amissah resides," Pattie said.

"Great information, but you still haven't answered my question."

"Your Honor, a number of weeks ago Thomas' parents handed him a portable CD player and told him that it was their going away present, because they were through with him. Unfortunately, that was the last time he ever heard from them.

"That's totally unacceptable," Judge Fanshaw said.

"Unfortunately, it happens all the time in Juvenile Justice cases," Pattie said.

Judge Fanshaw ignored Pattie's statement and turned his full attention to Annie.

"Now, Attorney Carey, has the defendant already been indicted?" He asked.

"Yes, Your Honor, for Gang Assault in the Second Degree."

Pattie cleared her throat and leaned over to Thomas.

"Gang assault? My God, that's a serious charge," she whispered.

"I swear it's not true. Frank made that part up!"

Pattie ignored him and addressed the Judge.

"Your Honor, whenever juveniles are held in custody on felony charges, a hearing is required within ten days of the arrest," she said.

Annie shook her head and gesticulated wildly.

"But Your Honor, we're not in the Family Court anymore. Remember? The case got transferred over here," she said.

"Your Honor, the transfer doesn't wash away my client's right to have a hearing within ten days," Pattie argued.

The furrow between Judge Fanshaw's eyebrows deepened.

"Well, when did the arrest take place?"

"Exactly ten days ago," Pattie said.

"Well, even if Defense Counsel is right, which she's not, the law may require a hearing, but it doesn't specify that the hearing has to be an evidentiary one," Annie said.

Judge Fanshaw looked at Pattie.

"Your Honor, of course the hearing has to be evidentiary. When you get right down to it, is there any other kind of hearing? A hearing is where we hear evidence," Pattie said.

"Yeah. Get it?" Thomas said, to Annie.

Judge Fanshaw frowned.

"Ms. Anwald, put a muzzle on your client and Ms. Carey, are you trying to stand there and tell me that simply scheduling a court date automatically protects a Defendant's Right to Due Process?"

"Your Honor, the Defendant's age and innocent face both belie his lengthy history as a Juvenile Delinquent," Annie yelled.

"I object! Everything Attorney Carey just said is irrelevant! Juvenile cases are anonymous and sealed for the purpose of preventing overzealous prosecutors like Attorney Carey from doing exactly what she did just now," Pattie yelled, equally as loudly.

Judge Fanshaw wagged his finger.

"Why, oh why, can't any either of you ever answer a direct question? And another thing! Keep your voices down!" Judge Fanshaw screamed.

Pattie cleared her throat.

"I'm sorry, Your Honor."

"Attorney Anwald, your objection is sustained. Attorney Carey's last statement is hereby stricken from the record. But, Attorney Anwald, if the representation you're making here today is true, as you claim, why haven't any of your colleagues ever brought this issue to my attention before, when faced with the exact same sets of circumstances?" Judge Fanshaw asked.

"Your Honor, I don't know why other attorneys do what they do. Maybe in those cases the ten-day period hadn't expired."

Reginald Reese stood and identified himself for the record.

"What is it, Attorney Reese? Are you somehow involved in any of this?"

"No, Your Honor and I'm not trying to stick my nose where it doesn't belong, but Juvenile Justice has own rules and regulations which are not well known to anyone who hasn't practiced it."

Judge Fanshaw nodded.

"Point well taken, Attorney Reese. Now, back to you Attorney Anwald. What is it that you are seeking?"

"Your Honor, I'm requesting that you order The People to go forward with an evidentiary hearing right now or else dismiss the case."

"Attorney Anwald, it's almost five o'clock and I still have a packed courtroom."

Pattie cleared her throat.

"I'm aware of that, Your Honor, but it's still no excuse to violate my client's right to Due Process."

"Well, would you consider waiving the hearing, so that we can go forward on another day?"

Pattie shook her head.

"No, your Honor."

The other attorneys in the Courtroom gasped.

"And even if The People were to go forward today, are you telling me that you're actually prepared to defend your client right now?" Judge Fanshaw asked.

Pattie nodded.

"Of course, Your Honor."

"Your Honor, she's insane," Annie yelled.

"Hey! I object to that characterization!" Pattie yelled back.

Judge Fanshaw banged his gavel and scowled at Pattie.

"Well sane or crazy, I don't like your strong-arm tactics at all, Attorney Anwald. I'm requesting, as a personal favor to this court, that you waive the right to a hearing today, so that we can schedule it for some other time in the near future."

"Your Honor, I already told you that I will not agree to that. Furthermore, if you do not permit an evidentiary hearing to go forward today, as is required by law, I will file an immediate appeal," Pattie said slowly enough so that everyone in the court-room could hear her.

Judge Fanshaw banged the gavel again. Then he stood and called a recess.

"All rise please," Ryan said.

Chapter Thirty
AND I WON

Twenty minutes later, Judge Fanshaw returned to the bench.

"I've reviewed this matter in chambers. As it turns out, Attorney Anwald happens to be correct. Therefore, the People must either proceed with an immediate evidentiary hearing or I'll be forced to dismiss the case."

Elliott Glutz sighed and leaned over to Reginald Reese.

"If Fanshaw turns these two bitches loose on eachother, their ridiculous cat fight could get us stuck here until midnight. I happen to know Pattie Anwald from one of my other cases and her tactics are disgusting," he whispered.

Reginald nodded.

"While I normally tend to empathize with anyone who hassles Annie, my empathy will vaporize fast if I end up getting stuck here," he said.

"Your Honor, I had sixty-five arraignments on the docket today. I have no assistant, which means I had to handle every aspect of every arraignment on my own. Furthermore, I only learned about the existence of this particular case this afternoon when the paperwork arrived," Annie whined.

"So what? This court does not wish to hear, nor does it have any sympathy for the People's pathetic Labor Relations problems. In accordance with the law, the People's case against Thomas Amissah is dismissed."

When he banged the gavel, Pattie grinned and every one gasped. Annie's mouth flew open so wide that her jaw looked unhinged. When the correctional officers removed the handcuffs from Thomas, he wrung out his hands and gave Pattie a high five.

"Thank God," Reginald Reese whispered.

Elliott Glutz nodded in agreement.

"Your Honor, The People aren't finished with this case," Annie said.

"Oh, yes they are," Judge Fanshaw said.

CHAPTER THIRTY-ONE
BETRAYAL

Bonnie Louden was upstairs in the bathroom that she shared with two other girls at Beau Rivage. She was expecting to see Kenny and she wanted to look her best for him, so she plugged in her double-barrel curling iron and primped while she waited for it to heat up. Meanwhile, outside, Willie intercepted Kenny, just as Kenny walked up the path to the main entrance.

"Yo. Kid. You here to see Bonnie?"

In spite of his bulk, Kenny felt intimidated. He knit his brow and wondered why the janitor was interrogating him, so in an attempt to be cautious and avoid trouble, he simply told the truth.

"Yes. Why? What of it?"

Willie winked.

"Well, did she put out for you yet?"

This confused Kenny even more.

"What?"

"All I'm trying to tell you, is not to let it go on too long without her putting out for you. Otherwise, you'd be letting her make a chump out of you. After all, she's put out for everyone else."

"How would you know?"

Willie crooked his finger.

"Follow me and I'll show you how I know."

He put his arm around Kenny in an avuncular manner and led him inside to April's office. He whipped out his key ring, opened the door and sauntered over to the file cabinet. He opened the drawer labeled "L" and rifled through it until he found Bonnie's file. Then he pulled it out, opened it to the appropriate page and pounded it with his index finger.

"There you go. I've done just about everything but read it to you," he said.

Kenny took a moment to read the page. By the time he slammed the file shut, his face was beet red.

"Oh, my God," he said.

Willie nodded.

"See? Almost everybody she's put out for is listed right there in them records. Lots of names are on it, but I couldn't find yours."

"Thanks man."

Willie smirked.

"Hey, don't mention it. Us guys have got to stick together against all of them whores and bitches out there."

He put it back into the cabinet and then led Kenny out of the office. He locked up and smirked as Kenny stormed up the stairs.

Bonnie pulled the plug on her curling iron, placed it in its holder so that it could cool down and applied the finishing touches to her mascara. When she spotted Kenny's reflection in the mirror, she gasped and turned to him.

"Oh my God! What are you doing up here? I told you, guests aren't allowed upstairs!"

"Oh really?"

"Yeah!"

He barged into the room, kicked the door shut and lunged at her.

"Well, I don't believe you. I found about you and now I want everything that's coming to me."

The color drained from Bonnie's face, as she picked up her curling iron.

"Look Kenny! If you're talking about what I think you're talking about, then you've got to know that I was a victim not a volunteer. So, just beat it," she said, as she brandished the curling iron in his face.

The door creaked open and Justin stood in the doorway.

"You heard what she said," Justin said, softly.

"OK I'll leave now, but I'll be back," Kenny said, to Bonnie.

He turned to leave and pushed Justin out of his way.

"Beat it asshole," he said.

Bonnie placed the curling iron back in its holder.

"Thanks Justin," she said.

"No problem," Justin whispered.

Bonnie closed the door, locked it and began to cry. She turned on the bath water, adjusted it to make it as hot as she could get it and while the bathtub was filling, she rifled through the medicine cabinet. When she found a small cuticle scissors, she grabbed it, placed it on the side of the bathtub and stripped. She slid into the steaming hot bath water and once she was fully immersed, she picked up the scissors and plunged it into her wrist.

Justin was downstairs when he heard Bonnie scream. He ran up the stairs and banged on the bathroom door. Then he tried the handle, to no avail.

"Bonnie?"

She ignored him and prayed that the sound of the running water would muffle her sobs. April came through the main entrance. When she heard the commotion, she dropped everything and bolted up the stairs.

"What's going on?" She asked Justin.

"I don't know exactly, but it sounds bad. We've got to help Bonnie!"

"Go get Willie," she ordered.

As soon as Justin ran down the stairs, April reached for the keyring in her pocket and unlocked the door. Through the steam, she saw Bonnie rocking back and forth on her haunches and sobbing as she held both of her bloody wrists under the tap. She whipped out her cell phone and dialed 9-1-1.

CHAPTER THIRTY-TWO

TOO YOUNG TO BE IN THIS MUCH TROUBLE

It was well past five o'clock by the time the arraignment court adjourned for the day. Pattie rushed into her office, tossed her files on her desk and grabbed her coat. Just then, Ryan showed up and they left the courthouse together. When they got outside, Thomas Amissah ran up to them. Ryan stood in Thomas' way, in order to block him from getting near Pattie. Pattie nodded at Ryan.

"It's OK, Ryan. Thomas and I go back a long way," she said.

Ryan moved aside and let Thomas approach Pattie.

"OK. Well, I'm late for class, so I might as well head over there now. I'll call you later," he said.

Pattie nodded.

"Great. Thanks."

Ryan gave her the universal OK sign and left.

"Hey, Attorney Anwald, I've been out here waiting for you all afternoon."

"You've got to be kidding. Why didn't you just wait for me inside the courthouse?"

"Remember the bully with the stun gun?"

Pattie nodded.

"Of course. Who could forget him?"

"Well, I hope you know that I never lied to you. The stun gun really was his. Anyway, his brother is the one who kicked me out of the courthouse. He said if I wanted to speak to you I had to wait for you out here."

"How could that be? Why would he come down here and order you around?"

"Because he works here."

"Really? Where?"

Thomas pointed at the Courthouse.

"He's the first person you see when you go through the main entrance. He works right at the metal detector."

"What's his name?"

"I don't know his first name, but his last name is Bakerman, same as the bully's."

"Bakerman. OK. Anyway, you wouldn't have waited out here all afternoon unless you had something important to say to me."

"That's right. What I wanted to say is thank you for getting me off the hook again. It was actually a blessing that the case got transferred over here, because at least I was able to have you as my lawyer again. I don't like that guy who replaced you."

"Why not?"

"Because he doesn't stick up for people or go out of his way for anyone, the way you do."

"Well, I'm not so sure that I'm doing you any favors in the long run by getting you off the hook all the time. You never seem to gain any insight from any of the lucky breaks you've enjoyed."

"Yes, I do!"

"How can you even say that, when every time I get you off the hook, you get arrested again and each time it's for a more serious charge? I have to tell you that I actually couldn't believe my eyes when I saw you up in that courtroom!"

"I know that I got into trouble again and I'm sorry, but I swear I'm not in any gang. Frank just made up an excuse so that he could transfer the case over here."

Pattie frowned and shook her head.

"It's really wrong of you to try to blame other people for your own shortcomings. Did it ever even occur to you, that one of these days I might not be able to help you anymore?"

He stared down at the tops of his sneakers and shook his head.

"No."

"Well, you'd better start entertaining that possibility, because like I've already said a million times, no lawyer can ever guarantee how any case will turn out. The only thing we can ever guarantee is that we will do our best."

"I know."

Pattie cupped his chin, lifted his face and stared into his eyes.

"Listen to me. What do you think will happen if you actually end up killing somebody one of these days?"

"What do you want me to say?"

"I don't want you to say anything. Don't try to manipulate me by spoon feeding me answers you think I might want you to say. Instead, take some sincere action and mend your ways."

"How?"

"That's why you're in Beau Rivage. Use them as a resource to help you answer that."

"How can I? They're not so great."

Pattie opened her mouth to respond, but her cell phone rang. She reached for it and glanced at the caller ID.

"Speak of the devil. It's April," she said.

"Well, don't tell her I'm still here."

Pattie ignored his remark and picked up the call.

"Hi Attorney Anwald. It's April Higgins. Can you meet Bonnie and me at the Knickerbocker Hospital Emergency Room?"

"Why? What's wrong?"

There was a pause on the other end of the line. Finally, April spoke.

"Bonnie tried to kill herself. The good news is that she's still alive."

"I'm leaving right now," Pattie said.

She hung up, tossed her phone into her brief case and hurried toward the subway station. Thomas followed her.

"Where are we going?"

"We're not going anywhere. For God's sake just go back to Beau Rivage and try to stay out of trouble! OK?"

"OK, but since I have to take the subway anyway, we might as well walk over there together," he said.

CHAPTER THIRTY-THREE
MATA HARI'S

Meanwhile, Judge Benchley and Judge Fanshaw were huddled together in their favorite booth at the back corner of Mata Hari's. Judge Fanshaw handed Judge Benchley a volume from the penal code.

"So anyway, read this and weep," he said.

Judge Benchley pored over the highlighted sentences and handed the book back to him.

"What gets my goat is that this whole God damn issue wasn't worth a rat's ass one way or the other," Judge Fanshaw added.

"Imagine that little bitch trying to strong arm you like that. Well anyway, at least you did the right thing in catering to her. You can't run the risk of any more reversals on appeal, especially in this late stage of your career," Judge Benchley said.

Judge Fanshaw nodded.

"I know," he said, "but it still galls me that some little nobody who's still wet behind the ears can come into my courtroom and tell me what I have to do. At first, I actually thought she was making this shit up in order to scam me, but she wasn't. The problem, is that she's the only one who knows anything about Juvenile Justice."

Judge Benchley nodded.

"I know. What a loser."

"Exactly and then when you combine that with her vindictiveness if I didn't rule in her favor, now you've got an idea as to why I drink," Judge Fanshaw said.

"You know, maybe we should be a little nicer to her. I mean, with all of the Juvenile Justice cases that are suddenly getting transferred over to us these days, we might need to pick her brain," Judge Benchley said.

"Yeah and then we'll still get the last laugh when we steal all the credit," Judge Fanshaw said, as he lifted his glass.

"As a matter of fact, I'll even drink to it!"

CHAPTER THIRTY-FOUR
EMERGENCY ROOM

Pattie rushed into the emergency room and ran up to April Higgins.

"How is she?"

"They just transferred her up to the Psychiatric Unit. She wants to see you alone. I'll take you up there," April said, as she led Pattie toward the elevator bank.

When they arrived on the unit, a nurse came from behind the desk and led them through a maze of hallways. The heavy iron door to Bonnie's room bore a thousand coats of beige paint and only had a tiny peephole, covered by a latch. The nurse slid the latch back so that Pattie could peer through the chicken wire and glass.

Bonnie was restrained in bed. Her arms and ankles were tied to the guardrails, both of her wrists were bandaged and an IV drip ran into one of the veins in the back of her right hand.

"Are all of those restraints necessary?" Pattie asked.

The nurse pulled out a set of keys, unlocked the door and smirked.

"Well, if we keep them on until she's stabilized, we'll never have to find out; now will we?" She asked, in a condescending way.

"Well, isn't she sedated?" Pattie asked.

"Of course, she is. Bang real hard if you need me," she said, as she slammed the door behind her and disappeared.

Pattie jumped, cleared her throat and walked over to the bed. Bonnie wore a pastel print hospital gown that failed miserably at trying to be cheerful. Even though her hair hung over her face, it did little to conceal her puffy eyes, splotchy skin and smeared mascara.

"Hi Bonnie, it's me, Pattie Anwald. Are you awake?" Pattie whispered.

Bonnie struggled to sit up. She winced and groaned at the pull of her restraints. Tears welled up in her eyes. Pattie fluffed her pillow behind her.

"Don't look at me, OK? I'm sure I'm a mess," Bonnie said.

Pattie turned away from her.

"OK. I'll keep my back turned toward the wall."

"Thanks."

"I came as soon I got the call from April. Do you want to tell me what happened?"

Bonnie broke into a sob. Her shoulders heaved and shook. After a few minutes she calmed down and told Pattie what had transpired between her and Kenny. She punctuated it with "and please don't say 'I told you so', because it will only make me feel worse."

"I'm not an 'I told you so kind of person' but that doesn't mean that I don't have something to say."

"I figured as much," Bonnie said.

"I'm sorry for everything you've gone through, every single bit of it; but the truth is that Kenny isn't worth killing yourself over. No one is."

"Don't you get it? This doesn't isn't even about Kenny. It's about the fact that no matter where I go, what I do or how long I live, I will never be able to escape from the reality of what happened to me and somehow I will always be the one to get blamed for it."

"That's not true. Of course, you will move beyond all of this. You're not even eighteen years old yet and you have your whole life ahead of you."

"Big deal."

"And when you're eighteen, the records will be sealed."

"So? Somehow, people always have a way of finding out things about everyone else. I mean if someone as dumb as Kenny can do it, anyone can."

"Bonnie, our pasts do not define us."

"Well it feels to me as if they do!"

"I understand that you feel this way right now, but I promise you that you won't actually feel this way forever."

"Well, what do I do in the meantime? I just need the pain to stop, because I really can't take it anymore."

"Well, that's why you're at Beau Rivage, so that they can help you."

"Oh please! All they ever did was get me landed here! And that's another thing. I need you to get me out of here, as soon as possible."

Pattie shook her head.

"I can't."

"Well, why not?"

"Because the law says that they have the right to keep you here as long as you say or do anything that gives them a reason to think that you might want to hurt yourself or someone else. Do you understand what I'm telling you?"

"Yeah. You're telling me to keep my mouth shut."

"No, because if you do that, they'll accuse you of being unco-operative. In the meantime, it's against the law for them to keep you restrained like this, so at least I can try to help you with that."

As if on cue, the nurse knocked on the door and stuck her head in.

"Just to let you know that the police should be here any minute."

She slammed the door and padded back down the hall.

Bonnie looked alarmed.

"The Police?"

Pattie grimaced.

"Yes."

"Why?"

"Well, I guess now would be the right time to let you know that suicide is against the law in New York State. So, on top of everything else that's happened to you, you're probably going to get arrested. If you're smart, you'll tell them nothing, except for what Kenny did to you."

"What if Kenny tries to get even with me later?"

"Don't worry. I'll get you an order of protection mandating that he stay away from you. The minute he violates it, he'll end up in jail."

"Can you stay with me when the police get here?"

Pattie nodded.

"Absolutely. I'll stick to you like glue the whole time they're here."

CHAPTER THIRTY-FIVE
ASCENT

Saturday finally rolled around. Pattie was dressed in black pants, a black scoop neck top and a pair of red and white striped socks. She glanced in her bathroom mirror and smiled. When she heard the knock at the door, she pulled her hair into a makeshift pony tail and grabbed her tote bag.

"I'll be out in a minute," she called through the door, as she scrambled for her keys. When she found them, she opened the door, slid through it and slammed it behind her. She double locked it, tossed her keys into her bag and finally turned around to face Jordan. He kissed her and pointed at her legs.

"I know I've seen tights like these before, but I can't place where.

Pattie smiled.

"The Wicked Witch of the West wore them in my favorite movie, 'The Wizard of Oz' and I think her sister did too."

He nodded.

"Ah yes! Now I remember."

He led her down the stairs and out into the taxi that was waiting for them around the corner. When they arrived at The Piers on the other side of the city, the driver removed Jordan's golf bag from the trunk.

"You'll never guess what I've got in store for us today," he said.

"Uh, golf?"

Jordan smiled.

"Good guess. There's a driving range here," he said, as he led her inside.

They got on the elevator and when the door opened, they stepped right out onto the top tier of a semi outdoor driving range. The sun felt warm and the air smelled clean as they looked across the Hudson River at New Jersey's Palisades. He smiled and pointed.

"Ah, isn't this view spectacular?"

She smiled back at him and nodded.

He bought a bucket of balls and when he returned he reached down and placed one of them on the tee. He selected a driver from his bag, gripped it and took his stance. Pattie watched as he drove the ball out into the distance. When he handed her the club she cleared her throat.

"I want you to know that I've never done this before," she said.

"Well, not to worry. I'll show you what to do."

He demonstrated the correct stance, then he stood behind her and showed her the correct grip. She felt his breath on the back of her neck as he placed his strong, warm hands over hers. He guided her in a practice swing, but she felt too nervous to pay close attention to his instructions. She cleared her throat again.

"I'm sorry. I'm afraid I have to ask you to explain this to me all over again."

He smiled and feigned an attitude of strictness.

"Now, now Pattie. Success with golf, like so many other things in life, depends largely on concentration."

She chuckled.

"All right. I promise to concentrate this time."

He repeated the demonstration and as promised, she listened carefully. Because he guided her swing, she was actually able to drive the ball out into the distance.

"Wow! I can't believe it," she said.

He smiled at her.

"Here. Try another one."

She managed to hit the ball on her own. After Jordan drove a few balls, a well-dressed man in his mid-thirties appeared from out of nowhere.

"Hey Jordan!"

"Pattie, meet Kevin Gordon, the golf pro here. Kevin, this is Pattie Anwald, a lawyer and first time golfer."

"It's nice to meet you", Kevin said.

Pattie smiled and shook his hand.

"It's nice to meet you too."

"Welcome to my neighborhood back yard."

"Kevin, Pattie is doing beautifully," Jordan said.

"Congratulations Pattie not only for doing so well, but also for having found a great teacher," Kevin said.

"You're too kind. Actually, I'm not a good golfer, but at least I'm an avid one," Jordan answered,

"You're way too modest," Kevin said.

"Pattie, Kevin's grandfather used to play at St. Andrews in Scotland."

Pattie smiled and nodded vaguely.

"How nice."

"Thank you. Anyhow, will you still be here in a few minutes?" Kevin asked.

Jordan glanced down at the half empty bucket of balls.

"At least."

"Great. I'll be right back."

After Kevin left, Jordan drove another ball out into the distance and helped Pattie do the same. Shortly thereafter Kevin returned and handed Jordan an envelope.

"Remember when I told you that my Grandfather helped to found a Golf Club in upstate New York?"

Jordan nodded.

"Yes and if I recall correctly it was modeled after St. Andrews. Right?"

Kevin smiled.

"Yes. You have a good memory. Anyhow, here is a pair of week long guest passes."

"Thank you. How thoughtful," Jordan said.

"My pleasure. They don't have an expiration date, so you can go up whenever it suits you and when you do, even though you'll be looking at this same exact river, it will feel to you as if you're in another world. At least that's the way it feels to me," Kevin said.

Jordan thanked Kevin again and when Kevin left, he and Pattie drove the remaining balls until they emptied the bucket. Then Jordan placed his driver back in the bag, slung the bag over his shoulder and led Pattie back toward the elevator bank.

"Do you think you're ready to try something more daring?"

Pattie cleared her throat.

"I don't know. It depends on what it is."

When they reached the main lobby, he led her across the plaza to a Spa and Health Club. Once they were inside, he led her down a long hallway and opened a door that faced a thirty-foot rock wall. It extended from the floor to the ceiling. Pattie stared at it, winced and cleared her throat.

"God, what is it?"

"Something we can climb. Of course, if you're uncomfortable with the idea, we can scrap it and do something else," he said.

"Well? Even though I'm used to being on the ground, as daunting as this looks, I'd be willing to give it a try. Just don't expect me to soar, at least not today."

He nodded.

"Fair enough By the way, what's your shoe size?"

"Six."

"I bet you'd have no trouble fitting into the proverbial glass slipper with those tiny feet."

"I wouldn't know. That's another thing I've never tried."

He rented shoes and a belt for her and handed them to her.

"Here. Put these shoes on and walk around to make sure that they fit you properly. There's nothing worse than sore feet."

Pattie chuckled.

"After looking at the height of this wall, I'm not so sure I agree with you."

She put on the shoes and walked around, while he reached into his golf bag and pulled out a pair of shoes and a belt for himself. As he was tying his shoelaces, she returned and nodded.

"They fit well."

"I'm happy to hear it."

He took hold of her hand and brought her closer to the wall. He pointed at the indentations, which were marked by various colors.

"Each color represents a different path where you can place your feet. As a first-time climber, you might want to concentrate only on the yellow indentations, because yellow is the path of least resistance."

She cleared her throat.

"Oh. OK."

He tied her legs into the belt, tugged on it to ensure that it was secure and then he picked up the rope.

"Don't worry. I'll be on the other end of this rope, belaying you."

"Excuse me? You'll be doing what to me?"

He chuckled.

"It's not as bad as it sounds. Belaying simply means that I'll be holding onto the other end of the rope so that you'll be safe when you climb."

"Well you can add being belayed to the ever-growing list of things I've never tried before."

He pointed to the yellow space closest to the floor.

"Start right there and remember. The first time is usually easier if you remember not to tense up."

She stared at the space for several seconds before she could will her foot into it. Once she did, he prodded her to place her left foot in the nearest yellow space above that.

"I think you know what to do now. Just keep following the yellow spaces and don't look down, no matter what."

She cleared her throat, nodded and spent the next forty-five minutes laboring slowly upwards, in accordance with Jordan's instructions. She broke into a sweat as she clung to the wall for dear life. When she was almost two thirds of the way up the wall, she made the mistake of looking down and immediately squeezed her eyes shut.

"Help!"

"I thought I told you not to look down."

"I know. I forgot. Just get me down!"

"No. Keep climbing. You're doing fine."

"I mean it Jordan!" Her voice was strident.

"All right then, but you'll have to let go of that wall or else I won't be able to pull you down."

"I can't!"

"Pattie, if you don't let go of that wall, you'll end up living a long, lonely life up there!"

"You mean a short life, don't you? It's already starting to flash before my eyes."

"Just trust me," he said.

"OK."

She let go of the wall and two seconds later she made a soft landing. Jordan immediately put his arms around her.

"Oh my God! I never thought I'd live to see Mother Earth again. I think my stomach is still somewhere up on the ceiling though."

"You'll be fully recovered in a few minutes. Take comfort in the fact that most people don't get as high as you did on the first try. You must really be strong."

"Thanks. People tell me that all the time. I guess what gets my goat, is that it took so long for me to climb up there and yet it only took two seconds for me to end up back on the ground."

He nodded.

"I'm sure there's a life lesson in there somewhere."

"For sure. Anyway, are you going to climb now?"

"I'd like to, if you don't mind."

"No problem. Do you want me to belay you?"

He chuckled.

"Well, as promising as that sounds, I'll have to decline for the moment. You see, you can't belay someone until you become an expert climber, because you're literally holding their life in your hands."

One of the male trainers walked by.

"Hi Jordan."

"Hi Felix. Pattie, meet Felix."

After Pattie and Felix exchanged greetings and shook hands, Jordan asked Felix to belay him. Jordan chose the hardest path. Pattie watched, as Jordan's body and breath worked in harmony to elevate him. Once he reached the top he asked Felix to pull him down.

"Wow, I'm impressed," Pattie said.

Jordan smiled.

"Thank you. I don't know about you, but I've worked up quite an appetite."

Pattie nodded.

"Me too."

"Well, why don't we go for a meal? There's a great micro-brewery not far from here."

She nodded.

"OK. Let's try it."

"Have you ever been to a microbrewery?"

Pattie shook her head and chuckled.

"My bucket list just continues to grow and grow."

CHAPTER THIRTY-SIX
COLD HEARTED SNAKE

After a brief cab ride, Jordan opened the door to the microbrewery and ushered Pattie inside. The hostess stood dutifully at her podium, attending to the busy work that Mel, the short, dumpy, fat, bald manager had assigned to her in order to prevent her from enjoying any down time. However, she received a small measure of consolation from the rock music that played in the background. She appeared to be in her late twenties. Her jet-black, dyed hair was even darker than Pattie's. When she heard the door open, she glanced up. The minute she saw Jordan walk through the door with Pattie, she frowned.

"Hello Darla. Table for two, please," he said.

Darla picked up two menus and led them through an almost empty restaurant to a table in the back corner. She lobbed the menus onto the table and without uttering a word, she marched over to a bleached blonde waitress, who was about her own age.

"Valerie! Look! There's that guy I was telling you about," she said, as she discreetly nodded in Jordan's direction.

Valerie spotted Jordan and gasped.

"Oh my God! I don't know how to break it to you, but he's the same guy I was telling you about!"

"It can't be!"

"Well it is. Jordan. Right?"

Darla nodded.

"Yeah. Well, did he ever call you afterwards?"

"Nope!"

"Me neither!"

"What a slime ball!" Valerie said.

"Wow! It sure didn't take him long to spread himself around Manhattan! I just can't believe it."

"Who does he think he is, dumping not just one of us, but both of us and taking up with that bitch? Look at her!"

"You should get a peek at her stockings!"

"I'll check them out as soon as I get over there. Right after I tear her hair out."

Darla could no longer keep herself from crying. Tears ran down her cheeks.

"You know the saddest thing about it? All this time I thought he really liked me," she said.

Valerie handed her a paper napkin, gave her a quick hug and patted her on the back.

"Well, try not to lose any sleep over it. The upside, is that at some point he'll probably dump her too. In the meantime, I'll get even by spitting in their soups," Valerie said.

She breezed over to their table, hovered over Jordan and smirked.

"Oh hello, Valerie. How have you been?" Jordan said.

"Don't ask."

She bent down, took a look at Pattie's tights and stood up again. Jordan and Pattie glanced at each other quizzically.

"What's the matter, Valerie? Did you drop something?" Jordan asked.

Valerie chuckled.

"Just you Baby, just you, but I digress. What would the two of youse like to drink?"

"Pattie, would you like an iced tea?" Jordan asked.

Pattie nodded.

"OK."

"I'm wondering whether you still carry that Czech style Ale?"

"From all those weeks ago? I don't know. I'll have to check."

"Very clever play on words there, Valerie. I'll have to check."

Valerie scratched her head.

"Huh?"

"Never mind."

Valerie shrugged and walked away and Pattie knit her brow.

"What's her problem?"

Jordan shrugged.

"God only knows," he answered.

"I'd like to wash my hands after all that golfing and rock climbing. Do you know where the ladies' room is?"

Jordan stood and pointed.

"Maybe over there?" It was more of a question than an answer.

"Thanks. I'll be right back."

She walked past Darla and Valerie who were huddled at the podium, whispering. They watched Pattie go into the ladies' room. After about a minute, they followed her in and hovered over the sinks. Pattie was already inside one of the stalls.

"Yeah. That lousy limey's got some nerve, coming back in here and flaunting his Bimbo du Jour after humping and dumping me only two short weeks ago. I didn't even get a phone call," Darla said, in a stage whisper.

"Well Honey, he did the exact same thing to me three weeks ago and he never called me either," Valerie said.

"Well, I guess we're no longer the flavor of the month," Darla said.

"Well, should we warn her about that cold-hearted snake?" Valerie said.

"Hell no. Let her find out the hard way like we had to," Darla said.

"In the meantime, I'll find a way to warm him up," Valerie said.

The door squeaked open and Mel the manager stuck his fat, round, bald head in.

"What's going on witch youse two? Youse are in here gabbin' an' laughin' and I'm seatin' the damn customers myself! I know a couple o' dumb broads that're gonna be out of their jobs in two minutes if they don't get their asses back out here pronto!"

"Sorry Mel," Valerie said, catching the door before it closed.

"You should be. Youse two ain't all that indispensable, you know," Mel said.

"Yeah, we know," Darla said, as she and Valerie followed him out of the ladies' room.

Pattie flushed the toilet and leaned up against the door of her stall. It took her a few minutes to compose herself and come out. Once she did, she glanced in the mirror and noticed that her décolletage was covered in splotches. She sighed, washed her hands and let cold water run on her wrists. Finally, she got a paper towel, soaked it in cold water and wrung it out. She patted her face and neck with it until she felt calm. When she returned to the table, Jordan stood, helped her into her chair and returned to his seat. He took one look at her and frowned.

"It felt like you were gone for an eternity. Is everything all right?"

Pattie glanced at him warily, nodded and cleared her throat. "Yes. I'm fine."

She sat there bemused, while he droned on about rock climbing, the Great Outdoors and Mother Nature. Eventually, Valerie reappeared and plunked their beverages on the table.

"Well, I'm ready to take your orders. By the way, today's soup special is beer cheese and it's on the house," she said.

"Thanks, but I'm not in the mood for any soup today," Pattie said.

"Neither am I," Jordan said.

Valerie sighed.

"Ah, gee. What a shame."

"I'll have a Chef's Salad without any dressing," Pattie said.

"How about an appetizer?" Jordan asked.

"No thanks," Pattie answered.

"I'll have a well-done steak with a side order of salad," Jordan said.

Valerie saluted him.

"You got it," she said and turned on her heel.

A few minutes later she returned with a platter of salsa and chips. She banged them down on the table so hard that Pattie jumped.

"Here. These are on the house," she said.

"My, the house is incredibly generous tonight," Jordan said.

Valerie smirked.

"That's right Jordan. Apparently, we're very well known for our free giveaways," she said, as she left to take the order of the people Mel had seated.

Jordan picked up a chip, scooped a generous amount of salsa onto it and popped it into his mouth. One second later he gasped, fumbled for his beer and gulped it. He mopped his brow with his napkin and gulped some more beer.

"Ouch! That salsa is bloody hot! I'll bet there's even steam coming out of my ears!"

He somehow gasped the words out, one raspy syllable at a time.

"I thought you said this was a nice place," Pattie said.

"Well, it used to be. Maybe some lunatic in the kitchen went wild with the red-hot chili peppers or something," he said.

Valerie returned with the entrees. She practically threw them onto the table and then pointed at the Salsa.

"Shall I take this away now?"

"By all means do," Jordan snapped.

After she was gone, Jordan sat and stared at his steak.

"I've never been afraid to eat a meal before," he said.

He took a tiny bite and it tasted fine. Pattie cleared her throat, picked up her fork and stabbed a lettuce leaf. The two of them continued their meal with no further incidents.

CHAPTER THIRTY-SEVEN
TREASURE CHEST

Pattie and Jordan weren't in the taxi very long before it pulled up in front of a beautiful high rise apartment building. As soon as Jordan got out of the taxi, the doorman rushed up to him.

"How are ya doin' today?" He asked.

Jordan smiled.

"Just great, Joe. And you?"

Joe nodded.

"Not too bad. Thanks for asking."

The driver popped the trunk and Joe retrieved Jordan's golf bags.

"Do you need me to carry them clubs up for you?"

"No thanks, Joe, but I appreciate the offer," Jordan said.

He led Pattie into the immaculate, elegantly furnished lobby. While they waited for the elevator, Pattie took a deep breath and admired the chandeliers, mirrors and sleek modern furniture. She basked in the glamour and tried to imagine what it must be like to take marble walls and floors like these for granted. When the elevator arrived, the door silently slid open to reveal a polished, walnut interior with a rosewood inlay. As they rode up to the eighth floor, Pattie took the liberty of running her fingertips over it, while silently hoping that Jordan did think she was too weird. When the door slid open at the eighth floor, he led her down the hall to his apartment. He unlocked the door and let her in. Once they were inside, he turned on the lights and stowed his golf bag inside the closet, while Pattie breathed in the details of her surroundings.

"It's such a relief to finally be able to get rid of this bag," he said.

Pattie frowned and nodded.

"I'll bet. It's so annoying when old baggage rears up its ugly head and drags us down," she said.

Jordan looked her strangely and shook his head. He walked across the room, opened the white floor length draperies and unlocked the French doors that led out to a terrace. They both walked out onto the terrace and stood by the railing.

"This faces north, right?"

He nodded.

"Right."

He stood behind her, watching her, as she gazed out. Even though the city below them was bustling, there was a sense of peace up on the terrace. The evening lights had just begun to twinkle and the first hint of a summer breeze gently fluttered against Pattie's skin. The orange sun hung low in the early evening sky. It spilled over the railing and onto the tiles. A skein of amethyst and rose clouds peeped in from the west at the cross streets. Pattie caught its reflection in the windows of the building across the street. As she leaned over the edge of the railing to look down, Jordan stepped forward and put his hand on her back. Her stomach flipped.

"Whoa! I wouldn't want a lovely girl like you to go overboard," he said, as he pulled her back.

She shook her head.

"Agreed. You know, in this high place with this magnificent view, it kind of lulls me into thinking that I don't have a care in the world."

He nodded.

"I know what you mean. That's exactly how I feel when I come out here," he said.

She pointed.

"Oh my God! Look! The Empire State Building just lit up!"

He smiled.

"Yes. Let's celebrate. I've got a bottle of champagne chilling."

"Do you have iced tea?"

"Oh dear. That's probably the one thing I don't have."

"Well you're British, aren't you? That means you have tea. If you brew it and throw some ice over it, I'll be set."

He nodded.

"I could do that. I even have ice, although don't ask me why. I've never understood the fascination you Americans have with it," he said.

She shook her head.

"Come on! Really?"

"Yes. From what I can gather you must all have cast iron stomachs or something," he said.

He walked back into the apartment and went into the kitchen. Pattie followed him inside, but she only got as far as the living room. When she saw his white leather couch, she sunk down into it, closed her eyes and melted into the cushions. A few minutes later, he returned with an assortment of cheese and crackers, which he had artfully displayed on a marble tray. When he left again, she sat up straight and studied the contents. A few seconds later he returned with another tray, which held a Baccarat flute filled with champagne and a Baccarat goblet filled with tea and chipped ice. He arranged everything on the cocktail table, then he dimmed the lights and turned on his CD player. Suddenly, the sound of love ballads filled the room and he was next to her on the couch. He handed her the goblet of iced tea, picked up his champagne flute and toasted her.

"Cheers," he said.

"Cheers."

They sipped their drinks and put their glasses down.

"Please help yourself to some cheese and crackers. I think you'll find them to be a lot more palatable than that fiery mess Darla served us earlier," he said.

"Thanks, but I can't. I'm still stuffed from dinner."

He smoothed her hair with his fingertips.

"From that little salad?"

She cleared her throat and nodded.

"Yes. Actually, it was actually quite filling."

He wrapped his arms around her and gently pulled her toward him. Tingling rays blazed through her as she melted into his caress. She felt his breath against her ear and then against her lips, as he kissed her tenderly.

"You have no idea how long I've waited to do that," he said, when he came up for air.

Then he kissed her again, this time with even more passion. He slid his right hand down her spine. When he reached the center of her back, he tried to remove her bra with one hand. That's when she broke away. Her face was flushed, her eyes snapped and she folded her arms across her chest.

"Hey you fresh thing! Just what the hell do you think you're doing?"

"Now, wait a minute. I was under the impression that you liked it."

"Well, that's still no reason for you to think that you can automatically make it to first base with me!"

"I don't even know what that means."

Pattie knit her brow.

"Tell me Jordan. Is that why you dragged me over here? So that you can add me to your collection?"

"First of all, I don't remember ever having had to 'drag' you anywhere and second of all, what do you mean by my collection? My collection of what?"

"Well shut that damn music off and then you tell me," she yelled.

Jordan stood, walked over to the CD player and turned the music off, while Pattie stood and walked over to an alcove that housed a black-lacquered, Chinese altar and a crystal Buddha.

"Anyway, I think I've had about as much excitement as I can stand in a day," she said, calmly.

"Yes. I gathered that."

"I can't help but like your living room though. It's like a museum in here and I mean that in a good way."

Jordan smiled.

"Well, that's at least something positive."

Pattie turned and walked toward the piano at the far end of the living room.

"Is this an antique?"

Jordan nodded.

"Yes."

She examined the Coat of Arms that hung above it. A muscular arm with a clenched fist rose out of a cloud, complete with a sword and buckle. Underneath, a motto read "Invictus Maneo".

"What does that mean?"

"Oh. Don't they teach you Latin in Law School?"

"Some, but none of us are fluent."

He chuckled.

"It's the Armstrong Clan's motto. It means 'I remain unvanquished.' Well, at least it was true up until just now."

Pattie chuckled.

"I guess you'll have to commission a new painting," she said.

He nodded and chuckled with her.

"You're a girl of much wit. I think I like it, at least most of the time."

"Thank you. I like your sense of humor too and I think it's really cool that you have your own clan. I wish I belonged to something."

"Don't you Anwalds stick together?"

She shook her head.

"No, not really."

"That seems to be the way families are nowadays," he said, absently.

She walked around and stopped near a bookcase, where a blue and white porcelain vase rested. It was almost as thin as tissue paper. She pointed to it.

"This looks Chinese to me."

"Well, actually, it's from Northern Italy."

A black and white etching of a couple in a nude embrace hung above it. She pointed to it and frowned.

"I don't like them. They're naked."

"Well, it's just art."

"Well, I'm still entitled to my own opinion."

"True. You don't drink. I've never seen you light up a cigarette and apparently, you don't engage in any other vices either."

"That's right. I don't."

"You know, if you didn't drive that little car of yours, I'd swear that you were an Amish woman."

"You know what? That's probably a good way to think of me and I'm going to teach you a lesson tonight."

"You're going to teach me a lesson? This should be good. What's the lesson?"

"The lesson is this. Just because you're good looking and smart and you own nice things, it doesn't give you the right to go around taking advantage of people."

"I didn't try to take advantage of you."

"People, Jordan. People. Are you hearing one word I'm saying?"

He frowned.

"I'm trying to, but none of them are making any sense."

"Well, then you need to let it all sink in, I guess."

"I'm afraid you sound a bit nutty."

She shook her head.

"Well, I'm not."

She bent down, peered into the bookcase and scanned the collection of leather bound classics by Freud, Jung, Adler, Robert Burns and others. When she was done, she walked back to the couch, picked up her glass and drained it.

"I'm ready to go home now," she said.

CHAPTER THIRTY-EIGHT
HOME SWEET HOME

Pattie and Jordan trudged up the stairs until they reached the landing in front of Pattie's door. Just as she turned to face him, he leaned over and kissed her chastely on the cheek. She pulled her keys out of her tote bag and unlocked her door.

"Well, good night you bad thing," she said.

"What went wrong tonight?"

Pattie bit her lip.

"You know, people often ask me things and then when I tell them the truth, they freak out. I really wish people wouldn't ask me things when they can't handle my answers."

"What makes you think I can't handle any answer you may choose to give me?"

"I don't know, but let's put it this way. I can't get into trouble for the things I don't say."

She opened her door narrowly, slid through it and slammed it, just as she always did.

Well, Good Night Irene, he thought, as he descended the stairs.

Once inside, she double bolted the door, pulled the string on her fluorescent light and surveyed her apartment. It felt as stifling to her as a sauna and she had neither a fan nor an air conditioner. Her breathing was shallow and she immediately broke out into little beads of sweat. She threw her tote bag onto the table.

All of a sudden, she decided that she hated every bit of her surroundings. It all seemed so desolate compared to the way Jordan lived. Instead of a nice, white leather couch, she had an unmade studio bed. The only other living thing besides her was the tea rose and that came from Jordan and the incessant dripping of her kitchen faucet reminded her that it was time to water it once again. Her only artwork was an unframed poster of Clarence Darrow, which she had thumb tacked to the wall. It read:

"I have lived my life and I have fought my battles, not against the weak and the poor—but against power, injustice, and oppression."

A makeshift set of shelves in the corner housed a collection of about twenty dolls of all types, sizes and price ranges. An old magic 8 ball from her childhood rested on top of it and her judo mat lay in front of it. She walked over, picked up the 8 ball and asked whether Roy and Penny Edwards had placed a spell on her. She shook it and waited for the answer to float to the top.

"My Reply Is Hazy," it read.

She sighed, placed the 8 ball back on the shelf and walked over to her closet. She removed her sweaty clothes, threw them into the pillowcase that served as a makeshift hamper and changed into a lightweight white gauze tunic. She glanced in the mirror, shrugged and walked over to one of the metal folding chairs that stood around her card table. She dragged it over to the counter and boosted herself up. She pushed her dingy white taffeta curtain out of the way and struggled to open the only window in her apartment, so that she could crawl through it and sit out on her fire escape, where it was at least ten degrees cooler. She positioned herself with her back to the building, closed her eyes and tried to ignore the fumes from the cars that whizzed and sped past her, just a few feet away on the FDR Drive.

Three Latinos were walking on the street below her. One nudged the other two and pointed up at her. They all whistled and cat called to her in Spanish. She opened her eyes, sighed and gave them the finger. Then she crawled back through the window, slammed it shut and locked it. Disgusted, she used the chair to climb down from the counter and she headed for her bathroom. She ran cold water over her wrists. Then she washed her face, braided her hair and turned off the light. She flounced into her studio bed, kicked the covers off of her and squeezed her eyes shut. She rested there in sweaty silence until the darkness crept in to envelop her.

CHAPTER THIRTY-NINE

"AFTER THE ECSTASY, THE LAUNDRY"

Jordan walked into his apartment, picked up the cheese tray and glasses and sighed. He brought everything into the kitchen, where he wrapped the cheese and put it away. He carefully hand washed the tray and the glasses and he carefully placed them on a towel to dry. Then he walked down the hall to his bedroom. He removed his shoes, reached into his pocket for his cell phone and glanced at the time. It was ten o'clock. He sprawled across his King-Sized bed and speed dialed Clint, who picked up on the second ring.

"Hey Buddy. How are you?" Clint asked.

"Not good. I had an awful night."

"I'm sorry to hear that. What's going on?"

"As you probably might have guessed, it was only a question of time before I asked that young attorney out."

Clint chuckled.

"I figured that might happen, but that should be good news, not bad news. What's the problem? Aren't things working out?"

"I guess not. We had an argument and she uses baseball terms to describe things."

"Well, of course she does. She's an American. Isn's she?"

"Yes."

"Well, there you go. After all, baseball is America's greatest past time."

Jordan laughed.

"That was beautifully stated, but it doesn't help me to figure out a damn thing she's saying."

Jordan could hear Clint's fiancée chiding him to hang up.

"Well, I'm sorry for your troubles. I hope things get better for you. I'll call you tomorrow night," Clint said.

"Thanks."

After they hung up, Jordan shook his head.

No help there, he thought as he walked down the hall, through his living room and out onto his terrace. He stood at the railing and watched the neon lights along Times Square.

CHAPTER FORTY
NIGHT CRAWLERS

Several hours later, while most of New York slept, the Seaport below Pattie's apartment sprang to life. The cacophony of noise and chaos added to the sound effects created by the endless stream of traffic on the FDR drive. The noise reached its crescendo when the armies of refrigerated trucks arrived to dump their two hundred fifty million pounds of fresh fish onto the docks. Unfortunately, fish wasn't the only thing they delivered. They also delivered the smell of oil and gasoline, which mingled with the fish odors to create an obnoxious stench that hovered in the stale air. The oil also leaked onto the cobblestones and mixed with the slime from the fish scales. Since few of the trucks had mufflers, another commodity they delivered was a rumbling din whose roar pierced the air.

Pattie was used to all of it, even the sounds of the stevedores, who cursed and used their forklifts to battle with each other. They unloaded and sorted their fish to the background noise of the competing radio stations that they blasted at top volume. She knew that it generally continued every night until dawn, when the jackhammers arrived to drown it all out with the sounds of their frenetic pounding. Those sounds interfered with Pattie's sleep, but they didn't worry her. What did worry her, were the other sounds she heard, sounds which were closer at hand. She tensed up and winced, as the battalion of rats began their nightly trek through the tunnels that they had been burrowing in her ceiling and walls for many moons now.

Her heart thumped and her flesh crawled as she lay surrounded by the literal rat race that went on above, below and all around her. At first, she pulled the covers over her head and listened in terror, as they gnawed at what she hoped wasn't an electrical wire or a supporting beam. The worst-case scenarios that her imagination evoked left her no peace. She finally forced herself to sit up and get out of bed. She scurried over to her tote bag and fumbled around until she found her cell phone. She turned it on and speed dialed her brother Lou. He picked up the call on the fourth ring.

"Hello?"

His voice sounded groggy.

"Did I wake you up?"

"No. I had to get up to answer the phone anyway."

"Very funny."

"I know. Anyway, what's the matter?"

"I'm having a panic attack!"

"Why?"

"Tons of rats are racing around inside my walls!"

"Just ignore them and go back to sleep."

"I'd do anything to sleep, but I can't. There's a distinct possibility that one of them could gnaw a hole through the ceiling. What if one of them lands on my face?"

"Stop thinking about it. Nothing's gonna happen. Your mind is stressing you out more than the rats are."

She started to cry.

"Listen, every night they get closer."

"I don't know what you want me to do. I have to get up for work out tomorrow," he said, right before he hung up on her.

Pattie shook her head.

CHAPTER FORTY-ONE
SUNDAY BRUNCH

Late the following morning, Pattie and Ryan sat together on a picnic blanket in Battery Park. The warm sun had brought some color to both of their faces. Ryan finished the last of his bacon, egg and cheese sandwich and wiped his mouth, while Pattie took the first sip of her White Chocolate Raspberry Latte.

"Yummy," she said.

Ryan pointed out at the Hudson River.

"What a great day this is turning out to be."

Pattie nodded.

"Agreed."

He pointed at the Statue of Liberty.

"Just look at Lady Liberty over there. She's like a guardian angel that watches over us. I always like looking up and knowing that she's there."

"Wow. I never thought of it that way."

Ryan shook his head.

"Well, after Nine Eleven I never take anything for granted anymore."

Pattie nodded vaguely.

"I guess you're right."

"You know, sometimes, when I can't get to sleep, I go up onto my rooftop, look out at the river and wait for the city to whisper her secrets to me," he said.

"That's such a poetic thought. You should write it down," she said.

He smiled.

"That's OK. I'll leave the poetry writing to you. Feel free to steal it if you want to. "

"Really?"

He nodded, leaned back and surrendered to the gentle breeze that floated in from the river.

"Why not? I don't mind."

"Thank you. I think I will," she said, as she reached into her tote bag for her black paged journal and gel pen.

The wind died down and as she wrote, Ryan reached into the picnic basket. He removed a blueberry muffin, a plastic plate and a serrated knife. He cut the muffin into quarters and set them on the plate.

"Gee that looks delicious," Pattie said.

He smiled.

"So, take one," he said, as he popped one of the quarters into his mouth.

She nodded, picked up a quarter and bit into it. When she finished it, he handed her another, which she polished off.

"More?"

She shook her head, wiped her mouth and smiled.

"No thanks. They were truly delicious, but I'm full."

"I had a feeling you'd say that. Anyway, how was your second date with Prince Charming?"

"I'm not sure."

Ryan gasped.

"Could it be that there's trouble in paradise?"

"Well, don't get me wrong. In many ways, he's a classy guy, but there's something wrong with him."

"Well, you're classy too and there's nothing wrong with you."

"Thanks."

"So, tell me. I'm dying to know what's wrong with him."

"I have a feeling he's got a lot of baggage."

"Well, the older you get to be the more baggage life makes you carry. It's a law of the Universe. Or some such thing."

"God, I hope you're wrong."

"But I'm not though."

"Anyway, he took me mountain climbing on a rock wall."

"Wow, I'm impressed."

She chuckled.

"Don't be. I was scared out of my mind. We also drove some golf balls."

"Even though that would seem a lot safer, it sounds like he gave you quite a work out. One day maybe you'll reciprocate by giving him a Judo Chop," Ryan said, as he popped the last quarter into his mouth.

"Hey, don't kid yourself. That might just happen. After all, what if he's just some guy on the prowl, who's trying to score as many one night stands as he can?"

Ryan grinned and wiped his hands.

"Oh my God! You mean he got fresh with you?"

"He tried, but he wasn't pushy about it and he didn't get very far. However, I heard some disturbing things about him through the grape vine."

"Wow. News sure travels fast in this city," Ryan said.

Pattie nodded.

"Doesn't it? Anyhow, no matter what, I just don't have the disposition to play rhythm guitar behind other girls."

"Well then, you'd better figure out everything you need to before you get in over your head. The last thing you need is a broken heart."

Pattie nodded.

"Tell me about it."

CHAPTER FORTY-TWO

YOU CAN'T ALWAYS GET WHAT YOU WANT

Early the next morning, Pattie sat at her desk and reviewed her arraignment files. She wore her most professional outfit, a brand new black suit with a white ruffled blouse and plain black leather pumps. Her hair was styled in a French Twist. Brad knocked on her door and sauntered in without even waiting to be invited. He waved two files at her.

"OK, listen up, Sweetheart. Both Jimmy and Teddy called in sick today. Plus, I just found out less than two minutes ago that at ten o'clock I'm gonna be picking a jury in People v. Poncetta."

"Sorry to hear that," Pattie said.

"Well, if you sincerely mean that, then you'll rise to the occasion and help me out here. Do the arraignments in the morning like you always do, but in the afternoon, handle these two pre-trials for me. Pre-trials are what give us defense attorneys a chance to find out how strong our defenses are when stacked up against the State's evidence."

"I know what pre-trials are, Brad. I did them every day of my life at the Family Court."

Brad stuck his right index finger into the left side of his mouth and made a popping noise against his cheek. When he removed it, he kept it upright and swirled it around in a circle.

"Well, big whoopdeeshit. Anyhow, don't lemme down, because this isn't that greasy kid stuff that you and your gal pal Annie are used to. You'll be up against Connor Dane himself."

Pattie frowned.

"That's interesting. Why isn't he prosecuting Poncetta?"

"Even though it's a complicated case, in his heart of hearts he knows he can't win. That's why he's sending Toby Barnett in. That way when they lose, Toby will be the one to look bad, not him."

Pattie shook her head.

"Gee, that's nasty of him to make Toby into his fall guy," she said.

"Well, that's the way the game is played, Sweetheart. It's a dog eat dog world out there, so wake up. Prosecutors only like to see their names in lights when it spells victory for them."

He lobbed the two files onto her desk, turned around and sauntered out. She picked up her arraignment files and headed for the arraignment court, leaving Brad's files right where they landed.

CHAPTER FORTY-THREE
SKULLDUGGERY AFOOT

After spending an uneventful morning in court, Pattie skipped lunch in order to review Brad's files. Once she was done, she took them over to Connor Dane's office to discuss them. She ran into Ryan on her way over there.

"Hey Pattie! You look like a million bucks today."

She beamed.

"Thanks."

"I've been going nuts trying to find you."

"I'm sorry. I skipped lunch."

"It's OK. I ended up eating with Judge Benchley's Court Officer Jerry. He told me that you were handling some Pre-Trials this afternoon."

Pattie beamed again.

"That's right."

Ryan assumed a boxer's stance, clenched his fists and pretended to shadow box.

"Now, listen up and take it from me. Be tough. See?"

He sounded exactly like Edward G. Robinson.

Pattie laughed.

"Sure thing, Little Caesar."

"Seriously though, Jerry told me that one of your cases might involve possession of cocaine. A dozen or so Colombians were indicted. Every one of them had private attorneys, except your guy."

"Really?"

Ryan nodded.

"Yeah. They were all were offered a really great deal, which they pled out to. I wrote it down."

He reached into his pocket and handed her a Post It. She read it, smiled and stuck in her pocket.

"Thank you. This is a really big heads up. What totally impressive spy work!"

"Well, you know I always have your back. That's why I want to let you know that Jerry overheard Connor saying how he didn't mind giving away the store to those other defendants, because he still had one fall guy. You."

"Me? Don't you mean my client? Vega?"

"No. I mean YOU personally. Jerry said that Connor even went so far as to specifically mention you by name."

Pattie gasped.

"Oh my God!"

Ryan nodded.

"I know. He even went on to say that it would be a cakewalk to convict your client, since the others are well represented and your client only has you. So, whatever you do, make sure you cover your ass with him."

"But, how though?"

"By making sure that your guy gets the exact same deal that's on this Post It, because if he pleads out to anything worse, you'll be forever branded as incompetent and that brand will follow you everywhere you go."

"Yeah, but from what you just said, it doesn't sound like Connor's planning to offer me the same deal."

He shrugged.

"So, then just put it on the trial list and let Brad deal with it later."

"Good idea. What's weird about all of this, is that Brad never mentioned any of this to me this morning, when he literally threw the files at me."

"Well, he may not have known about it. Isn't he on trial?"

"Yes, but it's also possible that he could be setting me up to look bad."

Ryan shook his head.

"I doubt it."

"Ryan, the guy doesn't like me and quite frankly, I wouldn't put anything past him. Anyhow, thank you. I really appreciate you letting me know all of this."

"Will I see you at Starbucks later?" Ryan asked.

"Sure. After Judo. How does nine thirty sound?"

"Perfect. I'll be waiting to hear what happens."

CHAPTER FORTY-FOUR
THE BIG BAD WOLF

The door to Connor Dane's office was wide open, showcasing him in all his glory, as he leaned back in his chair with his arms behind his head, smirking. He was a slim, well-dressed man in his early forties, whose dark, wavy hair hung over one eye. When Pattie knocked on his door, he bolted to an upright position and his hair fell away from his face, revealing cynical brown eyes. He flashed his pearly white teeth at her.

"Attorney Anwald?"

Pattie cleared her throat and nodded.

"Yes?"

"Brad told me that you would be handling this afternoon's Pre-Trials. Come on in," he said.

As soon as she entered his office, he sprung out of his chair and pointed to a chair across from his desk. When she sat down, he sat down too.

"What have you got?"

"Vega?"

"Yes. He's the one who got himself busted along with those eleven other morons."

Oh brother. This guy's worse than Brad, she thought, as she opened her file and removed the police report.

"OK, well, whatever you choose to call them, I hear that they all pled out to the deal of the century."

Connor licked his lips.

"So?"

"Well eighteen months suspended sentence with three years' probation is unheard of on a cocaine charge. So, I'm thinking, since the police report specifically states that my client had only walked in a minute or two before the police arrived, that he wasn't even part of the gang."

Connor smirked, snatched the paper out of her hand and crumpled it into a little ball. He lobbed it into the waste paper basket and leaned back in his chair.

"Well, I have a file too and my file says that he's a menace to society who's gonna go bye-bye for a long, long time. Let me give you a lesson in Criminal Law. The Fifth Amendment says that people only have the right to remain silent as long as the charges are pending against them."

"I know."

"Good, so, since the other eleven morons have all pled out, they no longer have any charges pending against them. As a result, I'll be able to use them to testify against your moron and I will, Hon, I will."

"OK, now that we discussed the Constitution, let's discuss something even more fascinating. My brother's a cop."

Connor frowned and perused his copy of the police report.

"On this case?"

"Of course not."

He yawned.

"So, then why should I care?"

"Don't you get it?"

"Get what? I never pledged any oaths requiring me to dole out special dispensations to people with relatives on the police force."

Pattie looked shocked.

"Oh my God! Is that what you think? Because, all I'm saying is that as a cop, my brother hangs out with a lot of other cops."

"I'll bet. We all know how insular cops can be, but why should I care about Police Anthropology?"

"I'm not trying to give you a crash course in Police Anthropology. I'm only mentioning it because some of my brother's friends on the force are narcs and everybody knows everybody, narc or not. And we know what every narc's worst fear is."

"What? That the likes of you will cross examine them? Don't flatter yourself."

"I'm not, but at the same time, don't underestimate me either. Anyhow, every narc's biggest fear, in fact, every detective's biggest fear, is that they'll get busted back down into a uniform. The Sixth Amendment guarantees my client the right to confront and cross examine every one of his accusers and when we go to trial that's exactly what I'll do."

"Yeah, well, that's what you're supposed to do," Connor said.

"Yeah well, imagine how ticked off those three narcs are gonna be when I call them to the stand. Because, right before I do, I'll make sure that the courtroom is packed with every known drug dealer in New York City. That way they all can get a good look at those narcs' faces and when I do that, there goes those narcs' anonymity for all future drug busts."

Connor sighed.

"Ho hum. I'll simply object to you packing the court with all of your client's cohorts and drug buddies."

"Well, you can huff and you can puff and you can certainly try, but in the end, you won't succeed, because, as everyone knows, unless a case involves a juvenile, Criminal Court is open and public. So in the end they're all coming in and I'll make sure I have all of those narcs back in uniforms before they even walk out of the courtroom."

Connor sized her up. After several seconds, he finally spoke.

"Oh, all right, Ms. Anwald. I'll be a gentleman and offer your guy the same deal that the other morons all got. How about that?"

Pattie grinned.

"Why, thank you," she said.

"You're not welcome. Remember though. The conditions are the usual drug testing and whatever else the probation officer deems necessary," he said.

"Do the others all have those exact same conditions?"

"Of course. They're always par for the course. I'm surprised that someone as learned as you didn't already realize that."

"Well, the rules around here keep changing so often it's hard to stay on top of them."

"Who have you got next?"

"Leland LeRucks?"

"That's pronounced LA ROO. They only say it your way in limericks," Connor said, chuckling at his own wit.

Pattie cleared her throat once again.

"Anyway, I looked through the file and guess what? The People never complied with the Motion for Disclosure that Judge Benchley granted."

Connor picked up his file and started rifling through it.

"What Motion for Disclosure?"

Pattie sighed.

"I guess we're back to The Constitution again."

"Yeah, yeah, yeah. All kidding aside, I've always been free-wheeling about letting you guys plow through all of our files."

"I know, which is why I find it so strange that we didn't even get a police report in this case," Pattie said.

"Are you sure? Maybe we did and you lost it."

Pattie shook her head.

"Oh no. The old 'you must have lost it' routine isn't going to fly. You see, Jimmy stuck a note in the file which says that, as recently as Friday afternoon, you still hadn't provided us with our disclosure."

Connor picked up his file, rifled through it and closed it.

"It's not in my file either," he said.

"Well then, where is it?"

"I don't know! Did you have a chance to talk to LeRoux yet?"

"No."

"Well, then maybe you should consider yourself blessed. In any case, talk to him and in the meantime, I'll get my secretary to track down your Disclosure."

"It works better for me when I've read the police report before I meet with my clients."

"Well, unfortunately we don't live in a perfect world, so you can't do that this time," Connor said to her as if she were an errant five-year-old.

Pattie stood.

"Fine," she said, "but I'll be back."

"Oh, I'm counting on it," Connor said, as he watched her walk out.

CHAPTER FORTY-FIVE
DESCENT

Like Persephone, Pattie took the stairwell that descended into the soulless bowels of the courthouse. She opened the cold, gray, steel door that led from the stairwell and walked down the hall toward the nether world of the lock up. She leaned against the door, inhaled deeply and exhaled before she rang the bell. When she heard the buzz, followed by the click that granted her entry, she used all of her might to push the heavy door open.

Dante Asmodeo, The Guardian of the Lockup, stood and nodded. He was rotund and even shorter than Pattie. His skin was a deep shade of olive. As he came from behind the control panel where he had been sitting in his comfortable, black leather chair, Pattie noticed that his stomach strained against the last notch of his belt, showcasing his waistline as the broadest part of his body. Even though his buckle was custom made to highlight his badge, it looked unsightly. He wore sunglasses, even though the lockup was dark. When Pattie looked closely at him, she realized that the lenses were mirrors, so instead of seeing his eyes, all she could see were two reflections of herself.

"What or should I say who, brings you down here to see me?"

His raspy voice was a hardly more than a whisper and he hissed whenever he pronounced the letter "s". Pattie shivered and cleared her throat.

"Hi, uh, I'm here to see Leland LeRoux."

"Really? That's interesting, because he hasn't enjoyed my hospitality yet today. Perhaps some bleeding heart bailed him out?"

"OK then, so what about Alejandro Vega?"

Dante shook his head.

"Well, the ice cream truck forgot to deliver him."

Pattie sighed.

"Are you kidding? It's almost two o'clock. I thought they had already brought everybody over here first thing this morning."

Dante shrugged.

"Well, somehow Mr. Vega must have slipped through the cracks. Relax. They made a second run especially for you."

"Thanks. I'll be back later."

"Don't I know it," Dante said, as he buzzed her out.

She found herself back in the hall. The light was so bright in comparison to the light in the dim, dingy lockup, that it hurt her eyes. She blinked several times to bring them back into focus before she ran back up the nine flights of stairs to the Legal Aid office. She stopped at Ceil 's desk.

"Have you seen Leland LeRoux?"

Ceil looked up from her word processing and pointed toward the waiting room on the other side of the Plexiglas partition.

"He's out there."

He could have been anywhere between thirty-five and sixty. He was lean, dirty and disheveled. He looked as if he hadn't been anywhere near soap or water in weeks. His complexion had an ashen pallor and he had a long, pointy nose. From what Pattie could see at that distance, his red rimmed eyes were a steely gray color. A tiny scar above his right eyebrow, revealed shades of an unfortunate encounter from some time in his past. Angry little patches of red and silver scales dotted his mouth and eyebrows. They were identical to the patches of scales that laced the backs of his hands, except that the ones on his face had broken open and oozed some kind of pus that had dried into a yellowish crust.

He wore a dirty, worn out, flannel shirt and a pair of even dirtier jeans. His faded orange construction boots were caked with dried mud. His mouse brown hair hung in greasy strings and curled awkwardly at his collar. It had little teeth marks, indicating where a comb had recently been applied to it and his fingernails were black with grime. Together they watched him through the glass, as he rooted and dug through three tattered shopping bags bearing the logo "Blissful Bug Extermination". The bags were all tied together with a series of thin, gray braided cords. Pattie tried to decipher his age.

Pattie looked at Ceil in horror.

"God, he looks like a weirdo, Pattie said.

Ceil nodded.

"Yup. Shit just got real. Try not to get too close to him, because we think the crap all over his face is impetigo and that's very contagious."

Pattie finally took a deep breath and walked through the door to the waiting room, which now smelled like a terrible mixture of mold and something else that Pattie couldn't quite identify.

"Hi Mr. LeRoux. I'm Pattie Anwald and I'll be representing you today."

Leland LeRoux ignored her and continued to rifle through his bags. When he finally finished, he stood upright, peered at her from underneath his eyebrows and slowly assessed her from her French Twist, right down to the soles of her shoes. When he was finished, he scowled.

"Why are you here? Where's Jimmy at?" He spoke in a thick Southern Drawl.

An obnoxious odor wafted from his mouth, which smelled like the sewers near Peck Slip after a heavy rainstorm and he only had about eight teeth in his head. They were gray and twisted, like old headstones in an untended, medieval graveyard.

She cleared her throat.

"Well, Attorney Farnsworth and some other members of our staff are out sick today, so I'll be covering most of their cases."

"Coverin' their cases or coverin' their asses? 'Cause if I know that dayum Brad they probably ain' really even sick. He's always sloughing me off onta the lowess rejecks on his totem pole so's they kin cut their teeth on my Civil Rights."

"I'm sorry that you're upset, but I honestly believe that I'm qualified to handle your case."

He twisted his sparse, bloodless lips into a sneer and winked.

"Well, why don't ya jess handle me instead?"

"Look, I'm not going to waste your time or mine. If you want me to handle your case, you can follow me into my office. Otherwise, you can go into the courtroom alone and ask Judge Benchley for an adjournment, so that Attorney Farnsworth can continue to represent you."

"Look, I jess want this over with as quick as possible so's I kin git my life and my bayul money back."

Pattie turned around and walked toward the glass partition and Leland followed her. Every time he took a step, clumps of dried mud dislodged from his boots, leaving a trail of dust. She unlocked the door with her electronic passkey and when she reached her office, he pushed past her, plopped down on the old wooden client's chair and tossed his bags on top of her desk.

"That el creepo downstairs done went through every dayum one of these here bags and he even stooped to clippin' my chill pills. Can you git 'em back fer me?"

Pattie frowned.

"Well, that's what you get for bringing controlled substances into the courthouse."

"Why? I came by 'em legit. The doctor down to the jailhouse done perscribed 'em fer me."

"All I can do is request that the judge order them to be returned to you, but I can't guarantee that he will do it. So, I wouldn't get my hopes up if I were you."

"Thank ya fer at least sayin' you'll try."

"You're welcome. Now who did you say took them?"

"That freak who works the metal detecktator down at the main entrance. What's his name? Sum'pn like Bakerman?"

He plunked his legs on her desk and crossed them at the ankles. She frowned and swatted at them with his file.

"Do you mind?" She asked, barely concealing her annoyance.

He slowly dropped each foot back down to the floor. Little remnants of dust remained on her desk. She used a tissue to wipe them off. Then she gingerly threw the tissue into the waste paper basket and glanced at her watch.

"So, uh, why don't you just tell me what happened when you were arrested?"

"I done been through the story of my arrest with Jimmy twice now and here you are comin' along, wantin' me to tell it all over again."

"Well, since Attorney Farnsworth isn't here, I need to know the details," she said.

"Well, didn't ya read the Pole-leese Reeport? That's the lease ya couldda did fer Gawd's sakes."

Pattie cleared her throat.

"I still need to hear your version of things."

"Well, it ain' a version. It's the facks. Besides, how do I know y'ain't gonna violate my confidence or nothin' if I tell ya the truth?"

"Because, I'm a professional."

"Well, I done heard all that confidentiality gibberish tons o' times before, but the reason I'm axin' is because everybody knows how much you gals jess love to gossip."

She stood and pointed at the door.

"OK, that did it. I'll just ask for the adjournment myself," she said.

"No. Wait. I'll tell ya whatever ya wanna know."

She sighed.

"Fine."

"Firss of all, lemme start off by reiteratin' what I already done tole Jimmy. A. I didn't do nothin' and B. I was the victim of pole-leese harassmenn, jess like I always am."

Pattie frowned.

"I can't imagine that the police would deliberately go around harassing anybody."

"Really? Why not? It's a lotta fun for 'em."

"Anyway, are you going to tell me what happened on the night of your arrest or what?"

He pursed his lips.

"Yes. So, anyways, on the night o' my soul called arress, it was Karaoke night down to El Diablo's Bar and OK, maybe I had a few too many beers that night, but I didn't think much about it, since I'd coated my stomach with some homemade ratatouille beforehand."

"How many beers is a few too many?"

"How in the hell should I know? Maybe a couple. Anyways, somebody done slipped me a Mickey which pervented me from keepin' track."

"Who slipped you the Mickey?"

"I dunno. I was with my friend Willie."

"Well, maybe he did it."

"I don't think so, because he was in worse shape than I was. I think somebody must a did it to us both, because he thought I should be the designated driver. He went ta take a leak and thew his car keys at me."

"Wow."

"Yeah, so anyways, he thew them keys at me an' done tole me ta wait fer him out in his car. Parkin' that night must a been a bitch fer everybody, cause when I first got outside, I couldn't even find where he'd parked the dayum thang. I finally did find it though, way over on them ole abandoned train tracks."

"I'm repeating back what you said. You said that you found your friend Willie's car on some old abandoned railroad tracks? Are you sure that's the way it went down?"

He nodded.

"Yeah. There's tons o' them abandoned train tracks all around this city."

Ceil walked in, holding a police report.

"Barbara from the DA's office brought this over and asked me to hand it to you right away."

Pattie smiled.

"Thanks."

Ceil nodded.

"Anytime," she said, as she hurried back to her desk.

"Anyways, I got in an' got hines the wheel an' before I even put the keys in the ignition, I payussed out. The necks thang I know, two o' New York's finess done knocked on the winda, woke me up and drug me the hell outta the car by my hair. Then they done breathalyzered and arrested me."

Pattie nodded, picked up the police report and read it. It corroborated Leland's version of the facts. Leland went into a long, drawn out coughing fit. He turned beet red and pulled an old handkerchief out of one of his bags. Then, just as Pattie stuck the report into the file, he expelled a profuse amount of dark green sputum into his handkerchief. It filled Pattie's office with a stench so vile, it caused the saliva to well up in her mouth. She clutched her stomach to fend off her nausea, but it didn't work. She gagged, ran out and bent over Ceil 's trashcan. Ceil got up from her word processing and placed her hand gently on Pattie's back, while Pattie vomited dry heaves. When Pattie regained her composure, she gently pulled Ceil into Jimmy Farnsworth's vacant office and closed the door.

"Oh my God, that guy's disgusting!"

Ceil nodded.

"That's why Brad and Jimmy meet our clients in those little cubicles outside of the courtrooms. Didn't any one ever tell you to do that?"

Pattie shook her head.

"No, but it's a really great idea."

"If you're not up to this, I'll just call the Judge and get it adjourned."

"No. It's all right. I'm OK now."

Ceil looked at her with a doubtful expression.

"Are you sure?"

Pattie nodded.

"I will be, if I can just take a breather for a while."

Ceil nodded.

"That's a good idea, she said, as she sat down.

She returned to her word processing and Pattie returned to her office.

"Well, Mr. LeRoux, why don't you go wait for me out in the hallway?"

Leland frowned.

"Why?"

"Because I have to discuss your case with the DA."

Leland took his sweet time fidgeting with the ties on his bag but eventually he stood up and left. Once he was gone, Pattie gingerly picked up his file and returned to Connor Dane's office.

CHAPTER FORTY-SIX
HAPPY CAMPER

Connor Dane stood and waved Pattie in.

"My, you look just like the proverbial happy camper."

Pattie smiled.

"Well, I guess you could say I'm in somewhat of a good mood."

"Well, have a seat and tell me all about it," he said.

She sat and Connor followed her lead.

"Well, I just had the opportunity to review the police report that your office was finally kind enough to provide. First of all, there's insufficient evidence to show that Mr. LeRoux even operated a motor vehicle and second of all, even if you could get him on operation, it wasn't on a road. The car was parked on railroad tracks, where DWI laws don't even apply."

Connor snatched the police report out of her hands. Then he skimmed it and threw it on the desk.

"Now isn't that a kick in the ass!"

"Yeah. Isn't it though? So, if you don't drop the charges I'll file a Motion to Dismiss right on the spot."

"Really? You mean to tell me that you'd go off on a half-cocked rant to protect a menace like that?"

"Oh please! You say that about everybody."

"I know, but this time I actually mean it. You haven't been here long enough to realize that Leland LeRoux is crazy. He can turn on anybody at any time, for no reason at all and that includes you, Sister, so it might actually behoove you not to go too far overboard for him."

"Wait a minute. Did you deliberately withhold the police report just so that you could torpedo him?"

Connor grimaced.

"Of course not! My God! You've jumped to the wrong conclusion!"

"So, then you'll drop the charges?"

"Do I have a choice?"

"Well, you'll sleep better tonight."

"No, I won't. That's just the point. None of us will sleep better tonight, with him on the loose."

She stood, so he followed her lead.

"Look, I don't want to hear this," she said.

"Well, you probably don't want to hear this either, but I'll say it anyway. You got me twice today, once on Vega and now again on LeRoux and I'm letting you know that I won't forget it."

"Bye," she said and left.

When he was sure she was gone, he stormed out of his office and went over to talk to his secretary, Barbara.

"Is everything OK?" She asked.

"No! That little Anwald bitch actually thinks she's smarter than I am. Remind me not to fall for her fake ingenue crap ever again!"

Barbara nodded and gave him the thumb's up sign.

"OK!"

CHAPTER FORTY-SEVEN
AFFIDAVIT

When Pattie left Connor's office, she found Leland in the hall-way, roaming around, so she directed him into an empty conference room.

"I have great news for you," she said.

"Ya done got my pills back fer me?"

"I already told you, I can't address that particular issue until I get before a judge."

"OK. Then, what is it?"

An older man opened the door to the conference room and stuck a piece of paper under Pattie's nose.

"Can you notarize this for me? It's a financial affidavit that says I'm poor enough to qualify for Legal Aid!"

"I'm sorry, but I can't right now. I'm with a client," Pattie answered.

"Well, I'm a client too or at least I could be one if you'd just notarize this damn piece of paper!"

"Why don't you take it downstairs and ask the secretary to help you?"

"Because you are the secretary," the man shouted.

Leland stood and walked over to him.

"No, she ain' no seckerterry an' she's with me, so beat it!"

He shoved the man through the doorway, slammed the door on him and flounced back into his seat.

The old man opened the door again and stuck his head back in.

"I'm going downstairs to report you for dereliction of duty," he said, as he slammed the door.

Leland broke into another fit. After a solid minute of coughing and hacking, he turned red again, pulled his dirty handkerchief out of his pocket and discharged some more green sputum into it. Pattie frowned and cleared her throat, just as one of the guards from the lock up opened the door.

"Hi, I'm sorry to interrupt you, but Dante told me to find you and let you know that Vega's down in the lock up," he said.

"Thanks. I'm right behind you," Pattie said.

She picked up her files and ran after him, grateful for an excuse to get away from Leland.

Leland stuck his head out of the conference room door.

"Hey! Git back here! Ya ain'done tellin' me my good news yet!"

CHAPTER FORTY-EIGHT
THE LOCK UP

Dante buzzed Pattie in and shoved a clipboard across the counter at her.

"Sign in," he said in a monotone.

She stared at the reflections of herself in his sunglasses. Then she glanced at her watch and complied. Afterwards, Dante led her through a cold, windowless, labyrinth of twists and turns. She shivered when they reached a dingy corridor that contained row upon row of dismal cells, whose sole function was to temporarily hold prisoners until they were called upstairs for their cases. One cell held a lone prisoner who wailed and bayed at no one in particular. Dante banged his nightstick against the bars.

"Shut up," he ordered.

"No! You shut the fuck up," a tattooed Biker in another cell responded.

Dante opened a heavy metal door at the end of the corridor.

"Voila`," he said, as he ushered Pattie into an eight by ten windowless cubicle that served as a makeshift conference room. It had no chairs, which meant that lawyers and clients were forced to stand for the duration of their meetings.

A sallow, underweight, man waited for her on the other side of the filthy plexiglass partition that ran through the center of the cubicle. Pattie noticed that his teeth were chattering. After Dante clanged the door shut behind her, Pattie asked the man whether he needed an interpreter. When he shook his head, she introduced herself, explained that she was covering for Jimmy Farnsworth and informed him that it was possible for him to be released from jail that very afternoon.

"That would be great, because I don't know if I can survive another day there."

"I can imagine. Anyway, in order to get out you would have to plead guilty to possessing the cocaine."

"I don't understand. The whole time when I said I was innocent, they kept me in jail, but now, if I say I'm guilty, they'll let me go home?"

"I know it sounds crazy, but that's the situation. There's a catch to it though."

He nodded.

"I knew there would have to be one. Tell me what it is."

"If you plead guilty you will end up going on probation for the next three years. During that time, you will have to do whatever your probation officer tells you to do and can't get into trouble again, otherwise you'll end up right back in jail and you'll stay there for eighteen months, minus whatever amount of time you've already spent there."

"And if I don't go along with this?"

"You don't have to go along with it. It's certainly your right to take your chances at trial and quite frankly if you are innocent, then I don't think you should plead guilty. If you didn't do it, you didn't do it and that's that."

"Yeah, but if I don't plead guilty then I have to go back to jail. Right?"

"Right, unless you can find someone to bail you out."

"Well, if I had any one who could do that for me, they would have done so by now."

"I should tell you that all of the other defendants in this case accepted the exact same offer that was just made to you and they're all in the process of being released, right now, as we speak."

"I was wondering why they never came back down here."

"One other thing. If you decide to plead guilty, you will have a criminal record after this, which could cause you to get deported at some point in the future."

"I don't care. I just want to get out of jail."

"OK then. When we get up to the courtroom the judge will ask you how you plead."

He nodded.

"Guilty."

"He will also ask you if you are pleading guilty voluntarily. Are you?"

"Yes."

"Also, you're going to have to tell him what happened, in your own words. That's called an allocution."

"Fine. I don't care what it's called. I just want to get out of jail."

"OK then. I'll see you in court very soon. By the way, since you really don't want to risk getting into trouble while you're on probation, you might want to consider making a new set of friends."

She turned around and banged on the door. A few minutes later, Dante unlocked the door and led her back to his desk, where he tapped on the ledger.

"You have to sign yourself out," he said.

She picked up the pen, stared at her reflections and signed herself out.

"I know, Dante. I do this every day. Remember?"

Dante pressed the button that slid the outer door open. As soon as she walked out, it clanged shut behind her. Once again, her eyes struggled against the light. When she regained her focus, she glanced at her watch and ran up the stairs. She opened the stairwell door and nearly bumped into Toby Barnett.

"Hi, Pattie."

"Hi. What a surprise to find you here. I thought you were on trial with Brad."

"I am, but court's still in recess right now. Anyway, how do you like it here?"

"Well, since you asked, I might as well tell you. I really miss my old job."

He handed a set of papers to her.

"Here's the Psychological Evaluation Dr. Armstrong just did on Justin," he said.

"Thanks."

She skimmed through it, turned to the last page and shook her head.

"Wow! 'After several sessions with the minor victim, Justin Edwards, it is my considered judgment that he is definitely strong enough to testify at trial without incurring any permanent psychological or emotional damage.' I can't believe it."

"Yeah. It sure as hell took him long enough, but actually I think it's good news."

"For you maybe, but not for Justin. How can anyone expect him to relive that ordeal?"

"Try to look at the bright side. Now that Justin can testify, there are no grounds for Elliott to get the case dismissed. I can also file a motion for a Pre-Trial, so make sure you're in court when it comes up on the docket."

Pattie nodded.

"I will be. By the way, if we don't resolve the case at that time, I'll be filing a motion for Justin to testify in camera."

Toby gave her the thumbs up sign.

"Good idea. Testifying in the Judge's chambers won't be as intimidating as having to testify in a courtroom with those parents of his leering at him. We'll videotape the in-camera testimony and play it for the jury," he said.

"Great. Of course, I'll do my best to shore him up before he goes into chambers."

Toby smiled.

"I know you will."

She waved good bye, ducked into an empty conference room and called Jordan. When she reached his voice mail she cleared her throat.

"Hi! I just received your evaluation on Justin. I don't mind telling you that I think it's really wrong!"

She hung up, sighed and returned to the conference room, where Leland greeted her with a scowl.

CHAPTER FORTY-NINE
SET UP

"Well, looky who's back after keepin' me a waitin' in suspense over her soul called good news," Leland said.

"Listen, you should be thanking me right now, because I convinced Connor Dane to drop all of the charges against you!"

Leland's scowl vanished.

"Now that's some right fine piece o' lawyerin', Ma'am."

Pattie smiled.

"I'm glad you're happy, but before we go into court, I need to complete some contact information for your file."

The scowl returned.

"Why? Jimmy knows everthin' he needs to know about me."

"Well, apparently, he never bothered to write any of it down."

"Because I done tole him not to."

"Where are you employed?" Pattie asked, ignoring the last comment.

"I got me occasional work with this Viet Cong Summabitch in exchange for my rent, electricity and cold water"---

"Doing what?"

"Whatever he tells me to do!"

"What's your telephone number?"

"Why?

"In case of an emergency."

"Well, din't cha jess git through sayin' you were closin' out the case taday? Besides, I don't have no phone yet, tho' I'm makin' playuns ta git me one."

"OK then, until you get a phone, please give me the number of your Vietnamese boss. At least I can put that down as your work number."

"The hell you can."

Pattie frowned and cleared her throat.

"Well, what about your friend Willie? What's his number?"

"I dunno."

"Well, how do you get a hold of him?"

"Well, since I don't own a phone, I never call him. We jess meet over to El Diablo's."

"Great, but since I have no plans to go to El Diablo's in the foreseeable future, tell me where he works and I'll Google his number.

"You'll do what?"

"I'll look it up."

"Well, he's a janitor at some place uptown called Beau Rivage."

"I have some clients who live there," she said absentmindedly, as she jotted down Beau Rivage's number from memory.

"Really? Willie done said it was fer wayward kids."

"They are kids. I used to represent them when I worked over at the Family Court."

CHAPTER FIFTY
VICTORY

Pattie sat in court for over an hour, while Connor Dane called all of the cases that involved privately retained attorneys. When he finally called Leland LeRoux's case, Leland strode up to the counsel table and stood next to Pattie.

"Your Honor, the People are going to drop the charges. We're in no position to prosecute. We can't even prove operation," Connor said.

Judge Benchley's ears perked up. He scanned the police report and shot Connor Dane a dirty look. Then he glared at Leland. His eyes were like two pinpoints of blue light.

"Well Mr. Dane, the report mentioned something about a switchblade and a Deck of Aleister Crowley Tarot Cards. Wasn't Aleister Crowley a Satanist from England?" Judge Benchley asked.

"Scotland, I think Your Honor," Connor answered.

"Well, where ever he came from, he was a real head case," Judge Benchley said.

"Your Honor, it's not illegal to possess Tarot Cards," Pattie said.

"Well, they're still weird, but let's forget about them for a minute and focus on that switchblade instead," Judge Benchley said.

Pattie cleared her throat.

"Well, Your Honor, the People won't be able to connect the switchblade to Mr. LeRoux. After all, it was found in his friend's car. This friend voluntarily gave the keys to Mr. LeRoux," Pattie said.

"Well since you're not admitting that the switchblade belongs to the Defendant, it's safe to presume then, that you won't be requesting its return," Judge Benchley said.

"Actually, Mr. LeRoux is requesting the return of the switch-blade, Your Honor. Under the Fruit of the Poisonous Tree Doctrine, since the underlying arrest was invalid, none of the evidence that the Police seized is valid either, no matter whom it belongs to."

"You two Attorneys are both pushing the envelope here to-day and enabling Mr. LeRoux to walk out of this courtroom Scot Free."

"Your Honor, believe me when I tell you that the People are not happy about this," Connor Dane said.

"Well, neither is this court, Attorney Dane. So, tell me, where is the car now?" Judge Benchley asked.

"It's been impounded," Connor Dane said.

"Well then, they'd better return it right away, because seizing cars in DWI cases was outlawed last year," Pattie said.

Connor pulled a piece of paper out of his file and handed it to Pattie.

"Not so fast, Attorney Anwald. The city has a lien on that car for over two hundred fifty dollars in back parking tickets," he said.

Pattie read the piece of paper, showed it to Leland and returned it to Connor. Connor walked it over to Jerry, The Court Officer, who, in turn, handed it to Judge Benchley. Judge Benchley read it and smirked.

"Well, at least justice is being served in some small way. The liens will hereby remain in effect until the fine is paid in full or until the car gets auctioned off to satisfy them, whichever shall occur first," Judge Benchley ordered.

"I object, Your Honor," Pattie said.

"Since the car doesn't belong to your client, you don't have standing to object. It's no skin off of Mr. LeRoux's nose at all. Therefore, your objection is overruled," Judge Benchley said.

"Thank you, Your Honor," Connor Dane said.

Judge Benchley nodded at Connor.

"Now, as far as I'm concerned, Mr. LeRoux you've been up before me too many times. So, unless you plan to go away for life under the repeat offender statute, I suggest that you never darken my doorstep again," Judge Benchley said.

Leland ignored Judge Benchley, jammed his elbow into Pattie's rib cage and whispered in her ear.

"What about them pills?"

Pattie cleared her throat.

"Your Honor, Mr. LeRoux received a lawful prescription for anti-anxiety medication by a staff physician over at Riker's Island and I believe that Court Officer Norton Bakerman, who works the metal detector by the main entrance confiscated them. Since they are Mr. LeRoux's lawful medicine, naturally he would like to have them returned to him," Pattie said.

"Do the People have any objection to this, Mr. Dane?"

Connor glanced at Pattie and shrugged.

"I guess not," he said.

"So ordered. Madam Clerk, during the next recess type up an order and I'll sign it. Court Officer Jerry Mitchell, will serve the order on Court Officer Bakerman."

Jerry nodded.

"Yes, Your Honor," the Clerk said.

"Since it looks like Mr. LeRoux is having a red-letter day, is there anything else we can do to accommodate him?"

"Nothing, Your Honor," Pattie said.

"Well, that's a relief. Mr. LeRoux you are free to go," Judge Benchley said.

"Hot Diggetty! Yer jess about the best little lawyer I ever done met!" Leland said.

He turned around and swaggered out of the courtroom before Pattie could thank him for the compliment. In the meantime, Connor Dane called the last case of the day, People v. Alejandro Vega.

CHAPTER FIFTY ONE
RATATOUILLE

Court Officer Jerry Mitchell arrived to serve Judge Benchley's orders on the short, reed like Norton Bakerman, just as Leland LeRoux approached the metal detector. Norton's dark brown greasy hair matched his strange, mud colored eyes. His skin was the color of clamshells. The sleeves on his uniform were so short, that they made his arms look like those of a chimpanzee. Every time he talked, his overly developed Adam's Apple jutted out of his pencil necked throat and kicked into gear. It was working overtime when he ranted to Jerry Mitchell about this latest indignity.

Norton tossed the switchblade and Tarot Cards into one of Leland's bags. However, as soon as he picked up the bottle of pills, Leland snatched it away from him, dumped its contents into his palm and counted every single pill. When he was satisfied that they were all present and accounted for, he grinned, closed the bottle and tossed it into one of his bags. Then he gave Jerry Mitchell the thumbs up sign and sauntered out of the building. He wended his way through the maze of Lower Manhattan's streets until he reached a rundown warehouse in Chinatown. He went in and walked down a long hall, where he had to duck every so often, in order to avoid being stabbed in the eye with the many dirty rags that had been slung over the low hanging pipes and twisted so that they would dry in the shape of sharp, pointy icicles. He pointed his index finger, chuckled and made a shooting noise at a rat that scurried past him. When he finally reached an office in the back of the building, he saw Nguyen Cong Duc arguing in his native tongue with another man.

"Hi, I hope I ain't interrupting nothin'," Leland said.

"Can't you see that you are? Now is not a good time for a chat. Come back here tonight at ten thirty," Nguyen said, in an accent so thick, someone could have cut it with a knife.

"Well, there's no need fer me ta come back. I jess came by to thank ya for bayulin' me out. Ya kin go straight to the courthouse and get all a yer bayul money back any time tomorra."

"Yes, you do need to come back tonight so you can work off some of the rent you owe me," Nguyen said.

"OK," Leland muttered, as he turned around and headed back toward the front of the building. Just as he reached the door, he spotted about two dozen nails of varying sizes on the windowsill. He swept them up into his dirty palm, slid them into his pocket and whistled all the way home.

By the time he turned the corner onto Christie Street, it was already dusky. He walked up the path of the run down, single story building he lived in. The building had four doors that led to separate apartments. Three of the doors were painted red, but one had an overlay of apple green paint and it was plastered with bumper stickers that jumped out like fun house demons. He went up to the door with the bumper stickers, put his bags down and stuffed his hand into his pocket. He wiggled his fingers down past the stolen nails until he found his house key. He pulled it out, but before he stuck it in the door, he glanced up and down the street to check whether anyone was watching him. Since the street appeared to be deserted, he slowly opened the door, picked up the bags and slipped inside.

The apartment was dark. He slammed the door, double bolted it behind him and turned the light on. He tripped over a broom and turned to see whether anyone had broken in. When he was confident that he was alone, he picked up the broom, put it back in place and gingerly carried his shopping bags over to his red, Naugahyde love seat. This was no easy feat, since the floor was like an obstacle course. He had to dodge a sea of yellowing newspapers, plastic grocery bags, food wrappers, egg cartons, milk bottles, empty beer cans, half eaten containers of food, bits of crumbled aluminum foil, unopened mail, newspaper inserts, rodent droppings and wads of fly paper that held the partially decomposed remains of its dead hostages.

The love seat was cracked and pock marked with tiny holes. He lobbed the shopping bags onto it. One of them knocked a broken banjo onto the floor. Annoyed, he stormed over to the banjo and kicked it against the wall. It clanged, as if in protest and boomeranged back at his feet, so he kicked it again. Then, once again dodging the litter on his floor, he made his way back across the living room and swaggered into his bathroom, where he pulled the string on a fluorescent light that hung over his filthy, ancient sink. His ball and claw bathtub was filled with stacks of mercenary soldier and UFO magazines. A broken shower rod hung halfway out of the wall. It was too unstable to even support the weight of a shower curtain.

He looked in the mirror, winked at his reflection and grinned. Then he turned off the light, went into his kitchenette and opened the door to his small, antiquated refrigerator. He pulled out a can of beer, snapped it open and chug a lugged as much as he could get down in one gulp. Then he sighed, let out an exaggerated belch and slid into one of the beach chairs at his kitchen table. He plunked his beer next to a can of Raid whose cap was missing, then he reached across the table for an oblong gift box and slid it over. When he ripped the cover off, a card fell face up onto the floor. He bent down, picked it up and flicked it onto the table.

"Merry Christmas, Come home soon. Love, Momma," the childlike scrawl read.

He reached into the box, pulled out his pellet gun and aimed it at the love seat. When he pulled the trigger and nothing happened, he placed the gun down and foraged around through the mess on the table until he found a box of ammunition and some fresh carbons. He loaded the gun, walked over to the love seat and placed the gun in one of his shopping bags. Then he picked up the bag, walked over to the door and stuck the broom under his armpit.

He peered out and scanned the street. When he was confident that no one was around to spy on him, he stepped outside, double bolted the door and walked down Christie Street. Although the sidewalk was dirty, it actually contained less litter than the floor in his apartment. He didn't even notice that he was actually following a trail of dried blood. At one point, he muttered a few curse words as he kicked some dried dog feces out of his way. When he reached the end of the block, he stopped, crossed the street and entered a park. He peered around and when he was sure that he wasn't being followed, he tiptoed toward a set of bushes at the back of the park.

Holding the broom, he quietly placed the bag down and crouched over the bushes. He listened for the squeaks and scuffling noises that came from inside. When he heard them, he stood and quietly removed the pellet gun from his bag. He clasped it in his right hand, while he used his other hand to plunge the broom into the heart of a huge rats' nest concealed within the bushes. He immediately felt the pressure as the rats attacked the broom. He peered in, saw the biggest rat and maneuvered the broom until he had separated him from the rest of the pack. Holding the broom in place with all of his might, he aimed the pellet gun and shot the rat between the eyes.

After the shot rang out, all but one of the rats raced away. One lone Alpha Rat remained and thrust his entire body at the broom, as if to protest the killing of his friend. He crouched and gnawed at the bristles. Leland frowned and kicked him. The rat stopped gnawing, but he didn't leave. The fur along his spine stood on end, as he arched his tail over his back and pointed his ears forward. Hissing, he spread his mouth into a wide "V" shape and flashed his huge lower incisors at Leland. Then he emitted a long, low growl, aimed his teeth at Leland's face and leapt at him. Leland jumped to his feet and moved to the side.

Ping! Leland shot him in the eye. The rat leapt and twisted in midair. Before he could recover, the second pellet knocked out his other eye. He died before he even hit the ground and he landed right next to Leland's left foot. Leland chuckled to himself, reached into the bag and removed a can of oatmeal. After he sprinkled it inside the bushes, he reached into his bag again, pulled out a handful of hay and sprinkled it over the oats. He sprinkled some beef jerky and peanut butter pellets on top of that. He knew that this recipe would ensure the remaining rats' eventual return, because rats can't resist peanut butter. He peered around and when he was sure that he was still alone, he walked to the bushes at the other side of the park and urinated in them to keep the rats from building an alternative nest there.

He walked back over to the first set of bushes, lifted the two dead rats by their tails and retrieved his belongings. Just as he was leaving, the lights in the park came on. Not wishing to be seen, he put everything back down on the ground and removed his pellet gun from the bag. He stepped back, aimed and took pot shots at every single street light. He chuckled when, one by one, each successful shot broke the glass, causing the light to sputter out. Before he could stop himself, his chuckle turned into a laugh. Then the laugh turned into a hack and the hack turned into a coughing fit. He punctuated his fit just like he did all of his other fits, by spitting a generous dose of green sputum. Since he didn't have his handkerchief with him, he shot it out onto the ground and headed home, swinging the rats by their tails. The blood that dripped from his quarry added to the trail of dried blood that led right up to his door.

CHAPTER FIFTY-TWO

WILLIE

Leland unlocked his door, peered around furtively and double bolted himself inside his apartment. He walked over to his table and flung everything down, including the rats. He took the last sip of his leftover beer, crushed the empty can and lobbed it onto the floor. He found a blank piece of paper and a pencil on the table and scrawled, "beer, peanut butter, grain and oats", then he shoved the list into his pocket. He foraged around in his bag until he found his switchblade. Then he picked up the rats and carried them over to the sink.

Click! The sharp thin blade gleamed in the dingy light. He cut the tails off of the rats and just as he started to chop the head off of one of them, a series of knocks and kicks at door interrupted him. He lobbed the rats into the sink and tightened his grip on the switchblade.

"Open up! It's me! Willie!"

Leland tossed the switchblade into the sink and opened the door to find Willie Hudson standing there towering over him, in his green janitor's uniform. Willie was a lot younger than he was and in far better shape.

"Hi"—Leland started to say, but Willie pushed his way into the apartment and lunged at him with such fury that it propelled him several feet backwards. He grabbed Leland's hair, dragged him over to the refrigerator and body slammed him into refrigerator door. He tried to kick Leland in the crotch with the steel tipped toe of his work boots, but Leland jumped out of the way in time. Willie pulled him back, ripped his work shirt and grabbed his left nipple. Then he twisted it until Leland yelped in pain.

"Come on!" Leland cried out.

Willie let go of him.

"I really ought to fuck you up! You know that? Where's my fuckin' car?" Willie screamed.

"I'm sorry ta tell ya this, but them cops done took it when they locked me up and that persercutor guy in court done said it has to stay down ta the impound. Apparently, there's some outstandin' tickets on it and ya can't git it outta hock 'til ya pay 'em."

"Well, how much will that cost, asshole?"

"Sumhmm like two hunnerd fifty dollars. Maybe even more by the time ya add up all them extra fees an' what not."

"Well, you'd better get it back for me ASAP."

"Look, I don't know what to say. You know with what that dayum Viet Cong pays me, I cain't hardly afford to buy nuthin'."

Willie squinted, pinned him against the refrigerator again and made a throat slashing motion with his right index finger.

"Look, don't hand me that shit. Just get the money. I don't care what you have to do to get it; just get it, because your ass is on the line here."

Leland nodded nervously.

"I know. I'm a see VC Charlie tonight at ten thirty, but what if he don't give it ta me?"

"Then, you'll be pushing up daisies. In the meantime, the least you could do is offer me a beer or something. So much for Southern hospitality, you ignoramus."

"OK. Let go a me and I will."

Willie released his grip on Leland, opened the refrigerator door and helped himself to Leland's last can of beer. He clicked it open, took an enormous swig and belched. Then he grinned, wiped his mouth on the back of his wrist and flexed his biceps.

"I feel like I'm suffocating in here with this heat," he said.

"Well, we all know this ain't the Ritz. Let's face it, if that da-yum Viet Cong don't gimme no heat or hot water, ya jess know he ain't gonna pervide no air conditionin'.'"

Willie sneered.

"Well, from the looks of things he doesn't provide a fan or maid service either."

"A fayun would be a nice idea, but ya know, I got better things to do than clean."

"Well, can't you at least get a fuckin' goat in here? He could do your floor and eat dinner, all at the same time."

"Well, I got me a new gal pal. Maybe she could come on over an' lend me a helpin' hand."

Willie chuckled with derision.

"You've got a girl friend? That will be the day!"

"Believe it or not, I do. Stack o' bibles and she's some winsome young piece a ayuss too."

"Oh, I have no doubt she's a real winner if she's stupid enough to hang with you."

"An' git this. On top of everthin' else, she's a lawyer."

"Yeah. Right."

"It's true, I'm tellin' ya. Ya shoudda seen 'er jess beggin' me fer my phone number. When I done told her I didn't have no phone, she made me take her card."

He went over to one of the bags on the love seat, reached in and dug around until he found Pattie's card. He pulled it out, walked it back over to Willie and handed it to him.

"Hmmm, Pattie Anwald. Now that's fascinating, because not too long ago I seen some lawyer bitch with the same name up at the halfway house where I work. Funny thing is, she was with some high fallutin' fancy Limey Doctor and you were nowhere to be seen."

"Well, maybe they done broke up since then, because she's with me now."

Willie drained the beer can, crushed it and threw it onto the floor.

"Blah blah blah. Anyway, if it is true, she's crazier than you are. And if that's the case, you should have no trouble making her give you the money for my car."

"Well, I kin try."

Leland coughed. As the coughing escalated, he turned redder. He spun around, raced toward the sink and emitted another large quantity of foul green sputum right next to the rats. Willie followed him and watched in horror, as Leland rinsed the sputum down the drain.

"Oh my God! What the FUCK are you doing?"

"Gittin' ready to perpare some homemade ratatouille and I don't mind braggin' on it that it's my own recipe. There's enough for us both if ya want to stay ta supper," Leland said.

"Are you fucking kidding me? I never heard that Ratatouille was made with rats! Isn't it made with eggplants or something?"

Leland waved his hand in dismissal.

"That's the vegan kind. I keep tryin' ta tell people that there's a lot of recipes you kin make outta rats. The thing is though, ya gotsta season 'em right or they don't taste good."

Willie shivered.

"You're really fucked up. You know that?"

"Why? I never seen ya turn yer nose up when it came ta takin' a few pot shots at 'em."

"I know. Because shooting them is fun. But honest to God, I never had any intention of eating them."

"Well then, I'm a better person than you are, 'cause I ain't the kinda guy what hunts jess fer sport. I usually wind up eatin' whatever I kill."

"Aren't you even scared of catching botulistic plague? After all, rats are disgusting and filthy. They even hang out in sewers for fuck's sake."

Leland waved the idea away.

"Ya don't even know what yer talkin' about. Rats is so smart they're actually brain food."

He picked up one of the rats and shook it in Willie's face until Willie slapped it out of his hand. When it landed on the floor, Leland bent down and scooped it up.

"Jesus Christ! The son of a bitch doesn't even have a tail!"

"That's 'cause I already done lopped it off."

"Holy shit! I gotta get the hell outta here, but I'll be back for my money later. So, don't let me down, because I need that car ASAP, like nowsville."

With that, he turned around, walked out and slammed the door, leaving Leland standing there and shaking his head.

"Dayum, now that's one janitor I wish they would keep in a drum," he muttered to himself.

CHAPTER FIFTY-THREE
BACK AT COSMO'S

By the time nine thirty rolled around, Ryan was seated in his favorite purple armchair at Cosmo's Astral Plane Café. A few seconds later, the door squeaked open and Pattie rushed in. When she flopped down into the chair that Ryan had set up for her, he asked her how she was.

"Worn out. I feel like everyone was sizing me up and trying to get a piece of me."

"Well, you know how it goes. The law of the jungle prevails. Everybody sizes up everybody, so that they can figure out whether they're going to be the dinner or the diner."

"Well, I guess you're right."

"Well, you shouldn't have any problems, what with the way you kicked Connor Dane's ass today."

Pattie tilted her head and frowned.

"Well, I couldn't have done it without the amazing head's up you gave me, but what concerns me is how you even know about it."

He sipped his coffee and waited a few seconds before he responded, so that he could create a feeling of suspense.

"Well, because there were no arraignments this afternoon, I was able to sneak into the back of Judge Fanshaw's courtroom and I watched you."

Pattie smiled.

"Connor Dane reminds me of the Big Bad Wolf in Little Red Riding Hood."

"Well then, just be glad you don't have red hair, like Annie does."

She chuckled.

"No danger of that. By the way, the only person I can stand in that office is Toby Barnett," she said.

Ryan nodded.

"I agree. I think that's because he's the only one who hasn't lost his humanity, yet. Anyhow, I felt sad when I watched you today, in spite of the good job that you did."

Pattie shook her head.

"Why?"

"Because it upsets me to think your phenomenal talents are being wasted on the likes of Leland LeRoux. He's like Hannibal Lechter out of his cage."

A barista came over with a black coffee for Ryan and a Raspberry Latte for Pattie. She winked at Ryan, before she returned to the counter.

"I hope you don't mind that I took the liberty of ordering for us," he said.

Pattie smiled, picked up her Latte and held it up in a toast.

"Of course, I don't mind. Anyway, here's to you for being the best friend ever.

Ryan smiled, picked up his coffee and toasted her back.

"You're very welcome and by the way, I have another head's up for you. Norton Bakerman was in the court officers' lounge at five o'clock today, ranting and raving about what a pushy broad you are and saying that he's going to make sure you get yours, whatever that's supposed to mean."

"You've got to be kidding! Why?"

"I don't know, Pattie. You tell me."

"I can't even begin to imagine. I've never even laid eyes on the guy."

"Well, it scares the hell out of me that you can actually go around making enemies out of people you've never even met."

"Me too! Plus, I have other issues."

"Oh? Such as?"

"Such as, I lost my employee's magnetic passkey."

"Now that really is bad news. It's going to take the Court Clerk something like six weeks to secure a replacement for you."

Pattie grimaced.

"How do you know that?"

He grinned and pointed to himself.

"Because I lost mine last year. So, I guess until you get a new one, you'll experience the joy of lining up with the rest of the humps who are forced to enter the building through the metal detector at the main entrance."

Pattie took a sip of her Latte.

"Mmmm, this is good. Gee, you'd think the Court Clerk would at least have a spare employee passkeys."

"Are you kidding me? That would make life too easy. Anyhow, I don't mean to scare you or anything, but the main entrance is where Norton Bakerman works."

Chapter Fifty-Four

BRAINCHILD

It was ten thirty sharp when Leland arrived at Nguyen's warehouse. When the outer door didn't open, he knocked and fumbled around in the pocket of his filthy jeans until he found what used to be Pattie's magnetic pass key. He slid it between the lock and the doorframe to see if it could unlock the door, but it didn't work. A few seconds later, Nyguyen opened the door, let him in and snatched the card.

"What's this?"

"I wanted ta show it ta ya earlier. It's a passkey ta the courthouse. It kin git me in there any time I want."

Nguyen put it in his pocket.

"Where did you get it?"

"My new gal pal done gave it ta me. She's a beautiful young lawyer."

Nguyen chuckled.

"No lawyer's stupid enough to hang out with you. Even fleas are too smart to hang out with you."

"Why don't anybody believe me?"

Nguyen walked down the hall and beckoned for Leland to follow.

"Never mind that. You need to get to work."

"Before I git started, I need ta ax a favor from ya. My friend Willie needs ya to lend him that bayul money when ya git it tomorra, so's he kin git his car outta hock."

Nguyen shook his head vehemently.

"No way."

When they reached a door in the back of the warehouse, Nguyen fiddled with the padlock, opened the door and shoved Leland into the room. Leland gasped when he saw the naked corpse displayed spread eagle in the middle of the floor. It had no hands, no feet and its head was missing. Gallons of dried blood and chunks of gray matter had oozed across the floor. A huge gray and red blob dripped down the back wall and it looked as if someone had sprayed gray and red speckles along the walls.

"Holy Shit! This is unbelievable. What the hell happened?"

"Someone asked me for one too many favors," Nguyen said.

"Well, why is all that chop meat strewn around like that?"

"That's not chopped meat. That's what used to be his brains."

"Well, where's the rest of him?"

Nguyen nodded and pointed to a sink. Underneath it stood a bucket, several sponges, stacks of towels, bottles of peroxide, gallons of bleach and heavy duty black plastic trash bags.

"Someone already took them parts. So, chop up the rest of him and stuff him into those bags. Then clean up this mess."

"Don't ya realize how hard it is to clean up dried blood? Why the fuck should I be saddled with this?"

Nguyen shrugged.

"Because if you don't, you'll be next.

Nguyen walked out, slammed the door and locked Leland inside.

CHAPTER FIFTY-FIVE
SINISTER

By the time Leland got home, it was five o'clock in the morning. He was exhausted and covered from head to toe in a mixture of blood, sweat and brains. He was carrying a bottle of peroxide and he pulled his house key out of his pocket, but before he could use it, Willie Hudson jumped him from out of nowhere and body slammed him into the door.

"OK, fork over my money!"

"I don't have it yet."

"Well, why the hell not?"

"'Cause times is tougher than ya realize, but keep the faith, 'cause I'm still workin' on gittin' it fer ya."

"Well you'd better. I have a big job to do for Roy and it's gotta get done by this weekend and I need the car to pull it off."

"Roy? Now, there's a blast from the past. I didn't even realize y'all were still friends."

"Well, we're not. I keep trying to avoid him but he keeps finding me and since he's not exactly the kind of guy anyone can say no to, I'm stuck. Anyway, stop grilling me before I fucking kill you."

"Jess do it then, because I had ta deal with a real mess tanight and I don't even have no way ta clean up after it."

Willie looked at Leland, sized up the situation and decided to finally let go of him.

"I guess I could sneak you into Beau Rivage and let you shower off, but then you'd have to hurry up and haul ass out of there, before any of them fuckin' brats wake up. And if you can't get my car out of hock, I guess I'm just gonna have to use you to help me solve Roy's problem."

Chapter Fifty-Six
HOMELAND INSECURITY

Even though Pattie was exhausted, it took her a long time to fall asleep. As always, the sounds and smells of the Seaport's activities lingered in the air outside. She no sooner got to sleep when her cell phone rang and jolted her back to consciousness, like a cold glass of water in her face. She moaned, opened one eye and kicked the matted wads of bedding out from around her ankles. She worked her way up to a prone position, opened her other eye and squinted at the bright morning sunlight that crashed through her window with all the grace of a sledgehammer. At that point, her phone had stopped ringing. She lumbered out of bed, walked over to the table where it was charging and fumbled for it. The caller ID registered a call from a "restricted line" at 5: 28 am, but the caller left no message.

She sighed, ate a few spoonfuls of yogurt and picked out an outfit for court. She decided on her red linen suit. Since she had extra time this morning, she decided to go all out with her makeup and accessories. She chose a ring, silver pendant and a stylish belt to accentuate her slender waist. She created a French Twist and fastened it into place with an exotic tortoise shell clip. She reached for the box that contained the brand-new pair of black leather boots she had bought to replace the pair she ruined on the night when she first met Jordan. They were knee high lace ups, so it took her several minutes to tie them. When she finally finished dressing, she inspected herself in the mirror and decided that she liked what she saw. She picked up her red brief case and hoped that everyone would notice how well it went with her suit.

When she arrived at the courthouse, she lined up at the front entrance behind the jurors, witnesses, victims, litigants and others who were there ahead of her. She glanced at her watch. It was eight twenty. She had plenty of time to get upstairs to her office without a problem.

For Norton Bakerman, this morning was no different from any other morning. The metal detector was his kingdom and he was never in any particular hurry to process anyone through it. If a person didn't like what he dished out to them, well, that was just too bad.

After twenty minutes of waiting in line, Pattie glanced at her watch again and sighed. The line had hardly moved at all.

"I can't believe this," the man behind her said.

"I been here before. This guy does everything but take blood samples and believe me, he don't give a damn if we're late. After all, HE'S on HIS job," the man behind him answered.

The man behind Pattie turned to him.

"Well, if he's doing this to people on purpose, then he's got a serious problem."

Aware of the comments, but unfazed by them, Norton continued to process people at a snail's pace. At about ten minutes past nine, he was ready to process the man in front of Pattie. He chuckled and pointed at the suitcase that the man was carrying.

"And what are you supposed to be? On the lam? Or just planning for a long prison stay?"

"No. These are all my worldly goods. I have a feeling I'll be getting evicted today.

Norton stared at the man and blinked.

"And?"

"Well, would it be all right if I left the suitcase here with you until I come out of the courtroom?"

Norton shook his head and pointed at the exit sign.

"No. You have to leave it outside on them steps."

"I can't."

Norton shrugged, blinked a few more times and popped the suitcase open. He rifled through every one of its nooks, crannies and compartments like a litter of puppies rooting through a sock drawer. He pulled out every item, inspected it and flung it onto the conveyor belt. Finally, he grabbed several pairs of jockey shorts and held them up to the light.

"Hey, who are you? Inspector Number Ten?" The man behind Pattie called out.

After every one finished laughing, another man called out.

"Yeah! Can we speed things up? Get along little doggie."

The people all laughed again. Norton blushed, waited for them to stop laughing and then stared every one down.

"Excuse me, but aren't you at least going to repack what you messed up?" The man with the suitcase asked.

"Some people expect concierge service. What is this? The fucking Hilton?" Norton muttered, as he gingerly picked up the items on the conveyor belt, jammed them into a ball and stuffed them back into the suitcase. He clicked the suitcase shut and tossed it onto the floor at the man's feet. Then he picked up a plastic yellow bowl and shook it in the man's face.

"What do want me to do with it?"

"Empty your pockets and put the contents in it. What did you think you think you were supposed to do with it? Pee in it?" Norton asked.

The man reached into his pockets, pulled out a handkerchief, a wallet, a comb and a Swiss Army Knife and placed them all in the bowl. Norton picked the knife up, opened it and ran his fingers along the blade. When he was done, he closed it, stuffed it into his own pocket and waved the man on.

"Hey! That's my knife," the man said.

Norton sneered.

"Not any more, not unless you want me to call the police and have them arrest you for carrying a concealed weapon into the courthouse."

The man shook his head.

"No. No. That's all right."

"That's what I figured. So, take your glad rags and beat it."

The man stuffed the remaining contents of the bowl back into his pockets, picked up his suitcase and walked toward the elevator bank. Pattie was next. She cleared her throat when Norton beckoned for her to step forward.

"Hi. I'm Pattie Anwald and I work upstairs at Legal Aid."

Norton's eyes lit up.

"No kidding! Well, wowee and even if that is true, then why aren't you using your employee pass key?"

As he spoke, he exhaled his stale breath into her face. That, combined with his body odor, made Pattie feel queasy. She did her best to conceal it.

"Well, unfortunately I misplaced it yesterday and I still haven't found it."

Norton shot her a dirty look.

"Well, I never seen you before in my life. So, do you know what that makes you? Nobody."

"Excuse me?"

He glared at her, twitched and grabbed her brief case out of her hands. He slammed it onto the conveyor belt and shoved it through the scanner. After it went through, he squinted, shook his head and muttered something unintelligible. Then he picked it up, slammed it onto the conveyor belt again and opened it. He counted her cash right down to the penny, scrutinized her driver's license, car registration and every one of her credit cards. Then tossed the wallet back into the briefcase. Next, he pulled out her cosmetics case, unzipped it and rummaged through it.

When he found three tampons, he scowled and held them up for everyone to see.

Pattie blushed, stared down at the tops of her boots and cleared her throat again.

"Please just tell me why you're deliberately trying to intimidate me," she said, hoarsely.

"I don't have to tell you nothing, because I don't answer to you," he answered.

He tossed the tampons into the trashcan behind him, chuckled and pulled out her eyelash curler. He opened it, fingered it and closed it.

"Whoa, now this thing looks lethal. What the hell is it?"

"An eyelash curler. Good God. Don't you know anything?"

He lobbed it back into the case.

"All I know, is that my eyelashes are naturally curly. Anyway, I'm warning you that if you don't shut your stinkin' pie hole I'll toss your ass right back to the end of the line."

Pattie reached for the eye lash curler, pulled it out and tossed it onto the garbage can.

"Look, I don't want it now that you've manhandled it."

He tossed the cosmetics case back into Pattie's briefcase without even bothering to zip it up. He pulled out an unopened pack of gum, ripped the seal on it and helped himself to a piece. Then he tossed the remainder of the pack into the trashcan. When Pattie reached for her cell phone he pointed to a sign and read it.

"All cell phones must be turned off while you are in this building."

"Well, I just thought it would be a good idea to call my boss Brad. He can verify that I work here."

"I thought I already told you to shut up."

"You can't talk to me like this."

"That's tellin' him, Sis," the man behind her said.

Norton grabbed the phone out of her hand and flung it into her briefcase. Then he proceeded to root through every other item he could find, just like he did with the previous man. When he was done, he slammed the briefcase shut and threw it back onto the conveyor belt. While it went through the metal detector for the second time that day, he picked up a little plastic bowl.

"Bling bling goes in here," Norton said.

She removed her ring, her pendant and her belt.

"I'm glad you're having fun," she said.

"Yeah. Right. Anyways, you forgot to take that bone out of your hair."

She loosened the tortoise shell barrette and let her hair fall loosely down her back.

"Are you happy now?" She said.

"No. I won't be happy until you take them boots off."

She was so nervous that it took her a long time to fumble with the laces. He tapped his toe while he waited for her.

"Come on, come on, you're holding things up," he said.

When she was finally done, he picked up the boots, slammed them down onto the conveyor belt and prodded her through the metal detector.

"Hey, don't touch me and don't slam my boots again either! They're brand new!"

The buzzer on the metal detector rang.

"What's causing that sound? You'd better not be trying to bring a weapon in here. Walk back and then come through again," Norton said, as he crooked his index and middle fingers at her.

She cleared her throat and walked through the metal detector again. When the buzzer sounded off for the second time, he picked up a portable detecting wand and waved it over the top of her head. He worked his way downward until the metal in her bra cased the wand to beep.

"Here we go," the man behind Pattie said.

"That did it!" Norton yelled.

He threw Pattie's belongings into her briefcase, snapped it shut and stashed it on a shelf under the conveyor belt, next to a taser. Then he pointed at the wall.

"Line up against that wall and stay there until they come to lock your ass up," he snapped.

"And if I don't?"

He pointed to the taser.

"Then I'll have no choice but to taser you."

"If you so much as reach for that taser, I'll make sure you never work anywhere again," she replied, as she walked over to the wall.

He picked up his radio and spoke into it.

"Hey, Madge?"

"Roger," a husky female voice squawked back at him.

"It's me, Norton. It looks like I've got a situation involving a disorderly female. She's using her attitude to undermine my authority, so I'm gonna need female backup."

"Yeah and this danger to society weighs about eighty-six pounds, soaking wet," the man behind Pattie called out.

"I read you Bakerman. Just keep her at bay until I can get there," Madge answered.

Norton ran the wand over her boots. When they didn't trigger the buzzer, he flung them at her. They bounced off of the wall and landed on the floor with a thud.

"Next," Norton said, as he beckoned to the man behind her.

Pattie put her boots back on and tied up the laces, as she watched Norton's every move. A few minutes later, a middle-aged Amazon, in a Court Officer's uniform, stepped out of the elevator and swaggered up to Norton. She appeared to be in her late fifties. She had a bulldog's face fringed by tiny, dirty-blonde pin curls. The pockets of fat strained and rippled against her uniform, so that it looked as if she was wearing riding breeches.

"OK Norton, I'm here now. Where's the no-good bitch who's giving you a hard time?"

He pointed at Pattie and handed her briefcase to Madge.

"That's her!"

Madge walked up to Pattie.

"Come with me," she said.

"Wait a minute. Don't you even want to hear my side of the story?"

"No, not really. I've heard stories like yours a million times before," she said, as she grabbed Pattie's arm roughly and muscled her down the hall.

"Look, this is not OK. You need to take your hands off of me now. I work upstairs at Legal Aid."

"Yeah, well, that's what they all say."

Madge opened a door, shoved Pattie into a tiny room and slammed the door behind them. She ran a wand over Pattie, which beeped when she reached Pattie's bra.

"I'm sorry, but now I'm gonna have to frisk you," Madge said.

After Madge finished frisking Pattie, she shrugged, handed Pattie her briefcase and pointed to the door.

"You're free to go."

"Oh really? Just like that? After you and your cohort put me through hell, made me late for work and totally freaked me out?"

Madge waved her hand dismissively and shoved Pattie's briefcase into her arms.

"Listen, unless you're planning for me to ruin your day, you'll just beat it now. And do yourself a favor. Keep that trap of yours shut," Madge said.

"I will not! You can't bully me," Pattie said, on her way out.

Pattie ran to the nearest ladies' room. Unfortunately, it was the one that the public used. The second she opened the door, a putrid stench assaulted her nostrils. The lights were so dingy that she could barely even see. She immediately wished that she had gone to the staff bathroom upstairs. Although it too was horrible, it was like heaven compared to this hellhole. In an effort to calm herself down, she went over to the sink, rolled up her sleeves and tried to run some cold water over her wrists. Unfortunately, no water came out of the tap. Disgusted, she closeted herself in one of the stalls and read the graffiti:

"The System is whack," someone wrote.

"You can say that again," someone wrote underneath it.

"The System is whack," the original writer wrote underneath that.

"Well that's cause y'all won't stop snitching on one another," someone new wrote underneath that.

Below that someone else had scrawled "for a wet ride call 212–555-4934. Someone had partially crossed out the comment with a black magic marker and wrote "Go get crunk" underneath it.

Pattie grabbed her briefcase, bolted out and ran toward the elevator. A few seconds later she smelled a beautiful scent. She turned around and saw Cara Forrester standing behind her, wearing an elegant peach colored silk suit.

"I know this is none of my business, but I saw that guard harassing you at the metal detector. All any one has got to do is take one look at you to know that you're not a troublemaker," Cara said.

Pattie attempted to smile.

"Thank you."

"The important thing to remember, is never to internalize any one's negative opinions of you."

Pattie nodded.

"That's sage advice."

Cara Forrester nodded back at her and smiled.

"It's the only advice."

The door opened and they got into the elevator.

CHAPTER FIFTY-SEVEN
BETTER LATE THAN NEVER

By the time Ceil buzzed Pattie into the Legal Aid office, Brad had been pacing and ranting for a long time. He greeted Pattie with his hands on his hips, a beet red face and a scowl. He silently put his hand on her back, pushed her into her office and closed the door. Then he spun the visitor's chair around, as if it were a pummel horse and crashed into it.

"A dillar, a dollar, a ten o'clock scholar. How awfully nice of you to finally grace us with your presence."

Even though Pattie was near the end of her rope, her intuition told her not to react, so she simply sat, cleared her throat and apologized.

"Look Brad, I'm sorry for being late, but Norton Bakerman put me through hell down at that metal detector," she answered, in the most stoic voice she could conjure up.

"Yeah, well, what were you doing down there anyway?"

"I don't know how to tell you this, but I misplaced my employee pass key."

Brad sighed.

"Oh Jesus. That's a breach of security. So now you'll have to go see the Chief Clerk and fill out a form so that can she requisition a replacement for you."

"I'll do it right away."

"Court already started without you. In addition to that, some old man filed a complaint against you. He claims that you were rude to him yesterday by refusing to notarize his financial affidavit and that on top of it, you sicked Leland LeRoux on him."

"Oh my God! That's not what happened at all! When the man interrupted my consultation with Leland LeRoux, I politely suggested that he ask Ceil to notarize his affidavit."

"Anyhow, both the incident as well as today's lateness are now a part of your permanent record."

She looked at him as if he had just sucker punched her.

"Wow, that's kind of harsh, isn't it?"

"Well, maybe I can soften the blow with some good news. Leland LeRoux stopped by this morning to sing your praises. He told me how much he appreciated the great job you did for him yesterday."

"Wow. Thanks."

Brad nodded.

"He also came up with a great idea, which I think I just might implement. He wants me to make you his personal attorney in case he ever gets arrested again."

Pattie cleared her throat.

"Well, I'm not quite sure I'm ready for that."

Brad sneered.

"Who cares what you're ready for? Your opinions are irrelevant. Besides, if you can't stand the heat, may I suggest that you get back in the kitchen?"

He stood, swung the chair around and left, so she rested her head on her desk. Leland LeRoux knocked on her door and swaggered into her office before she had a chance to calm down. He wore a clean, white Oxford shirt, with the same filthy jeans and boots from the day before. His hair was washed and combed. He had covered the sores on his face with Band-Aids and he grinned just like the cat that swallowed the canary. He flounced down into the chair where Brad had been.

"Yes?" Pattie asked.

"I jess dropped in ta say hi an' also let ya know that I done praised ya to the Big Kahuna."

His breath wafted across the desk and she nodded vaguely, while she tried to fight her nausea.

"Well, thank you," she said.

He lifted his legs and plopped both of his feet onto her desk. She frowned, grabbed a file and swatted his legs with it.

"How many times do I have to tell you not to put your feet up on my desk? It's my desk and even I don't do that!"

Leland shrugged.

"OK. OK. There's no sense in bein' that territorial," he said as he slowly dropped each foot to the floor.

As she watched him, a violent chill passed over her body. She glanced at her watch and in an effort to gain her composure, she gripped her briefcase, stretched her fingers out over it and suppressed a desire to scream at the ceiling. She snapped her briefcase open, stuck her files in it and stood. When she left for court without saying a word, he pursed his lips and followed her.

CHAPTER FIFTY-EIGHT
LUNCH

Pattie and Ryan spent their lunch hour at the deli. Ryan wolfed down a Pastrami Sandwich on Rye while Pattie twirled a lettuce leaf with her fork and regaled him with the details of her morning at the metal detector.

"Anyway, you turned out to be right about Norton Bakerman. He really does seem to have it in for me. Either that or he's a real head case."

"Probably a little bit of both, but seriously, what a disaster. I'm really sorry you had to go through that."

"Well now, I've got him living rent free in my head, because I can't stop obsessing about what he's going to do to me tomorrow."

"Well, give me some time to come up with a plan and I'll level his Karma. In the meantime, just go around to the employees' entrance and call me from your cell phone. I'll come down and let you in."

Pattie smiled, lifted her glass of ice tea and toasted him.

"Gee, I hate to be a burden, but thanks," she said.

CHAPTER FIFTY-NINE
A PLAN

Early the next morning, as the nocturnal sounds at Peck Slip gave way to the sounds of the jack hammers, Pattie's cell phone rang and once again it jarred her awake. She moaned, forced her eyes open and sat up.

"It must be a déjà vu moment," she mumbled, as she extricated herself from her tangled bedding. By the time she got to her phone, the call had gone over to her voicemail. She squinted at the bright morning sunlight that barged through her window like an iron fist. Even though her window was closed, the smell of fish permeated her apartment. She yawned, rubbed her eyes and squinted to see where the call had come from.

"Restricted Line."

She sighed and checked her voicemail, but the caller left no message, so she put the phone down, walked over to her refrigerator and pulled out a container of Wild Cherry yogurt. She ripped the lid off, licked the yogurt that clung to it and flung the lid into the garbage. She walked over to her utensil drawer, removed a teaspoon and plunged it into the yogurt. She flopped into a chair and the phone rang again. She sighed and picked up the call without even bothering to look at the Caller ID.

"Who is this?" She screamed.

"Christ, Pattie!" Ryan said.

"Oh. Sorry," she mumbled.

"Did I wake you up or something?"

"No. Someone else beat you to it. They called here from a blocked line and didn't bother to leave a message."

"Oh."

"So, anyway, what's up?"

"I told you I'd call you once I came up with a plan to level Norton Bakerman's Karma."

"Wow. So quickly?"

"You know me. I'm never one to let any grass grow under my feet. Anyhow, meet me at the drug store across the street from the courthouse at about ten after eight."

"OK."

"And don't wear any make up."

She groaned.

"Why not?"

"Because, it's part of my plan. So, trust me and by the way, leave your briefcase home too. Carry your stuff in that old black tote bag."

After they said their good byes and hung up, Pattie decided that she wasn't hungry, after all, so she threw her uneaten yogurt into the trashcan. She went over to her closet, put on a one piece black dress and slipped into her black velvet Mary Janes. She threw a lime green jacket over the outfit, which made her un-made-up face look ghostly pale. Trusting Ryan, she transferred her belongings from her briefcase into her tote bag and put on her sunglasses. She decided not to wear any jewelry, because she didn't relish the idea of having to take it all off and then put it back on again at metal detector. She grabbed her keys, took one last look at herself in the mirror and two seconds later she was out the door.

CHAPTER SIXTY
TURNABOUT IS FOUL PLAY

At exactly eight twenty that morning, Pattie and Ryan left the drug store, laughing and giggling.

"Are you ready for this?" Ryan asked.

"I sincerely doubt it," she answered.

He winked, crossed the street and turned the corner that led to the rear of the courthouse. She waited a minute or so, crossed the street and walked up to the main entrance, where she took her place at the end of the line, just like she did the day before. Forty five minutes later, Norton beckoned to her.

"Next," he said, as he shoved the plastic yellow bowl at her. He whipped out his flashlight and pointed at the bowl with it.

"Bling bling goes in here," he barked, as if he'd never seen her before.

Pattie cleared her throat.

"I'm not wearing any," she said.

He beamed the flashlight right into her eyes.

"Hey!" She yelled out, as she tried to wave the light away.

He pointed at the canister hanging from his belt.

"Don't make me mace you."

"You just try it and see what happens," Pattie said.

He twitched, smirked and ripped the tote bag out of her hands.

"Gimme that rag bag," he muttered, almost under his breath.

The second he yanked it open, Pattie began to imitate one of Leland LeRoux's coughing fits. She whipped a tissue out of her right pocket, pretended to cough some phlegm into it and then feigned an exaggerated sigh of relief. Norton gave her a dirty look. Then he reached inside her tote bag, gasped and pulled his hand out. A wad of wet, sticky tissues, clung to it and they had a slight green tinge.

"What the fuck," he yelled, as he frantically tried to pull the slimy bits of tissue off of his hand. Unfortunately, only the tiniest pieces of tissue tore off. They floated to the floor, like pale green parakeet feathers, but the remainder stuck to his fingers like glue. He panicked, as he manically rubbed his hands back and forth, to no avail. A few seconds later, Ryan came from around the corner.

"Hey Attorney Anwald! How the hell have you been?" Ryan asked.

Pattie shook her head, imitated Leland's coughing fit again and then waved her hands frantically like Norton did.

"I don't know. I feel like hell. I just got tested for SARS, but I don't have the results yet," she answered.

All of the color drained from Norton's face. Then turned to Ryan and held up his hands.

"Who the hell keeps SARS infected tissues in their bag?" He asked.

Ryan shrugged.

"Beats me."

"Oh gee, I'm sorry. Did I do that? I must have done that when I was still delirious," Pattie said.

Ryan beckoned her to come closer. When she did, he put his hand on her forehead.

"Wow. You're really burning up," he said.

"I am not. What do you think Officer Bakerman?"

She moved closer to Norton and stood on her toes. She craned her neck, stuck her face an inch away from his and feigned another coughing fit before he had time to back away from her. She reached into her other pocket and pulled out another pile of tissues, just as he shook his tissue laden hand in her face. She spat into the tissues again and flung them onto the conveyor belt.

"Just take your snot rags and get the hell outta here! I don't care if you've got a fuckin' B-52 in your bag, no job is worth me dying over!"

"Oh. I don't know about that. I think just about any job in this world would be worth you dying over," Pattie said calmly.

She picked up her tote bag, walked through the metal detector and headed for the stairwell, leaving Norton to pluck bits of tissue from his hand. Ryan followed her. When the door closed, they gave each other a high five, leaned against the wall and laughed so hard that Pattie's eyes watered.

"That'll teach him to mess with us," Ryan said.

"Thank you, Ryan. I never knew that tissues, lime juice, egg whites and rubber cement could be put to such creative uses," she said.

Ryan winked.

Chapter Sixty One
CONFRONTATION

It was Saturday night and Jordan snuggled up to Pattie in the booth they shared at the elegant French Restaurant not far from where he lived. He turned to her and smiled at the way her face glowed in the soft candlelight.

"Did I ever tell you how beautiful you are?"

She shook her head.

"No, but thank you for saying it right now. I'm flattered."

"I didn't say it to flatter you. I said it, because I really do mean it."

She smiled.

"That's sweet."

"Last Saturday you seemed rather preoccupied, as if something was preying on your mind. I wish you would tell me what it was."

She cleared her throat.

"OK. I know this might sound crazy, but I'm wondering whether you're leading some kind of a double life or something."

He looked at her quizzically.

"What?"

"OK then, let me put it another way. How many people are you dating right now? Including me."

"Only you. Would it make you happy to know that I haven't even looked at any one else since we started seeing one another?"

"Yes. Actually, that would make me feel ecstatic."

"Well good, because it's true, but I'd like to know what would cause you to even ask me such a strange question in the first place."

She shook her head.

"No particular reason."

He picked up a tray of smoked oysters.

"Would you like one?"

"No thanks, I'm already way too full and by the way, something else is preying on my mind."

"What is it?"

"The issue of Justin's evaluation."

"I was wondering when you were going to bring that up."

"Really? Didn't you get my message the other day?"

"No. Did you leave me one?"

"Yes!"

"Where?"

"At school."

"Look, don't call me there. You know I can't retrieve any of my voice messages."

"Still?"

"Yes."

"Anyway, I'm not exactly comfortable discussing this here. Would you mind coming back to my flat and discussing it there? I even managed to get you some sweetened raspberry iced tea."

"Well, right now you're saying that we're going there strictly for the purpose of discussing Justin's evaluation, but I have a feeling that once I get there, we won't end up talking about Justin at all. I'll wind up having to fend you off, just like I did the last time."

"All right then, we'll discuss it here. You hired me to evaluate him, which I did and I furnished you with my expert opinion and whether or not you agree with it, I'm not inclined to change one word of it. You hired me to tell you what I believe, not what you want me to say."

"I understand that and I respect your integrity, but I'm letting you know that I don't like it at all."

"Well then, I guess this will be one issue, where we will simply have to agree to disagree."

Pattie nodded.

"Agreed."

He smiled.

"Well then, having gotten that out of the way, I'd like to ask you if you'd be willing to give me another chance and return to my flat again. I promise, that if I say or do anything awful, you can always leave."

She chuckled.

"Well, since you put it that way, OK."

"Great," he said, as he motioned for the check.

When he led her out of the restaurant, he pointed at the low hanging full moon, whose glow lit their way.

"That moon looks close enough for us to reach up and touch," he said.

Pattie looked at it and nodded absently.

CHAPTER SIXTY-TWO

INTERRUPTION

Once Pattie was comfortably situated on Jordan's couch, he left her and went into the kitchen. A few minutes later he returned with a bottle of champagne and two glasses.

"This has been chilling since early this morning," said, as he set the tray down on the coffee table.

She cleared her throat.

"Wait a minute. I was sure you said you bought sweet raspberry iced tea especially for me."

"I did, but I thought you might like this better."

She shook her head.

"No, thank you. If it's all the same to you, I'd rather just have the iced tea."

He nodded, retreated into the kitchen and returned a few minutes later with a huge silver tray. On it was a crystal goblet, a pitcher of sweetened raspberry iced tea, two linen napkins, two dessert plates and a plate filled with oversized, chocolate dipped strawberries. He smiled and placed the tray squarely in front of her.

"I hope you realize that I packed your glass with as much ice as it could hold. There's also more where that came from."

She smiled.

"Thanks."

She picked up a strawberry by its stem, removed all of the chocolate with her front teeth and bit the remainder, except for the stem, which she discarded onto one of the plates. Then, she slid her pumps off and dug her maroon colored toenails into the fluffy, white carpet. He turned on the CD player and sat back to allow the velvety sounds of love ballads envelope them.

"The last time I was here I got to see your terrace at sunset. I'll bet the city looks even more awesome when it's all lit up at night."

He smiled.

"You be the judge", he said, as he walked over to the draperies. He drew them open and unlocked the French doors. She joined him and they walked out onto the terrace together. As they gazed out into the city, she turned to him.

"Do you ever use this terrace in the winter?"

"I must admit that I did when I first moved here. I used to come out here with a heavy woolen comforter, but the novelty soon wore off. After all, this is a northerly exposure."

He put his arm around her, gently drew his lips to hers and kissed her. He rubbed her back with the palm of his hand and waited to see her reaction. Her cell phone rang before he had the chance to find out. She sighed and broke the embrace.

"Sorry," she said, as she ran inside.

She reached into her tote bag, pulled her phone out and looked at the Caller ID.

"It's Beau Rivage. I wonder what they could possibly want from me on a Saturday night."

"I don't know, but it can't be good. Maybe you'd better pick it up."

She nodded.

"Hi, Attorney Anwald. This is April Higgins calling with bad news again. This time it's about Justin."

Pattie cleared her throat.

"What's wrong?"

"He's been missing since late this afternoon. We notified the police, but they didn't think he was gone long enough for us to be alarmed."

"Do you think he ran away?"

"I doubt it, but we can't rule it out at this point either."

"Well, I hate to be rude, but there's no other way to say this, but three of my clients were placed under your care. Not only have you failed to help any of them so far, in addition; all three of them have met up with some sort of serious calamity. One was arrested, the other tried to kill herself because of an altercation with a High School Senior whom you didn't perceive of as a problem and now another one is missing."

"Listen Attorney Anwald, I don't know what you're trying to insinuate, but Beau Rivage enjoys a superb reputation."

"So, I've been told and by the way, I'm not insinuating anything. I'm coming right out and expressly stating that it boggles my mind that you don't know where Justin is. Please tell me in all seriousness, what are the odds of something like this happening?"

"Actually, the odds are quite high. After all, the reason your clients are here is because they were classified as 'high risk' in the first place."

"Well, that actually sounds like a cop out to me."

"Our entire staff consists of nothing but responsible professionals who do more than adequate jobs," April countered.

Then she hung up.

Pattie threw her cell phone into her bag and turned to Jordan, who was frowning.

"Did you hear that?"

He nodded and led her back to the couch. When they were both seated, he clasped her hands in his.

"Pattie, I know that you have a soft spot in your heart for Justin."

She nodded.

"You're right. I do and now I'm worried sick about him."

"I understand. I feel the same way. That's why it's important for both of us to keep a positive attitude and know that where ever he is, he'll be found."

She looked into his eyes.

"Do you actually believe that or are you just saying that?"

"I actually believe it. Otherwise I wouldn't have said it."

"Can I ask you something?"

He nodded.

"Sure."

"What is your honest opinion of Beau Rivage?"

"Well, I know that you don't you trust them, but quite frankly, although April and Ken are good therapists, they're not miracle workers. None of the clients in their charge got messed up overnight, so it's unreasonable for anyone to expect them to straighten out overnight either and by the way, arguing with April isn't going to enhance anything."

She nodded.

"I know, but I'm frustrated and worried. If Justin didn't run away then does that mean he was kidnapped? I mean what are the alternatives?"

"Well, maybe he just lost track of the time."

"That doesn't seem likely. What if he did run away? I've never dealt with runaways before."

"Well, I have. After all, Scotland doesn't get too much sunlight and what it lacks in sunlight it makes up for in rain."

"Oh my God. Is that your way of telling me that you were a runaway?"

"In a manner of speaking, yes, but at least I was an adult at the time."

Pattie stood and slipped her pumps back on.

"Wow. Well, you promised me that we would talk about Justin tonight, but I never expected the conversation to be anything like this. I guess we should just call it a night," she said.

Chapter Sixty-Three
EMOTIONAL RESCUE

After Jordan dropped Pattie off at her door, she slithered into her apartment, locked herself in and pulled the string on her fluorescent light. She went into her bathroom, waited while the light flickered and removed her makeup. When she came out, she changed into a red satin peignoir. Just as she was about to turn the light off, her cell phone rang. She jumped, clutched her chest and reached for it. She didn't bother to look at her Caller ID, because she was sure it was April Higgins calling with an update on Justin.

"Hey, what's happening?"

It was Ryan.

"Jordan and I had a dinner date. As a matter of fact, he just dropped me off a few minutes ago. Anyway, I'm not feeling all that well."

"Why?"

"Lots of reasons."

"You didn't have another fight with him or anything. Did you?"

"No. Nothing like that, but every time he drops me off, I open my door as narrowly as I can get away with and then I slide in. I know he wants me to invite him in"—

"I'm sure he does."

She chuckled.

"Well, I never do. Instead, I invariably end up slamming the door in his face. So far I've actually managed to keep from slicing off his nose."

"Why do you do that? Don't you like him?"

"Actually, I like him so much that I can never let him see the inside of this place. He'd die if he knew how I lived."

"Well, I have a feeling that at some point you're going to have to."

"I suppose your right."

"Well, as a bona fide hardware store heir, I can honestly say that decorating is no big deal when you have the money."

Pattie chuckled.

"I know that, but what good does it do me? I don't have one thin dime to call my own."

"But here's the secret. A true genius can decorate without money."

"I agree with that too, but as we all know, I'm no genius either. So, it looks like I'm screwed all the way around."

"Not necessarily, especially when you've got me to come to the rescue!"

Pattie chuckled.

"What do you mean?"

"I mean, I'm going to help you paint your apartment. Believe me, even though I'm not a professional painter, painting really isn't all that hard. I managed to paint my own digs."

"Wow. I don't even know what to say. You really are an amazing friend."

Ryan chuckled.

"Just say thanks."

"Thanks!"

"You're welcome and the best part of all, is that Dear Old Dad will be supplying the paint."

"Gee, that's nice of him."

"No, not really. He doesn't even know it yet."

"Gee, now I feel guilty. I think the least I could do is pay for the paint."

"You will. Someday, when you're an overpriced, highly paid, private defense attorney. Until then, don't sweat it."

"I have to, because that day may never come."

"Yes, it will. You'll see. Anyway, what colors should I hit Dad up for?"

"I don't know. No one has ever bothered to ask me what I like."

"On one level that's kind of sad, but you have to start somewhere, so since you like Jordan's apartment, what color are his walls?"

"White."

"Well, white's a nice safe color and it will make your apartment look bigger."

"No. I don't want to imitate Jordan. Besides, I know I couldn't sleep if I were surrounded by white walls."

"Why not? After all, once you turn off the light, they'll look just like your favorite color. Black."

Pattie chuckled.

"How about pale lavender walls with an off white trim? After all, lavender is close to purple and purple is my third favorite color."

"I know. Right after black and maroon. But yes, lavender with white trim sounds really pretty."

CHAPTER SIXTY FOUR
GREAT NEWS

No sooner did Jordan walk into his apartment, when his telephone started to ring. He ran into the bedroom and answered it.

"Hey Buddy! What's going on up there?" Clint asked.

"Not much. I just dropped off my brilliant, little, attorney friend."

"Oh. I'm surprised you're still seeing each other after the things you said about her."

"Well, she's slowly starting to thaw. In the meantime, I'm following your advice and remaining optimistic."

"I'm glad to hear that, because I'm an optimist myself. As a matter of fact, that's why I'm calling. I have some really great news.

"You set the date!"

"How did you know that?"

"I didn't. It just popped into my head. Anway, Congratulations!"

"Thank you. So, please keep the first Saturday in December free, because that's the big day and we both want you here."

"Of course, I'll be there. Thanks for inviting me."

"The printed invitations will follow once we get closer in time," Clint said.

They chatted for a few more minutes and hung up.

PART TWO
APPLE BLOSSOM TIME

Chapter Sixty-Five

SOME THINGS NEVER CHANGE

Pattie breathed a sigh of relief when Judge Fanshaw finally called the lunch recess on Monday. She was delighted that she had no cases on the afternoon docket, because she needed to return some calls and catch up on her paperwork. However, no sooner did she return to her office, when Brad strode in with a stack of files.

"Listen Sweetheart, I don't know whether you heard about it or not, but Judge Jamieson is retiring from the Appellate Court. Anyway, since he got his start as an ADA right here in this courthouse, everybody who is anybody is planning to attend his retirement luncheon."

Pattie smiled.

"Oh, how nice. I don't recall being invited though. When is it?"

"You don't recall being invited because you weren't invited. You're not anybody; you're nobody. Get it?"

Pattie cleared her throat.

"So, then why tell bother to me about it?"

"Because it's happening right now and I'll be needing you to cover our cases at the Criminal Motions Calendar at two o'clock."

He lobbed the files onto her desk.

"See ya," he said.

Then he left.

CHAPTER SIXTY-SIX
HANG 'EM HIGH

Judge Fanshaw was on the telephone in chambers. He swiveled around in his chair and stared at the autographed poster of Pat Hingle that hung on the wall behind his desk, while he listened. The poster read read "Hang 'Em High," which accurately reflected Judge Fanshaw's sentiments. Ryan knocked and Judge Fanshaw swiveled back around and waved Ryan in. His face was red and his scowl seemed deeper than usual. He pointed at his phone and circled his index finger as if to indicate that the person on the other end of the line was crazy.

"Listen pal, what the hell do you mean I've GOT to do it? I laid out sixty bucks for this shindig, so who the hell are you to screw me out of it?" His voice was like a roar.

He slammed the phone down so hard that Ryan jumped. They were both so shocked that neither of them noticed Norton Bakerman hovering and eavesdropping outside in the hallway.

"Did you break it yet?" Ryan asked.

Judge Fanshaw picked up the receiver, listened for the dial tone and shook his head.

"Nah. Not yet. These old land lines are too well made."

Ryan chuckled.

"Are you ready for Judge Jamieson's farewell luncheon? I thought we could walk over there together."

"Yeah, well, so did I, but we can't."

"Why? What's going on?"

"It was all settled that Johnny Nichols was going to preside over the Motions Docket this afternoon, but at the last minute he called The Chief Judge and said that he's going home sick, so the Chief Judge just called me and mandated me to stay here."

Ryan shook his head.

"Wow. Why you?"

Judge Fanshaw shook his head.

"I don't know. I'll bet Johnny isn't even sick. It's probably just some passive aggressive stunt he decided to pull at the last minute."

Ryan nodded.

"Well, that goes without saying."

"Hey listen, I've got an idea that could be right up your alley!"

Ryan chuckled.

"What is it?"

"Well, since you're a Drama Major, why don't you take my robe, throw it over yourself and pretend to be me on the bench this afternoon? That way I can still get to the luncheon?"

Ryan smiled.

"I'd actually like that. There are a ton of people I would hold in contempt. Plus, I'd rule against Annie every chance I got."

Judge Fanshaw scowled again.

"Why did you have to bring her up? Don't tell me she's covering the Motions Docket."

Ryan nodded.

"Yup."

"Oh God, that's terrible. It's just keeps getting worse and worse. Who's covering for you?"

"Norton Bakerman."

"Oh God. It might as well be Norman Bates."

They both chuckled.

"Listen, if you want me to stay here, I don't mind skipping the luncheon. I'll just tell Norton to scram."

"No. Go on over there and enjoy yourself. You can tell me all about it later."

"Are you sure?"

"Sure, I'm sure. I love living vicariously through someone who's actually still young enough to have a life."

Ryan smiled and shook his head.

"Thanks. By the way, if you're not able to attend, would you mind if I bought your ticket and used it to take Pattie Anwald?"

Judge Fanshaw's face looked as if he had just bitten into a lemon.

"You mean that thing that dresses up like a vampire?"

"I know her taste in clothes sometimes falls on the Gothic side, but it's still not right to judge a book by its cover. She's actually a very nice person."

"Is that what they call it? Being Gothic?"

Ryan nodded.

"Yeah. It's a very popular look right now and it actually has been for quite some time."

"Well, it's ugly. Anyway, I don't think she's a nice persona at all. I still haven't forgotten the way she threatened me on that case involving that thug kid who was transferred over here from the Family Court."

Ryan shook his head.

"Come on now, Judge. She was only trying to do her job."

"Well, you can invite her if you want to, although I'd advise you against it. You don't even have to buy the ticket. I'll just give it to you."

Ryan smiled.

"Really? That's very nice of you, Judge. Thanks."

He pulled his cell phone out of his pocket and dialed Pattie's number.

"Hello?" She picked up the call with a sigh in her voice.

"Thank God I caught you. Is everything all right?"

"No. Not really."

He invited her to the luncheon and after she explained that she would be covering the Motions Docket he sighed and expressed his disappointment. When he hung up, he let Judge Fanshaw know that Pattie would be representing Legal Aid.

Judge Fanshaw shook his head.

"I don't know what the hell I must have done in a past life, but it must have been a real doozy, because I can never seem to escape from those two annoying broads."

"You know Judge, if you could only find a way to zoom through the docket, you might still be able to make it to the celebration in time for dessert."

Judge Fanshaw broke into a smile.

"That might just happen, because something you said earlier has inspired me."

CHAPTER SIXTY-SEVEN
BASTILLE DAY

Pattie hung up from Ryan, picked up her files and walked over to The District Attorney's office. Barbara wasn't there and the lights were out, but she heard the sounds of a computer coming from one of the offices in the back.

"Who's out there?" Annie called from the back.

"Pattie!"

"Come on back!"

Pattie walked back to Annie's office. As she stood in the doorway, she noticed that Annie's office was about the same size as hers and it had similar furniture, but somehow Annie had managed to make her office look nicer. An antique Colonial flag with the original thirteen stars and a black and white photograph of a policeman walking next to a toddler on a pony, hung in silver frames, which graced the wall behind Annie's desk. Pattie pointed to the flag.

"What an interesting flag."

Annie minimized her game of "Mine Sweeper" and glanced up from her computer screen.

"Thanks. It's been in my family since Colonial Times," she said.

Pattie pointed to the photograph.

"Is that you on the pony?"

Annie nodded.

"Yeah, from when I was a kid up upstate. That's my father. He's now the Chief of Police."

"Oh really? I'm from a law enforcement background too."

"Yeah. Someone mentioned that to me, but I forgot who. By the way, I've been meaning to ask you something."

"What?"

"Do you know a guy named Jordan Armstrong?"

"Yes. Why do you ask?"

"No particular reason. How well do you know him?"

"He's my boyfriend," Pattie answered.

Annie bit off her right thumb nail and spewed it out into her waste paper basket.

"So, I guess you're here because they've got you handling the Motions Calendar?"

Pattie nodded.

"Yes and from the looks of things I guess you are too."

"Yup," Annie said.

"So, I have an idea. Let's make it Best Deal Day."

Annie frowned, looked at her calendar and shook her head.

"Is it the fourteenth of July already? My, how time flies. Anyway, no one outside of France ever celebrates Bastille Day."

"I didn't say Bastille Day. I said Best Deal Day."

"What's that?"

"The day that you and I work out the very best deals ever!"

"Now, why would I want to do that, when everyone knows that criminals, especially Legal Aid clients, don't deserve any deals, good or bad, because they already enjoy more than their fair share of Constitutional loopholes and presumptions of innocence? So, whether you call it Bastille Day, Best Deal Day or any other kind of day, there is no way any clients of yours will ever go free on my watch!"

"Oh, for God's sake, Annie!" Pattie said.

"And by the way, I haven't forgotten your distinct lack of gratitude on that Robert Foreman case. So you really have some nerve barging in here and making demands on me!"

With that, Annie bolted out of her chair, picked up her files and pointed at the door.

"Now, wait just a minute. I wasn't trying to make demands on you. I was just trying to streamline things," Pattie said.

"Well, let 'em eat cake. Now beat it," Annie said, as she turned out the lights and left.

Still shaking her head, Pattie stood, gathered up her files and headed for the courtroom.

CHAPTER SIXTY-EIGHT
LAWYERS DO IT WITH MOTIONS

By the time Pattie reached the courtroom, Annie was already in place at the prosecution table. The rest of the courtroom was filled with private defense attorneys. The only vacant seat was the empty chair next to Elliott Glutz, so Pattie cleared her throat and sat.

"Hi, have you heard any news about Justin?" She whispered. He frowned.

"Well, as his so-called Guardian Ad Litem, shouldn't you be the one to answer that question for me?"

Before she could respond, Norton Bakerman knocked on the door. A scowling, red faced Judge Fanshaw pushed past him, burst into the courtroom and opened the court session himself. Annie called the case of People v. DeVittorio. Reginald Reese stood and walked up to the Counsel table. Pattie remembered that Bonnie Louden was one of the victims in this case. She glanced down at her décolletage and noticed that she was covered in splotches.

"Good afternoon Your Honor," Reginald said.

Judge Fanshaw nodded.

"Good afternoon, Attorney Reese."

"Your Honor, you have before you, the Motion in Limine I filed, along with a supporting brief. It was necessary for me to bring this motion, in order to keep The People from clogging up the court's time with evidence of extraneous and irrelevant wrong doings on the part of my client. Besides, it's bad public policy for prosecutors to wave everybody's dirty laundry in front of a jury."

Annie stood.

"Excuse me, Your Honor, but the Defendant's prior bad acts can hardly be called irrelevant. After all, they illustrate the true character of a judge gone wrong," Annie said.

"Your Honor, on page seven of my brief, I cited a case entitled State v. Apao, which sets a precedent for keeping this kind of evidence away from a jury, if it is more prejudicial than probative. I believe that the facts of our case fall squarely within the four corners of Apao, because, like the excluded evidence in Apao, the evidence The People intend to bring would be more prejudicial than probative. If allowed in, this evidence would not only ruin Judge De Vittorio's career, it would jeopardize his very liberty."

Annie rustled through her copy of Reginald Reese's brief until she reached page seven.

"Please, Your Honor! Is that the best he can do? Cite a Hawaiian case that has no bearing at all in our jurisdiction?"

Judge Fanshaw perused the brief, frowned and waved his hand.

"Yes, I've read it. The Defendant asserts that The People are only attempting to vilify him with details of his prior bad acts, because they're not confident that they could convict him any other way."

"Well, Your Honor, Assistant District Attorney Toby Barnett wrote a brief supporting The People's Objection to Attorney Reese's Motion and unlike Attorney Reese, he actually cited case law from right here in our own jurisdiction," Annie said.

"Your Honor, the cases that Attorney Barnett cited were significantly different from either this case or Apao."

Judge Fanshaw nodded.

"Yes. For that reason, The Defendant's Motion in Limine is granted and evidence of all prior bad acts is hereby disallowed," Judge Fanshaw said.

"Thank you, your Honor," Reginald Reese said.

"You're welcome. Madam Clerk, call the next case."

Arguments between Annie and various defense attorneys ricocheted throughout the courtroom for the next hour as Judge Fanshaw summarily granted one defense motion after the other. He denied every one of Annie's requests and overruled every single one of her objections. At three o'clock he banged his gavel, called a recess until Monday morning and shed his robe on his way out of the courtroom. Pattie walked over to the prosecution table and tried to comfort a deflated Annie, who was quietly gathering her files.

"I want you to know how sorry I am about today's result in De Vittorio," Pattie said.

Annie stared at her.

"Yeah. Right."

"No seriously. I represented one of the victims when I worked over at the Family Court."

Reginald Reese and Elliott Glutz walked over to the prosecution table and joined them.

"Attorney Anwald, I've never had the opportunity to introduce myself before. I'm Reginald Reese."

Pattie shook his hand.

"Hi. It's nice to meet you."

"It's nice to meet you too. You did a fantastic job today. Congratulations on winning every one of your motions."

Pattie beamed.

"Thank you!"

Reginald reached into his wallet and handed Pattie his card.

"Here's my card. Keep it for a rainy day."

Pattie read the card, stuck it in her jacket pocket and nodded.

"This is great. Thanks again."

"You're welcome. And as for you Annie, either you're the most atrocious prosecutor that ever lived or Fanshaw really hates your guts."

"Well, why should Fanshaw be any different from the rest of us?" Elliot chimed in.

Reginald chuckled, Pattie gasped and Annie blushed so hard that her face almost matched her hair.

"Excuse me, but you've got no right to talk to me like this," Annie said.

"Well whether we do or we don't, I must say that I can't remember ever having had this much fun at the Motions Docket. Watching Judge Fanshaw wipe the floor with you just made my day," Reginald said.

Elliott nodded.

"Agreed Reginald! Too bad stuff like this can't happen every day. The only thing I regret is that we all didn't make Motions for outright dismissals in everything," he added.

"Yes, that would have been nice. Oh well. Hindsight is always twenty twenty," Reginald said.

"You're both out of control," Annie said.

Reginald stuck his index finger in her face.

"No, Baby Girl. You are," he said.

"Maybe next time it would help to make yourself available to resolve motions beforehand," Pattie said, quietly.

Reginald nodded.

"Good point," he said.

Norton shooed everyone from the courtroom, except for Annie who stood at the prosecution table, shaking. When she regained a small measure of her composure, she bit her left thumbnail and tore into it.

CHAPTER SIXTY-NINE

THE CAB RIDE FROM HELL

On Saturday night Pattie and Jordan walked hand in hand through the lobby of the theater where they had just seen the hottest new musical on Broadway.

"So, what did you think?" Jordan asked.

Pattie was all smiles.

"It was great. I loved it. I'm amazed that you were even able to get tickets."

"I must admit, it wasn't easy. Anyway, are you hungry?

"Yes."

"Where shall we go for a meal?"

"My best friend works at Elvis in the Village. It's a very popular place."

"Well then, let's try it out! I've never been there and it will be interesting to meet your best friend."

They opened the door and when they stepped out onto the street, a blast of hot, humid air assaulted them and Jordan's hair immediately curled up.

"Good God, this must be the hottest night of the year," he said.

"Well I love hot weather. I guess that's because I'm always so cold. I confess I also like what it does to your hair."

He patted his hair and frowned.

"I can't imagine why. It probably looks terrible."

"Au contraire. It's actually kind of cute when it's all wild and woolly like this," she said, as she gently pulled one of his curls.

She giggled when it sprang back into place. A taxi passed them and Jordan tried to hail it, but the driver immediately lit up his off-duty sign. Jordan pointed at the night sky.

"That full moon looks like a judge, holding court amongst the stars," he said.

"Oh, I can tell. You've been doing too many reports for the Family Court."

He chuckled.

"You may be right and I'll tell you something. It's really not the same without you there."

She nodded.

"I miss it too."

Another taxi whizzed by, but it was filled with passengers. After several minutes and several tries, a taxi driver finally pulled over. Pattie and Jordan got in and noticed the butt of a handgun protruding from a newspaper on the front seat. The driver turned around and glared at them.

"Maybe we should wait for the next one," Pattie whispered.

"God only knows when that will come along," Jordan whispered back.

"Where are you going?" The cab driver asked, in an unbelievably thick accent.

When Jordan said Elvis in the Village, the driver nodded, faced forward and jerked away from the curb with a screech. When he turned the corner onto Seventh Avenue, he nearly grazed a man and a young girl in the crosswalk. The man clenched his fist and shook it.

"Hey! Slow down!" The man yelled.

The driver gave him the finger.

"You won't be saying that when I back over you," he screamed.

Afterwards, he slowly inched the taxi down Seventh Avenue. The only time he sped up was when he aimed the taxi at an enormous pothole. Jordan and Pattie bounced around the back seat like a pair of dolls and Jordan mopped his brow.

"Is it hotter in here than it was outside or am I just hallucinating?" Jordan asked.

"You're definitely not hallucinating, although in view of this ride a good hallucination wouldn't be a bad idea," Pattie answered.

Jordan tried to crank the grimy window open, but it didn't budge. After trying it a few more times with no success, he finally tapped on the partition that separated them from the driver.

"How can I get the window to roll down?"

The driver turned back to look at Jordan, while he still continued to drive.

"Are you talking to me"?

"Yes."

"You cannot open the windows. It interferes with the air conditioning. Makes them all work like hell," he answered.

"Well, it already feels like hell. I didn't realize that you even had air conditioning. Why don't you turn it on?"

"Because it's broken and cannot be fixed until after the fare increase."

The driver turned his CD on as loudly as he could, in order to drown out any further attempts at communication.

"Can you believe this bloody nonsense? I'd always thought that taxis were the best mode of public transportation in this city," Jordan said.

"Well they're not. That's why I have my own car and if you weren't so damn stubborn we could be riding in it right now," Pattie answered.

Jordan looked appalled, as the driver continued to crawl down Seventh Avenue. The attractive woman with long blonde hair who was driving the red Mercedes convertible behind them honked her horn so many times, that he slammed on his brakes and screeched to a halt at the next yellow light. This caused

Pattie and Jordan to slam back against their seats. The woman tapped their bumper and they lurched forward again.

"Good God, I feel like I'm in a bloody rocking chair," Jordan said.

The taxi driver turned around, yanked the emergency brake and grabbed his pistol. He leapt from the taxi and ran back to the Mercedes. The driver hurried to get her top up, when she saw him rushing at her, brandishing his pistol, while Pattie and Jordan watched.

"I will kill you and shoot off your nose to spite your face," he screamed.

"It looks like I'm going to wind up with a new client," Pattie said.

"I doubt it. He's probably not eligible for Legal Aid. No doubt his father is some oil rich Sheik with billions stashed away in several Swiss bank accounts."

Once the Mercedes driver got her top up, she reached for her cell phone. The taxi driver opened her door and snatched it from her.

"Hey! You give that back to me," she screamed.

He aimed his pistol at her. She screamed and covered her face with both of her hands. He spat at her, slammed her door shut and banged her hood with the butt of his pistol. Then he stormed back to the taxi. By this time, the traffic light was yellow again. As soon as it turned red, he sped through it, leaving the woman screaming and sobbing behind him. On the next red light, he opened his door and tossed her phone onto the street. When he finally stopped in front of Elvis, Jordan paid him and tipped him and they disembarked.

"Well, that was awful," Jordan said.

"Oh, it could have been worse," Pattie answered.

"I can't imagine how."

"Well, for one thing, he didn't kill the woman. Did he kill her?" Jordan shook his head.

"No."

"And second of all, he didn't drive down here by way of Omaha in order to jack up the price. Did he?"

"Well that's only because he rigged that meter of his to spin like a bloody top."

Jordan's eyes lit up when he spotted an aqua, two-tone, 1957 Chevvy parked on the sidewalk in front of the entrance to the restaurant. He walked over and admired it.

"Now this is what I call a work of art," he said.

CHAPTER SEVENTY
JEALOUS GUY

Jordan led Pattie inside and they immediately got on line behind several other people. The restaurant was cool, but noisy. Every table was filled to capacity and the servers all moved quickly. An aqua and white sign hung overhead, which read, "Please Wait in Line Until Your Car Hop Seats You."

"Busy place. I guess we're in for a long wait," Jordan said.

Pattie texted Ryan. A few minutes later, Ryan appeared at the end of the line, dressed in his server's uniform, consisting of a white button down shirt, black pants and a black bow tie. He smiled warmly at Pattie, kissed her on the cheek and greeted her. Then she introduced him to Jordan.

"It's so nice to finally meet you," Ryan said.

Ryan led them toward the back of the restaurant and when some of the other people on line noticed this, they grumbled. A big burly man, with a shaven head, jumped up and punched the sign.

"What the fuck? Can't none o' youse read? The line forms to the rear and that guy ain't even a car hop!"

"Sorry," Jordan said, as he passed by.

"You should be," the man hollered back.

"This is embarrassing," Jordan whispered to Pattie.

"Why? It beats waiting on line forever. Doesn't it?"

"I don't know. Does it?"

When they reached the back of the restaurant, Ryan seated them at a corner table that was in the process of being cleaned.

"Have a seat. I'll be back in a jiffy," he said.

He left and returned a few minutes later, carrying two menus, an ice filled glass and Pattie's favorite raspberry flavored iced tea. Pattie smiled and lifted her glass to toast him.

"Thanks so much."

"My pleasure. Now, Jordan, what would you like to drink?"

"What kind of beer do you have?"

Ryan clapped his hands together.

"You name it; we've got it."

"Well then, surprise me," Jordan said.

"You got it," Ryan said, as he disappeared.

"When you told me that your best friend worked here I thought you were referring to a girlfriend."

Pattie shook her head.

"Well then, you must have connected the dots wrong."

"Quite frankly, I've never heard of a platonic relationship that remained that way."

"Really? I have. Besides, just because you never heard of something, that doesn't make it non-existent."

"How do you know him?"

"He's a court officer where I work."

"How interesting that you and he coincidentally work together at the same courthouse."

Pattie smiled.

"Actually, the same courtroom, but in case I never told you, I don't believe in coincidences. Anyway, I knew Ryan way before I ever went to work in that courthouse. He's the one who helped me get the job there."

Jordan picked up his menu, snapped it open and peered over the top of it.

"How sadistic of you to flaunt him at me," he said.

She cleared her throat and picked up her own menu.

"I don't know what you're talking about," she said.

A few minutes later he put his menu down and stared at her.

"Have you decided?"

"Of course. I want you."

Jordan chuckled nervously.

"No. I meant for your meal."

"Oh, I don't know. I usually get the Chicken Enchiladas. You know Jordan, if I didn't know any better, I could swear that you were jealous."

"No. Not really."

A carhop led the burly man and his entourage past them and seated them at a nearby table. The burly man gave Jordan the "evil eye", just as Ryan returned with a pale ale.

"I'm sorry this took so long," Ryan said.

"No problem," Pattie said.

Ryan glanced uneasily at Pattie, took their orders and disappeared.

"This is mind boggling," Jordan said.

"Yes, it is. I can't believe the way you're hassling me about my friendship with Ryan."

"Let me ask you something. Do you and he share that flat over on Peck Slip?"

Pattie shook her head.

"Are you kidding? I live there alone and Ryan lives all the way across town in a building in Hell's Kitchen that his family has owned for generations."

"Well if that's true, then, why don't you ever let me into your flat? I've shown you my digs."

"Believe me when I tell you that it has nothing to do with Ryan."

Just then, Ryan appeared with their food. After a long, tense, silent meal, he came back and bussed the table.

"Can I interest either of you in a coffee or dessert?" He asked.

"I'm a tea drinker," Jordan said.

The tension between Pattie and Jordan continued. Ryan returned and set a mug of cappuccino in front of Pattie and a mug filled with tepid tea water in front of Jordan. He opened the paper on a tea bag and plunked the tea bag into the mug. When it floated on top, Jordan stared at it in horror. Finally, Ryan put his hands on his hips and leaned over Jordan.

"I'm sorry. You did say you wanted tea. Right?"

"Well?"

"And? So? What's the problem?"

"And so, when I make tea it comes usually comes loose. Then I pack it in tea balls and pour boiling water over it."

"Ouch, that must hurt," Ryan said.

Pattie chuckled.

"Sorry?" Jordan said.

"Wow! I never even realized that tea had balls. You learn something new every day in this job."

Jordan frowned and shook his head.

"I don't understand. I'm British."

"Well, get over it," Ryan said.

Ryan winked at Pattie, handed Jordan the bill and left.

After a silent cab ride to the South Street Seaport, Jordan asked the driver to wait for him, so that he could walk Pattie upstairs. He only broke the silence when the reached her landing.

"You don't have to tell me. I already know I'm not welcome inside," he said.

Then he planted a quick kiss on her cheek and jogged down the stairs.

Once inside, Pattie glanced at her watch. It was almost two o'clock in the morning. She wasted no time in removing her makeup and getting into bed. She lay under the covers and tensed up, as packs of rats raced and fought in the ceiling above her. She managed to fall asleep in spite of them.

CHAPTER SEVENTY ONE
PAINT YOU A SONG

The following morning, Pattie woke up and stretched, as she watched the sun rise above the easternmost corner of the night sky. Its rosy tip ignited the darkness and transformed it from pitch black to navy blue. As it continued its ascent, the sky lightened to a rosy hue and by the time the sun was completely above the eastern horizon, it was so bright that it bathed Pattie's counter and kitchen floor in a pool of bright light. The knock on her door drowned out the sound of the cars that whizzed up and down the East Side Drive.

"Hey wake up! It's me," Ryan called to her through the door.

She jumped out of bed, threw her robe on and opened the door. Ryan was dressed in overalls and a painter's cap and he was grinning from ear to ear.

"Hi Ryan," she said, as she leaned on the door and yawned.

She stood there while he made several trips in and out of the apartment, each time returning with paint, primer, rollers, brushes, drop cloths, black plastic lawn and leaf bags and on the last trip, a box of donuts and enough coffee to fuel an army.

"It's OK now. You can close the door. I've got everything," he said.

She cleared her throat and closed the door behind her.

"God Ryan, I'm sorry. I guess I'm just not awake yet."

He peered at her uneasily.

"Did you forget that I was coming today?"

"No. It's just that my mind is preoccupied with Jordan's crazy behavior at the restaurant last night. Although he denies it, I could swear that he's jealous of you or something."

Ryan pointed at himself and feigned an expression of shock.

"Oh, that's rich. He's living on Easy Street and he's jealous of moi?"

"In a word, yes."

Ryan opened the container of coffee and poured its steaming hot goodness into two cardboard cups. The rich aroma permeated the entire apartment. He handed Pattie a cup.

"Here. This should wake you up," he said, as he picked up the other cup.

She smiled and lifted her cup to toast him.

"Thanks. Anyway, here's to the best friend I ever had," she said.

He smiled.

"Right back at you."

"So, how was the retirement luncheon on Friday?"

"Fun!"

She nodded.

"I wish I could have gone with you."

He chuckled.

"That's what everybody's been saying. Anyway, how did you make out in court?"

"Oddly enough, I won every single motion."

Ryan's eyes lit up.

"How come I'm never around when good things happen?"

She smiled.

"You would have loved it. Instead of saying that I won every motion, perhaps a more accurate accounting is that Annie lost every single motion, not only to me but to everyone."

Ryan grinned.

"You've got to be joking."

"I'm not though. It was almost surreal. Want some yogurt?"

Ryan shook his head and chuckled.

"Hell no. Why would I want yogurt when I have these delicious donuts?"

"I don't know. Because yogurt tastes good and it's healthy?"

"I guess I'll just have to take your word for it," he said, as he bit into a jelly donut.

Pattie got up, took two small plates from the cabinet and set them on the table. Then she walked over to her white, vintage refrigerator, opened the door and peered inside. When she eventually settled on a container of fat free vanilla yogurt, she tore the lid off, licked the yogurt and flicked the lid into the trash.

"Wow. That was delicious. Maybe tomorrow I'll try blueberry."

They both chuckled.

"I wouldn't put it past you," he said.

She brought the yogurt over to the table, sat and picked up one of the plastic spoons that Ryan had brought. They both ate and when they were finished, Ryan stood, retrieved a black plastic bag and walked it over to Pattie's doll collection. He grabbed one of the porcelain dolls by its left leg and then lobbed it into the bag head first. Pattie ran over to him and placed her hand on his arm, just as he was about to grab the second doll.

"Ryan, many of these dolls are collector's items, so please, let me be the one to move them out of harm's way. OK?"

He nodded.

"Sure. No problem."

She carefully placed the dolls in the bag, while he walked over to her window. He wound his fingers around the tension rod and pulled it down, curtains and all. Pattie watched him in horror.

"Oh my God! What the hell are you doing?"

"Pattie, I don't know how to break it to you, but these have got to go. They're ugly. You deserve better curtains."

"What are you talking about? I made them myself in home ec. class, when I was in the eighth grade."

"Yeah? Well, they look it."

She sighed, gently put the bag of dolls down and walked over to a drawer, where she fished around until she found a tape measure, a note pad and a pencil. She handed them to Ryan.

"Do me a favor and write down the exact measurements, so that I can at least buy the right size when I replace them," she said.

He nodded, complied and handed the pad back to her.

"Of course, you'll need a new curtain rod too, but don't worry. I'll snag one from the store. When I bring it over I'll hang the curtains for you at the same time."

She smiled.

"Thank you. You're such a doll."

He smiled back at her and pointed to the bag.

"Well, just don't throw me in there though."

Before she could answer him, a loud scurrying sound traveled across the ceiling and he looked at her in shock.

"What the fuck was that?"

"I'm surrounded by rats. Didn't you know?"

"Oh God. Really?"

She nodded.

"Yes!"

"Well then, let me go down and get the ladder. I have to inspect the ceiling for holes, before I prime and paint, because if, God forbid, I find any, I'll have to spackle them. Rats' teeth and claws are so strong that they can actually penetrate wood, metal and even human bones."

Pattie frowned.

"I know and I'm relieved to hear that someone besides me gets this."

"Don't worry. My father sells some electronic rodent repellents that people can plug right into ordinary wall sockets. They emit high frequency sounds that humans can't hear, but it scares rats and meeses away."

"Wow."

"On the other hand, you could always get a cat."

Pattie shook her head.

"I'd never be able to take care of one. I'm never here. I have all I can do to keep that tea rose alive."

"You don't have a smoke alarm either. I'll liberate one of those from my father too. Then I'll install it for you too."

Pattie smiled.

"Hey, if you keep this up, you're liable to turn this rat's nest into a home," she said.

"I'll do my best, but the one thing I won't be able to fix is that ever present fish smell. I think you need to go out and buy some scented candles or something. It really is disgusting," he said.

"Really? I'm so used to it, that I don't even smell it anymore."

CHAPTER SEVENTY-TWO

"THE LAW IS A ASS"

Early the next morning, while Annie sat hunched over a pile of loose papers on her desk, Connor Dane breezed into her office, carrying a stack of files. He lobbed them on top of the papers, pounded on them and silently watched, with his hands on his hips, as Annie lunged to grab them before they slid to the floor.

"I'm curious to find out exactly how you managed to lose every single motion, because that takes real talent!"

Annie looked up at him and raised her arms in supplication. She shivered when she realized that his eyes gleamed at her like those of a hungry wolf."

"I have no idea what happened, Connor. In fact, I spent the entire weekend trying to figure it out. Maybe Fanshaw screwed up because he only handles arraignments?"

Connor sneered and shook his head.

"Oh, so now it's Fanshaw's fault? Fanshaw doesn't know the law but Anne Carey's OK? I doubt it."

Annie nibbled at the cuticle on her right thumb.

"Well, maybe it's just that Fanshaw hates me."

"Yeah, well he hates Anwald too, but even she managed to mop the floor with you, which is ridiculous when you get right down to it! "

"Is it? Please don't force me to remind you that it wasn't very long ago when she kicked your ass too. Besides, I hate that bitch."

"Why?"

"Well, do you remember a couple of months ago, when we were all at Frank Bernard's birthday party?"

"Yeah. So? What does that have to do with anything?"

"Well, do you remember that cute hot Brit that played the piano for me when I sang?"

"What is this? Twenty Questions? Yeah, I remember him."

"Well, he could have been my boyfriend by now, except Anwald came along and snatched him right out from under me."

Connor chuckled.

"I hope you mean that figuratively and not literally."

Annie rolled her eyes.

"Tsk. Of course."

"Well, let me tell you something. Whoever he is, he can't be much if he settled for the likes of her and although your love life is not my problem, your professional inadequacies are. So, don't come in here and tell me that you can't concentrate on your work because you have the hots for some English piano player who likes Anwald better than he likes you."

"Wait a minute. That's not what I said. You're twisting everything around."

"No, I'm not. You as much as said that you basically hate Anwald because you're jealous of her boyfriend and you don't know what to do about it. Well, I'll tell you what to do about it."

"And what, pray tell, is that?"

"When you want to take revenge against an asshole, you have to stop whining and biting your nails, for God's sake and then just do what I do. Grow a spine and take every ounce of your wrath out on their clients. By the way, I've got something important to take care of before I forget and while I'm doing it, clean up this mess!"

He pounded on her desk again and stormed out. This time he succeeded in knocking all of her files to the floor. Once she fiished picking them up, she shoved them onto her desk, in no particular order. Then she bit down on her right pinky nail and tore it off in slow motion. She spat it into her trashcan. Then she pulled a crumpled tissue out of her pant suit pocket and wiped away the tears that trickled down her cheeks.

Connor stood in Pattie's doorway and silently watched her work. When he knocked, she looked up.

"Hey Connor," she said.

He walked into her office, stood in front of her desk and tilted his head to the right. His eyes gleamed just like they did in Annie's office.

"You aren't reviewing the arraignment files by any chance. Are you?"

"Yes. As a matter of fact, I am."

"Good. Did you get to Alejandro Vega's yet?"

Pattie knit her brow and sighed.

"Oh God. Don't tell me he's back again so soon."

"Yup. New York's finest picked him up last night. He's probably already down in the lockup."

"What were the charges?"

"Illegal sales and brace yourself, because I'm not making any deals with you this time. In fact, I'll be moving for as much additional prison time as I can get, hopefully all in consecutive sentences. Then, once he's finished serving them, if he ever is in this lifetime, I'll be notifying immigration, so that they can deport him."

Pattie moaned.

"But this is only his second arrest."

He waved his hand in dismissal.

"Tell it to the Judge."

"Why are you being so vindictive?"

"Because the time has finally come for me to kick your ass! Figuratively speaking, unfortunately. You thought that you were so high and mighty lording it over me on the day you handled his pretrial."

Pattie shook her head.

"You're kidding, right?"

"No and I have an additional reason. You stole Annie's boyfriend! And that's just bad female behavior!"

Pattie's mouth hung open in shock.

"What you talking about?"

He turned around and left without answering her. She quickly rifled through her files until she found Alejandro Vega's. As she pored over the police report, there was another knock on her door. She frowned and without looking up, she spoke sharply.

"Now, what?"

"Hello, may I come in?"

Jordan stood in the doorway, holding a vase with a dozen red roses.

She stood, smiled and walked over to him.

"By all means, do. I'm happy to see you. Your visit is the first nice thing that's happened to me today," she said, as she kissed him on the cheek.

He walked over to her desk, cleared a place for the vase and gently placed it down.

"I'm sorry. You were right about my being jealous of your friendship with Ryan."

"Hah! I knew it, but there was no need for you to go to all this trouble, even though the roses are beautiful. Thank you so much!"

She walked over to her door and struggled to close it as far as she could. When she turned to face him, he put his arms around her and kissed her.

"I also want you to know that I trust you and I'm not jealous anymore."

"Really? Just like that? Why the one eighty?"

"Well, it's not as sudden as you might think. I spent all day yesterday giving this issue a lot of thought. Anyway, will you accept my apology?"

She nodded.

"Of course."

"Shall I phone you tonight?"

"That would be great."

"All right. Talk to you then," he said.

He walked over to the door and struggled to get it open.

CHAPTER SEVENTY-THREE
A PATTIE'S EYE VIEW
OF THE WORLD

The following Saturday, Pattie and Jordan walked out of the South Street Seaport Museum, into perfect summer weather. The baby blue sky was dotted with puffy cumulus clouds, which all had silver linings. Jordan slid his arm around Pattie's waist and led her through the crowd toward a souvenir shop. When they came out a short while later, Pattie was wearing a baseball cap and a pinstriped baseball shirt, with the name "Pattie", embroidered across the back. The front was open, revealing her sunny yellow halter top. Jordan took her by the hand and led her toward the pier at the edge of the water, where they watched the bright yellow sunlight glisten on the surface of the East River. Passengers on pleasure boats drifted past them and waved. They smiled and waved back. Finally, he turned to her.

"You really impressed me at that museum with your incredible knowledge of this city," he said.

She smiled.

"Thank you. That's such a nice thing to say, but you overestimate me. There's a lot I don't know."

"I find that hard to believe."

He removed his cell phone from his pocket and snapped a photograph of her, with the Brooklyn Bridge as her backdrop. She smiled when he showed it to her.

"You're a great photographer."

He shook his head and pointed at the Brooklyn Bridge.

"You're entirely too modest Anyway, Labor Day Weekend is almost here and I have an idea! Why don't we drive over that bridge and spend it relaxing on some Long Island Beach Resort?"

She frowned and shook her head.

"That sounds like a complete waste of time."

"Really? I can't see how recharging one's inner battery could ever be considered a waste of time."

"Well, for openers, I don't know how to swim."

"Well, if you can learn law, judo, performance poetry, golf and rock climbing, you can certainly learn how to swim."

"I doubt that. Besides, this is as close to water as I ever hope to be, unless I'm in the shower or doing laundry."

"You don't know what you're missing. Swimming is one of the healthiest sports around. Plus, it's a lot of fun and like golf, people can do it well into their eighties. Speaking of golf, we could always make use of Gordon's guest passes."

She shrugged.

"Let's not and say we did."

"Pattie, let me ask you something. Have you ever even been anywhere outside of New York City?"

She cleared her throat.

"Oh, for God's sake Jordan, what the hell kind of a question is that?"

"A straightforward one, which I notice you haven't answered."

"Well, if I answer your question, can we change the subject?"

"Yes. We can even go for lunch."

"All right then, no. I've never been anywhere outside of this city."

"I just want you to know that I would never judge you, if it turned out that you had any phobias or anything."

Pattie chuckled.

"Gee, what a relief. Now where's my lunch?"

He pointed to a building on the other side of the pier.

"Do you see that building over there?"

She nodded.

"Yes."

"Well, the third floor houses a restaurant with a wonderful view and I believe that's where your lunch awaits you."

"OK, but if we go there, will I be in for any surprises?"

He shook his head.

"None that I can think of. Why? Is it your birthday or something?"

She smiled.

"No. Not until the end of January. I was just wondering whether I'll have to fend off any long-lost staff members, like Darla and Valerie."

"I never even came to this part of the city until I met you."

"Well, that's good."

They walked along the pier and just before they reached the restaurant, Pattie spotted a store that specialized in items from New York City.

"I can't resist," she said, as she ran inside.

"Look at this stuff! Every single item has something to do with New York!"

"I can't believe that you live within a minute's walking distance of this place and you've never been inside."

"In all honesty, I never even knew it existed. See? That proves I don't know everything about New York."

"Actually, all it proves is that you're a girl who never learned how to have any fun."

"That's not true. I have fun whenever I'm with you."

He held up a laminated map that depicted New York City as the center of the world and her face lit up.

"Wow! I recently had my apartment painted and that would be the perfect piece of art to jazz it up!"

"I'll buy it for you, as a sort of a housewarming gift," he said, as he brought it up to the cash register.

CHAPTER SEVENTY-FOUR
NIGHTS IN WHITE SATIN

Pattie and Jordan finished their lunch and walked back out onto the pier. Jordan once again slid his arm around Pattie's waist and they headed for her apartment. When they reached the third-floor landing, he drew her close to him, gently cupped her face in his hand and kissed her. She closed her eyes and melted into his kiss. When the kiss was over, she pulled her key out of her tote bag and stuck it in the lock.

"Come on in," she said.

He smiled.

"You mean I'm finally being allowed into the Sanctum Sanctorium?"

She smiled back at him.

"Yes."

Once they were inside, she closed the door and pulled the cord that turned the light switch on. He noticed the pale lavender walls with the ivory ceiling and trim which matched the lavender and ivory tablecloth, curtains and comforter. Her sheets, lay in their usual knot at the foot of her bed.

"It's lovely," he said.

"Thanks. I'm actually relieved that you like it, because I'm well aware of the fact that it's light years away from the elegance of your apartment."

Rain beat against her windowpane, even though the sun was still shining.

He pointed at the window.

"Look at that! A sun shower. They're pretty rare," he said.

She nodded.

"I know."

He pointed at her doll collection.

"Oh my, you have quite a doll collection."

"Thank you."

He once again pulled her against him and kissed her. She closed her eyes, wrapped her arms around his neck and clung to him. As they kissed, he slid his hand gently, yet firmly down her back. She blushed, broke away from him and cleared her throat.

"I'm sorry. I misunderstood. I thought you were ready for this to happen," he said.

She nodded.

"I am. If I weren't, you'd still be out in the hall."

He smiled and helped her slip out of her baseball shirt and halter top.

CHAPTER SEVENTY-FIVE
THERE'S GOT TO BE A MORNING AFTER

The next morning, while Pattie and Jordan lay together entwined in the arms of Morpheus, sunlight blazed through her window. Her new curtains were no more effective in blocking it out, than her old ones had been. Once she woke up, she lay still and watched Jordan sleep. Finally, she got up, slipped into her baseball shirt and tiptoed into the bathroom. After she shut the door behind her, she pulled the string on the fluorescent light and inspected her face in the mirror. She looked to see whether it had changed, but to her surprise, she looked the same way she always did. When she returned to bed, Jordan was also awake, propped up by his elbow and the pillows. She climbed in next to him.

"You've never done anything like this before. Have you," he asked.

She cleared her throat.

"Is it that obvious?" Her voice was a whisper.

He smiled.

"You know, as I watched you walk across the room, I realized that this is the first time I've ever actually seen your legs."

She stuck her leg in the air and pointed her toes.

"I hide them because my mother always says they look like broomsticks."

He shook his head.

"No, they don't."

She smiled and ran her fingers lightly through his hair.

CHAPTER SEVENTY-SIX
MOTION TO DISMISS

The next morning everyone was already in the arraignment court, waiting for Judge Fanshaw. Even though it was well past ten, neither he, the clerk, Ryan nor any of the other court officers were in sight. A few minutes later, Toby Barnett appeared in the doorway, holding some papers. He spotted Pattie and walked over to her.

"Hi. Did you get a copy of Elliot Glutz's latest motion?" He asked.

"No. As you know, he's not in the habit of sending me anything. What's he up to now?"

He handed her the papers.

"He filed A Motion to Dismiss the case against Penny and Roy Edwards."

"On what grounds?"

"He says that we're depriving them of their Constitutional right to a speedy trial by delaying it. Since Justin is our only witness, I have no other choice, but to delay it until after he returns. After all, I can't win if the only witness isn't around to testify," Toby answered.

"So now what happens?"

"Well, naturally I'm going to fight it. Justin's absence is an extraordinary circumstance and delaying the matter doesn't impose any real hardship on the Defendants. After all, it's not as if they're incarcerated or anything."

Pattie nodded.

"Yeah. Unfortunately, they're still walking around loose. Do you think that Judge Benchley will grant the Dismissal?

"Well, if he does, I'll appeal."

"You know I'll support you."

Toby smiled.

"Thanks. In the meantime, though, I have to file an Objection."

"Good. I'll file one too. Can I ask you something?"

Toby nodded.

"Sure."

"Do you even think that Justin is still alive any more?"

Just then Ryan, Judge Fanshaw, the Court reporter and the Clerk appeared in the doorway.

"Let's talk more about this later," Toby said, as Ryan knocked on the Courtroom door.

"All rise please," Ryan said and every one stood.

"Please be seated," Ryan said, after Judge Fanshaw took the bench.

Once Ryan opened court, Toby disappeared.

CHAPTER SEVENTY-SEVEN
INVITATION

That night, Pattie waited for Ryan at Cosmo's. She glanced at her watch. It was nine forty. She sipped her Vanilla Frappuccino, eased back into her chair and closed her eyes. A few minutes later, Ryan rushed in.

"Hey Pattie, I'm sorry I'm so late."

"No problem. I don't think the coffee I bought you is too, too cold yet."

He smiled.

"Thanks."

He sat, removed the lid and lifted the cup in a toast to her. She smiled and clicked his cup with hers.

"It's so nice to finally relax. Court sucked more than usual today," he said.

"I know. I'm exhausted too. I no sooner got through the insanity of today's docket when my mother called to remind me that it's almost Labor Day."

"Oh God. You mean it's time for the annual Labor Day slash birthday party for Lou? Emphasis on the word slash, of course?"

Pattie chuckled.

"My family is so predictable, even in their unpredictability. How many ways can you spell dysfunctional? A-N-W-A-L-D."

"It's true of all families to some extent."

"I know, but mine goes beyond the pale with it. Anyhow, you're welcome to join us if you'd like."

"Well, I was hoping to put in a few hours at Elvis that day, but if you need me for moral support or to act as a buffer, I'll blow them off."

She shook her head.

"No. I don't want you to lose a day's pay. Besides, something tells me that Lou might bring his girlfriend, Cheryl."

"Good. Maybe her presence will serve as a buffer."

She nodded.

"One can only hope."

"What about Jordan? Have you invited him?"

"Gee, I hadn't thought about that yet."

"Well, he'll have to meet them at some point, lucky guy."

Pattie chuckled.

"Don't say that."

"Listen. He's a Psychologist, right? So, he's probably smart enough not to judge you by what your family does," Ryan said.

"I hope you're right, because I'm nothing like them. Do you think that when I was born, maybe someone in the hospital mixed me up with some other kid?"

Ryan nodded and smiled.

"What a monumental screw up that would have been, but stranger things have been known to happen. Imagine if some wonderful family was forced to raise an Anwald and a nice girl like you got stuck with Chet and Edie?"

Pattie chuckled.

"Talk about your classic case of bad karma. Well, I guess if Fate says I'll have to bite into the old sour apple and invite Jordan, I guess there's no time like the present. What makes it worse is that he probably comes from a perfect family, where every body's normal and they all get along."

She reached into her tote bag and pulled out her cell phone. Ryan placed his hand on her arm to stop her.

"Listen, you don't have to do this tonight."

She shook her head.

"I might as well," she said, as she speed dialed Jordan's cell phone number. She reached his voicemail.

"Hi Jordan, I know I should have told you this before, but one of the reasons I didn't want to go away with you for Labor Day Weekend, is that every year my parents throw a combination Labor Day slash Birthday Party for my brother, Lou. Anyway, I plan to be there and I'm hoping that you'll come with me."

She hung up and put her cell phone back in the tote bag. Ryan knit his brow.

"I don't understand you. If Jordan invited you to go away with him for Labor Day Weekend, it would have been a great way for you to side-step this year's madness with your family. Sometimes I could swear that you're your own worst enemy.

She nodded.

"I know, but sadly, I'm not the only one. Not to change the subject or anything, but, what is your opinion of a male boss who calls his female employee 'Sweetheart' all the time?"

"Are the boss and the employee dating?"

Pattie shook her head and looked down at her feet.

"No. In fact they don't even really like each other."

"Well then, how does the female employee feel about it?"

"Well, frankly Ryan, I hate it."

Ryan sighed.

"You mean, it's you and Brad?"

She nodded.

"Yes and at least once during most of our interactions, he drops the Sweetheart bomb on me. Actually, he's been doing it ever since I first started working there."

"What's up with that?"

She shook her head.

"I have no idea."

"Well, can't you just politely tell him to knock it off?"

"I'm afraid that if I do, he'll retaliate against me by doing something worse. He's not really using it as a term of endearment and as you know, I can't really afford to be unemployed."

"Well he can't just up and fire you. After all, you do have some rights."

CHAPTER SEVENTY-EIGHT
WASHBOARD BOOGIE

It was well after midnight by the time Pattie returned to her apartment. She watered her tea rose plant, leaned her nose into its petals and breathed in their heady fragrance. Then she did the same thing with the roses that Jordan had brought to her at the Courthouse. She stripped her bed, stuffed her sheets and used towels into a pillowcase and sorted the rest of her laundry. When she was done, she grabbed her laundry powder from underneath the sink and stuffed it into one of the pillow cases, along with her cell phone, a change purse full of quarters and the thriller that she was currently reading.

The basement always reminded Pattie of an underground dungeon. The ceiling and walls were made out of cinder block that no one had ever bothered to paint. The cement floor hadn't been swept in years and light bulbs of a dubious wattage were screwed into the ceiling. Each socket was covered with a cage, as if to protect them from some imperceptible threat. As she walked past the small garbage room, the stench from the overflowing dumpster mingled with the ever-present fish odors and she choked back a gag. She heard a series of intense squeaks, which stopped her dead in her tracks. She turned around and noticed two rats fighting for scraps in front of the dumpster. She wasted no time in scurrying past them.

She had the laundry room all to herself. She inserted her coins into both washing machines, filled them with her laundry and opened the box of soap powder. She couldn't help but sniff it, because she loved its lemony scent. She smiled and poured some into the dispenser. Then she sighed, collapsed onto the unpainted wooden bench and rested her back against the cinder block wall. She reached for her book and read for about twenty-five minutes, until it was time to transfer her clean, wet laundry into separate dryers. Once that was done, she placed her light-colored clothes into the washing machine and sat back down again.

Within minutes, the laundry room felt like a furnace. The poorly installed vents on the dryers caused them to disgorge blasts of heat and lint. Beads of sweat collected on Pattie's forehead, chest and arms. A few minutes later she heard a squeak and put down her thriller. It wasn't a rat. It sounded more like the hinges on a door. She felt chills on the back of her neck. Her heart thumped. The door to the outside slammed shut and she heard the sound of approaching footsteps.

My God, some one's here!

She picked up her phone to call the police, but because she was underground she couldn't get any reception. She cleared her throat and faked a call to 9-1-1. The sound of the footsteps receded. The door to the outside squeaked open and once again it slammed shut.

She jumped up and ran over to the machines. Wet, damp or dry, it didn't matter. She pulled all of her laundry out, hustled it into the pillowcases and grabbed her other belongings. Like a demented Santa Clause, she dragged her bags up the stairs. When she reached her apartment, she slammed herself behind her rickety door and listened as the trucks pulled up to deliver their nightly supply of fish.

She stuck her phone into its charger and with the exception of three wash cloths and two towels, she draped her damp laundry across the backs of the chairs and table. Hot and upset, she took the towels and washcloths into the bathroom, stripped and stepped into her antique bathtub. She pulled the clear, vinyl shower curtain around her and turned the water on. At first the shower head only gurgled and spewed forth cold water, but Pattie didn't care. She closed her eyes, stood underneath it and let the water beat down onto the crown of her head. She pretended that she was under an enchanted waterfall in Hawaii and she willed the healing waters to wash away all of her stress and anxiety. Her visualization worked. Little by little, as the water temperature rose, she began to feel better. She relaxed under the stream and let it soothe her frazzled nerves. She shampooed, rinsed and applied a deep conditioner to her hair. Leaving it in place for maximum effect, she reached for her loofah with one hand, curled her other hand around a bar of soap and scrubbed herself briskly.

She shivered, groaned and wondered why she felt so weird. Then she shrugged and chalked it up to an overactive imagination. Once she felt clean and refreshed, she rinsed the conditioner out of her hair, turned the water as hot as she could stand it and held the wash cloths under the shower head. She wrung them out when they were saturated and draped them around both of her shoulders, in order to enable their moist heat to draw any residual tension out of her body. Then she turned the temperature back down and cooled herself off. Once she felt completely de-stressed, she turned the tap off, stepped out of the shower and wrapped herself in one of her damp towels. She grabbed another damp towel and dried her hair. Then she combed it, arranged it in a loose ponytail and threw on a clean nightgown. She removed a clean set of dry sheets from her linen closet, made up her bed and sank into it. Eventually the sounds of the fish market lulled her to sleep.

CHAPTER SEVENTY-NINE
LIGHT MY FIRE

The sound of scuffling feet right on the other side of Pattie's door woke her up. She knew that they belonged to a human. Fortunately, no rat in the world was big enough to make noises that loud. Knowing that her paper-thin door offered her virtually no protection against whoever was out there, she lay as stiff as a board, paralyzed by fear. She gulped when she heard the sound of liquid being spilled. She sniffed and inhaled the acrid odor.

It couldn't be gasoline! Or could it?

A moment of silence went by, punctuated by the sound of a kick on her door and followed up by the striking and subsequent sizzle of a match. There was a flurry of footsteps down the stairs, a popping sound and finally, the sound of flames crackling. The space underneath her door glowed like a jack o' lantern. Pattie smelled the pungent smoke that seeped through it and she watched it billow around the room, in an upward spiral. It came to rest on the ceiling and then it proceeded to fill the room, from the top down.

Pattie used all of her inner strength to push through the terror that paralyzed her and she forced herself to sit up and lumber out of bed. She reached for her robe. It was still damp, but she put it on anyway. She couldn't find her slippers, so she tiptoed to the door in her bare feet. She checked to see whether her door was still locked, but since it was made out of metal, as soon as she touched it, it scorched her fingers. She recoiled in pain and wrung her hand.

The smoke's thick tentacles reached down from the ceiling and gripped her. The smoke detector went off and its shrill din caused her to jump. The temperature in the apartment was unbearable. Her face was flushed. Beads of sweat rolled down her forehead, stinging her eyes. Between the sweat, smoke and her tears, Pattie couldn't see at all. Flames crept up the lower third of her door, turning it into hot, smoldering ash. The flames licked and devoured the threshold and without a door to keep them out, they were free to dance their way into the apartment. Pattie groped blindly in the smoke so that she could get as far away from them as she could.

She bumped into something. Startled, she opened her mouth to gasp and smoked filled her throat. She coughed and jumped back. With a trembling hand, she reached out again and realized that it was only one of her bed sheets. She tripped over her brief case, but one of the chairs broke her fall. She fumbled for her cell phone. She knocked it out of its charger and picked it up, but she couldn't see the numbers through the smoke.

She dragged a chair over to the counter by the window and hopped onto it. By this time, she could barely breathe and tears were rolling down her cheeks. Her nose and throat burned and when she pushed her curtains aside, the blisters on her right fingers stabbed her. Using the palms of her hands, she tried to pry the window open. Its wooden frame was so swollen from the heat, that it wouldn't budge. Her heart pounded wildly as she tried to loosen it.

Smoke filled her lungs and choked her. Every time she coughed, each hack burned her lungs and throat. She jumped down from the chair and knelt on the floor in the hopes of getting some decent air into her lungs, but all she managed to do was to breathe in more smoke. Knowing that she was closer to death with every passing second, she frantically groped for the faucet, turned it on and doused the hem of her bathrobe under the running water. She wrung it out slightly, covered her nose with it and literally breathed a sigh of relief. She climbed back onto the chair, made her way back onto the counter and accidentally bumped into the tea rose plant. She struggled with the window once more. When she still couldn't get it to open, she gingerly grabbed the tea rose by its porcelain pot, turned her face away and smashed the windowpane. When she finished creating a hole wide enough to fit through, she crawled out onto her fire escape.

CHAPTER EIGHTY
FIRE ESCAPE

Once Pattie was out on the fire escape, she dropped her hem, scurried to the railing and leaned over it. Gasping and heaving, she looked into the distance, where the first vestiges of dawn lit up the sky's easternmost tip. She inhaled as much clean, smoke free air as she could, but before long her lungs went into spasms that triggered another coughing fit. When her coughing finally subsided and she could once again breathe, she turned on her phone and called 9-1-1 to report the fire. Pressing the buttons felt like torture to her scorched fingertips.

She snapped her phone shut, clung to the railing with her left hand and began her long trek down the cold, metal stairs that led to the street. Every step she took felt like crushed ice shooting up from the soles of her feet and the pain shot halfway up her calves. Wincing all the way, she pressed on until she reached the lowest floor, where she stopped to catch her breath again. Down on the street, an overweight, aging hippie turned the corner.

"Pattie, are you all right?" He called up to her.

"Hi Gus, I'm stuck up here. Can you do me a favor and pull on that ladder?" Her voice sounded hoarse.

He nodded.

"Sure."

She watched and waited while he panted and struggled with the ladder. It was stuck, as if it had been glued into place. No matter how much Gus pulled on it, he simply couldn't get it to budge. All of a sudden Pattie heard a creak and a groan behind her. Then some gravel hit the pavement below. She turned around and gasped. The bricks and grout on one corner of the fire escape, had crumbled and fallen and the fire escape tilted downward by about an inch.

"Oh God! Now what do I do?" Pattie cried out.

"I don't know. Do you want to try to take a chance and jump into my arms? You're light enough that I could probably catch you!"

She shook her head.

"No!"

"You're like my wife. She's still on the fire escape over on our side of the building."

"Do you mean to tell me that the ladder on your side is stuck too?"

"No. I managed to get ours open. That's how I made it down, but Martha was too afraid to climb down with me."

"Oh God, I hope the fire department gets here before we all die," Pattie said.

Gus nodded.

"Me too. Let me go check on her. I'll be right back," he said, as he ran around the corner.

A siren wailed from afar, but after a few seconds the siren got closer. Eventually, a fire engine peeled around the corner and roared onto Peck Slip. Two firefighters jumped down from it and ran into the building with fire extinguishers. Another firefighter jumped down, connected a hose to the fire hydrant and dragged it into the building. Right after that, an ambulance arrived. It was followed by another fire engine. Two firefighters jumped off and ran into the building. Pattie watched, as the stevedores and other spectators began to mingle on the street. A young woman with a porcine face, sauntered out of the building, wearing nothing but a black, see through baby doll peignoir and black, silk, marabou slippers. Her kitten heels showcased her perfectly shaped legs.

"Hey! Do you live in this building?" Pattie called down to her.

She glanced up at Pattie and nodded.

"Yes."

"Well, how come you didn't have to climb down the fire escape like everybody else?"

"I'm lucky. I live on the first floor and the fire is up on the third floor. All I had to do was walk outside."

She spoke with a thick Eastern European accent.

Pattie pointed at the window behind her.

"Is this the window to your apartment?"

She nodded.

"Yes!"

"Well, I'm stuck here. Can you go in and open your window, so I that can climb through it? That way I can make it out onto the street like you did."

The girl smiled.

"Sure."

She started to enter the building, but one of the firefighters blocked her. She pointed up to Pattie. Just then, Gus returned and they both explained that Pattie was stuck there. As the firefighter tried to pry the ladder open, Gus called back up to Pattie.

"Listen! I came to tell you that I have to go to the hospital! Martha went into cardiac arrest!"

Pattie cleared her throat.

"Oh no!"

Two EMTs came from around the corner, carrying Martha on a stretcher. Gus followed them and watched as they slid her into the back of the ambulance. Then he climbed in after her. Once he was inside, The EMTs slammed the doors shut, got into the ambulance and sped away.

"Miss? I can't pry this open. We're going to have to prepare an extension ladder for you," the firefighter called up to Pattie.

"This is unbelievable," she muttered.

He turned around and bumped into another firefighter. They both ran back to the engine and drove it alongside the building. Pattie's attention was diverted from the mayhem on the street by several loud noises that came from her apartment. She turned around and peered up. All she could see was the thick, black, smoke that trailed from her window.

"Excuse me, Miss? Here's what I need you to do"—one of the firefighters on the street called up to her.

As she turned to him, another firefigher stuck his head out of her window and called down to her.

"Uh, Miss?"

She turned around, looked up and cupped her hands around her eyes.

"Hi up there. I can't see you, but whatever you do, could you please get my laptop out of harm's way before you turn on the hose? I don't want it to get water damaged!"

"Don't worry about it. The fire is out."

"Does that mean I can come back inside now?"

"Yes."

She breathed a sigh of relief.

"Thank God, because I really didn't want to climb down an extension ladder," she muttered.

She made the torturous climb back up to the third floor. When she reached her window, the firefighter was there, with an extended hand, waiting to pull her through.

"I'll help pull you through. Be careful of your feet, with those shards."

"Too late. They already cut me on my way out. You be careful when you touch my hands, because my fingers are burned."

He gently grabbed her around the waist, lifted her and carried her through the window. Then he sat her on one of the chairs by her table. The room was still filled with smoke, but at least she could see the outlines of her refrigerator. She began to cough again and she tried to wave it away.

"It takes a while for the smoke to dissipate. By the way, Your laptop is right on the table in front of you."

She nodded, gently patted it, nodded and continued to cough. When her coughing fit subsided, she asked him to put the light on.

"I can't. We turned off the main circuit breaker off in order to keep the building from blowing up. It will probably be switched back on in a few minutes."

"Thank you."

"By the way, I'm Charlie Brunner."

"It's nice to meet you," she said.

"It's nice to meet you too."

"Thanks."

He nodded, switched his flashlight on and inspected her hands and feet."

"You're right. There are tiny little slivers of glass stuck in the soles of your feet," he said, as he checked her forehead to see whether she had a fever.

"So, do I have a fever?"

"It's hard to tell. Anyway, you did yourself a real favor by getting out of here when you did. People don't realize that the number one cause of fire related deaths is smoke inhalation."

She nodded.

"I had to fight my way out onto the fire escape.

He beamed the light into her eyes and she winced.

"I'm sorry I had to do that, but I wanted to check out your eyes. They're red and puffy. Also, would you mind opening your mouth for me?"

She nodded.

"Sure. My throat is killing me," she said, as she opened her mouth wide.

"Well no wonder. It's pretty raw. Do you feel nauseous at all?"

She nodded.

"Kind of."

"Well, I have a feeling you may have smoke poisoning. I definitely think you should get it checked out at the hospital."

She nodded.

"OK."

"Get dressed and I'll take you."

"Thank you."

"Would you like for me to radio for a female EMT to help you?"

Pattie shook her head.

"No. I think I'll be all right."

He helped her down, then she tiptoed toward her closet. On the way, she noticed that her door was missing. She pointed at the gaping doorway.

"Where's my door?"

"Out on the landing."

She shook her head and when she reached her closet, she used her left hand to pull out a maroon skirt and a black jersey pullover. She took them into the bathroom and closed the door. Charlie followed her and stood outside.

"Can you hear me in there?"

"Yes."

"I need to know your name for the report."

"Pattie Anwald."

"OK Pattie, are you the one who reported the fire?"

"Uh huh."

"And this is your apartment. Right?"

"That's right. Or do you think I just happen to store my clothes in other people's apartments?"

"Sorry. Sometimes I'm forced to ask ridiculous questions."

A few minutes later she tiptoed out of the bathroom, fully dressed. She went over to her bed and found her bedroom slippers.

"I know I look crazy, but I don't think I can stand anything else on my feet right now. By the way, there was an intruder in the basement last night around midnight."

"How do you know?"

"Because I was down there doing my laundry."

"Wow, isn't that a bit late to be doing laundry?"

"Hey! This is America, so I can do my laundry whenever I want to. Besides it's the only chance I have to do it."

Before he could respond, Lou burst through the doorway. He frowned, glanced around and shook his head. Pattie cleared her throat.

"Jesus Christ, I can't believe my eyes. Who are you?" Lou asked.

Charlie dug into his wallet and handed a card to Pattie and Lou.

"Hi, I'm Charlie Brunner. FDNY."

Lou nodded and flashed his badge.

"Lou Anwald. Fifth precinct. She's my sister," Lou said.

"Well, your sister got lucky. It was only a tiny fire, as fires go. It was mainly confined to the little area outside of her door."

Lou looked at Pattie.

"How did it get started?"

"Arson. A real amateur job too, thank God. Like I said, she got lucky," Charlie answered.

"Pattie, what do you know about this?" Lou asked.

"All I know is that I woke up in the middle of the night , because I heard sounds outside my door."

"Well, whoever set the fire singled out your doorway, so I have to ask you whether you know of anyone who might have a motive to harm you?" Charlie asked.

"She's a lawyer for Legal Aid. Does that answer your question?" Lou said.

Charlie shook his head.

"No, not really, because criminals don't usually go after their defense attorneys. They need them too much," Charlie said.

"Well, I'm relieved that you know so much about the workings of the criminal mind, but she must have stepped on somebody's toes in order for this to have happened," Lou said.

"Why is it that whenever anything goes wrong in this world it's automatically my fault?" Pattie whined.

"I don't know. Since you seem to be the prime target, you tell me," Lou said.

"Well, I think she gave me as much information as she had and she's got some smoke poisoning and a couple of minor injuries, so I need to take her over to the ER," Charlie said.

"Don't bother. I'll take her myself. I've got an unmarked cruiser downstairs."

"Would you mind handing me my cell phone? It's on the counter next to my brief case. Also, go into my brief case for me and get out my wallet," Pattie said.

Lou nodded.

"Sure."

"I can carry you down the stairs," Charlie offered.

"Don't bother. I'll do it," Lou said.

CHAPTER EIGHTY-ONE
LOVE THY NEIGHBOR

When they got downstairs, Charlie held the doors so that Lou could carry Pattie all the way out to the cruiser. Once Lou placed her gently down on the front seat, Charlie closed the door.

"Well, good luck at the hospital. I'll be in touch," he said.

Pattie waved good bye and a few seconds later, a taxi dropped Gus off. He walked up to her.

"Hi, Pattie. What's going on and why are you getting arrested?" Gus asked.

Pattie shook her head.

"I'm not, Gus. This is my brother Lou. He's taking me over to the hospital."

Lou and Gus shook hands and greeted each other.

"Martha is still over there. They sedated her and told me they're keeping her for observation. I came back here to see if I could get into the building and grab some of her personal things."

"Well, they're letting people back in and the lights should come back on soon. I hate to add to your burdens, but the door to my apartment is literally gone. Before you return to the hospital, could you do me a favor and get my computer and my dolls and store them in your apartment until I get back?"

"Sure. No problem. I'd be happy to do that for you."

"Thanks."

A thin, older woman in a faded blue bathrobe and rimless glasses came from around the corner. Her gray hair was wound around tiny, pink foam curlers.

"Oh God, it's Gladys. Let me get upstairs before she does, so that I can head her off at the pass. God knows I've waited all my life for a chance to head someone off at the pass," Gus said.

Pattie and Lou chuckled and Gus rushed into the building, just as Gladys ran up to the cruiser. She peered in and when she spotted Pattie, she wagged her gnarled index finger in Pattie's face.

"I'm glad you're arresting her, Officer! She could have gotten us all killed with her bull shit in there," she yelled.

Lou frowned.

"Excuse me? I have no idea what you are talking about," Pattie said.

"Well, I'm talking about you, you whore! The fire happened in front of your apartment. What were you doing in there, free basing?"

"Sleeping!"

"Yeah. Right. Anyway, I'm sick to death of you and the way your tricks and johns keep me up all night!"

Lou flashed his badge at her.

"You shut the hell up and watch your mouth, before I lock you up for harassment, you nasty old bitch!" Lou bellowed.

Gladys stuck her index finger in his face and smirked.

"What's the matter, copper? Did Big Brother send you over to kick my ass for exercising what's left of my right to free speech?" She said, in an imperious tone.

Lou pushed her hand away.

"Look, I'm telling you right now to keep your fucking finger to yourself, because if you don't, I'm gonna snap it off, poke both your eyes out with it and then shove it down your throat! Got that?" Lou bellowed.

"Yeah!" Pattie echoed.

Lou got into the cruiser and slammed the door.

"Nice lady," he muttered.

Pattie nodded.

"Tell me about it. Can you give me my wallet and phone now?"

He nodded and handed them to her.

"Here. I'll call that rattletrap slumlord of yours after we get to the hospital. I can't wait to tell him off," he said, as he peeled away from Peck Slip.

"Thank you."

"That entire building is nothing more than a fucking tinder box, if you ask me and every one of those wooden doors is a separate code violation."

"After you call my landlord, would you do me a favor and call my boss? I have a feeling that I won't be going in to work today."

"Sure. No problem," Lou said, as he sped through the streets of Lower Manhattan, complete with the siren and flashing lights.

Pattie picked up her messages with her left hand. The first, was a voicemail that came in from a blocked line. The caller hung up without leaving a message. The rest were emails, all from an email address 'Lightning Bug'. The subject line on the first read, "Inferno." She opened it. It contained only one sentence.

"Let's get toasted."

She gasped.

"Oh, My God!"

"Now what?" Lou snapped.

"I'll show you when we get to the hospital."

The subject line on the second email read "Die". There was no text, only a picture of Pattie, naked, in the shower, shampooing her hair, with her eyes closed.

Pattie gasped and rocked forward in her seat. Lou bent over to look at it and the car swerved.

"Jesus," he muttered, as he regained control of the car.

Pattie's hands were shaking when she opened the third email. Untitled, it contained only text.

"Those who worship the beast have no rest day or night and the smoke of their torment will go on forever."

Just as she broke into tears, her cell phone rang.

"It's from a blocked line."

"Well, pick it up and put it on speaker," Lou said.

Pattie nodded and picked up the call.

"Hello?"

"Yeah, hello. I wasn't sure you'd still be alive at this point," the voice hissed, in a stage whisper.

"Who is this?" Pattie shouted.

"The only reason your Karma's a bitch is because you're one," the voice hissed.

Click. Dial tone.

Lou grabbed the phone out of Pattie's hand.

"Level with me, Pattie. What the fuck is going on?"

Pattie glared at him.

"Nothing!"

"Then why is all of this bullshit happening to you?"

"I don't know. Why do you keep acting like any of this is my fault?"

"First of all, that guy Gus seemed to think you were getting arrested."

"Well, he was confused. Give the guy a break. His wife just had a heart attack, for God's sake."

"Yeah, well, what about the old battle ax? Was she confused too when she called you a whore and then accused you of free basing in your apartment?"

"Well I guess so. Besides, who the hell cares about anything she has to say?"

"No one, but I'd still like to know why she said it or why you would let someone take a naked picture of you in the shower. If you'll pardon the expression, where there's smoke there's fire."

"Yeah, very clever. Anyway, as you probably already noticed, Gladys is nuts to the point of being half senile and as far as the picture goes, I'm as concerned as you are about it."

"Well how did they get into your apartment? Don't you lock that rattle trap door of yours?"

"Of course. I guess they must have broken in."

"Yeah well, then, how did they get your email address and your phone number?"

She shook her head.

"I don't know. I just wish you'd stop punishing the victim."

"I'm not punishing the victim. I just want to know what the hell is going on. And why."

"Well, you're the cop. Find out, because I'm terrified right now."

"Believe me, I will. In the meantime, I'm wondering whether you should play it safe and move back home."

She shook her head vehemently.

"Hell no! Just the thought of that makes my skin crawl."

Lou came to a screeching halt in front of the emergency room. He shut off the siren, left the lights on and carried Pattie inside.

CHAPTER EIGHTY-TWO
UNSOLVED MYSTERY

On a sweltering evening three weeks later, Ryan and Pattie sat together in Cosmo's, nursing their usual beverages. Pattie held her hand up to show her fingers to Ryan.

"See? They're almost healed."

Ryan smiled.

"Wow. Thank God. And how are you feeling otherwise?"

Pattie shrugged.

"Pretty good for the most part, but because I inhaled so much smoke, my lungs will be vulnerable for the rest of my life."

Ryan shook his head.

"Gee, what a shame."

"I know, but things could always be worse. At least I'm still alive."

Ryan nodded.

"I agree with you there and I'm grateful for that."

"Thanks. The one silver lining in this great big storm cloud is that Lou actually forced my landlord to give me a fireproof door, but the bad news is that they broke my mirror when they installed it."

"Would you like another mirror? I'll snag one from Dear Old Dad and install it tomorrow night, after work."

She smiled.

"Wow. That would be great, but I hate being a burden to you."

"You're never a burden. You're a good friend and I'm sure that if the tables were turned, you'd do the same thing for me."

She nodded.

"That's true. I would, but in the meantime, I just wish my life would get better."

Ryan smiled.

"It will."

She smiled back at him.

"Well, thank you for saying that and I hope you're right."

Her cell phone rang. It was Lou.

"Hi Pattie. Have you gotten any more weird calls or emails lately?"

She chuckled.

"You mean other than this one?"

"Very funny."

"Seriously though, there's been nothing since the day of the fire."

"Well, whoever the hell did it, did it from an untraceable phone and email address, so I haven't been able to catch them. I haven't given up though."

"Thanks for letting me know. I appreciate it."

"A friend of mine who works over in vice emailed them something from a pornographic sounding email address. I'm hoping they'll snatch the bait. That way we can reel them in."

"That would be great."

"By the way, do you think it might be that rattletrap slumlord of yours?"

She shook her head, even though he couldn't see it.

"I doubt it."

CHAPTER EIGHTY-THREE
BIRTHDAY BASH

Labor Day was one of those "ten best weather days" that meteorologists all love to boast about. Pattie turned her car onto West Twelfth Street and managed to find a parking space next to the chestnut tree in front of her parents' house. She wore a plain, black cotton mini dress with a scoop neck. Her black leather belt accentuated her tiny waist and her black fishnet pantyhose, black boots and dramatic make up all hinted at her Gothic taste, without going too far overboard. Jordan looked collegiate in his pale-beige, linen pants, plaid, button down sports shirt and Docksiders.

Pattie took a deep breath, cleared her throat and glanced at her watch. It was almost two o'clock. She turned the car off, opened her door and stepped out into the warm, afternoon sun. She opened the hatchback, retrieved Lou's birthday present and waited for Jordan to pick up the small potted plant he had bought for Edie. Once he did, she locked the car and led him up the Hosta lined brick walk toward the three-story brownstone. A flower box overflowed with geraniums under each of the diamond shaped, lead-paned, glass windows. The wreath that graced the massive walnut door was made out of a straw hat that Edie had decorated with every fresh flower in season.

The fox terrier that lived next door bounded up to the wrought iron fence that separated the Anwald's property from his. He wagged his tail and barked at them. Pattie ignored him, but Jordan crouched and stroked him through the bars. He stood on his hind legs and licked Jordan's hand.

"What an adorable doggie. You're a nice doggie, aren't you?" Jordan crooned.

He looked up at Pattie and continued to pet the dog.

"This is some house," he said.

"Thanks."

He came back to a standing position.

"So, if you don't mind my asking, why are you living over on Peck Slip when you could be living right here?"

Pattie cleared her throat and as if on cue, Edie opened the door. She struck a pose by standing on her left leg and arching her back, while pressing the sole of her right foot against the door. This showcased her new, black, patent leather flip flops, which were dotted with oversized faux jewels. Her lime-green, spandex tank top barely stretched across her ample cleavage, leaving hardly anything to the imagination. Her lime-green and black print polyester shorts, revealed a pair of shapely, but well-padded legs. She wore more makeup than Pattie did. Her lipstick was fuchsia colored. She held a jumbo sized margarita in her left hand. An unlit cigareette was stuck behind her right ear. She silently glared at Pattie and Jordan, while licking generous portions of salt from the rim of her glass. When Pattie introduced them, Edie inserted her cigarette behind her ear and extended a limp wrist.

"Enchante`," she said, slurring her words.

Jordan shook her hand.

"Hello. It's so nice to meet you. You have a beautiful daughter," he said.

Edie rolled her eyes.

"I don't know about that. I think she overdoes her makeup a little. Plus, like I've told her a thousand times before, she's way too scrawny," Edie brayed.

She poked Pattie in the back and prodded her into the house. Once they were all inside, Edie slammed the door and cut in front of them. Her cleavage jiggled in her push up bra as she led them down the hall and back to the kitchen in the rear of the house. The soles of her feet flapped against her flip flops, which clicked against the black and white tiles. When they reached the kitchen, Jordan handed Edie the plant and Edie unceremoniously plunked it onto the counter. She removed the cigarette from behind her ear and held it out for Jordan to light.

"Oh Madam, I'm so sorry. I don't have a lighter."

Edie chuckled.

"Madam. Hey, that's a good one," she said.

She walked over to the table, picked up her favorite white plastic lighter and lobbed it at him. She smiled when he caught it.

"Read the slogan," she said.

"As Long as You Have Your Wealth," he read.

She winked and once again held her cigarette out to him. As he lit it for her, she drew the nicotine in and held her breath. Several seconds later, she blew a mixture of smoke and carbon dioxide into his face. Pattie squinted, cleared her throat and waved the smoke away.

"Anyway, everything is set up outside," Edie said.

She opened the back door and motioned for Pattie and Jordan to follow her. Once they were outside, Jordan spotted a hummingbird feeder, a birdbath and several other bird feeders housed amidst a wealth of Chestnut, Apple, Maple and Lilac trees. A Cherry Tree stood at the southwest corner of the property. Across from it, a tree house nestled in the boughs of an oak tree. A weather-beaten sign on the bottom rung read "Louie's Tree House." Ornamental shrubs, black-eyed susan's, roses, mums and begonias dotted the landscape. Their collective scents hung in the air and co-mingled with each other. A jade fountain graced the garden's center and added to the general sense of tranquility. As the water flowed, Jordan noticed that it pushed a floating clapper around and he smiled.

"I'm impressed with your garden. I haven't seen anything like it in ages. Is it your creation?"

Edie beamed.

"Of course. Anyway, if you think it looks beautiful now, you should have seen it back in the spring," she said, as she blew more smoke into his face.

"Hey Pattie, don't you think it's high time you got your friend a drink?"

Pattie nodded.

"What would you like, Jordan?" Pattie asked.

"I'll have a beer, if you've got one, thanks."

"Hey it's nice to know that you're not a teetotaler, like some people I know," Edie said, giving Pattie a sidelong glance.

Pattie walked toward the beer cooler, which was set up next to the brick grill where her father, Chet, stood grilling an assortment of meats. Chet was stocky and he had gray hair, which matched the color of his dull, lifeless eyes. He wore a T-shirt that read "Abominable Party Animal." As soon as Pattie got near him, Edie called him.

"Hey Chet! Get over here and meet Pattie's veddy impawtent sounding friend, Jawdan," she yelled, mimicking a British accent.

Chet took a long sip of his beer, put it down and limped over to Jordan. Then he pumped Jordan's hand.

"It's swell to meet you. Welcome to our son's surprise birthday party," he said.

"Thank you. It's nice to meet you too. I didn't realize that it was a surprise party, because Pattie mentioned that you do this every year."

Chet smiled.

"We do, but every year we tell him that it's only a Labor Day Party and then we give him a later arrival time. That way we can keep on surprising him year after year."

"It's amazing that he keeps falling for it," Jordan said.

Edie beamed.

"Yes, well, he is amazing. We're very proud of him. As a matter of fact, he's up for a promotion to Detective Third Grade," she said.

"Oh, how wonderful," Jordan said.

"Sure it is, because now he'll be able to put his brain to good use," Chet said.

Pattie returned and handed Jordan a glass of beer. He smiled at her.

"Well if his brains and work ethic are anything like Pattie's, I'm certain he'll have no problems," Jordan said.

"So, tell me, Jordan. How you can stand her?" Chet asked.

"Well, she certainly doesn't bother me. I hardly know her. After all, she's your wife," Jordan answered.

Chet suppressed a chuckle and pointed at Pattie.

"Actually, I was referring to this one over here," he said.

Pattie cleared her throat.

"Excuse me?" Pattie eked out the words.

"I don't understand your question," Jordan said.

Chet sniffed.

"Well then, I'll explain it. Louie and all them other cops are putting their lives on the line in order to collar the skells that go around ruining our beautiful city. Then along comes Pattie and all them other bleeding heart defense attorneys to make sure that the judges undo their collars, by cutting them all loose on account of some off the wall Civil Rights technicality," he said.

"Oh yeah. The judges really listen to us defense attorneys. Most of them are rubber stamps for the Prosecutors," Pattie argued.

"Well, at least we got the Death Penalty back," Edie chimed in.

"Please, let's not talk about that? You know how much I hate it," Pattie said.

"Of course, you do! But WE like it," Edie said.

"Well then God have mercy on your souls," Pattie said.

"No! God have mercy on your soul for the way you make life difficult for your poor brother down at that Fifth Precinct," Chet yelled.

Pattie cleared her throat again.

"Excuse me?"

"I'm referring to that comedy of errors that you created last spring with Ralph Carmen's loony toon of a future ex wife. Doesn't that ring any bells for you?"

Pattie shook her head.

"No."

"Well, it should. After all, you fought on her side in court and wound up getting her off the hook, for God's sake! Poor Louie has to see that guy at work every day and he still hasn't lived down the disgrace of it!" Chet said.

"You know, I always hated it when you represented those pint-sized hoods, but you really went from bad to worse the day you graduated from them and started representing adults," Edie said.

Then she turned to Chet.

"You'd better go and check on that meat and while you're at it, turn the corn," she added.

With that, Chet sniffed and limped back to his place at the grill, while Edie strutted over to her chaise lounge and flounced down on it. Even though her breasts jiggled, she miraculously managed to avoid spilling so much as a single drop of her margarita. Jordan and Pattie sat in the wicker love seat directly opposite and Jordan reached over and gently curled his hand around Pattie's.

Edie crossed her cankles, took a huge gulp and licked a wad of salt from around the rim of her glass. She used her thumb and forefinger like pincers, to forage the depths of her glass for the biggest piece of crushed ice she could find. Then she gingerly fished it out, arched her back and slowly ran the ice cube along the contours of her neck. When she was done, she licked the ice cube a few times, popped what was left of it into her mouth and pulverized it with her back teeth. Two orioles flew by and landed on one of the bird feeders. Edie removed another cigarette from the pack in her pocket and held it out for Jordan to light. Once again, Jordan complied. She took the first drag and chuckled on the exhale.

"Forgive me. I get these aggravating hot flashes," she said.

"Don't they have a medicine for that?" Pattie asked.

Edie shook her head.

"Ice works better. Anyway, Jordan, what do you do for a living?"

"I teach Psychology at Omnia University."

Edie's face lit up.

"Does that mean you can write prescriptions?"

Jordan shook his head.

"No. That's a psychiatrist's job."

The corners of Edie's mouth drooped downward in disappointment.

"Oh well, that's too bad. Can you at least hypnotize people?"

"Yes."

She tilted her head in Pattie's direction.

"Did you ever do it to her?"

"Do what to her?"

"Hypnotize her, of course. What in the hell did you think I meant?"

"Actually no. I've never tried to hypnotize Pattie."

Edie took another long drag on her cigarette and blew the smoke in their direction. Once again, Pattie cleared her throat and waved the smoke away.

- 308 -

"Well, maybe you should sometime and while she's under your spell, you could get her to act normal, because that's something I've never been able to do. I'll bet she runs to you all the time with dozens of fake horror stories about me."

Jordan shook his head.

"Actually, she's never mentioned you to me at all."

Edie sighed and raised her left eyebrow, just as the long ash from her cigarette fell onto the ground.

"Well, maybe that's because she doesn't want the truth to come out. She gave me such a hard time as a kid and now that she's supposed to be all grown up, she actually believes that she's better than I am, what with her fine legal mind and all the rest of that crap," Edie said.

Pattie cleared her throat.

"Since you never paid one cent toward my education, my attitude shouldn't concern you at all."

Edie glared at her and stubbed her cigarette out with a vengeance.

"That's not the point. The point is, that you are throwing your whole life away defending a bunch of lowlifes when you don't even have a clue as to how to get your own needs met. The only thing you've got to show for all of your efforts is a stupid mountain of unpaid student loans!" Edie said. Her voice was at battle pitch.

"Again, it's none of your concern, since I pay them all back singlehandedly," Pattie yelled.

Chet sniffed and limped over to the group.

"Jesus, Pattie, you just don't listen to anybody. You're really not happy unless you're causing trouble. Are you!" His voice boomed so loudly that he the terrier ran up to the fence and barked hysterically.

"You shut the hell up! Pattie, go get my gun!" Chet screamed.

"Jesus Christ! Don't shoot him. They'll charge you with cruelty to animals," Edie brayed.

"I'm not gonna shoot him. I'm only gonna bop him on the snout with it," he said.

"Never mind that. Just do what I do," Edie said.

She slid a coffee can out from underneath her chaise lounge and picked it up. The top of it was secured by an entire roll of duct tape. As soon as the terrier spotted it he ran away to the other side of his yard.

"What the hell is that?" Pattie asked.

"It's a fucking coffee can that I filled halfway up with pennies and every time that miserable little son of a bitch over there barks at me I shake it right in his kisser!"

"Oh. OK. I get the picture," Pattie said.

"Watch and I'll show you how it works," Edie said, as she got up.

She walked over to Pattie and stared at her with a mean glint. Foamy spit formed in the left-hand corner of her mouth and the right-hand corner of her bottom lip hung down. When she shook the can in Pattie's face, Pattie winced and jumped backwards to get out of her way. The heat rose up on Pattie's décolletage, neck and face, as she broke out into angry red welts. She burst into tears and ran into the house. Edie chuckled, tossed the can down and reached for her margarita glass, which she managed to drain in one gulp. Jordan ran into the house after Pattie. He arrived just as she slammed and locked the old, oak bathroom door. He knocked on it and called to her.

"Lovie, are you all right"?

"No! I feel like I'm ready to jump out of my skin," Pattie answered.

Edie staggered into the house.

"Why the hell are you calling her Lovie? Who do you think you are? Thurston Howell the Third?"

Jordan ignored her.

"Pattie, if you won't come out, then at least let me come in," he said.

Edie shoved Jordan out of the way, peered through the crack in the door and banged as hard as she could. Chet lumbered into the house, pushed past Jordan and Edie and pounded on the door, just as Pattie broke into sobs.

"Jesus Christ, Pattie, I hope you don't cry like this in court, beecause, if you do, they'll all have a field day laughing at you!" Chet hollered.

"They probably do anyway!" Edie said.

Pattie's sobs grew louder.

"I can't see where any of this is helping," Jordan said.

"Well, you're the shrink. You fix her!" Edie bellowed.

Someone knocked on the outside door. Edie staggered down the hall, opened it and saw Cheryl standing there. She wore no make up on and she was dressed in a plain tan, cotton dress. She was holding a box from a nearby bakery. Edie frowned and let her in.

"Who is it?" Chet bellowed.

"The little brown wren!" Edie bellowed back, before addressing Cheryl.

"What the hell did you bring a cake for? I thought I told you on the phone that I always bake all of my son's birthday cakes from scratch," she said.

"They're only cookies," Cheryl whispered.

Edie turned to Chet.

"Get me another Margarita," she ordered.

Chet sniffed and went back outside.

"By the way, Cheryl, this is Pattie's boyfriend Jordan," Edie said.

Jordan greeted Cheryl and knocked on the bathroom door again.

"Pattie, let's go for a walk. Shall we?"

Pattie blew her nose.

"Give me a minute. OK?"

"Sure. I'll wait for you outside," he answered.

He walked down the hall and went outside, without uttering another word.

"What's going on?" Cheryl asked.

"Oh, Pattie's hysterical because this is Louie's Big Day and nobody's paying any attention to her," Edie said.

"Oh. I hate people who make everything all about them," Cheryl said.

Edie nodded.

"So do I! Now hang on a second, while I go and check on what that bastard is doing outside," she said.

She walked down the hall and opened the front door. Jordan was leaning on the iron fence with his back facing the house. When he didn't turn around, Edie slammed the door and locked it.

CHAPTER EIGHTY-FOUR
YOU DON'T KNOW ME

Eventually, Pattie came out and joined Jordan. Her face, neck and chest were still dappled with hives.

"Oh dear," Jordan said, when he saw her.

Instead of responding, she silently slid her hand into his and led him on a walk toward the Hudson River. The sun danced along its whitecaps and lit the cobblestones beneath their feet. When they finally reached a park by one of the piers, Pattie walked over to a bench, sat on it and stared at the Palisades for several minutes.

"Look, I'm really sorry about everything that happened back there," she said, when she finally spoke.

He brushed her cheek gently with the back of his hand.

"Why? You certainly didn't do anything wrong."

"I know, but I still feel bad about it."

"Well, we're not responsible for what other people do, even when we're related to them.

"Believe me, I understand that intellectually, but somehow I haven't caught up with the idea, emotionally."

"Well, at least I understand why you prefer to live on your own."

She nodded.

"I moved into the dorm, just to get the hell out of there, even though I could have commuted to college and Law School on foot."

He shook his head.

"What a shame, although I can't say that I blame you."

"My mother criticized and nitpicked the hell out of me for as long as I can remember. No matter what I did, it was never good enough, but I have to say that lately it's gotten worse."

"I hope you don't jump through hoops just so that you can win her approval one day, because that's not likely to happen. If anything, she'll just keep setting the bar higher."

Pattie knit her brow and scratched her head.

"Why? Am I that awful?"

"Not at all. You have to stop thinking that any of this has anything to do with you. She acts the way she acts because of who she is, not because of who you are."

"Really? Because she doesn't act this way towards my brother. If anything, she's opposite."

"That's probably because he does whatever she tells him to do, but if he ever stops, you'll see her turn on him with a vengeance. People like your mother dangle and withhold their approval as part of a big mind game. Their goal is to be in control."

"Are you saying that my mother doesn't approve of me because I won't dance to her tune?"

He nodded.

"That's exactly what I'm saying. Plus, it's obvious that she's jealous of you for having surpassed her in life."

"Well then, what's my father's excuse?"

"He probably approves of you inwardly, but he's forced to keep his mouth shut, because he doesn't want to incur your mother's wrath. He probably knows better than anyone what she's capable of."

Pattie nodded.

"Wow. So now what do I do?"

"Continue to follow your own North Star, just as you've always done and accept the fact that your mother's not likely to change. Once you stop seeking her approval you'll be able to walk away from all of her mind games in the future."

"OK, except I don't always know what my North Star is."

"Get quiet, dig deep within your heart and listen for your own Inner Voice. That's where you'll find all your answers."

She smiled for the first time that afternoon.

"Wow."

He smiled back at her and nodded.

"Wow is right. Once you learn to follow the advice that your Inner Voice gives you, you'll never need anyone else's approval again, because you'll automatically approve of yourself."

"Thank you for explaining this to me. It's all so new that I feel like a revolutionary."

He patted her hand.

"You're welcome. The reason you feel like a revolutionary, is because this whole concept is extremely freeing."

"I have a question though. What if I wind up making a mistake?"

"Well, we all make mistakes at some point, but so what? We learn and move on from them with greater wisdom. There's no need for any self-blame or self-abusive thoughts."

"You mean it's not a disgrace or anything?"

He chuckled.

"Of course not."

"Really? I always thought I had to be perfect."

"No one's perfect. Just because we make a mistake, it doesn't mean that we are a mistake. All we need to do is just relax and do our best."

"But what should I do when my mother lies about me? I mean, she lies about me all the time."

"Well, ridiculing people and putting them into a negative false light is all part of the same mind game. The same power struggle. Just remember, their end game is always about Power and Control."

"Well, how can I stop her?"

"Unfortunately, you can't. The only person you can ever control is yourself. That's why it's so important to never, ever, EVER, let any one else label or define you."

"But it upsets me to think that there's nothing I can do to stop her."

"Remember, the game ends the minute you walk away from it and you can walk away at any time."

"Yes, but that won't stop her from saying mean things about me."

"All right, let me find another way to explain this. The truth is that we can never stop anyone from saying or doing anything. All we can do is stop ourselves from believing or internalizing it."

Pattie knit her brow.

"What?"

"I am not made by the things that happen to me, but only by my reaction to them."

"I think I've just been hit with a very deep statement."

He nodded.

"Remember, the only power anyone has over us, is the power we give to them."

"So, in other words, I never have to give my power away to my mother again."

"That's right, nor to anyone else either and it doesn't matter what anyone says about you. Just because someone says something, it doesn't make it true. For example, if your mother called you a maple tree would that make you one?"

She smiled.

"Of course not."

"That's right. So, if calling you a Maple Tree doesn't turn you into one, then calling you anything else doesn't turn you into that, either. Besides, you'll find that once you stop letting other people define you, you'll have room to define your own self, in ways that work for you and give you mastery over your life."

Pattie's splotches were finally gone.

"I think I'm finally starting to understand this."

He smiled and kissed her on the cheek.

"Good. By the way, for what it's worth, everyone over at the Family Court really misses you. They're constantly extolling your virtues and wishing that you were still there."

"Well, doesn't that work in reverse though?"

He frowned.

"Doesn't what work in reverse, Love?"

"The things people say. Just because someone says something good about me, that doesn't make it true either."

He shook his head.

"In the final analysis, we're the only ones who get to choose what we internalize about ourselves. We have the same right to internalize the positive things, that we have to reject the negative things. That's what's so beautiful about being empowered."

She nodded and cleared her throat.

"Well, I guess we should get back to the house before we ruin Lou's surprise party."

He looked at her as if she were crazy.

"Are you serious, after all we just talked about today?"

She nodded.

"Yes. Why?"

"Well, first of all, it's hard for me to believe that your brother is smart enough to become a detective, when he's not even smart enough to figure out that the surprise party he gets every year is the same surprise party he gets every year."

"OK, you have a point, but so what?"

"Well, the point is, that I have no intentions of ever going back there."

"Please? You've got to! I really don't think that I can face them without you."

"Exactly and I don't think anyone should ever have to subject themselves to that kind of abuse. That's the reason why I'm not going back there."

She shook her head.

"Well, I have to."

"No, you don't."

"Well, I'm going to."

"But not with me. I'll just walk home from here."

When he stood, and walked away, Pattie chased him. When she caught up with him, she got in front of him and tried to block his path. He silently side stepped her and stormed off. She shook her head and watched him cross the street. Then she slowly walked back to her parents' house.

CHAPTER EIGHTY-FIVE
ON THE LAM

Pattie opened the door and walked straight back to the kitchen, where Edie was hovering over one of her gas jets. She was trying to light the cigarette that was clenched between her teeth. Chet hovered behind Edie and Lou hovered behind Chet, with his hands in the pockets of his neat, creased khaki pants. The box of cookies that Cheryl had brought and all its contents were strewn across the faded linoleum floor, along with several broken plates, a pile of wet dishrags and a butter knife. Pattie gasped when she saw the mess, causing Edie to stand up straight and turn around. She removed the unlit cigarette from her mouth, as Chet switched the gas jet off.

"Well, how about that! You managed to ruin your brother's surprise party after all," Edie bellowed. Her speech was more slurred than it was when Pattie left.

"Yeah! You're so late all the time, it's a wonder them judges don't throw you in jail for contempt of court. Maybe them judo teachers ought to teach you how to commit Hari Kari or whatever it's called when they disembowel themselves," Chet added.

"Oh, shut up Chet! Who the hell cares about Hari Kari? The only thing I wanna know is where that lousy Limey ran off to," Edie brayed.

Lou shook his head.

"Who are we talking about?"

Edie turned to Lou. Her mouth was twisted into a snarl.

"Some Casanova she dragged in here. He's supposed to be English, but he didn't even kiss my hand when I held it out for him. I even said enchante` and everything!"

"Well, that's because he's probably Eurotrash," Lou said.

Edie nodded and pointed through the windowpane at Cheryl, who was sitting outside, sulking.

"Exactly. But who are you to talk? Take a peek at that dipstick you've got out there. She's plainer than a bowl full of mushrooms," Edie said.

"Hey! Don't compare Cheryl to some English desperado," Lou shouted.

"Why not? I honestly don't know where either of you two kids gets your taste in people," Edie shouted back.

Probably from me, Chet thought, as Pattie peered out of the window to get a good look at Cheryl.

"By the way, Jordan's from Scotland, not England," she said.

"Well, who cares? It's the same fucking island, isn't it? Anyway, where is he?" Edie yelled.

"He went home."

"Why?"

"Who cares? Good bye and good riddance," Chet chimed in.

"Well, I care. I care passionately at this point," Edie said.

"Well, I'd be more concerned about why he left England in the first place," Lou said.

"He's probably on the lam for being a thief," Edie said.

"A thief?" Pattie repeated.

"Yeah. After all, he stole my God damn lighter! Who knows what the hell else he did?"

The hives and splotches returned to Pattie's face, neck and chest.

"Oh, come on! This is ridiculous. Go to the Dollar Store and get yourself another one if you love it that much," Pattie said.

With that, Edie lunged at Pattie, but Pattie turned around and ran out before Edie could reach her.

"Should I go out after her?" Lou asked.

Edie waved her hand in dismissal.

"The hell with her, but do me a favor. Next time you're down at the precinct, pull up that Limey's rap sheet! His name is Jordan Armstrong and he works at Omnia University," Edie said.

"I'll see what I can do," Lou said.

Edie turned around, switched on the gas jet and finally lit her cigarette.

CHAPTER EIGHTY-SIX
MAKING UP IS HARD TO DO

The following morning, Jordan wandered through the courthouse in search of Pattie. He finally found her. She was alone in the law library, researching some old records on microfiche. She was so involved with her work that she didn't even hear him approaching. When he put his hand on her shoulder she jumped. She stared at him. He looked as drawn and as careworn as she felt.

"Oh, my God, Jordan! You scared me."

"I'm sorry for scaring you. Anyhow, it wasn't easy to find you. The guard at the metal detector said he'd never even heard of you."

"That's because he's a weirdo."

Jordan chuckled.

"Anyway, I looked for you in every courtroom, but they were all empty."

"There's a judge's convention in Atlantic City, so there's no court today."

"Well anyway, I'm glad I finally found you. I wanted to tell you how sorry I was for leaving you in the park yesterday."

"I forgive you, even though I felt like you'd abandoned me."

"Do we have time to get a cup of coffee and talk about this or do you need to get right back to work?"

"I'm free."

As she gathered her notes and files together, she spotted Norton Bakerman hiding in one of the stacks. She cleared her throat, ignored him and led Jordan out.

PART THREE
HARVEST TIME

CHAPTER EIGHTY-SEVEN
ALL THE LEAVES ARE DOWN

Ten weeks had flown by. The November wind swept a pile of dried leaves into a miniature cyclone on the sidewalk in front of the deli, where Pattie and Ryan planned to have lunch. Ryan side stepped them and held the door for Pattie, who was dressed in her favorite purple knit dress suit and matching purple suede boots. Once they were seated, Ryan ordered an egg salad sandwich on a poppy seed bagel, along with his obligatory black coffee and Pattie ordered a small coleslaw and her usual iced tea.

"Gee, I wish Veteran's Day fell on a Monday."

Ryan nodded.

"Agreed."

"Another weird thing is that the docket feels like it's thinning out," Pattie said.

Ryan nodded.

"That's because it is. Most people don't realize that Criminal Law is a seasonal business.

Pattie knit her brow.

"Seasonal? How can that be?"

"In the summer, when it's nice out, people are out and about getting into all sorts of trouble. But once it gets cold outside, they hibernate indoors and hunker down for the winter. Also, when summer temperatures go sky high, people get a little crazy with the heat."

Pattie nodded.

"Wow. That's pretty interesting. I never put two and two together like that."

"Trust me. I'm right. Do me a favor and don't turn around," he said.

Pattie turned around and noticed that Annie had just come into the deli. She was wearing a Kelly green woolen pants suit with a silk, jungle print scarf and she was heading straight over to their table.

"Oops," Pattie said, as she turned around to face Ryan.

"I thought I told you not to turn around."

"I know. I'm sorry. But whenever someone says 'don't turn around' I automatically wind up turning around," she said.

Annie stood next to Pattie and Ryan's table and towered over them. She looked down, squinted and stuck her ravaged index finger in Ryan's face.

"Listen Pilgrim!"

Ryan bored a hole right through her with his eyes.

"Wow. I have to say, that's got to be the worst John Wayne imitation I ever heard," he said.

Pattie tried to suppress a giggle and Annie shot her an evil look.

"Oh, what wit," Annie said.

"OK. So now that you've got my attention, what do you want?" Ryan asked.

"Norton Bakerman tells me that you go around the courthouse calling me a bitch every chance you get," Annie said.

"Well, you know the old saying. Don't believe everything you hear."

"Are you calling Norton Bakerman a liar?"

"No, but I'm accusing him of understatement. I mean, after all, if he wants to go around quoting me, I think the least he could do is get the quotation right. You see, I didn't just call you a bitch."

"Well, then what did you call me?"

"I said you were a real bitch."

Pattie suppressed another giggle.

Annie sighed.

"Look you idiot. I don't want you talking about me behind my back."

"Don't worry. I won't any more. After I did it that first time, you turned out to be such a boring topic of conversation, I was forced to change the subject."

Pattie shook her head, as Annie stormed off. When the waitress arrived with their lunch, Pattie pushed hers away.

"You know what? I think I lost my appetite."

"Oh, for God's sake. Don't let that bitch, uh, er, I mean that real bitch ruin your lunch," he said, as he bit into his sandwich.

"It's not just her. I'm nervous, because I have to meet Toby Barnett in Judge Benchley's Chambers."

"Really? Why?"

"Because Elliot Glutz filed a Motion to Dismiss the Edwards case and it's on this afternoon's docket," she said.

"Ah. Well. No wonder you look so snazzy."

Pattie smiled.

"Why, thank you, kind sir."

"You're welcome. Now if you wait for me to finish my lunch, I'll walk over there with you," he said.

She smiled.

"That would be great."

Chapter Eighty-Eight
MOTION TO DISMISS

Judge Benchley instructed his court officer to clear the court-room, except for the lawyers and parties involved with People v. Edwards. Elliott Glutz stood at the Defense Table with Roy and Penny Edwards, while Pattie stood next to Toby Barnett at the prosecution table. Pattie's pulse raced. The little hairs on the back of her neck stood on end when she realized that Roy and Penny Edwards were once again relentlessly shooting daggers of hatred at her. She felt a wave of revulsion overcome her. She wished that she could simply curl up into a ball and roll out of the courtroom. She shuddered and turned toward Toby Barnett.

"Attorney Glutz, I've had the opportunity to read your Motion to Dismiss and your supporting brief, along with the Objections filed by both The People and The Guardian ad Litem in this matter. Now, unless some one wants to add something that is not already included in these papers, I'm actually ready to rule," Judge Benchley said.

"Your Honor, I filed this motion way back in August when the People's only witness had already been missing for a long period of time. Three months have gone then and my Motion is only now coming up on the docket? I'd really like to know what's going on," Elliott Glutz shouted in his loud, nasal voice.

Judge Benchley frowned.

"First of all, Attorney Glutz, I don't run the clerk's office, therefore I have no control over what gets docketed or when.

Although it seems to me that twelve weeks for a motion to come up on the docket is a very long time, the truth is that the Defendants posted bail immediately after their arrest. So, since they've been free to rumba around the city, there's no proof that a delay has caused them any undue hardship at all."

"Well, it is a hardship, Your Honor. My clients were arrested seven months ago, which means that this case has been hanging over their heads for all this time. And they were ordered not to leave the jurisdiction, which means that they haven't even been able to go on vacation."

Pattie cleared her throat.

"The Defendants ought to spend more time worrying about whether their son is dead or alive, instead of worrying about going on vacation. Their sense of misplaced values, boggles my mind," Pattie said.

"I agree with Attorney Anwald," Toby Barnett added.

Defendant's Motion to dismiss all charges against Roy and Penny Edwards is not warranted and is therefore denied," Judge Benchley said.

He jumped out of his chair and left, before Elliott Glutz could utter a word in protest.

"All rise, please!" The Court Officer announced.

Elliott spun around and stormed out, with his clients close on his heels.

"Thank you for supporting my Objection," Toby said.

Pattie smiled and made the thumbs up sign.

"Hey! Anytime! I'm just glad we won."

Toby nodded.

"Me too."

Toby ran into Brad on the way back to his office.

"Hi Brad, it looks like you made a real find with that Pattie Anwald," he said.

"Yeah! Right!" Brad said, in a loud manner that was inconsistent with his usual flat affect. Then he stormed off.

Chapter Eighty-Nine

LET ME CALL YOU SWEETHEART

By the time Pattie returned to her office, Brad was already there, pacing in front of her doorway. She cleared her throat and greeted him, but instead of answering her, he placed both of his hands squarely on her shoulders, spun her around and steered her inside. He struggled with the door until he closed it all the way, snatched Justin's file out of her hands and skimmed through it. Then he tore her brief out of its clip and waved it back and forth in her face.

"I don't know what to say, except that this actually had the potential to be an excellent brief, if only—if only, it had been written by a prosecutor instead of a criminal defense attorney," he sputtered.

Pattie cleared her throat.

"Well Brad, Judge Benchley appointed me as Guardian Ad Litem for the victim in this case way back when I still worked over at the Family Court," she answered, as calmly as she could.

"Yeah, well, you haven't worked over there in almost six months."

"I know, but since the case hasn't been resolved yet, I'm still involved."

"Yeah, well, I don't like you 'being involved' on my dime."

"I'd be happy to make up the time."

He waved his hand in dismissal.

"That's not the point. The point is that you looked insane standing next to Toby at the prosecution table."

"Well, where was I supposed to stand? I couldn't very well stand next to Elliott Glutz and his clients when I was opposing them in court. Now that would have looked crazy."

"Listen Sweetheart, we all know you're one of those prosecutor wannabees who hails from a long line of cops. So, any time you want to cross over to the dark side and work for them, don't let the door hit you in the ass. And another thing that got my goat is that prick, Jeffrey locking me out of the courtroom."

"The judge ordered him to clear out the courtroom because the victim is a minor," Pattie said, trying to reason with him.

"Well, that still doesn't mean that I have to like it any more than you're gonna like it the day I kick you out of here," he said.

"I guess this is the part where I'm supposed to feel threatened," she said.

He shook his head.

"Oh no, Sweetheart. It's a promise, not a threat."

He marched over to her door, fought to get it open and then left, without saying another word.

Chapter Ninety

DREAM JOB

Bright and early Monday morning, Lou and ten other brand new detectives sat in a conference room at the precinct. They were dressed in their best civilian business attire and they each had a thick loose leaf manual in front of them.

"Some of you may already know me. For those of you who don't, I'm Lieutenant Dale Purdy, second in command of the Detective Division. Chief Joe Braden is our commander and we all take our orders from him," the man at the front of the room said.

Chief Braden rose to his feet.

"I'd like to welcome and congratulate each and every one of you on having successfully attained the title of Detective Third Grade. Lieutenant Purdy and I are pleased to have all of you in the division. Unfortunately, I have a conflicting meeting at the mayor's office, therefore I will leave you in Lieutenant Purdy's capable hands for the remainder of this orientation," he said.

Once Chief Braden left, Lieutenant Purdy addressed the group again.

"I think you'll find that Chief Braden and I are both fair. Please know that we consider all of you to be the cream of the crop," he said.

He instructed the new detectives to open their manuals, locate the name and photograph of their newly assigned partner and team up with them. Everyone did, except for Lou who kept glancing around the room, to no avail. Eventually, Lieutenant Purdy picked up a manila folder and walked over to him.

"Your partner is in the hospital recovering from an emergency appendectomy. So, until he's back on duty, the Chief and I will either assign you to work with another set of partners or we'll send you out on nice, easy cases that you can handle on your own."

"Thank you," Lou said.

Lieutenant Purdy nodded and handed Lou the file.

"Read this file and get on it right away. The minute anything goes wrong, call for immediate back up. I'll be ending this orientation in a few minutes anyhow."

CHAPTER NINETY-ONE
STING

L ou got into an unmarked police cruiser, shoved the file under the seat and sped over to Nguyen Cong Duc's warehouse. When he reached the front entrance, he slammed on the brakes and barged in. He dodged and weaved between the man-made icicle-rags that dangled from the pipes and walked to the back of the warehouse, where he finally found Nguyen Cong Duc. Nguyen looked up at Lou and scratched his head.

"Do I know you?"

"I don't know. All I know, is that you're Nguyen Cong Duc. Right?" Lou answered, brusquely.

"Who wants to know?"

Lou flashed his badge in Nguyen's face.

"I do. I'm Detective Louis Anwald, with Manhattan's Fifth Precinct and I'm here to investigate a complaint about a trail of blood that has been emanating from one of your apartments over on Christie Street."

Nguyen thoughtfully rubbed his chin between his thumb and index finger.

"Sounds like strange goings on over there."

"Well, who lives there?"

"Tennans."

"No shit. What's the tenant's name in Apartment A?"

Nguyen shook his head.

"I don't remember."

Lou frowned and wound his fist around Nguyen's shirt collar. He backed Nguyen up against the wall and slammed him into it with such a force that it took several seconds for Nguyen to regain his equilibrium.

"Don't hand me that phony, baloney bull shit. Do you really think I look dumb enough to fall for it? Now, I'm asking you again, nicely, what the tenant's name is," Lou barked in a voice that sounded like car tires backing over gravel.

"Lerand Leroux."

Lou frowned. He whipped out a pen and notepad and shoved them into Nguyen's hand.

"Yeah? Well, write it out for me on this pad and be sure you spell it with American letters."

Nguyen scrawled Leland's name and handed the pen and notepad back to Lou.

"OK. Bye. Have a nice day," Nguyen said, as he turned to walk away.

Lou grabbed his shirt collar again and yanked him back.

"Listen, stupid. Don't get cute, because I'm not through with you yet. You keep pissing me off and I'll huff and I'll puff and I'll crawl up your God damn ass with a toenail clipper and believe me, I won't stop poking you with it until I pull you and your house of cards down," Lou bellowed.

"Tell me what you want."

"What I want, is for you to fork over a key to that shit hole, so I can get to where LeRoux lives. And it had better work," Lou said.

"When?"

"Right now! When do you think I might want it? Next year?" Lou barked.

"You wait right here. I look," he said.

"Well, I'll go back there with you and we'll both look until we find it."

Nguyen scurried down the hall, with Lou following closely on his heels.

Unbelievable, Lou thought as he stood in the doorway. Nguyen removed a key from a hook and handed it to Lou.

"Here," he said.

"Thanks," Lou said, as he handed Nguyen his card.

"Now the next time LeRoux comes over here, whether it's to work, play or scratch his God damn ass, you get on the phone and call me at this number and until I call you and tell you otherwise, you better see to it that he doesn't leave town," Lou said.

"But, how can I keep him from leaving if he wants to?" Nguyen asked meekly.

"Hey! That's your fuckin' problem. And another thing, make sure that our entire conversation stays private," Lou barked.

With that, he turned around and left. Nguyen Cong stood there, scratching his head.

CHAPTER NINETY-TWO
SHIVER ME TIMBERS

Pattie and Ryan sat in the front row toward the right side of the stage in the underground party room at Cosmo's. Pattie's long hair hung loose and she was dressed in black from her beret to her ballet slippers. Even her eyeliner was black. A solitary spotlight shone directly on an empty stool in the center of the stage, whose backdrop was a red, brick wall.

"You look really great tonight," Ryan said.

Pattie smiled.

"Thanks. I tried."

"Are you nervous?"

She nodded and cleared her throat.

"I haven't done any performance poetry since before I changed jobs. What if I get up there and forget everything? Or worse, what if I get a case of laryngitis at the exact moment I try to speak?"

Ryan smiled.

"Then you'll understand why I always urged you to take that mime class."

She smiled and swatted at him playfully.

"Very funny!"

He touched her wrist.

"Wow. Your pulse is racing. Seriously though, you'll be fine."

"I hope you're right."

"Of course, I'm right. I'm always right."

Dante Asmodeo appeared from out of nowhere. He was dressed in a black hoodie, black jeans, black cowboy boots and his mirrored sunglasses. He spotted Pattie and Ryan and approached their table. Pattie frowned, nudged Ryan and whispered in his ear.

"Oh God! What's he doing here?"

Ryan shrugged.

"I don't know," he whispered back.

"I've always wanted to know something. Technically speaking, is he a dwarf?"

Ryan chuckled.

"I don't know the answer to that either. Nobody knows anything about him."

Dante nodded at the two of them.

"You look beautiful tonight, Attorney Anwald."

Pattie cleared her throat.

"Thank you."

"What's going on?" Dante inquired.

Ryan smiled.

"Pattie's going on stage to perform her poetry in a few minutes," Ryan said, cordially.

"Well, shiver me timbers," Dante said.

As Pattie and Ryan looked at each other to figure out what Dante meant by that, Dante busied himself by dumping himself into a chair. Then he whipped out a lighter, lit the black candle on their table and reached for Pattie's stack of poems. He skimmed through them and looked up at Pattie.

"Always remember, my Dear, when you hit rock bottom, you need to stop digging; because at that point, the only place you can go from there is up," he said, slowly and without much animation.

Pattie cleared her throat.

"What? Are you trying to tell me that my performance is going to tank tonight?"

"No. It's just general advice for future reference. Don't ever think you have to thank me for it either," he said.

Pattie leaned over and whispered in Ryan's ear.

"He's making me really nervous."

Before Ryan could say anything, the lights went out and Cosmo took the stage to introduce Pattie. She stood, took a deep breath and went on stage, while the audience applauded.

Shiver me timbers is right, she thought.

Chapter Ninety-Three
ANGELS WITH DIRTY FACES

Leland LeRoux, after spending the evening at El Diablo's bar, turned the corner onto Christie Street and headed for home. It was raining, so he walked fast. A disheveled, homeless man in a moth-eaten overcoat was leaning up against a streetlight not far from his apartment. When Leland peered at the homeless man, he peered back at Leland and snapped the brim of his beat up gray fedora. Leland pretended to ignore him and fumbled for his key.

"Hey Buddy, that's some outrageous door you've got there," the homeless man said, in a tough New York accent.

Leland spun around, shoved his hand in his pocket and clenched his fist around the nails he had stolen from Nyguyen many months before. He pointed them through his pocket as if they were a gun.

"I ain't yer Buddy, ya dayum white trash dirt bayug, so buzz off and get the hell away from me--before I blow yer fuckin' lungs out," Leland snarled.

The homeless man held out a tiny spoon.

"Come on, give me a break here. I'm lost and my lighter's dead. Can't you spare me some heat?"

Leland opened his door, slipped through it and slammed himself inside. He double locked it, crept over to the window and peered out. He breathed a sigh of relief when the homeless man shuffled down the street.

Once he was around the corner and safe inside his unmarked police cruiser, Lou removed his fedora and coat.

"Yeah dispatch, this is Anwald. Can you pull up a rap sheet on any and all occupants living at 260 Christie Street?"

He turned the ignition and peeled out of his parking space.

Chapter Ninety-Four
THANKSGIVING EVE

It was quarter to five on the day before Thanksgiving and most of the people in the Courthouse just wanted to get home to start their Holiday Weekend. After Pattie's last case concluded, she glanced at her watch, struggled to lift her huge stack of files and rushed back to her office. It had been a long day and she was glad it was over. Her stack of files got heavier with each and every step she took and by the time she reached her office, her arms were aching. She couldn't wait to put the files down. When she walked into her office, she found Brad ransacking her desk. The contents of her drawers were strewn all over and mixed in with the trash from her upended waste paper basket. Her desktop was so cluttered with this debris, that there was no place for her to even put her files down. Sweat broke out on her forehead, as she finally decided to stack them with care on the visitor's chair. Then she cleared her throat, which caused Brad to look up and stop his rummaging. She gingerly removed the garbage can from her desk and placed it upright on the floor.

"Why are you going through my garbage can?"

Brad stopped his ransacking and shrugged.

"Why? What's it to you?"

She picked up her trench coat, which Brad had apparently flung onto the floor.

"Well, it's kind of weird."

Brad chuckled to himself, as if laughing at a private joke.

"Look who's talking about weirdness. Anyway, I hope you're ready for your six-month review."

"You mean now? On Thanksgiving Eve?"

"Well, I can't put it off too much longer. After all, you're dying of SARS Aren't you?"

"Oh, come on, Brad! That was just a joke."

"Oh yeah? Anyway, I don't believe you. I knew something was up with you, right from the very first day you used Ryan Pilgrim to claw your way in here."

She shook her head.

"What brought all of this on?"

"Listen Sweetheart, the list of bones I have to pick with you is endless, starting with the day you chose to side with that stupid black prostitute who cried rape against one of our own clients."

"You mean Cara Forrester?"

"Yeah. That's right. She's the one."

"I didn't 'side with her' against anyone. It's just that I felt bad about her circumstances."

"Well, then, that's siding with her. Then the next incompetent stunt you pulled was to lose your employee's strip."

"Big deal. I'm not the first one that did that!" She yelled in a voice so loud that she even surprised herself.

"Pipe down, you fucking nut! Don't go all postal on me or I'll call the laughing academy and have you locked up for the weekend and trust me Sweetheart, I can make that happen," he yelled back.

His face was beet red. Little pieces of spit formed in both corners of his mouth. Pattie chuckled nervously.

"Be careful, Brad. When they get here, they might end up carting you off instead. After all, you look and sound crazier than I do right now."

"Are you sure? Because you're the one everybody laughs at. I crack up every time I get a visual of you standing out there on line like a chooch and coming in here an hour late for work."

Pattie gasped.

"Oh really? Well then, if you find that amusing, you must be pretty sick."

"The funniest part about it was that you were too stupid to even figure out how to go around to the back of the courthouse and wait for someone to let you in. Anyone with a half a brain could have done that. You're so stupid you couldn't even figure out how to use your cell phone to call someone to come down and get you."

Pattie shook her head.

"I tried to, but Norton wouldn't let me!"

"Really? And I suppose it's his fault that you were kissing Toby Barnett's ass on that Guardian ad Litem case you've got going on?"

"Uh Brad, I thought I already explained that it's an old case from when I worked over at the Family Court."

"Well that hooker wasn't one of your old cases from the Family Court. You know, when I stop and think about it, you're always kissing the prosecutors' asses and taking their side against ours. What about that time you commiserated with Annie when she lost that Motion in Limine on the De Vittorio case?"

"Well, I really wasn't siding with her. I just happened to feel sorry for one of Judge De Vittorio's under aged victims, who also happened to be a client of mine at the Family Court."

"Listen Sweetheart, it's always about you and your God damn Family Court! You have all the sympathy in the world for everyone on the other side, but you treat our clients like dog shit, especially when they're senior citizens. And let me tell you something else, you're gonna go to hell for the way you treated that poor old man."

"Which poor old man?"

He tilted his head at her and his eyes popped.

"Don't you remember that old man you sicked Leland LeRoux on, when he asked you to notarize his financial affidavit?"

Pattie sighed.

"Believe me, I never sicked Leland LeRoux on anybody. I just so happened to be in the conference room with Leland when the guy barged in and started badgering me."

"Yeah, right. Now you listen to me, Sweetheart. Do you know what happens to old people when you sick the likes of Leland LeRoux on them? They have heart attacks and fucking die!"

"Well, if I'm as big a problem as you claim, why have you waited until now to bring all of these so-called blunders to my attention?"

"Because I'm a patient soul who gave you every opportunity to straighten yourself out, but now I'm at the end of my rope. And while we're on the subject of your blunders and shortcomings, let's not forget that unauthorized three-day vacation you gave yourself last summer."

"Vacation? Oh, my God Brad, I've never taken any vacation. I happened to be in the hospital recovering from smoke inhalation as a result of the fire in my building!"

Brad nodded.

"Yeah, well, you probably set the damn thing yourself so that you that could go and fuck around on some nude beach with that British boyfriend you snatched right out from under Annie! And I guess you thought that getting The Police Department to call in sick for you gave it some stamp of legitimacy, but I have news for you Sweetheart, it didn't."

Pattie looked shocked.

"I can't believe you're even twisting things like this. First of all, you tell me that I'm buddying up to Annie and then in the next breath you accuse me of stealing her boyfriend. And oh, by the way, that cop who called in sick for me wasn't calling in any official capacity. He just so happens to be my brother."

"And that's another thing, Sweetheart. You work in an office where cops arrest our very clients. Meanwhile you're related to them."

"So?"

"Well, to my way of thinking that just screams conflict of interest! So, even if you didn't have any of the other countless defects I called you out on, that one thing alone gives me enough grounds to terminate you."

"I want to know why you're deliberately trying to sabotage my career, Doll Face."

"Hey! What's up with the Doll Face bit?"

"Well, I'm calling you Doll Face, since you keep calling me 'Sweetheart'. I mean if calling people cutsie belittling nicknames will help me to fit in here better, then I'll just have to get with the program, starting right now."

"I can call you whatever I want, Sweetheart and no you'll never fit in, which is my exact point. In other words, I think you need to quit," he said.

Pattie's hands were shaking. but Brad couldn't see them, because she was still holding her trench coat.

"No, Brad. I'm not falling for any of this. I won't quit and you can't fire me either, because I have rights. How dare you try to violate my rights, impugn my integrity as a person and destroy my professional reputation with nothing more than a bunch of trumped up charges and vicious, irrelevant slander?"

With that, she picked up her briefcase and ran out. Brad chased her. When they reached Ceil 's desk, Brad stood there panting, with his hands on his hips, but Pattie kept running. She opened the door that led to the waiting room and ran through it.

"What's going on?" Ceil asked.

He waved his hand in disgust.

"That God damn nut! I mean if she wanted to quit that badly she could have simply handed me a letter of resignation. Why go through all of this drama, especially on the eve of a holiday?"

He returned to his office, slammed the door and slid Millard's application out from underneath his blotter. He reviewed it, smiled and picked up the phone. In the meantime, Pattie ran down several flights of stairs, through the main lobby and out past Norton Bakerman. Once she got outside, she stopped running, put her raincoat on and began her half mile trek home.

CHAPTER NINETY-FIVE
A COKE AND A SMILE

Annie was the only one left in the District Attorney's office. Everyone else had left for the weekend. Once she was sure she was alone, she grabbed her briefcase, closeted herself in Connor Dane's office and locked the door. She eased herself into the folds of his chair, leaned back and ruminated about some vague time in the future when she would sit here for real. Eventually, she dozed off until a series of knocks interrupted her reverie and caused her to sit upright.

"Who's there?"

"The candy man."

She stood, straightened out her clothes and walked over to the door. She unlocked it and opened it a crack.

"Did everybody finally go home?"

Norton Bakerman nodded.

"Uh huh. Except for us."

Annie smiled.

"Good. So, I hope you brought me some candy."

Norton grinned and nodded.

"I sure did. A Colombian dude tried to smuggle some really good shit through the metal detector and now it's ours."

"Oh Goody."

"You know, it's not like me to just show up naked."

Annie chuckled.

"No. That part comes later."

"Listen, are you gonna let me in or what?"

She opened the door all the way. When he came in, he put his arms around her and walked her backwards until she was up against the wall. He kissed her collarbone and gradually worked his way up the nape of her neck. When he reached her mouth, he jammed his tongue as far down her throat as he could and they French kissed for almost a minute.

"Any gossip or anything I need to know about?" Annie asked, when they broke up the kiss.

He shook his head.

"Not really, except Anwald ran out of the building at five o'clock, like a house on fire."

Annie waved her hand in dismissal and sunk back into Connor's chair.

"Ugh. I didn't think SARS patients could run. Don't they get winded? Or something?"

Norton nodded and chuckled.

"One can only hope."

Annie removed a small, rectangular mirror from her briefcase and placed it face up on Connor's desk, while Norton reached into his pocket, pulled out a glassine bag and tore it open. He tapped a chunk of chalky white powder onto the mirror, pulled a razor blade out of his pocket and chopped the powder as finely as he could. After that, he used the edge of the razor to sweep it into a thin, straight line.

She reached down, pulled a twenty dollar bill out of her briefcase and rolled it into the shape of a homemade straw. She stuck it into her right nostril, thrust her head down and sniffed the entire line in one fell swoop. She sighed, eased back into the chair and waited for the rush to kick in. When it did, she nodded and grinned.

"This really is some shit of distinction," she said.

He grinned at her, sprinkled some more powder onto the mirror and chopped it up. She leaned forward, snorted the line with her left nostril and giggled. He prepared two lines for himself, took the twenty-dollar bill and snorted them.

"God it's stuffy in here," he said.

Annie nodded. Her nostrils were red and they had a powdery residue around them. Mucous dripped from them.

"I know. I don't get why the windows in this place have to be so hermetically sealed," she said.

"I don't know either. Let's get the hell out of here. This whole scene is giving me claustrophobia."

"Why?"

"Because if anyone ever catches us, we're through," Norton said.

"I thought you just said we've got the place to ourselves. Besides, I have more at stake than you do. So, if I can hang tough, why can't you?"

Norton scratched his head.

CHAPTER NINETY-SIX
IT'S ALL TOO MUCH

Pattie was almost home when the sky suddenly turned battleship gray and let loose a torrent of rain that drenched her. She tried to hail a taxi, but the minute the driver spotted her, he turned his off duty sign on and sped away. By the time she reached her apartment building, she was soaking wet and chilled to the bone. Her hair hung around her in wet strings and her mascara and eyeliner were smudged. She opened the door, stepped inside the little vestibule and thanked God that she was finally out of the deluge. She stamped her feet, shook herself off as best she could and stopped to collect her mail. She tensed up when she heard the outside door open behind her. When she turned around, she realized that it was Jody Flynn, a process server she sometimes used at work.

"Hi Jody! What are you doing here? I don't have any papers for you to serve."

Jody handed her a set of papers.

"I know, Hon. You got it backwards. Pattie Anwald, it's 5:40 p. m. and I'm serving you."

He watched, while she pored over the papers. Little by little, as she read them, the color drained from her face. Finally, the papers slid through her fingertips and landed on the dirty tile floor.

"Why?"

Jody shrugged.

"Hey, these are trying times. Life lesson? In the end, it's best not to take anything too personally."

"Well of course I'm taking it personally."

"I know you are. That's why I'm telling you not to."

"Well, why shouldn't I? After all it's my name on the Eviction Notice."

"Yeah, but it doesn't really involve you. Arvid's just following his lawyer's advice to take advantage of a once in a lifetime business opportunity."

"Which is?"

"My God, don't you read the newspapers? Manhattan real estate prices have skyrocketed. As a result, Mayor Mike figured he'd close the Fish Market at the end of 2005 and move it up to a brand-new location in the Bronx," Jody explained.

"And?"

"And with no noise or fish stink, that automatically upgrades the entire neighborhood and everything in it, including this old dump. That's why Arvid decided to kick all of youse low lifes outta here and use the insurance settlement he got from the fire to gut the joint and sell the units off as individual loft type condos. He's even lined up European craftsmen to renovate it, in keeping with the neighborhood's original look."

Pattie squinted.

"Excuse me, but did you just call me a low life?"

Jody shook his head and chuckled.

"No. Once again, you're taking everything way too personally. Everyone knows you're a silk purse."

Just then, the girl with the porcine face and European accent, clickety clacked down the stairs in her kitten heeled slippers with their Marabou trim. Her bright green and yellow wrap around dress draped her exquisitely shaped body and showcased her curves. Her face was made up, her shoulder length hair was smooth and sleek and she smoked a Gauloise. Next to her, Pattie looked like a little drenched water rat. Once her cigarette smoke clogged up the vestibule, Pattie tried to wave it away. The girl stared at Pattie and frowned.

"Hey, you look like some kind of a raccoon," she said. Then she turned her full attention to Jody.

"If you're here to serve the Eviction Notices, you may as well serve me mine. It's only a formality in my case, because I'll just keep moving from one apartment to the other during the renovation."

"See? Now that's the way to look at it. If everyone looked at it this way, my life would be a hell of a lot easier," Jody said to Pattie.

"I don't believe this. How come you're getting the option to live here and I'm not?" Pattie asked.

The girl dragged on her Gauloise and answered Pattie on the exhale.

"Because I'm one of the architects on the project. When the renovation is complete, my parents will send me the money to put a down payment on the loft of my choice and then they will come over here and live with me. After all, this is waterfront property," she said.

She bent down, picked up Pattie's crumbled Eviction Notice and gingerly placed it on top of Pattie's other mail.

"Hey! Maybe you should have gone in for Architecture, instead of Law," Jody said.

"So, anyway Sis, what's your name?" He asked the girl.

"Tereza Novak."

Jody rustled through his paperwork.

"Tereza Novak, it's 5:45 and you have been served," he said.

Pattie felt a numbness creep over her, as if she were a deer caught in a pair of headlights. She turned and ran up the stairs, without even saying good bye.

"Hey, Happy Thanksgiving!" Jody called after her cheerfully.

"Yeah, right," she muttered.

When she reached her landing, she unlocked the new metal door that Arvid had installed for her, threw the Eviction Notice and the other mail onto her table and placed her briefcase against the wall. She looked at the streaks of harsh, dirty rainwater that had ruined it, shook her head and went into the bathroom and stripped. She threw her wet garments over the shower rack, blew her nose, and removed what was left of her makeup. Then she washed her face and towel dried her hair. She combed it into place, changed into a track suit and flopped into a chair. She picked up her mail, tore into one of the other envelopes and read the contents. Shaking her head again, she got up, walked over to her briefcase and pulled out her cell phone. She returned to the table with it and used its calculator function to crunch a series of numbers.

"Great," she mumbled.

A knock on the door startled her.

"What now"? She snapped.

"It's Jordan, Love."

She tossed the papers and the calculator onto the table, ran to the door and opened it. Jordan was standing there, holding a huge basket of fruit from Top Cat Epicures.

"Oh hi. Come on in," she said.

He entered the apartment.

"I'm sorry to pop in on you this way. Anyway, this is for you," he said, as he handed her the fruit basket.

She brought the basket over to the table.

"Wow! Thank you! Out of season peaches and everything."

He smiled.

"You're welcome. I hope you'll enjoy them."

"Oh, I will."

"How are you tonight?"

"Don't ask. I've had a really rough day."

Jordan picked up a strand of her wet hair and let it fall.

"Rougher than usual?"

She flopped back into her chair and nodded.

"In a word, yes. Anyway, have a seat."

"You poor thing. Seeing you with wet hair like this reminds me of the night we first met. Perhaps I should have bought you an umbrella instead fruit."

"Actually, the fruit is perfect. In any case, I hope you're having a better day than I am."

Jordan smiled and nodded.

"I suspect I might be. Now that I'm here, I need to run an important question past you. I received a wedding invitation from my friend Clint in Florida and I'd like to attend."

"When is it?"

"Well, they didn't give their wedding guests much notice. It's going to take place on the first Saturday in December, which is only ten days from now."

"You're right. That really is short notice."

"I know, but I'm hoping that you'll accompany me anyway."

She shook her head.

"I can't."

"I had a feeling you'd say that. I had another thought too. What if we finally put Kevin's guest passes to use and just hit the road this weekend?"

"Wow. That's even shorter notice."

"All right. I admit that, but sometimes it's fun to be spontaneous. Wouldn't you agree?"

She shook her head.

"No. I wouldn't, but I have a few ideas of my own. Why don't you just go up there with Anne Carey? And while you're at it, you can take her to your friend's wedding too!"

He knit his brow.

"Who's Anne Carey?"

"Don't you dare play dumb with me!" Pattie yelled.

"I really don't understand what you're talking about Pattie."

"Stop it! Stop it! Stop it," she yelled.

His face turned red. He walked over to her and grasped her by her shoulders.

"I'm beginning to wonder whether you're crazy," he said.

His words sounded crisp and harsh, like ice cubes falling into a glass. She shook her head vehemently. When a strand of hair fell into her eyes, he gently reached out to brush it back. Thinking that he was reaching out to strike her, she ducked back as if to fend off a blow. Then she wrapped her arms around his neck and maneuvered him into a chokehold. He winced, pushed her elbow out of his way and deftly extricated himself. He stared at her and pushed his arm against her shoulder to hold her at bay for several seconds. Then he shook his head, dropped his arm and stormed out of the apartment. She ran out after him and watched him race down the stairs, while Gladys opened her rickety old wooden door, popped her head out, and spied on Pattie.

CHAPTER NINETY-SEVEN
SONG OF DEFEAT

Pattie locked herself inside her apartment, pressed her face against the new mirror that Ryan had installed for her and reached out to her reflection with both hands. When that feeble attempt to comfort herself failed, she slid to the floor and wept for several minutes. When she was finished, she stood, walked over to the table and called Jordan.

"Jordan, I think we need to talk about this. Why do you always run away whenever things don't suit you? Please call me back as soon as you get this message, no matter how late it is!"

Then she hung up and called Ryan. When he didn't pick up either, she burst into tears, cried into his voicemail and hung up without leaving a message. She snapped her phone shut, collapsed into her folding chair and tried to process the day's events. By the time she had convinced herself that she would end up jobless and homeless, someone knocked on her door. She got up, ran over to it and found Ryan standing there with a worried look on his face. He was dressed in a hoodie and jeans and he was holding a dripping umbrella. She pulled him into the apartment, kicked the door shut and stood his umbrella against the mirror. When he removed his hoodie she hung it over the back of a chair to dry.

"I heard you crying. What's going on?"

"Oh, Ryan, you know the saying 'when it rains it pours'?"

Ryan nodded and pointed at his umbrella.

"Yeah. How could I not?"

"Do you want some coffee or fruit?"

"Sure. I'll take a black coffee if you've got it."

She nodded.

"Sit down while I make it," she said.

He sat and watched her brew the coffee.

"So, tell me what's going on," he said, when she joined him at the table.

"Everything. First of all, when I woke up this morning, I realized that today is the six month anniversary of my client Justin's disappearance."

Ryan shook his head.

"Wow. Really?"

She nodded.

"Yes and it's like everyone but me has forgotten about him. At this point even I'm beginning to think that he might never come back."

"Oh, come on now. Don't give up hope. You've got to believe that he'll come back."

"I want to. Did I ever tell you that the very first day I made that motion to have him evaluated, his parents followed me out of the courthouse, surrounded me on the street and told me that they put a curse on me?"

Ryan looked shocked.

"You're kidding!"

"I wish I were, but I'm not. They said that I would never know a minute's peace as long as the case was pending against them."

Ryan waved his hand dismissively.

"Well, they probably only said that to scare you."

"Well then, they succeeded, because it's happening. The truth is that I really haven't known a minute's peace ever since they said it."

"Well, I don't believe in curses. I only believe in prayer."

"Then pray for me, Ryan. Pray really, really hard and pray for Justin too. Pray that he gets found alive and well."

Ryan nodded.

"You know I will. Starting tonight."

"Thanks."

She cleared her throat, rifled through the pile of mail on her table and handed him a piece of paper.

"Here. Read this and weep," she said.

He scanned it and looked up at her.

"Wow! A love letter from the student loan people. They're claiming that you owe them two hundred twenty seven thousand dollars!"

She nodded.

"Yup."

Then she handed him her Eviction Notice. He read it and shook his head.

"Wow. What did you do? Forget to pay your rent or something?"

"No. No matter what else went on, Arvid always got his money on time and I never broke any rules either. Yet, this is what I get in return for being a good tenant."

"What a guy. In any case, I can't say I blame you for being upset."

Pattie went on to explain his plans for the building.

"Wow. The fire happening just when the neighborhood finally skyrocketed in value is really too much of a coincidence."

She nodded.

"That's right and you know I don't believe in those."

"Neither do I. It sounds like arson to me."

"Actually, since he knows his way around the building, he had opportunity too. As I learned in Law School, motive and opportunity are the two necessary components for the commission of any crime."

"Well, did you call that guy Charlie over at the Fire Department and tell him about it?"

She shook her head.

"No. Not yet. I only got served an hour ago."

"Well, I hope you call him on Friday and while you're at it, be sure to tell your brother too."

"The only problem with our theory is that Jody said Arvid is using the insurance money to foot the bill for the renovations. I don't think the insurance company would have paid out on a claim where they suspected foul play."

"Well, just because he didn't get caught, it doesn't mean he's innocent."

Pattie nodded.

"You're right and what gets my goat even more is that he's making out like a bandit while I'm on the verge of homelessness. After all, I not only got burned. I got permanent lung damage."

Ryan nodded.

"Wow. It sounds like he got the elevator and you got the shaft. However, you can't get a pay out if you didn't make a claim."

"I didn't think to make one. After all, my medical insurance paid the hospital."

"Yeah, but you're not thinking like a lawyer here. You just got through saying that you suffered permanent lung damage."

Pattie nodded.

"You're right. Also, one of my neighbors was so scared, she ended up having a heart attack."

"That's horrible. Is she OK?"

Pattie nodded.

"Yes, so far."

"Well, that's at least good. But what about the three days when you were displaced because of the smoke? You should add everything up, sue for it and include your hotel bill as part of the law suit."

"I didn't have a hotel bill. I was in the hospital for the entire three days."

"Oh yeah. That's right. Anyway, do you have any idea where you will move to?"

She shook her head.

"No. I just hope I don't end up living out on the street."

"That will never happen. As a matter of fact, I just came up with another one of my stellar ideas! How well do you get along with Reginald Reese?"

She nodded.

"Pretty well, I guess. He once gave me his card and told me to save it for a rainy day."

"Well take a look around. I doubt it can get much rainier than this. Besides, nobody can shake the money out of a situation the way he can."

"Really? I thought he only did Criminal Law."

"Hell no. He's great at any kind of litigation. If I were you I'd call him first thing Monday morning and run the whole scenario past him."

Pattie nodded.

"I will."

"He can probably hold up the student loan people and your eviction process too, but the real pay dirt will be your lawsuit."

"Well, as you know I'm not a materialistic person."

"I know, but extra money always comes in handy when people need consolation and right now it's safe to say that you need some serious consolation."

Pattie nodded.

"You don't even know the half of it. I've got other problems I haven't even brought up yet."

"For instance?"

"Well, like Brad, for instance."

"Why? What did he do now?"

"Well, his hatred of me has finally reached a new crescendo or should I say a crush endo?"

"What happened?"

"He staged a huge, ugly fight with me a week and a half ago and then he staged another one again today right at five o'clock. He accused me of being crazy and then he threatened to call the men in the little white coats to come and take me away. What was weird was that he was the one who was actually starting to become unglued."

"What an asshole."

"I know, but my nerves are so shot at this point that part of me wonders whether he's actually right."

"Of course, he's not right and what's more, he knows it. He's just gaslighting you. Don't let him."

She nodded.

"He had me so nuts that I'm not sure whether he ended up firing me or not. He talked about it, but he never actually came out and said it, so I don't even know whether I'm supposed to return to work on Monday or whether I should just report straight to unemployment."

"This is disturbing. I guess the best thing to do is to call in sick and then report straight to Reginald Reese. He'll tell you what to do next."

Pattie nodded.

"Good idea. Thank God, you're my friend. By the way, at one point Brad was so out of control, that he actually accused me of setting fire to this place in order to spend time a nude beach, with quote unquote the British guy I snatched out from under Annie."

Ryan chuckled.

"Snatched out from under? He may be a whacko, but if nothing else, he sure knows how to turn a phrase. Anyhow, I didn't know that Jordan used to date Annie."

"Neither did I and when I brought it up to Jordan, we got into a fight and that's when I got called crazy for the second time today."

"Pattie, do you love Jordan?"

She stood, walked toward the coffee maker and poured Ryan's coffee. Then she carried it back to him and flounced into her chair.

"I'm absolutely in love with the guy."

Ryan sipped his coffee and pondered the situation.

"Well then, stop fighting with him all the time and if it turns out that he was with Annie in the past, so what? She's was his past. You're his future," he said.

"Do you think it's possible that he could be two timing us both in the present?"

"Pattie, I have no reason to give that guy the benefit of the doubt, but I will, because I honestly believe he deserves it."

"Ryan, I lost everything in my life today, except for you and my car."

"I don't think that's true, although it's obvious you're over-whelmed, so it probably seems that way to you. I think you need to take something to soothe your jangled nerves. Do you have any anti-anxiety medicine in the house?"

She shook her head.

"I used to have a bottle of pain killers from when I had my root canal, but my mother stole it."

"Jesus. Why would she snag your pain killers?"

"She said she needed it to add to her collection."

Ryan frowned.

"Her collection of what?"

"Of antidepressants, anti-anxiety pills and pain killers."

He shook his head.

"Why does she collect them?"

"So, she can grind them all up, mix them together with sea salt and line the rim of her margarita glass."

Ryan laughed nervously.

"Holy crap! With all that you'd think she'd have a more mellow disposition."

Pattie nodded.

"Yes. In a perfect world that would be the case, but as we all know, she doesn't."

"Well, do you at least have some sleeping pills?"

She shook her head.

"No. I don't even have aspirin. Actually, I wish I did because I have a migraine right now."

"If I were you I'd put them at the top of your grocery list," he said, as he drained his coffee cup.

She nodded, stood and walked behind his chair.

"I know. Anyway, it's Thanksgiving Eve and you belong with your family."

He stood and turned toward her.

"Are you kicking me out?"

She shook her head.

"Don't think of it that way."

"Why the sudden need to be alone?"

"Because misery really doesn't always love company. It's hell on friendships and besides, I want to sleep off this migraine."

"Well, what if I told you that I don't feel right about leaving you alone right now?"

She walked over to his hoodie and umbrella and handed them to him.

"I'd tell you not to worry about me."

"Then, why can't I stay here a little longer?"

She sighed.

"You can, if you want to, but I really just want to lie down right now."

He put his hoodie and umbrella down, hugged her and turned out the light. As soon as she went to bed, he poured himself another cup of coffee and then sat in the dark and drank it.

CHAPTER NINETY EIGHT
CHOKE HOLD

A series of knocks startled Pattie out of her sleep. She stumbled out of bed, opened the door and jumped for joy at the sight of Jordan. She fell into his arms, but when they kissed, his lips were so dry and scaly she opened her eyes. Horrors! She wasn't kissing Jordan at all! She was staring into the face of Leland LeRoux! She pushed him away in disgust and watched, as he coughed up a wad of vile green sputum. She grabbed his throat. It felt so good to squeeze and knead his leathery flesh. She blinked and within a split second, Leland had turned into her mother. She quickly recoiled and let go of Edie's throat and Edie pointed at her.

"Look at you! You're no better than your own worst criminal," she brayed.

Then she broke into gales of laughter that were so loud; they jolted Pattie out of her sleep. Pattie's heart was racing, but her migraine from the night before still gripped her head like vise. She sighed, sat up and swung her legs out of bed. She found her robe, slipped into it and dragged herself over to the window. The sky was one gigantic storm cloud that blocked the sunlight completely. As a result, even when she turned her light on, her apartment looked more desolate than ever.

She picked up her cell phone and checked the time. It was ten after seven. She checked her voice mail. No messages. She sat at the table and switched on her laptop. Nothing from Jordan nor anyone else. Apparently even the email spammers had decided to take the day off. A few seconds later she heard a ding. Someone had just sent her an instant message!

Mnaghten730: Good morning & Happy Thanksgiving!

Blanche: Happy Thanksgiving back 2 u.

Mnaghten730: I hope u don't mind, but I left soon after u fell asleep.

Blanche: I don't mind. I think u did the right thing.

Mnaghten730: Good. How r u doing? R u OK?

Blanche: Yes. I still have the migraine tho.

Mnaghten730: Did u hear from Jordan?

Blanche: No. I just woke up.

Mnaghten730: I'm so sorry u r going thru so much right now. Try not 2 worry. OK?

Blanche: I promise I'll only worry a little. How are u?

Mnaghten730: Tired but otherwise good. I didn't get very much sleep. Did u?

Blanche: Yes, complete with nightmares and everything.

Mnaghten730: Pick up your phone when it rings. It will be me. It's easier for me 2 talk than 2 type.

About ten seconds later, Pattie's cell phone rang. She picked it up on the first ring.

"Hey," she said, in a flat affect.

"I came up with another caper that you might like even better than our last one," Ryan said.

Pattie smiled.

"I still laugh whenever I think of that last one. Norton Bakerman will never be the same."

Ryan chuckled.

"That was an all-time classic, even if I do say so myself. Anyway, here goes. If you don't hear from Jordan by Monday morning, dress yourself up to the nines, barge into his office and refuse to leave until you and he straighten out everything that's gone wrong between you."

Pattie sighed.

"Oh Ryan, that's the kind of thing he does whenever we have a fight."

"Yeah well, obviously it works. Right? Except this time, you'll beat him to the punch."

"I guess I could try it. At this point I have nothing to lose."

"My other thought is that you should spend Thanksgiving with my family and me."

"I think it's better for me to spend the day with my own family, although I would like to stop by and have coffee and dessert with you. How does that sound?"

"Cool. I'll tell my mother to expect you around seven, but I'll also keep my phone on in case you need me before then."

CHAPTER NINETY-NINE
KNOCKOUT

Since it was Thanksgiving, Leland LeRoux decided to wear a clean pair of khaki pants and a brand-new navy blue and beige T-shirt. He picked up a baseball cap, placed it on his head in a jaunty style and opened his door ever so slightly. He peered out furtively with his left eye, then stuck his entire head out so that he could sniff the crisp Thanksgiving air. He checked to see if anyone was watching him and when he was sure that he had the street to himself, he stepped outside, closed the door behind himself and used his key to double bolt the lock. He shoved his key into his pocket and hurried over to Nguyen's warehouse. Before entering, he peered over his shoulder to see whether any one had followed him. No one. Good.

"Nguyen?" He called out as he walked down the hall.

Nguyen was annoyed when he heard Leland's voice. That cop had done such a thorough job of intimidating him, he realized that he had no choice but to drop what he was doing and comply with his demands. The question was how. He went out into the hall to find out.

"What do you want?" Nguyen barked, when he saw Leland.

"I hate to bother ya, this bein' Thanksgivin' and all, but I'm afraid Ima have to ax you fer some cash. I'm in a kinda hurry too. I need ta git goin' and pick up my nephew from outta town."

Nguyen shook his head.

"Don't worry, I'll get it for you, but why you wait til the last minute, when you know it's a holiday?"

"I dunno. I git absent minded sometimes, I guess."

Leland paced while Nguyen went back into his office. Finally, after what felt like an eternity Nguyen returned with a handful of cash and a sly expression on his face. The cash slipped out of his hand and floated to the floor. Leland shot him a dirty look, as he lunged down to retrieve it. His claw like fingers had no sooner entwined themselves around it, when Nguyen pulled a .38 caliber pistol from out of his back pocket and used it to crack Leland's skull. Leland's knees buckled and he dropped down to the floor. Nguyen snatched the money, shoved it into his pocket and ran back to his office. A few minutes later he returned with some rope and tied Leland up.

Chapter One Hundred

BREAKFAST IN BED

Lou was in an uncharacteristically cheerful mood, as he yawned, stretched and luxuriated in bed. He thanked his lucky stars, because, in spite of his lack of seniority, through some miracle, he managed to get the holiday off with pay and he intended to savor every minute of it. His cell phone rang, right when he was toying with the idea of getting Edie to make him her Special Holiday French Toast. When Nguyen's name and number popped up on his caller ID, he sprang to attention.

"What?" He snarled into the phone.

"This is Nguyen Cong Duc. Lerand Leroux is here now," he whispered.

Shit.

"Well, just make sure he doesn't leave before I get there," Lou snapped.

Nguyen muttered something in his native tongue, but instead of responding, Lou hung up, bolted out of bed and threw on some clothes. He decided not to bother shaving, but he quickly raked a comb through his buzz cut, strapped on his gun and gathered his wallet. Almost as an afterthought he remembered to take his badge and key ring, which included the duplicate key to Leland's apartment. When he stepped out into the chilly, gray morning, the fox terrier next door ran up to the iron railing and gave him a thorough tongue lashing. Ignoring him, Lou locked his door, ran over to his custom purple pickup truck and peeled out of his parking space with a screech.

CHAPTER ONE HUNDRED ONE
MY HEART'S IN THE HIGHLANDS

Even though Jordan looked sporty in his black cashmere pullover, gray woolen pants and high end mountain boots, he didn't feel sporty at all. As a matter of fact, he felt like a zombie, who was moving in slow motion. He closed his suitcase, whipped out his cell phone and called Clint. Feigning cheeriness, he wished Clint's voicemail a Happy Thanksgiving. Not knowing what to say after that, he simply shrugged and hung up. Just as he was about to stuff the phone into his coat pocket, the candid shot he had taken of Pattie back at the South Street Seaport, popped up onto his screen. Wishing to exorcise all memories of her, he sighed. He put Kevin's passes in his wallet, threw his coat on and picked up his baggage. Then he retrieved his golf clubs from the closet, locked the door and left.

He was pleasantly surprised when the clerk at the car rental agency accepted his UK driver's license without any hassles. He stashed his golf bag and luggage in the trunk and once he got used to the idea of driving on the right-hand side of the road, he was on his way.

CHAPTER ONE HUNDRED TWO
FAMILY TIES

Ryan's extended family occupied an entire five story building on the Southeast corner of Ninth Avenue and West Fifty Fourth Street. Pilgrim Hardware, the family business, took up the entire ground floor. Ryan's parents lived in the comfortable apartment which spanned the entire second floor. Ryan's sister Wendy, her husband, Joe and their three children, Melanie aged eight, Susie, aged five and little two-and-a-half-year-old Christopher, occupied the third floor. Ryan's brother, Zachary rattled around on the fourth floor by himself and Ryan, who inhabited the top floor, found it inconvenient that this "Hell's Kitchen Building" had no elevator.

He finished dressing, grabbed his cell phone in case Pattie called and descended the three flights of stairs that led to his parents' apartment. He went straight back to his mother's cozy kitchen, knowing that he would find her there. As he walked down the hall, he tried to identify the homey aromas that tantalized his nostrils. He could identify vanilla cookies, apple and pumpkin pies and cinnamon scents, along with nutmeg, turkey and the unmistakable aroma of his mother's fresh, home baked bread. It all smelled like home to him. He found his mother at the kitchen sink, peeling carrots in a lilac silk dress, pearls and an apron. He walked up to her and kissed her on the cheek. She smiled, wiped her hands on her apron and hugged her youngest child.

"God, it smells great in here! I can't wait until dinner time," he said, as he grabbed a raw carrot.

"Thank you. What happened to you this morning? Didn't you wake up in time to make it to church?"

"Actually, I did, but I wound up talking to Pattie instead," he said, as he crunched the carrot.

"Oh really? How is she doing?"

He shook his head.

"Not very well. I'm concerned about her. She's about to get kicked out of her apartment," he said, when he finished the bite of his carrot.

"Oh, that's terrible. I will put the poor little thing on my prayer list so that she can come up with a way to pay her rent."

"Now wait a minute. You're connecting the dots all wrong here by making it sound like she messed up and failed to pay her rent, when that isn't the case at all. Do you see the way rumors get started?"

"You're right. I'm sorry. So, then why is she getting kicked out?"

"Because her landlord wants to turn the building into condos."

His mother looked surprised.

"Are you kidding? Who in their right mind would ever be crazy enough to buy one?"

"It's amazing what people will waste good money on these days. Anyhow, I think we should invite Pattie to come here and live here with us. After all, we certainly have enough room to accommodate her."

She frowned.

"Ryan, you know that won't work."

"Why not? She's a good person who's going through a bad time."

"Have you discussed this with her yet?"

"Of course not. I wanted to run it past you first."

"Good. By now you should know now that you can't live under this roof with someone you're not married to."

"Didn't you ever watch 'Three's Company'?"

"No. It reminded me too much of Sodom and Gomorra. Besides, all that Hollywood stuff has little to do with real life."

"Well, why don't I talk to Zachary about moving in with him so that I can give my apartment to Pattie?"

"You're really determined to do this. Aren't you?"

He nodded.

"Yes. I am. What's the point of going to church and trying to be a good person if you don't put the teachings to good use in real life? The spiritual life shouldn't just be some theory."

"Well, you have a point there. Zachary's at church. You can talk to him later and see how he feels about having you as his roommate."

Ryan smiled and gave her a kiss on the cheek.

"Thanks. By the way, Pattie may stop by for dessert later."

"Well then, go inside and prepare another dessert setting."

Smiling, he went into the dining room and placed Pattie's dessert setting on the sideboard. Afterwards, he went into the family room, sat on the piano bench and checked the ringer on his cell phone to make sure that it was turned on. When his mother called him back into the kitchen, he left it on the piano bench and went in to see what she wanted.

CHAPTER ONE HUNDRED THREE
TIES THAT BIND

Lou parked his truck around the corner from Christie Street and headed straight for Leland's apartment. He was relieved to see that the street was deserted, because he didn't want anyone to witness what he was about to do. The search warrant hadn't come through yet, a delay that would no doubt be blamed on the holiday, Lou thought. He drew his gun, shook his head at the sight of Leland's outrageous door and tried to open it. When he discovered that it was locked, he used Leland's key to unlock it. Then he turned the door handle ever so slightly and opened it without making a sound. Once he was inside, a vile stench, consisting of mold, bad body odor, urine and excrement, assaulted his nostrils. He gagged, whipped out a handkerchief and shoved it over his nose to keep himself from vomiting.

With his sidearm at the ready, he tiptoed around to see whether any one else was in the apartment. When he was sure he was alone, he returned to the living room, whipped out his cell phone and took pictures of the debris that covered every horizontal surface in the apartment. As he was saving the pictures, he heard what sounded like a whimper coming from behind a door and frowned.

How could I have been stupid enough to overlook a door that was in plain sight?

He walked over to the door and jerked it open. It turned out to be a closet. The concentrated stench of stale urine, vomit and old blood hit his nostrils so hard that he jumped back. Two mice squeaked, scurried out and ran into a hole in the living room wall. Lou shuddered, turned his flashlight on and directed it into the closet.

A ghostly pale preteen boy was bound to the pole above him with braided, gray, leather-like strands. Filthy from head to toe, he was shaking with terror and the smells from his scalp, body and shoulder length hair, all added to the obnoxious odor in the closet. He wore dirty jeans and a t-shirt that he had long since outgrown. His hair hung over his eyes and because he was bare-foot, it was easy for Lou to spot the scratches and bite marks that covered his ankles and feet. Some of them had already healed, leaving scars in their wake, but most of them were surrounded by swollen red bumps and rashes.

Underneath his feet, was a crude hand painted pentagram inside a circle. When Lou aimed his flashlight to get a better look at it, he noticed that three plastic storage boxes had been stacked against the wall. He picked one up, opened it and found dozens of tiny pointed skulls and bones. Underneath them was a list of dates indicating when they had been placed in the storage box. Another box contained a pile of grayish brown fur pelts and the last box contained rows and rows of long, tapering, leather like strands, just like the ones that bound the boy. The list inside revealed that they were rat tails.

Lou shuddered as a second wave of nausea overcame him. He pushed the boy's hair away to get a glimpse of his face. Duct tape had been stretched tightly over his mouth and he had the faded remains of a black eye. Lou took a picture of the boy and the pentacle, as well as the contents of the storage containers and their corresponding lists. Finally, he removed a knife from his utility belt, hacked hacked through the braided rat tails and turned around to walk toward the sink. As soon as he turned his back, he heard the boy running toward the door. He spun around and pointed his gun at the ceiling.

"Stop! I'm a cop!"

The boy froze in place. He was shaking and both of his knees buckled. He lunged for the wall and used it to support himself. He peered up at Lou in terror, as Lou went over to him, grabbed his arm and flashed his badge.

Lou walked him over to the sink and gagged for a third time when he saw a dead rat and a clot of dried sputum festering next to it in the sink. He jerked his head away, forced himself to regain his composure and then crouched down to open the cabinet door under the sink. He looked for a bottle of hydrogen peroxide, so that he could pull the boy's gag off with a minimum of pain. He saw a brown bottle next to a bottle of pills that had been prescribed to Leland from the jailhouse dispensary six months before. He opened it and counted eleven pills. He closed it, stuck it in his pocket and poured some of the contents of the brown bottle over his left index finger. He licked it gingerly. Relieved to discover that it was actually hydrogen peroxide, he poured a generous amount onto his right index finger. He wedged his finger underneath the duct tape and rubbed back and forth as gently as he could, until he loosened it. When he pulled the tape off, he noticed that the boy's teeth were chattering. He also had several red sores around his mouth.

"I didn't do anything wrong," the boy said, in a hoarse voice.

"Don't worry. I believe you. Tell me your name."

"Justin."

"Justin what?"

"Edwards."

Lou called dispatch.

"Cheryl, is that you?"

"Yes."

"I'm at 260 Christie Street. I've got a male juvenile in bad shape over here and I need a bus to take him over to the ER. I hate to admit this, but I also need backup."

"Weren't you supposed get the day off?"

"Yeah, but you know how that goes. A cop's work is never done. Anyway, tell them to look for the apartment with the anxiety ridden door."

"Did you say 'the anxiety ridden door'?"

Lou chuckled.

"Yeah. Believe me, there's no other way to describe it. Also, do me a favor and call my mother?"

"What do you want me to tell her?"

"Just let her know I'll probably be late for dinner, but I'll do my best to get there as soon as I can."

"OK and before I forget, Lieutenant Purdy told me to let you know that Judge Nicholas signed your warrant to search 260 Christie Avenue. It's already been faxed it over to us."

"Thank God. I'll call you later and thanks," Lou said.

He hung up, turned to Justin and patted him gently on the back. Tears washed clean streaks down the boy's dirty face and dropped onto the filthy floor.

"I'm freezing," Justin said.

Lou nodded.

"I can tell. The worst is over now. You'll go to the hospital and everything will be OK after that."

"Yeah well, the last time someone told me that I was going to the hospital, I ended up here instead."

Lou shook his head.

"That's terrible. Why don't you tell me about it while we wait for the ambulance?"

CHAPTER ONE HUNDRED FOUR
KIDNAPPED

Justin began his tale of woe, while Lou wrote everything down. He explained how, one Saturday back in the spring, he had borrowed his friend Thomas' bike, so that he could ride over to another friend's house, where he was expected for dinner. When he reached his friend's street, a terrible, awful looking man lunged at him from out of nowhere and blocked him. Justin hit the hand brakes, but not in time to avoid accidentally knocking the man to the ground. When Justin realized what had happened, he got off of his bike and tried to help the man.

"Are you all right?" Justin asked.

Leland LeRoux stood, pulled up his pant leg and pointed at a mass of red and silver scales above his ankle.

"Does this look like I'm all right? Jess look at what ya done to my leg! Now me and you are gonna have to go to the emergency room, unless you want me to call the po-leece and have you arrested as a hit and run driver," Leland said.

He grabbed Justin's arm and whistled for a taxi.

"Look, I'm sorry. I'm not a hit and run driver. I stopped to help you," Justin said.

Leland pinched him hard.

"You jess shut the hell up boy," he hissed.

Leland flagged down a taxi and when it pulled over to the curb, he yanked the door open and shoved Justin inside.

"Take me to 260 Christie Street and step on it," he told the driver.

After that, no one spoke until the driver dropped them off in front of Leland's apartment. Leland slid out, pulled Justin out by his ear and counted out the exact fare. When the driver balked at being stiffed on a tip, Leland left the door open and hustled Justin toward his apartment.

"This doesn't look like any hospital," Justin said.

"I also thought I done tole you to shut the hell up," Leland said.

He pinned Justin up against the door and held him by the ear with one hand, as he unlocked the door with the other. Once the door was open, he shoved Justin so hard, that Justin landed on the floor. He double bolted the door, reached down and pulled Justin to his feet by his hair. He dragged Justin across the room and flung him into the love seat with a bang.

"Now you jess set there," he said, as he walked backwards towards his kitchen table.

Dodging the litter on the floor, he kept his eyes locked on Justin, while he groped around blindly on the table for his pellet gun. Once he found it, he wrapped his claw like fingers around it, aimed it at Justin, and walked backwards towards the sink. He grabbed a dead rat, walked it over to Justin and when he was about a foot away from the love seat, he stuck the pellet gun in Justin's face. Justin ducked, so Leland lunged at him and used the nose of the pellet gun to inch his head forward. When Justin started to shake, Leland grinned and tossed the rat in his lap.

"Don't you never away look away from me or try to git away from me boy or you'll end up jess like that there rat."

Justin shivered. His breathing was heavy. Tears welled up in his eyes and rolled down his cheeks.

Leland walked backwards until he reached the closet door. Once he opened it, he pulled out a plastic storage container, walked it back toward Justin and lobbed it onto the love seat next to him.

"What is it?" Justin asked.

"A box o' rat tails. I want ya ta hurry up and open it, take out six tails and make two sets of braids of 'em. An' they better be tight."

He kept the gun pointed at Justin while Justin complied. When Justin was finished, he stuck the gun between his knees, tested the tails for tautness and bound Justin's hands. Justin tried to fend him off, so he reached into his pocket, pulled out a switchblade and nicked Justin's left arm with it. He licked it the blood that trickled out, dipped his finger in the wound and smeared it across Justin's lips.

CHAPTER ONE HUNDRED FIVE
LONG HOT SUMMER NIGHT

Lou heard the wail of a siren. As it got closer he nodded and patted Justin on the shoulder.

"You have a lot of courage kiddo," he said, without revealing his revulsion for Leland or his compassion for Justin. Before Justin could answer him, there was a loud boom at the door and two uniformed officers busted in.

"Hey Lou!"

"Hey Ralph. This is Justin Edwards. He's freezing," Lou said.

"Hang on a minute. The bus just arrived. I'll get a blanket to wrap him in," Ralph said.

Ralph went outside just as two EMTs arrived with a stretcher.

"Take him over to the ER while I go and collar the dirt bag who did this to him. I have a good idea where he is right now," Lou said.

Officer Ralph Carmen returned with the blanket and wrapped it around Justin.

"Thank you," Justin said.

Lou nodded.

"You may as well start to seal off the place off and dust it for prints," Lou said.

Ralph nodded.

A look of terror crossed over Justin's face as the two paramedics strapped him down on the stretcher.

"Help! I'm scared. They're tying me up!" Justin screamed.

"Whoo hoo! Look at these magazines!" Ralph called out from the bathroom.

Ignoring Ralph, Lou bent down and did his best not to gag from the smell of his hair.

"Trust me and try not to be scared. They're only strapping you down so that you don't roll off the stretcher," he whispered.

"Tell them not to? Tell them I'll hold on tight. Better yet, tell them I'll even walk out to the ambulance."

"Let them do their job. OK? When you get to the hospital, the nurses will call your parents so that you can be reunited with them."

Another look of terror flashed across Justin's face.

"Please don't call them? I don't live with them anymore."

Lou frowned.

"What do you mean?"

Justin explained how he came to live at Beau Rivage, while Lou took more notes. When Justin was through, he nodded.

"OK. So, when anyone at the hospital asks you who your parents are, don't tell them. Just have them contact Beau Rivage. In the meantime, I'll do what I can to track down your social worker."

"I forgot to tell you something. He keeps a ton of dead rats in the freezer," Justin said.

Lou gulped and nodded.

"Thanks for the head's up kiddo," he said and signaled to the EMT's to get going.

"It's just a short ride to the hospital. You won't be strapped down for very long," the first EMT said, in a gentle tone of voice, as he and his partner carried Justin out.

Once they left, Lou walked over to the refrigerator, opened the freezer door and peered in. He found about seventy-five skinned rats that had been individually packaged in clear cling wrap. They were dated and neatly stacked on top of one another. Lou shook his head, shut the freezer door and looked in the refrigerator. He found a six pack of beer, a deck of Aleister Crowley Tarot cards, a red notebook with the word "Grimmery" scrawled across the cover and a box. He pulled out the notebook and opened it. A red wax candle that had been crudely carved into the shape of a female had been placed inside a page entitled "A spell to Make Her Your Love Slave." Cheap black wig hair had been glued to the top of the candle. He put it back so that the uniformed officers could collect it as evidence. He opened the box. Inside he found a pellet gun, ammunition, carbons and a card.

Hmmm, now this puppy is definitely a top-notch item. Outlawed in New York State for sure, but it would be such a waste to let it be destroyed as contraband.

He read the card, shook his head and closed the box. Then he took it out, along with a can of beer. Holding the beer in one hand and the box in the other, he kicked the refrigerator door shut and quietly left the apartment. When he reached his truck, he stashed the box under his seat, opened the can of beer and pulled the pill bottle out of his pocket. Shaking a tablet into his hand, he popped it into his mouth and chased it down with a mouthful of beer. Then he peeled away from the curb.

Chapter One Hundred Six
WALK THE LINE

Lou broke every speed record on his way over to Nguyen's warehouse. When he arrived there, he was thrilled to discover that Leland was already tied up.

"I don't know who y'are, but thank Gawd yer here! Help me! This here crazy VC sumbitch done knocked me the fuck out and hog tied me," Leland yelled.

Lou flashed his badge and pulled Leland to his feet.

"You're under arrest," he said and then he read Leland his rights.

An unstoppable flood of indignation poured over Leland.

"Now you wait jess a minute! Ya mean to tell me he done this to me and I'm the one who's gittin' arrested?"

He tried to squirm away from Lou and when that failed, he spat in Lou's face. Lou grabbed him by the scruff of his neck and pushed him face down onto the cement floor. When he knelt down, Leland saw this as his chance to use his to head to ram Lou in the groin. Lou doubled over in pain.

"You're resisting arrest!" Lou eked out the words. Then he frisked Leland and called Ralph Carmen for backup.

One of Leland's pockets contained a five-dollar bill, a handful of nails and an assortment of loose change and the other contained his housekey. Lou pocketed the money and shortly thereafter Ralph Carmen and his partner arrived on the scene.

All three of them escorted Leland out to the police cruiser. Ralph Carmen opened the back door, while Lou pushed Leland's head down and shoved him inside.

"Watch your head," he warned.

"You sheddapp," Leland countered back.

When Lou shut the door, Leland crouched on the rock-hard seat. Nguyen's ropes bit into his wrists. He reclined and kicked the window in an effort to escape. Lou opened the door and peered in.

"I'm asking you nicely to pipe the fuck down," he said in a not so nice tone of voice. Then he slammed the door.

Ralph came around and got into the driver's seat. Once the other officer was seated, he drove to the precinct and Lou followed them in his truck.

"I am praying for the imminent destruction of this evil world and for the salvation of only the righteous. Amen," Leland prayed.

When he finished, he cursed and screamed at the top of his lungs. By the time Ralph dropped him off at the precinct, Lou rushed over to the cruiser, opened the door and dragged Leland inside.

"I demayund ta know where the fuckin' phone is at so's I kin at lease call my Goddamn lawyer," Leland said in an imperious tone, which belied his inner nervousness.

"You can call your lawyer later. After all, I'm sure no decent lawyer is hanging around waiting for you to fuck up their Thanksgiving," Lou said stonily, as he escorted Leland to the interrogation room.

"Well, this one will, 'cause she's not only my lawyer, she's also my fiancée. You jess wait 'til she hears what ch'all done ta me. She's not gonna take it lyin' down."

"How many times do I have to tell you to shut the fuck up?" Lou hollered.

"YER THE ONE WHO'D BETTER SHUT THE FUCK UP!" Leland screamed.

Without saying another word, Lou opened the door to the interrogation room, dragged Leland over to the wall and slammed him down onto the concrete floor, where an iron ring had had been bolted into the wall. Before Leland knew what happened, Lou placed one handcuff around the ropes that bound him, secured the other cuff to the ring in the wall and blasted Leland's eyes with a generous dose of mace. Temporarily blinded, dazed and in unrelenting pain, Leland crashed against the wall and crumpled into a heap. Tears ran down his face and mucous dripped down the back of his throat, as Lou rushed out of the cell.

Lou clanged the iron shut door shut and headed back down the hall toward his desk.

"Well, at least he's quiet," he told Ralph.

"That's good, because I'm gonna take my break now," Ralph said.

Lou nodded and worked on his report, while Ralph and the other officer went down the hall to the break room.

"I've got to leave, but I'll be back later. Can you call ACS and track down the victim's Social Worker for me?" Lou asked, when Ralph and the other officer returned from their break.

Ralph nodded and jerked his head in the direction of the interrogation room.

"Sure, but in the meantime what do you want me to do with looney toons in there?"

"Wait until I'm gone, unbolt him from the wall and then process him. Since he asked to speak to his lawyer, there's no way we can interrogate him. On the other hand, since he resisted arrest and butted me in the groin, at least try to delay his phone call until after you get through to ACS," Lou said.

Ralph nodded.

"Why don't they just let us shoot guys like him?"

"Because then we'd end up getting charged for a human," Lou said, as he picked up his car keys and left.

Ralph went down the hall to the interrogation room and opened the door.

"OK Mr. LeRucks come along with me. It's time for mug shots and prints," Ralph said.

"Dammit, that's supposed to be pronounced LeRoux. Don't ch'all even know howdda read?"

Ralph shrugged.

"Whatever," he said as he unhooked Leland from the wall.

"Kin ya at least tell me why he hadda mace me like that? Don't that violate my Civil Rights?"

Ralph shrugged.

"I don't know what you're talking about. I didn't see him do nothin'."

"That figgers," Leland said.

CHAPTER ONE HUNDRED SEVEN
MY HEART'S NOT HERE

Jordan had seen more trees in the past hour of driving, than he had seen since the day he left Scotland. They were bare, but an early ice storm from the night before had left them with a coating that looked like glass. The beautiful silhouette they formed against the charcoal sky somehow managed to give Jordan a distinct sense of peace and comfort. He felt as if the Universe had put up some early Christmas decorations in an effort to ease his troubled heart. When he approached Bear Mountain, he saw a smattering of snow on the peak that loomed large in the distance. Raindrops pelted his car. He struggled to find the switch for the windshield wipers and wound up swerving on a patch of black ice. When he slammed on the brakes, the car spun out of control. The squeal of his tires, combined with the fact that he was now facing backwards, scared Jordan. He thanked God that he was the only car on the road. He turned the car around, continued his journey and breathed a sigh of relief when he finally arrived at The Golf Club. The smiling desk clerk and blazing fire in the spacious, elegant lobby offered him a cheery welcome.

"Happy Thanksgiving. My name is Carl Drummond. Is this your first time with us?"

"Yes," Jordan answered, as he handed Carl the guest passes.

"I'll summon the bellman to take your things and show you to your suite."

"There's actually no need for one. My golf clubs are out in the car and I'm only bringing in this one bag, which I can certainly handle myself."

Carl smiled and handed Jordan the key to the suite.

"Well, then, here you go. The dining room is open twenty-four seven for your convenience. Please dial zero if there is anything we can do to enhance your stay."

Jordan smiled and nodded.

"Thank you."

Jordan walked around his pleasant, spacious suite and admired its décor. The ornate tapestries were beautiful, the mahogany furniture gleamed and the entertainment center was state of the art. Although he wanted to luxuriate in the over-sized jade green Jacuzzi, he decided that he had to take care of his hunger first. He went downstairs and realized that he was the only guest in the dining room. When he asked the waiter about it, the waiter explained that they were usually empty on Thanksgiving.

"But don't worry. More people will be arriving tomorrow," he said, as he handed Jordan a menu.

Jordan scanned the menu and smiled when saw a full Scottish Breakfast. Feeling a little homesick, he decided to order it and forego the Traditional Thanksgiving Turkey dinner, even though it was way past the breakfast hour. The waiter smiled and nodded.

"That's a great choice. We have a full assortment of juices. What would be your preference?"

"Orange juice would be lovely."

"Well, since oranges are in season now, you're in for a treat. You'll have freshly squeezed orange juice in just a few minutes."

Jordan nodded, smiled and glanced around. Thoughts of Pattie competed with thoughts of his homesickness and he knew that he needed to distract himself with something positive. When the waiter brought the juice, he savored the taste. A few minutes later, the waiter removed the glass and he replaced it with a tea pot filled with piping hot tea, a bowl of brown sugar, a creamer containing milk and a smaller pot of boiling water. He left and returned again with a tray of steaming porridge, plain yogurt, golden raisins and a jar of locally grown wildflower honey. The yogurt reminded Jordan of Pattie, so he pushed it aside. He splashed the milk into the porridge and stirred in some raisins. Then he topped it off with a heaping teaspoon full of brown sugar. It tasted heavenly. He no sooner finished it, when the waiter returned with a lazy Susan that held an assortment of crisp toasts, three different types of scones, butter, clotted cream and organic jams and marmalade.

"I must tell you, that was the smoothest porridge I've tasted since I left Scotland," Jordan said.

"I'm glad you like it," he said, as he disappeared.

He returned a few minutes later with a platter containing two grilled tomato halves that were drizzled with Cheddar cheese, a rasher of ham, three bangers, a helping of sautéed mushrooms, baked beans, two eggs over easy and a portion of black pudding.

Jordan smiled.

"My God, this is enormous!"

The waiter smiled.

"It's Thanksgiving. Enjoy yourself."

By the end of the meal, Jordan was so full, he knew that his only defense was to go outside and work off the calories.

CHAPTER ONE HUNDRED EIGHT
HER SONG

Pattie took special pains to apply her make up in her favorite "Gothic" style. She started with a pale foundation. Then she lined her eyes with extra generous doses of thick, black eyeliner and even thicker, blacker mascara. She finished the job with a shade of deep maroon lipstick. When she finished, she teased her hair at the crown, in order to create the illusion of height. She put on a lacy thong, a matching bra and her silver gothic pendant and ring. She carefully removed the price tags from her brand-new maroon and black velvet empire dress, stepped into it carefully and slipped into a pair of black fishnet stockings. She finished her look with the laceup boots that Norton Bakerman had flung at her. Then she gave herself a manicure. She smiled when she saw how the tips of her puffed sleeves tapered to a point, showcasing her long, black nails. She read while she waited for her nails to dry and then she picked up her cell phone and glanced at the time. It was already two thirty. She checked her voice mail and emails and she sighed when there were no new messages. She primped, inspected and put the last of the finishing touches on herself, until she was completely happy with the way she looked.

I can't be late. I can't give them any ammunition, she thought, as she tossed her cell phone into her tote bag. She picked up her keys, grabbed the novel she was reading and lobbed that into her tote bag as well.

CHAPTER ONE HUNDRED NINE
CORNUCOPIA

Ryan's sister, Wendy, carried the "Horn of Plenty" centerpiece that she had spent most of the morning arranging and set it down in the middle of her parents' dining room table. Her husband Joe came downstairs with their three children, just as she was put the finishing touches on it to make it look "just right". Melanie went straight into the family room where her grandfather, Arthur J. Pilgrim, was watching a classic Thanksgiving movie and her brother and sister, Susie and little Christopher trailed along behind her.

"Hi Grandpa. Happy Thanksgiving!" Melanie said.

Arthur smiled.

"Well, well, well, Happy Thanksgiving to you too!"

"I want to sing and play a new Thanksgiving song that I learned from my piano teacher."

"OK, but first I need my hug," he answered.

He stood, picked her up and hugged her. Then he kissed her on the cheek, put her back down and repeated the process with Susie. Little Christopher watched and pulled at his grandfather's pant leg.

"Look at that! The little guy wants a hug too. C'mere you", he said, as he scooped Little Christopher up and hugged him.

Melanie went over to the piano, climbed onto the piano bench and slid Ryan's cell phone out of her way. She sang and played a

Thanksgiving song in a style that was typical of any average first year piano student. Arthur put little Christopher down and sat on the couch. Christopher toddled over to the piano bench. As he got ready to climb up and join his sister, the sight of Ryan's cell phone distracted him. It was such a fascinating object that he couldn't resist it. He picked it up with both hands and clutched it to his heart with joy. Then he rocked from side to side with glee. When Melanie finished her song, Arthur applauded.

"You're a talented pianist, young lady and a talented singer too, I might add."

Melanie beamed.

"Thank you. Should I play something else? I know another song too."

"Sure. Why not?"

"Well, it's not about Thanksgiving, though."

"Oh well, that's all right," Arthur said.

Melanie played and sang while Christopher waddled down the hall as fast as his legs could carry him. When he reached his grandparent's bedroom, he darted inside, fell backwards and landed on his diaper padded seat. He giggled because it didn't hurt and he hadn't dropped his wondrous, new prize. He remained where he landed and began to explore it. He flicked the ringer switch on and off. Then when he heard his Uncle Zachary come through the front door, he wondered whether or not he should go to him for a hug and a piece of candy, but he decided to do that later. He pulled the antenna. When it didn't come off, he pulled it harder. When he reached the point where he couldn't force it off, he bent it and worked on it until he finally succeeded in snapping it off. He stuck it in his mouth, shook his head and stuck his tongue out.

Ew. Nasty.

He shoved the antenna under the bed and worked on the latch for the battery case. He slid it back and forth until he successfully pried it open. The little square battery was attached to two tiny wires. He patiently worked on each one until he finally liberated the battery. He tried equally as hard to reconnect the wires to it, but he was interrupted by the sound of his Uncle Ryan walking down the hall. Scared, he shoved the entire mess under the bed, stood and waddled toward Ryan, who waited for him with open arms.

"It looks like someone wants a hug," Ryan said.

CHAPTER ONE HUNDRED TEN
MOUNTAIN CLIMBING

Jordan parked at Little Stony Point and got out of the car. The sky was overcast and even though he wore enough woolen layers to spearhead an expedition to the North Pole, he nonetheless felt chilly. He inhaled the sharp, crisp air and removed his rucksack from the trunk. It was time to explore. He hiked for a while, then followed a trail that led upward toward a cliff. About an hour later, he stopped to catch his breath. He a looked down at the rain soaked valley below him in the distance. As the wind picked up, white caps began to bob and weave on the surface of the river and an eagle swooped down and skimmed their white peaked crests. Jordan was amazed, because he had before never seen a wing span that wide. When the eagle finally soared up and out of view, he took it as his cue to begin hiking again.

After he trekked on for a while, the gravel beneath his feet turned to earth. The only sound he heard was the sound of the twigs and leaves that crunched beneath his hiking boots. It brought back childhood memories of pleasant hikes he took with his grandfather. He continued walking until he reached the base of a gigantic, cone shaped rock. He gazed up at the humpbacked marvel that dominated the landscape and decided that it had to be the most splendid rock on earth. He admired the way it shot up into the sky like a spire against an infinite backdrop. He smiled at the puffy cumulus clouds that wrapped themselves around its heavily snow laden peak and he appreciated its impressively climbable outline.

How disappointing that he had no suitable climbing partner. Not a soul could be found, aside from the skeleton crew over at the club. Thoughts of Pattie intruded again. He tried to exorcise them by taking deep breaths and then he decided to climb the rock with or without a partner. After all, it was his only companion on a dreary afternoon when everyone else was spending the day with loved ones. Even Pattie preferred the company of her crazy family to him, he thought, suddenly resenting that fact. That's when he knew for sure that climbing this rock was his only defense against his negative thoughts, so he began his ascent in a brisk, orderly fashion. He also knew that the rock was formed from pure granite, which would make his climb easier.

It was a stimulating stretch for him, but not an uncomfortable one. After he reached two hundred feet, the rock's angle grew steeper. He worked and struggled but eventually he made it to the highest plateau. He was completely out of breath and the only sound he could hear was that of his own heartbeat. He removed his ruck sack, spread a blanket on the ground and sat with his back against the rock. He reached for another blanket and draped it over himself. Although the air was thin, it was the purest air he had breathed in a long time. He decided to surrender to the beautiful atmosphere that surrounded him and as he did, he felt an extraordinary sense of peace. He breathed it in and let it wash over him until he eventually dozed off.

CHAPTER ONE HUNDRED ELEVEN
THANKSGIVING

Pattie glanced at her watch. It was exactly ten past three when she arrived at her parents' brownstone. She knocked, opened the door and walked down the hallway. When she reached the dining room, she noticed that the table was set for four people with Edie's usual olive green tablecloth and orange place mats. She stood in the doorway and silently watched, as Edie struck several poses and admired herself in the mirror. Edie picked up her glass and watched herself artfully use the tip of her tongue to scoop up a generous portion of salt from the rim of her Margarita glass. She was so absorbed, that she didn't even notice the dangerously long cigarette ash that fell onto her skin tight, fuchsia, polyester dress, nor did she notice Pattie standing in the doorway, watching her every move.

"Good afternoon and Happy Thanksgiving," Pattie finally said, interrupting her mother's reverie.

Embarrassed by the intrusion, Edie jumped, squinted and scrutinized Pattie.

"Jesus Christ, you scared the shit out of me. Just look at that getup on you! Didn't anybody bother to tell you that this is Thanksgiving, not Halloween?" Edie said. She punctuated her comments with an exaggerated drag on her cigarette.

The faint, but unmistakable slur in Edie's speech and the way the lower right hand corner of her mouth drooped, let Pattie know that Edie was already drunk.

"Gee thanks for the cheerful greeting, Mom. You look amazing too. Actually, it feels more like Groundhog's Day than anything."

"And don't bother to go running to Lou, either. That American Domesticated Shorthair he's sleeping with just called to tell me that he's not gonna get here until later."

"Oh really? I thought he had the day off."

"Wrong again. He's probably shacked up with her. Tell me, why is it that neither one of you kids can ever make your own phone calls?"

Pattie shrugged.

"I don't know," she said, thinking to herself that everything Jordan said was right after all.

Edie turned on her heel and retreated into the kitchen, while Pattie went into the living room. She sat down next to Chet, who was totally engrossed in a football game that was being played on the biggest flat screen television that money could buy. He had a glass of beer and a bowl of cashews in front of him. Sitting there in his comfortable, royal blue velour sweat suit and calf-skin slippers somehow made him look out of place on the worn out black and gold plaid couch. When he saw Pattie, he sniffed and hit the mute button.

"Oh, I didn't realize the circus was in town," he said.

Pattie frowned and cleared her throat.

"What?"

"There you go again, wearing another vampire costume. Don't you own any clothes that don't scare people?"

Before she could answer him, he turned the sound back on and continued to watch his game. Pattie reached into her tote bag, pulled out her book and soon found herself transported to another world, where people were actually nice to one another. Her good mood lasted until the front door slammed.

Lou came crashing into the dining room carrying his night-stick and handcuffs in one hand and a plastic bag in the other. He carelessly lobbed the items onto the sideboard. Then he removed his gun from his holster and tossed it down next to them. Pattie stood and went into the dining room. When she spotted the switchblade inside the plastic bag, she gingerly picked the bag up by its corner and dangled it.

"Wow. This thing looks lethal," she said.

"You're God damn right is. It can slice some body's jugular to shreds," Lou said.

"Where did you get it?" Pattie asked.

"Off the dirt bag I collared."

Edie came out of the kitchen. She and Lou exchanged Thanksgiving greetings amd when she stuck her cheek out for Lou to kiss, she caught sight of the switchblade. She frowned and the corner of her lower lip hung down even more than before. She snatched the bag out of Pattie's hands.

"Is this yours or hers?"

Lou shrugged.

"It's evidence."

"You know, things can go wrong when you carry evidence around with you. You should have logged it in."

"Yeah, well, I'll log it in later. I didn't want to be late for dinner."

He walked into the living room and slammed himself into a beat out old lounge chair. He landed so hard that it actually groaned under his abuse. Chet hit the mute button and stared at him.

"The nerve of you showing up for Thanksgiving Dinner all unshaven. You never saw me looking less than my best back in the day," Chet said.

Lou gave Chet a dirty look.

"Didn't you get the message? I got called into work at the last minute this morning. I didn't have time to primp myself," Lou said.

"Well, I also had to go out and work on more holidays than I care to remember. Now go home and fix yourself up," Chet said.

Lou waved his hand in dismissal. He sat sideways, dangling his legs over the arm of the chair and Chet turned the sound back on.

"Yo, Pattie, since you're up, can you bring me a beer?" Lou called out.

When Pattie appeared with the beer a few minutes later, he took it from her without thanking her and gulped it.

"Ahhh. Now that's good," he said.

"By the way, it's your last one," she said.

"No, it isn't. I have several more six packs stashed in my truck. Do me a favor?"

She shook her head.

"No way. I'm not getting anything else for you. I'm not your freaking maid, you know."

"Fuck you."

With that, Pattie turned around, charged out of the room and locked herself into the bathroom. Chet looked up, pressed the mute button and sniffed again.

"Here we go again. Why in the hell does that damn kid spend so much time in the bathroom? Does she have some kind of a kidney problem or something?" Chet asked.

"Oh, who knows? I just hope she washes some of that shit off of her face while she's in there," Edie brayed.

Chet pointed at Lou.

"We can't get this one anywhere near a bathroom and we can't get the other one out. Go figure," he said.

Lou sighed, got out of his chair and walked out of the room. A few seconds later the front door slammed.

"Well, I can get her out. After the stunt she pulled last time, I went and had a key made," Edie brayed, as she charged down the hallway.

"Look Pattie, you'd better straighten up and pull yourself together, because I need your help today," she yelled.

"Go away!" Pattie said.

"Like hell I will! This is my house!" Edie yelled.

She removed the bathroom key from a hook in the closet, unlocked the door and found Pattie standing over the sink.

"Do you mind?" Pattie screamed.

Edie lurched the medicine cabinet open, revealing an actual pharmaceutical cornucopia. Every shelf was tightly packed with bottle upon bottle of just about every prescription and over the counter drug available. Pattie gasped when she spotted the various tranquilizers, antidepressants, sleeping pills, amphetamines, painkillers, codeine cough syrups and mood altering substances. Edie snatched a bottle of tranquilizers, fought with it to get it open and finally shook two pills into her palm. She used her free hand to turn on some lukewarm tap water. Then she filled a dusty old bathroom glass, shoved the pills into Pattie's mouth and gave Pattie the glass. She slammed the door and staggered back to the dining room, as Pattie stood there stupefied. Finally, Pattie spat the pills into the sink and watched the running water send them spiraling down the drain. After she washed and dried her hands, she turned off the water and returned to the dining room. Lou came in right behind her, carrying a six pack of beer in one hand and Pattie's cell phone in the other. Pattie's key ring was clenched between his teeth. He spat it onto the sideboard and shook his head.

"Not only did you leave your car unlocked, you left your cell phone and your car keys on the seat in plain view for anyone to steal! It's actually a clever racket when you stop and think about it. First you tempt the dirt bags to steal stuff and then you get paid to defend them," he said.

Pattie's cell phone rang in his hand and he jumped in surprise.

"Give me that! I'm waiting for a call," Pattie said.

Instead of handing her the phone, he snapped it open and jammed it up against his ear.

"It's your dime. Spill it," he barked.

His face grew whiter as he listened to the caller. Finally, he turned to Pattie and looked at her in disbelief.

"Who is it?" Pattie asked.

"Your fiancé! So, why am I the last one to find out that you're engaged to the worst skell in Manhattan?"

"Oh, my God! Are you still running around with that thieving Limey? I thought I told you to dump him months ago!" Edie yelled.

"No, it's not the Limey. If you knew who it was, you'd be begging her to bring the Limey back," Lou said.

"Well, if it's not the Limey, then who the hell is it?" Edie asked.

"Will the two of you please stop calling him that?" Pattie shouted.

"It's the Goddamn dirt bag I collared this morning! Pattie, I know you've done a lot of off the wall things, but getting yourself hooked up with this asshole brings you to a new low!"

"What?" Pattie and Edie yelled at the same time.

"You heard me! I just got finished busting his ass for kidnapping a twelve-year-old. I'll just bet he's the same guy who emailed you those naked pictures of yourself last summer!" Lou yelled.

Edie gasped.

"Naked pictures? What the hell is going on?"

Both Pattie and Lou ignored her, but Lou was so hot under the collar, he hurled her phone at the gilt-edged mirror that had graced the Anwald dining room for more than one hundred years. It crashed and splattered into a spider web of a thousand shards, which covered the sideboard and part of the floor. The eagle that adorned its top keeled over and crashed onto the sideboard, landing right next to the switchblade.

"Oh, my God!" Pattie cried out.

"Oh, my God is right you freak! Look at what you just made Louie do!" Edie yelled.

"That's seven years of bad luck on your head, not mine, you phony bitch!" Lou screamed.

Edie snatched the eagle from the sideboard, cracked it against the left side of Pattie's skull and flung it onto the sideboard. As a sea of pain washed over Pattie, her eyeballs rolled back in her head and she reeled into the sideboard. She grabbed hold of it it in order to keep her balance and she realized that people actually do see stars when they get hurt.

Chet sniffed, reluctantly turned the television off and tore himself away from the couch. He picked up his beer and limped into the dining room. Edie snatched the eagle and handed it to him.

"Here! Just look at what your precious daughter did!" Edie yelled.

"Oh, my God! How can you stand there and lie like that when you know Lou was the one who broke it? You even watched him do it!" Pattie yelled, as she stood there rubbing her head.

Chet stuck the eagle in Pattie's face.

"God, damn it! I've tried to be patient with you, but even I have my breaking point."

"Hello? Didn't you even hear one word I just said? I told you I wasn't the one who broke it."

Chet shook his head.

"Why must you ruin every holiday with your bull shit and your antics? Don't you know that John Mueller of Nueremberg hand carved this fuckin' eagle back in 1841? Don't you even care?"

"Of course, she doesn't care! She doesn't care about anything except her selfish self!" Edie yelled.

"Well she'll have to care when the repair bills start coming out of HER salary!" Chet bellowed.

At that moment, the only thing Pattie cared about was the throbbing on the left side of her head. She lumbered over to the sideboard and picked up her cell phone.

"Hello? Who is this? Is anyone still even there?" Pattie asked, in a hoarse voice.

"Yeah. I'm still here, so listen up!"

Pattie thought she was hallucinating.

"Leland?"

"Yeah and by the way, I done heard everything y'all said, but I'm a fergit that fer right now, 'cause I need ya ta help me! So, if ya have even one ounce a humanity left in ya, please come over to the jail an' git me the hell outta here!"

"Don't you mean Central Booking?"

"No! I mean the jail! They done hauled my ass all the way over here ta hassle me I s'pose," he said, as he slammed down the phone.

Pattie quietly hung up and placed her phone on the sideboard next to Lou's pistol. She stood motionless for several seconds and waited, as each heartbeat brought a fresh supply of blood, oxygen and pain to the throbbing on her head. Finally, she turned to Lou and stared at him.

"Not that it's any of your business, but the person who just called happens to be one of my clients! Do you really think that I could ever be engaged to someone like that?"

"Who knows? Why not? At this point I think you're capable of just about anything," Lou said.

"Well, if that's what you think of me, then you really don't know me at all."

Lou picked up the cell phone, spat on it and flung it to the floor. Then he stomped on it and crushed it under his heel.

"Look what you did," she cried out, as tears ran down her cheeks.

"You know what? I'm outta here," Lou muttered.

He stormed out, slamming the door behind him. Edie followed him, leaving Pattie and Chet alone in the dining room.

"My head is killing me and the room feels like it's spinning. I think I'm going to faint," she said.

Chet held his glass under her nose.

"Here. Take a sip of this. It'll do you some good."

Gagging at the smell, she grabbed her keys.

"Hey you! Where do you think you're going?" Chet hollered.

Almost as an afterthought, Pattie pulled the switchblade out of its plastic bag and waved it at Chet. Then she ran out.

"Hey, that's Lou's evidence," Chet hollered, limping after her.

Pattie ran all the way to her car, but Chet only got as far as Lou's pied a terre. He banged on the door and beckoned for Edie and Lou to come outside.

"Well, if we don't eat soon the turkey's gonna be all dried out!" Edie brayed.

Pattie shoved the switchblade under her seat, sped away and watched, as their reflection in her rearview mirror got smaller and smaller.

Chapter One Hundred Twelve
JAILHOUSE BLUES

The streets and highways were deserted, which gave Pattie a chance to drive from her parents' house to Riker's Island in record time. Upon her arrival, a clerk handed her a copy of Leland's police report. She plowed through it, in spite of the migraine which had returned to her and the incessant throbbing from the bump on her head. She was amazed to read that Lou had charged Leland with seven separate offenses: kidnapping, risk of injury to a minor, obstruction of justice, assaulting a police officer, possessing a weapon and cruelty to animals. Because the kidnapping victim was a minor, his name had been redacted from the report. In view of Leland's previous record and the number and nature of his current charges, the bail was high. Although the Bail Bondsman didn't care much for Leland, he had a soft spot in his heart for Pattie.

"I can tell that you're kind. After all, you took time away from your family to come over here for the likes of Leland LeRoux."

Pattie nodded, smiled weakly and thanked him. Drained from feeling like an imposter, she walked outside and filled her lungs with some fresh, crisp air. She propped herself up against the chain link fence in order to keep herself from collapsing. She needed to stay alert long enough to get to a telephone, so that she could call Ryan and ask him to meet her at the emergency room. The air that blew in from the steel gray East River was so cold that it kept her awake, yet, at the same time, it chilled her right to the bone. She distracted herself by blowing rings in the air every time she exhaled. She noticed the sparrows perched on the barbed wire fence that separated the island from the river and wondered how they could sit there like that without feeling any pain. Her thoughts then flew to Leland LeRoux. She wondered how he could have stooped so low as to have kidnapped a twelve-year-old and that led her to think about Justin. Ryan told her to pray and have faith in God, so she said a prayer for Justin to still be alive and well. No sooner had she finished the prayer, when a huge, full, double rainbow filled the sky. It was bigger, brighter and more exquisite than any rainbow she had ever seen. Its two arcs formed a cross and created a bridge that beckoned her to step aboard and explore it. She gasped at its awesome beauty. However, her heart sank when the jailhouse door opened and discharged Leland. The second he waved and swaggered over to her, the sparrows peppered the sky with their hasty flight.

"I'm surprised ya even bothered ta wait fer me," he said.

She looked at him and turned away. His red, swollen eyes and the blisters around his mouth were too painful for her to even look at. He sneezed, snorted and blew his nose onto the back of one of his sleeves. She distracted herself by pointing out into the distance.

"Did you see that amazing double rainbow just now?"

He stared out at the gray, empty sky and shook his head.

"What rainbow? Where?"

She pointed out to the horizon.

"Right there in front of us! It must be a sign or an omen of something inspirational."

"Well, I didn't see nothin', but I could sher use yer inspiration to git me off a them trumped up charges."

Pattie shook her head and sighed.

"Oh well, it's gone now at any rate," she said.

- 411 -

"Oh Mayun. Either yer makin' this shit up ta try ta distrack me from how mayud I am atcha or yer Thanksgivin' cocktails must a' packed a mighty wallop."

She knew that the time had come for her to permanently distance herself from Leland. She clicked the lock on her car and walked toward it.

"I don't drink. Anyway, I'd better get going. Bye and Happy Thanksgiving," she said.

Leland dogged her every step. When they reached her car, he gave it the once over and whistled.

"Dayum if this thang don't look jess like a little ole hearse," he said.

She shot him a dirty look.

"It does not," she snapped.

He walked around to the back, peered into her rear-view window and pointed at her license plate.

"Looky here. 'Illsueu2'. Now that's funny," he said.

Pattie nodded.

"Yeah, sometimes I can be a real laugh riot."

He pointed at the bumper sticker Ryan had given to her last Spring.

"Now, this here bumper sticker makes me thank ya might have somethin' the matter with yer horn."

She nodded again.

"Yes. Sometimes it cuts out on me."

He nodded along with her, as if he were filing that information away.

"Mmm, hmm. Well, I muss say, this is a cute little car. I like that little hatch back ya got there."

She nodded vaguely.

"Thanks."

"Well, yer not the only one who needs ta git off a this here island, ya know."

"I'm sure that's true, but didn't they issue you a bus pass to 59th Street? After all, that's standard procedure."

"Nope. They'd done run out on accoun' a' it bein' a holiday an' what not."

Pattie's face looked crestfallen. Anxiety gnawed away at her solar plexus and the little voice inside her head screamed for her to just jump in the car, lock the door and speed away. Instead, she abandoned her instincts.

"OK. Hop in," she said, with a sigh.

"Kin I drive?"

"No. I'm not insured for that. Isn't it enough that I'm giving you a lift?"

"Hell yeah. It's right kind a ya."

She nodded.

"Good. I'm glad you see it that way."

When she opened her door and got in, he walked around to the passenger's side and did the same thing. It only took a few seconds for his rank stench to fill her car. She tried not to gag as she turned the ignition. When she opened the sunroof and windows, cold air whooshed into the car, so she cranked the heat on full bore in an effort to fight it. Then she turned on her CD player and hoped that some music might form a buffer between Leland and her frazzled nervous system.

"Dayum if y'ain't crazy openin' all them windas in this da-yump weather," he said.

"Hey, this is my car, so if you don't like it, that's just too bad. Besides, I feel messed up right now, so the last thing I need is aggravation from you," she said.

"Well, you won't git none if you remember not ta take yer shit out on me," he snapped.

She cleared her throat, shook her aching head and drove toward the long, narrow bridge that led her away from the four-hundred-acre compound at Riker's Island.

"What's your address again?"

"260 Christie Street."

"Well, when we get onto the FDR drive, you'll have to tell me which exit to take."

He winked. "Sure thang, Honey."

After that, he didn't say much during the long ride home, nor did he even turn toward Pattie, but from time to time he lifted his left eyebrow, rolled his left eyeball all the way over to the left corner of his eye and spied on her. When she finally exited the bridge, she drove past the churches and parks that dotted Queens borough's banks of the East River. Traffic became increasingly heavier, so it took a while for her to cross the second bridge that led her onto the FDR Drive. By the time they reached lower Manhattan, the sun had begun its descent, which changed the late afternoon sky from gray to a dusky periwinkle twilight. Leland directed her to turn left at the bottom of the ramp.

"After this here stop sign, drive to the first light and turn right onto Christie Street."

Pattie nodded and followed his directions.

"OK, which one is your apartment?"

He spread his scaly index finger out like a proud magician who had successfully completed an intricate trick and pointed at his graffiti ravaged door.

"That one."

Pattie pulled up to the curb and left the engine running. Since she was practically frozen and expecting him to leave any second, she decided to close all the windows.

"Finally," he said.

It took all of her inner strength not to react to him nor to comment on the condition of his door.

He peered out and scanned the street. Not a soul was to be found. He clutched the handle, but made no move to open it. Instead he sighed, leaned back into the seat and closed his eyes.

She cleared her throat and jabbed his arm.

"Uh. This is where you get out. Remember?"

He opened his eyes and stared straight ahead.

"Right. This is exactly where I get off," he said.

He stretched his left arm and flopped it onto her right thigh, with his palm facing upwards.

Pattie flinched.

"Uh, excuse me, but I don't like it when people touch me," she said.

He glared at her, flipped his hand over and squeezed her thigh.

"Well, git used to it," he said. His voice sounded raspy and harsh.

"What?"

He chuckled.

"Yer scared now. Ain't ya?"

She shook her head.

"Of course not."

"Yes ya'are. I can smell fear. Anyhow, the jig is up."

"What jig?"

"You'll fine out," he said, as he shoved his face within an inch of hers.

She recoiled and backed as far away from him as she could get. When he pressed his head directly under her nose, she tried to suppress her impulse to gag. The swollen, throbbing bump on her head hurt her so much, she winced.

He turned the volume on the CD player as high as it would go. When she reached out to lower it, he gripped her wrist with his scaly claw. When she tried to pull away, he clenched it even harder. A sharp stabbing sensation moved up her arm, but she tried not to react. He lifted her wrist, forced her hand up to his lips and kissed it. Then he used his free hand to reach behind her and lock the door. He dropped her wrist, grabbed her shoulders with both of his hands and lifted her off of the seat. Then he slammed her back against the door and plunked her down in such a way that she had no choice but to face him. She groaned and shuddered when the handle stabbed her tailbone.

"You're hurting me," she cried out.

He leaned over, turned the ignition off and pocketed the keys all in one fell swoop. He inched his way closer to her and slid on top of her. The full force of his weight moved her further down on the seat. This time the door handle stabbed her in the left shoulder. He bent his knee, shoved it between her legs and forced them apart. Then he pressed her head down onto the seat with his elbow. He tore her bodice open, shoved his scaly claw into her bra and pulled out her breasts. He grinned and drooled, as his eyes lit up with excitement. When his saliva dripped down onto her left breast, he squeezed it, licked the saliva off and looked up at her. Then he stuck his face in hers and kissed her. This time it was impossible for her to suppress her gag reflex.

Her gagging was the last straw as far as he was concerned. He flew into a rage and slapped her so hard that her head banged into the door handle.

"Did ya ever have someone sneer down at ya like y'ain't worth nothin'? Like yer lowlier 'an a piece a shit?" His voice was loud enough to be heard over the music.

She nodded, as tears rolled down her face.

"I'm sure we all have at some point. The world can be a very cruel place sometimes," she whispered.

"Yer dayum right it is and it hurts like hell! Especially when it's it you who's doin' the sneerin'!"

She opened her mouth to respond, but he clamped his mouth on it, thereby forcing her to kiss him. She shook her head to ward him off, but he jammed his tongue down her throat.

Moaning, he unzipped his fly and struggled until he was able to expose his red hard penis. He grabbed her hand and pressed her fingers around it. When she tried to pull away, he held it firmly in place. He stopped kissing her, planted his mouth on her left shoulder and bit down so hard that he broke her skin.

Once again, she cried out in pain. It hurt her so much that she had to struggle to even breathe. She noticed that his entire pubic area was covered with the same scales that ravaged his face and hands.

She banged down on the horn several times, but no sound came out. She dug the nails of her free hand into his scalp. Without knowing it, it was the exact place where Nguyen had hit him with the gun.

He recoiled in pain, let go of her and clutched his head in agony. Then he backhanded her in the face again and shoved her down on the seat as far as she would go. The door handle banged against her head again and by this time her face, neck and chest broke out in red splotches.

When he hitched his torso up and yanked his pants down around his knees, she saw it as an opportunity to escape. She reached back with her left hand, fumbled until she found the lock and clicked it open. Then she found the door handle, opened the door and slid out of the car, head first.

He watched her until she was halfway out, then he laughed, grabbed a good-sized chunk of her hair and used it to pull her back into the car. Once she was completely inside, he slammed the door behind her, clicked the lock and pulled her face up to his. He pinched her nostrils together and when she opened her mouth to breathe, he forced another kiss on her. Before she could get away, he flung her dress up, raked her thong and fishnets down to her knees and thrust himself on top of her. The scratches on her thighs felt as if someone had cut her with a knife.

Knife! Wait a minute!

She suddenly remembered that she had stashed a switch-blade under the seat. Taking pains to be as subtle as possible, she stretched her left arm, reached as far under the seat as she could and slowly stretched her fingers. She trolled for the switchblade and when she found it, she seized it and raised her arm. Click. She opened it. She forced its sharp tip against the side of Leland's neck and pressed it as hard as she could, without actually breaking the skin.

His eyes opened in shock.

"Hey! That's my knife!"

"And now it's your turn to be scared."

"Well, I ain't," he gasped out the words.

"Well, why not? You should be, because I'll kill you right now if that's what it takes for me to get the hell away from you," she said.

Before he could answer her, she wrapped her other arm around his head, pinned him down with her elbow and propped herself up. She tried to keep from shaking, as she held him down with all her might.

"OK. You win," he gasped, as he tried to break away from her.

Finally, he pressed the steel tipped toe of his right boot against the lock, wriggled and worked with it until he got it unlocked. Then he wedged his toe against the door handle and opened the door. By now, it was almost dark.

CHAPTER ONE HUNDRED THIRTEEN
DOUBLE TROUBLE

Willie Hudson turned the corner onto Christie Street, just as the bells from a nearby church pealed to let Lower Manhattan know that it was five o'clock. He walked up to Leland's apartment and kicked his door with a vengeance.

"Open up, fuck face! It's me!"

He heard a car door open behind him, so he spun around and watched as a pair of legs shimmied out of a little black car. A few seconds later, when Leland stood up, he went into verbal attack mode.

"What the fuck is going on?" Willie demanded to know.

"I jess had a near death experience," Leland said.

"Well, since you're still alive, pull your fuckin' pants up and close your fly," Willie said.

Leland looked down, blushed and complied.

"Whoops, sorry."

Pattie opened her car door, got out and held the knife up. Leland glanced at Willie for a cue as to what should happen next. Willie looked back at him and chuckled.

"Wow! She must have really shown you a good time. Maybe it's my turn to indulge in a little mayhem," he whispered to Leland.

"I need my keys," Pattie called out.

Willie stepped forward and took control of the situation.

"Listen you bitch, he'll give you the keys after you hand over that switchblade."

Pattie frowned and squinted at the diamond stud that sparkled in Willie's left ear. It looked vaguely familiar and she found that somewhat disturbing.

"Don't I know you from somewhere?" Pattie asked.

Willie grinned and pointed at her breasts.

"Nice tits," he replied.

She looked down and and gasped. Holding the switchblade in one hand, she did her best to put herself back together. Willie used that as his opportunity to sprint around to her side of the car and charge at her. Ignoring her inner terror and refusing to cry out, she waited until he got within arms' distance and then she gave him a karate chop. The shock of her bravado kept him at bay for a few seconds, but then he lunged at her again and tried to grab her by the throat. She fended him off with a swift kick to his shin.

"Oh, you no good fucking bitch," he muttered.

He clenched his fist and blindsided her, before her foot even had a chance to return to the ground. The second his ring smashed into her jaw, she passed out and crumpled to the ground in a heap. The switchblade landed next to her and Willie scooped it up.

"Hand over them keys, so I can stuff her in the car!" He said to Leland.

When Leland pulled the keys out of his pocket, Willie snatched them, opened the hatchback and stashed them in his pocket. Then he heaved Pattie up, tossed her into the car like a sack of cornmeal and checked her pulse.

"Maybe I should slit her throat and finish her off, because I don't think she's dead," Willie said.

Leland looked horrified. He pressed the back of his scaly hand against her neck and held it there for a few seconds. Then he shook his head.

"She don't have a pulse and she's stone cold. She's dead all right. Besides, slitting her throat would be too messy."

Willie shrugged.

"So?"

"Well, it's only right to let the dead rest in peace. Leave her intact and let this be her sacred hearse."

Willie shook his head, removed her jewelry and stashed them in his pocket.

"Yeah well, maybe you're right. Now that I've killed her, I have to think about that old saying. 'Don't leave any living witnesses'," he said, as he slammed the hatchback.

Leland frowned.

"Do what?"

"You heard me. Besides, Roy has a hit on you."

"Why?"

"Why? Well, first of all, he asked me to get that pain in the ass kid of his out of the way until after his trial was over, but you prevented me from doing that by getting my car impounded. Then he asked you to do it."

"Well, I done it! Besides, it ain't as if I lost yer car on purpose."

"Yeah, you did it all right, but today you got caught and now the kid is back in circulation, blah blah blabbing to the police, no doubt and whether you lost my car on purpose or not, it doesn't matter, since they auctioned it off last night."

Leland pointed at Pattie's car.

"So then jess take this one."

Willie patted his pocket.

"Don't worry. I intend to."

"So, there you go. Problem solved."

Willie's pupils narrowed to tiny pinpoints that bore a hole right through Leland.

"How much of this did you blab to that bitch lawyer of yours?"

Leland shook his head and waved his hand in dismissal.

"I didn't tell her nothin.' As a matter of fact, even if ya hadn't a deep sixed her jess now, I was gonna break it off with her. Turns out she was two timin' me, not only with that English doctor ya done tole me about, but with a cop too, of all things."

Willie spat on the sidewalk next to Leland's left boot.

"Yeah. Right. Roy also told you to burn her in her sleep last summer, but you fucked that up royally too."

Leland held both of his hands up, as if to surrender and then clasped them in prayer.

"I'm sorry I jess ain't the kind of guy who goes around killin' the thing he loves. But, please, please don't kill me over it."

Willie shook his head, gave him a steely look and waved the switchblade in his face.

"It's already a done deal. Even if I didn't hate you for losing my car, Roy already made it clear to me that if I don't kill you, he'll send someone after us to kill us both. You know how it works."

One look at Willie told Leland that he was doomed. His only way out was that little pothole he spotted behind Willie. He gave Willie a good hard shove.

Willie lurched backwards into the pothole, twisted his left ankle and lost his balance. When he flailed his arms to regain his equilibrium, he accidentally sliced a gash in Leland's right thigh.

The blade was so sharp, it didn't even hurt at first. Leland ran down the street, but by the time he reached the corner, his thigh started to throb. He glanced down and watched the blood gush out of it. He could no longer run, so he limped around the corner, ducked into the nearest doorway and crouched there. He poked his dirty fingers through the tear in his jeans and inspected his wound, praying in French the entire time.

Willie chased him down the street and he had no problem gaining on him, even with a twisted ankle. All he had to do was follow the trail of blood which led him around the corner and right up to the doorway where Leland was praying. He grabbed

Leland by the scruff of his neck, pulled him to his feet and pointed the knife at his throat. He dragged Leland back to the car and slammed him against it.

Leland held his hands up as if to surrender, but instead instead of backing off, Willie jabbed the switchblade into Leland's left palm. Leland cried out, as his blood spilled onto the sidewalk. Spurred on by his own adrenaline, Willie lunged at Leland, repeatedly slashed and tore at his palms, like a demented version of Zorro. Finally, he thrust the switchblade at Leland's stomach in the hopes of disemboweling him, but Leland successfully blocked him with his shredded hands. He aimed for Leland's stomach again and when Leland once again moved to protect it, Willie shifted direction. Using every ounce of his strength, he plunged the switchblade into Leland's carotid artery. It caused a gnashing sound as it tore into Leland's flesh. He slashed the entire length of Leland's throat. Leland was in agony, but with no voice, his inchoate scream imploded, sounding like nothing more than a muted gulp.

When Willie removed the blade, several ounces of blood gushed forth from Leland's throat like a geyser, splashing onto Willie's face and chest. The stench assaulted Willie's nostrils and he could taste it all the way at the back of his own throat. A few seconds later, a huge blood clot and an ounce of putrid green sputum plopped out of Leland's mouth and splattered onto the sidewalk. Every time Leland's heart beat, his body spewed forth more blood and sputum. Enraged by the mess, Willie reached out and sliced off the tip of Leland's nose. Then he plunged the switchblade so deeply into Leland's neck again, that Leland lurched, keeled over and landed on the hood of the car. This drove the blade in even deeper.

Willie watched as Leland's right eye swelled and spewed an ounce of blood. As it ran down Leland's face, his eye deflated and drooped. Both of his eyes remained open. One eye stared upwards at the sky and the one that drooped stared straight at

Willie, as if to confront him. Willie opened the passenger door and heaved Leland onto the seat, causing blood to splatter all around the car's interior.

Leland grew paler as blood and sputum continued to surge out of his hands, ears and the gaping wounds in his neck. A few seconds later, blood oozed out of his nostrils and across his crotch, spreading down both of his pant legs. Eventually he went into shock as the last vestiges of blood and life completely left his body. His mouth unhinged and a blood clot burst forth from the right side of his mouth and finally, his bowels and kidneys let loose. Now that his body was completely drained of any life force, it looked bizarre in contrast to the baseball cap that managed to remain perched so jauntily on top of his head.

Willie gripped the switchblade with both hands and yanked it out of Leland's neck, which created another gnashing sound. He watched Leland's upturned hand twitch as if in protest and he plunged the blade into Leland's palm, in order to get it to stop.

Blood was everywhere. Several blood clots even managed to splash onto the ceiling. Some of them congealed and hung like stalactites that pointed down at the clots on the dashboard and floor. Willie rifled through Leland's pockets in an effort to distract himself from the mess and the smell, so that he wouldn't end up vomiting. He flew into a rage when he realized that all Leland had to offer the world was a bus pass from Riker's Island and a handful of nails. He cursed and shoved Leland's body down into the foot well on the passenger's side of the car. Then he kicked Leland for good measure and slammed the door. He peered up and down the street, hurried over to the driver's side and got into the car.

Even though he was satisfied with himself for having single-handedly rid the world of two pests, he was uncertain about what to do next. He needed to get out of harm's way and lay low for a while in order to avoid the wrath of Roy and since it was Thanksgiving, he suddenly felt homesick for Moriah, his hometown in Upstate New York. Moriah struck him as a great idea, because it would enable him to dump the corpsicles in Lake Champlain, so he turned the ignition and aimed the death mobile toward the Northbound entrance ramp of the FDR drive.

Chapter One Hundred Fourteen
BAD NEWS

The chill in the air and the faint rumbling of Jordan's stomach woke him up. He reached into his rucksack and pulled out a jar of cashews and a bottle of spring water. He heard the faint sound of an oncoming train down in the valley. He stood and munched, while he watched it make its way southward down the tracks on the other side of the river. A strong gale came out of nowhere and scoured his face with cold air. The dampness and drizzle made his hair look wilder than ever. He took a sip of his water and watched, as the sky turned rosy, silver and finally gray. He remembered that sunset happened more quickly in the mountains, so he decided to return to the inn.

He spotted a trail that led out of the woods. Even though it was only two feet wide, his instincts told him that it was the best route back down to Stony Point. Shortly after he began his descent, the drizzle turned to rain. Halfway down the trail he heard the sound of running water. Intrigued, he followed it. It led him across a wooden bridge, past a street called Patty Cake Lane. The name stabbed his heart like a knife. He turned away from it and continued to follow the sound until he reached a waterfall. It was amazing. He couldn't stop staring at it. It was over ninety feet high. Even though it was still raining, he stood there and breathed in the energy from the endless supply of pure, clean, water and prayed that it would drown out his sadness, but it didn't.

A gray overcoat spread across the sky and muted the rosy colors of the twilight. He slung his rucksack off and dug around in it for his cell phone. When he got a signal, he checked his voice mail.

"It's Clint. Sorry I missed your call. Happy Thanksgiving right back at you, Buddy."

End of messages.

He returned Clint's call and reached Clint on the first ring.

"Hey, what's going on up there?"

"I had another row with Pattie last night. She insisted on spending today with her family and I can't stand to be around them. Believe me, they're all madder than hatters, especially her mother."

A beep interrupted him.

"Are you getting another call? If that's her, take it. You can always call me back later," Clint said.

"No. It's a number I don't even recognize. Besides, if I hang up now, who knows when I'll get another signal?"

"Why? Where are you?"

"I'm rock climbing in Upstate New York."

"Who's with you?"

"I'm alone."

"That's dangerous. Isn't it?"

"Yes."

"So then why are you doing it?"

"I have no idea."

"Look, it's obvious that you're tormenting yourself like this to take your mind off of what's going on with your girlfriend. The problem is that you could wind up killing yourself in the process. Wouldn't it just be easier to try to work things out with her or just call it quits?"

"Neither option would work, because she's nuts. Trust me when I tell you, in another twenty years she'll be her mother."

Clint chuckled.

"Well, you know the old saying. In twenty years, they all end up morphing into their mothers."

"Please don't taunt the wretched."

"Trust me, I'm not! You're doing it all to yourself. Just think though, if every man broke up with the woman he loved because he thought her mother was a hot mess, the human race would have died out hundreds of thousands of years ago."

Jordan chuckled.

"Be serious."

"I am being serious. You know, if you make an anagram out of the word 'mother in law' you end up spelling 'woman Hitler'."

"Please tell me that you didn't sit down one day in order to figure that out."

"Actually, Laurie did... the day after she met my mother."

They both laughed.

"Here's the thing. Mother or no mother, last night when we were arguing, I gently reached over to whisk a stray hair out of her eyes and she reacted by putting me into a headlock. Now if that's not nutty I don't know what is."

Clint chuckled.

"Hmmm, she sounds like a real little wild cat."

"Plus, our age difference doesn't help. At first I thought it wouldn't matter, but the whole thing's become too much."

"Well, people are like wine. We all start out immature, but then we improve with age. Remember, 'Love Conquers All', but only when we let it."

"Do you really believe that?"

"With all my heart. Otherwise I wouldn't be getting married next week. You're still coming to the wedding, right?"

"Yes! I'm looking forward to it."

"Good. Me too. Now in the meantime, slow down."

"Slow down?

"Yes. Happiness is trying to catch up with you. Why don't you just surrender and let it?"

"But Clint, why do you care so much about whether I go back with her or not?"

"Because, I happen to know exactly how shut down you were before you met her and I can see that your whole life has opened up since then and personally, I'd like to see it stay that way. That's why."

Jordan thanked him and they said their good byes. Afterwards, Jordan checked his voice mail.

"Hello Jordan, this is Warren Lindsay, your father's solicitor. I'm phoning you with regard to your father's estate. I hope you get this message and return my call."

He left his number and asked Jordan to return his call as soon as possible.

Jordan replayed the message, took a deep breath and hit the redial button

"Hello, it's Jordan, returning your call. Is everything all right?"

"I'm so sorry to have to give you this news, Jordan, but your father and his wife, Ella, were killed in a common disaster. They were en route to Luxembourg on business this morning and the engine on their aircraft failed. Their bodies were found late this afternoon."

"Does any one know what caused the engine to fail?"

"Investigators haven't finished inspecting the wreckage, so no one has all the details as yet. From what I can gather, your father was able to make contact with the tower right before the end, though."

Jordan shook his head.

"I'm having such a hard time processing this."

"I can only imagine. I need to let you know that I drafted both of their Wills right after their wedding. In spite of your heartbreaking departure, with the exception of a few bequests to certain people in your father's employ, you are now the sole heir to an estate in excess of 76 million pounds."

"Well, it's a holiday over here and I'm in the mountains right now, but I'll make arrangements to return first thing tomorrow morning."

"Good. Once you get your flight information, contact me with the details and I'll collect you at the airport myself. In the meantime, do your best to let go of any hard feelings."

"I will."

"What's done is done. In the end, love is the only thing that matters. In fact,"—

The wind blew, the call got dropped and Jordan was unable to get another signal. He shrugged, stashed the cell phone in his pocket and stood there, shivering and staring into space.

CHAPTER ONE HUNDRED FIFTEEN
MEMORIES

Jordan said a little prayer for his father and Ella and thought about his childhood, growing up under the mist of a gray Scottish sky. He could taste the sweet, damp air in his food and he felt it in his clothes. He was lucky, however, because he grew up in material comfort, which colored his early perceptions of how the world worked.

One of his earliest memories came to mind. He couldn't have been more than four years old at the time. He was angry with his father, because he had found a photograph of a woman in a sterling silver frame. The woman was beautiful and she wore a diamond necklace. When Jordan inquired about her, his father explained that she was Jordan's mother. He went on to say what a wonderful woman she was and that he regretted having lost her when Jordan was two years old.

When Jordan asked how she "got lost", his father refused to discuss it, so Jordan decided to run away and find her. When he ran out the door, his father chased him and when his father got close enough to scoop him up, Jordan rolled down a hill. The gatekeeper caught Jordan at the bottom of the hill, dusted him off and returned him to his father. Once they were inside the house, his father questioned him.

"Why must you always run away whenever you don't get exactly what you want?"

"Because I only like it when I do get what I want," Jordan answered.

"Well it never suited any one to be that stubborn, you know," his father said.

Jordan was a teenager by the time he discovered that his mother wasn't "lost", but that she had actually died. He never understood why his father felt the need to be so cryptic.

Jordan then pondered his last encounter in Scotland. With his studies complete, Jordan had hopes of proposing to his girlfriend. He walked arm in arm with her through the lush gardens and wooden trails on his family's estate. Colorful blossoms swayed in the cool breeze. Dappled sunlight filtered through an ancient weeping willow tree and they stopped to rest. To him, she was every bit as graceful than the deer that grazed in the distance. Her back formed a silhouette against the wrought iron fence that surrounded the estate. He took a deep breath, clasped her hands and knelt.

"You're the most marvelous woman in the world. I love you more than words can ever say. Will you marry me?"

She pulled him to his feet.

"Oh Jordan, I've been trying to figure out the right way to tell you something for the past few days and I still don't know don't know how to go about it. I know how hard it will be for you to accept this, but the truth is that I can't marry you."

Jordan turned ghostly white.

"Why not?"

She shook her head.

"Because there's someone else."

Jordan looked shocked.

"Who is it, Ella?"

"Your father, Jordan. Believe me when I tell you that we never set out to fall in love and of course neither of us ever wanted to hurt you. It's just that sometimes things happen."

"You never wanted to hurt me? Well, you haven't hurt me. You've managed to devastate me."

The despair in his voice rang out into the woods. The deer stopped grazing and looked up at them. Ella reached under her high lace collar, pulled a diamond necklace out from under it and held it out to him. Jordan gasped. It was the same necklace that his mother had worn in the picture with the sterling frame. He reached out to grab it, but before he could, she turned away from him and ran into the house. Once she was gone, the deer resumed their grazing.

A few days later he set sail for the United States, where he applied for a job teaching at a college in Florida. Clint, the Department Chair hired him on the spot. In spite of that, he was able to drown out the memory of Ella's betrayal.

CHAPTER ONE HUNDRED SIXTEEN
CHECK OUT TIME

The air turned cold just as the last vestiges of sunlight sunk beneath the peaks. Jordan snapped out of his reverie and began his long trek downward. By the time he returned to his car, his hands were numb from the cold. He slung off his rucksack, stowed it in the trunk and got behind the wheel. He cranked up the heat, blew on his hands to warm them and returned to the inn as if he were driving on automatic pilot. When he informed the desk clerk that he needed to check out right away, the clerk looked surprised.

"Oh, I'm sorry to hear that. Is everything all right?"

Jordan shook his head.

"Unfortunately, there's been a family emergency."

The clerk checked Jordan out and filled out another guest pass, so that Jordan could return in the future. Jordan thanked him and inquired about the quickest route back to New York City.

"It's pretty straightforward. Turn right out of our driveway onto Route 35. Then stay on Route 35 until you see a sign directing you to The Taconic State Parkway Southbound."

Jordan nodded.

"Thank you. Then I just take that?"

"Yes and stay on it, until you see the signs for New York City. Just remember, as long as you keep heading Southbound you'll be fine."

Jordan thanked him again and went up to his room to pack. Before he left, he decided to return Pattie's call. He reached her voicemail and left a message stating that he wanted to meet with her later that evening. Then he asked her to call him back as soon as possible.

CHAPTER ONE HUNDRED SEVENTEEN
WHERE IS SHE?

Ryan and his mother were the last two people left at the dinner table. Ryan ate the last bite of his pie a la mode and finished his coffee.

"I guess Pattie decided not to show up after all," his mother said.

Ryan nodded.

"I guess not and what worries me is that this isn't like her at all.

"Well, maybe you should call her and find out what happened."

Ryan nodded.

"You're right."

He stood, reached in his pocket for his cell phone and frowned. He patted all of his pockets, searched the dining room and then went into the kitchen to look for it. When he couldn't find it, he searched the living room. Finally, he went upstairs and looked for it in his own apartment. When he realized that it wasn't there either, he returned to his parents' apartment and dialed his number from their landline. When he couldn't hear it ringing, he hung up and used his parents' landline to call Pattie. When she didn't pick up, he hung up without leaving a message. Then he called Edie's landline.

CHAPTER ONE HUNDRED EIGHTEEN
DO OVER

Lou, Chet and Edie sat around the dining room table, ignoring the shards and slivers of glass on the sideboard and floor. Just as Lou ate the last forkful of his pumpkin pie, the old, red dial phone in the kitchen rang. He stood and ran into the kitchen to answer it. Edie and Chet followed him.

"If that's Pattie tell her to get her ass back over here and clean up this mess," Edie brayed. Her speech was more slurred than ever.

Lou held his hand up to quiet her and picked up the call. A few seconds later, he cupped his hand over the mouthpiece.

"It's only Ryan," he whispered.

Edie sighed.

"Sheesh what a stooge! I wonder what excuse she told him to give us this time!"

Unlike Lou's discreet whisper, Edie's tone was loud and belligerent.

"Tell your Mother that the stooge hasn't heard from Pattie since early this morning and he can't reach her on her cell phone either, so now the stooge is worried," Ryan said.

"Well, I don't know what to tell you. She was here earlier but she left several hours ago," Lou said.

"That's weird. Where did she go?"

"She didn't say."

Lou's cell phone rang.

"I'll bet that's her now," Edie brayed.

Lou hung up on Ryan and picked up his call.

"Hello, Anwald? This is Lieutenant Purdy. I'm at the precinct."

"Hello Lieutenant Purdy. Happy Thanksgiving."

"Thanks. You too. Sorry to disturb you, but I read your report and you made it sound like you had the Christie Street case all wrapped up," he said.

Lou beamed.

"Yes and I'm proud to say that I even solved a kidnapping!"

"Yeah well, that was in the past."

Lou frowned and scratched his head.

"Excuse me?"

"Well, the perp's back out of his cage and the original complainant called me to report that when she returned from Thanksgiving dinner at her son's house, the sidewalk along Christie Street was filled to the brim with more blood than ever."

"How could that have happened?"

"You tell me. Someone with the last name of 'Anwald' arranged for the perp's bail. Any relation?"

"What's the first name?"

"Pattie."

"That's my sister."

"Well that means we've got a problem. I can't keep you on the case. It disturbs me to think that any relative of yours could even be found consorting with a character like that."

"Well, she's a lawyer over at Legal Aid."

"I guess that makes her the perp's attorney then. I still have to take you off the case, though."

Lou shook his head.

"Why?

"Conflict of interest," Lieutenant Purdy said.

When he hung up on Lou, Lou sighed and snapped his phone shut.

"Pattie strikes again!"

"Why? What did she do this time?" Edie asked.

"You know my collar from this morning?"

"Yeah," Edie said.

"Well, she bailed out my perp and now I'm off the case."

Edie gasped and shook her head

"You mean the guy who called her? You're kidding!"

"I wish I were."

Edie lit a cigarette with a plain black plastic lighter and exhaled the first puff in Chet's face. Chet sniffed and coughed.

"That God damn son of a bitch! This is outrageous! I'll bet she did that on purpose to torpedo you," Edie said.

"Yeah. She is really getting out of control sticking her nose where it doesn't belong. By the way, I forgot to mention that when she left here earlier, she took your switchblade," Chet said.

"She probably gave it to that Limey. Now he's got your switchblade AND my lighter," Edie said.

"You know, between having your case blown and your evidence stolen, you're liable to end up getting busted back down to a uniform," Chet said.

"My name will end up being mud when Lieutenant Purdy finds out that I never even logged the switchblade into evidence. Anyway, the victim is a twelve-year-old kid and I promised him that I'd visit him at the hospital tonight, so if you don't mind, I'd love to take him a little of our Thanksgiving dinner."

"OK, I'll do it, but you're getting almost as bad as Pattie worrying about these stray little birds with broken wings. I'm not the International Red Cross you know," Edie said.

She put a Thanksgiving dinner together, added a generous slice of her homemade pumpkin pie and wrapped it.

"Here you go," she said, as she packed it into a shopping bag and handed it to Lou.

"You know what you should do? Stop by the precinct and pick up some baseball paraphernalia to give to the kid," Chet said.

Lou nodded.

"That's a good idea."

"And stop stop back here when you get home tonight. I'll try not to pass out," Edie said.

He gave her a kiss on the cheek.

"OK," he said, as he picked up the bag and left.

CHAPTER ONE HUNDRED NINETEEN
HOSPITAL ROOM

Justin Edwards was propped up in bed in a private room in the pediatric wing at the hospital. He was hooked up to an Intravenous Drip and luxuriating in a fluffy heating blanket. The television was on, but the volume was muted so that he could chat with his visitors, Bonnie and Thomas. Bonnie's hair was now a natural honey blonde color. All traces of her previous bleach were gone. She wore blue jeans, a white pullover and white clogs. Her makeup consisted of a light coat of mascara and the faintest hint of peach colored lip gloss. She had gained some weight but she was curvy, not fat. Thomas looked the same as ever.

"Don't worry. The nightmare is over. Everything will eventually work itself out and the memories will soon fade," Bonnie said.

Thomas nodded.

"Bonnie's right. From now on, things will just keep on getting better and better. You'll see."

"Plus, you know we're all here for you," Bonnie said, pointing to the doorway where April Higgins stood chatting with Justin's ACS social worker, a counselor from the hospital's Assault Response Team and the two uniformed police officers who were assigned to guard Justin.

"I think this IV is making me woozy," Justin said. He smiled at Bonnie and Thomas.

"I remember when I was in the hospital. I had an IV just like that. It could have been a cool feeling, except I kept trying to fight it."

"Well, I'm going to fight it too. I'm afraid that if I go to sleep I'll wake up and find out that being rescued was only a dream."

"It's OK, Justin. It wasn't a dream. You can doze off and we'll all still be here," April called out.

"You even have twenty-four-hour protection," Justin's Social Worker added.

"That makes me feel important," Justin said.

"Well, you are important," April said.

"I never thought I'd see the day when I'd actually be relieved to see cops," Thomas said.

The elevator door opened and Lou walked down the hall toward Justin's room. When he flashed his badge, the two uniformed officers nodded and let him through. He walked right over to Justin and smiled.

"Bonnie and Thomas, this is the detective I was telling you about," Justin said.

Bonnie smiled.

"Hi. It's nice to meet you," she said.

Thomas tugged on Bonnie's shirt and pulled her toward the doorway.

"Uh, we'll let you two talk in private," he said.

"Thanks kids," Lou said.

As soon as Bonnie and Thomas left, Lou removed a big serving container from the shopping bag and uncovered it. Justin smiled when he saw the massive turkey leg, stuffing and mashed potatoes that were smothered in a smooth turkey gravy. He also noticed the peas, creamed onions and Edie's special homemade cranberry sauce.

"Wow! I didn't even realize that it was Thanksgiving until I got to the emergency room," Justin said.

When the nurse's aide walked into the room, Lou asked her where he could heat the dinner.

"I can nuke it for you," she offered.

"Can I eat the pie now while I wait?" Justin asked.

"I don't think that's such a great idea. Why don't you wait and have it after your dinner?"

"OK."

"I notice you have the football game on."

Justin nodded.

"I'm not really paying attention to it though. I can turn it off if you want me to."

Lou smiled.

"It's not a problem. Do you like football?"

Justin nodded.

"Yes."

"Do you like baseball too?"

"Even more so."

"Good, because this is for you," he said, as he handed the other shopping bag to Justin.

Justin reached inside and pulled out a brand-new catcher's mitt. He held it up to his nose and ran his fingers over it.

"Wow. Nothing feels or smells as great as a new mitt," he said.

Lou nodded.

"Agreed."

Justin reached into the bag again, pulled out a baseball and read the autograph.

"Oh, my God! Derek Jeter! Thank you so much."

Lou smiled.

"My pleasure."

"I don't mean just for this, but for saving my life."

A doctor walked in and Lou asked to speak to him out in the hallway.

"Who are you?" The doctor asked, defensively.

When Lou flashed his badge, and explained that he was the detective who found Justin, the doctor dropped his guard and shook his hand.

"Nice work detective," he said as they passed the group in the doorway and stepped out into the hall.

"I know I should have asked you first, but I hope it's OK for Justin to have some solid food. My mother made it herself," Lou said.

"Well, he was pretty dehydrated when he first arrived in the ER and his fever was high, but since he's doing well, I suppose we can give it a try."

"Thanks. The nurse's aide is heating it up as we speak."

"If it's the one I think it is, she'll probably eat it herself," the doctor said.

They both chuckled.

"Is Justin in any pain?" Lou asked.

"Not really. He's mildly sedated though. His vital signs are stable, but in spite of that he's still got some serious physical and emotional issues."

Lou nodded.

"I can imagine. His condition was unspeakable."

The doctor nodded.

"His feet and ankles are covered in mouse bites, some of which are infected. Plus, he's got Parvo."

Lou squinted.

"Parvo! I thought only dogs got that."

The doctor shook his head.

"A common misconception. People can get it too and what's even worse, is that we had to start him on a course of rabies shots."

Lou winced.

"I hear they're the most excruciating thing on earth. Don't they go directly into the stomach or something?"

"Not so much anymore, since the technology has improved. Now they're just regular injections in the arm. Not that they're a walk in the park or anything, but at least they're better than they used to be."

"May I have your card? I'll need it in order to complete my report," Lou said.

"Ditto."

The nurse's aide walked past Lou and the doctor as they exchanged cards and she served Justin his Thanksgiving dinner.

"Let me go check on him now, so that he can eat his dinner while it's still warm. I still have other patients to see. It's been like a three-ring circus around this place ever since seven o'clock this morning."

Lou nodded.

"Unfortunately, I can relate. No rest for the weary," he said.

He joined the group in the doorway until the doctor left. Then he returned to Justin's bedside. Justin was already eating. The baseball was cupped inside the mitt on the bed next to him.

"This is so delicious. It even has the perfect amount of salt and pepper," Justin said.

Lou smiled.

"Well, I'm glad you like it. I'll let my mother know. By the way, I expect to get together with you to play catch once you get out of here."

He removed another card from his wallet and stuck it in the mitt. Justin picked it up and read it.

"Your last name is Anwald?"

Lou nodded.

"Yup."

Justin smiled, just as Bonnie and Thomas returned.

"What a coincidence. My lawyer's name is Anwald too. Pattie Anwald," Justin said.

"Pattie Anwald is our lawyer too!" Bonnie said.

"She's the best lawyer ever," Thomas said.

"She's my sister," Lou said.

"Really?" April called out from across the room.

Lou nodded.

"Yes!"

"How ironic. Pattie's been worried sick about Justin for these past six months. I left her a voice mail to let her know that he's been found and that he's basically OK, but she hasn't gotten back to me yet, which is really out of character for her."

"Pattie was worried about me?" Justin asked.

April nodded.

"God yes."

Justin smiled.

"You know what? My kidnapper told me that no one cared enough about me to even bother looking for me."

"Well, he was lying, because as you can see, a lot of wonderful people care a great deal about you," April said.

Bonnie smiled.

"That's right Justin. We all care about you. You and Thomas are like the brothers I never had."

"Thank you. You guys are like my brother and sister too. Speaking of sisters, Detective Anwald, when you see your sister again, please give her a hug for me," Justin said.

Lou nodded and gave Justin the thumbs up sign.

"I haven't seen her since this afternoon. Her cell phone was broken, so she probably hasn't been able to pick up her messages yet, but the second I see her I'll give her the good news. I'm sure she'll come running right over here and hug you in person when she finds out," Lou said.

On that upbeat note, he waved good bye, walked down the hall and waited for the elevator. He kept wondering where Pattie was and he prayed that she wasn't in any danger. With that lunatic LeRoux back on the streets anything could have happened to her. He regretted losing his cool and breaking her cell phone. When the elevator door opened, he got in and rode down to the lobby alone. Once he got outside, he stared into the cold dark night and knew that he had to find Pattie, even if it meant asking Lieutenant Purdy to issue an All Points Bulletin.

CHAPTER ONE HUNDRED TWENTY
CAN'T FIND MY WAY HOME

The journey back to the city took a lot longer than Jordan expected. First of all, the shock of suddenly losing his father took its toll on his nervous system, so he wasn't thinking clearly. Also, visibility was terrible. Blinding sheets of rain slowed him down to a near crawl and street lights were few and far between. The wet roads shone like patent leather in the dark. Although he did his best to follow the desk clerk's directions, he somehow managed to miss the entrance ramp to the Taconic State Parkway. Last, but not least, Jordan was starting to develop a nervous feeling about Pattie. He was concerned about her, yet he couldn't pinpoint exactly why.

After about an hour of driving southbound on Route 35, the rain stopped and he saw a sign that read "Welcome to Peekskill." That's when he realized that he was lost. He drove past a street called "Armstrong Avenue". Ordinarily such a sign would have piqued his curiosity, but he knew that there was no time to stop and explore it tonight. The only time he slowed down was when he approached a Presbyterian Church that reminded him of his own church back in Scotland. The sign on it read "Enter to Worship - Linger to Pray - Depart to Serve". Since it looked as if it was still lit up, he got out of the car and tried the door. An old man opened it and greeted him with a smile.

"You're late, my son. The service ended hours ago."

"I stopped in because I need to get back to New York City as soon as possible and I seem to have lost my way."

The old man nodded.

"I can tell by your accent that you're a long way from home."

"Yes, I am."

"Ah well, you're not as lost as you think. Just turn left out of the driveway and continue Southward on Route 35. Right after you pass the reservoir you'll see the sign for Route 684 Southbound."

Jordan frowned.

"I thought I was supposed to take something called the Taconic Parkway."

"You probably were, but since you already passed it and you've gone too far South, you can't turn back now. Just stay on the route you're on and take 684 and you'll be fine. May God bless you and light your way."

Jordan thanked him and returned to his car. He tried to call Pattie, but he reached her voice mail again. This seemed odd to him, which compounded the gnawing he felt in the pit of his stomach. He was beginning to wonder whether Pattie was in some kind of trouble and when he tried to shake off the feeling, he realized that he couldn't.

CHAPTER ONE HUNDRED TWENTY-ONE
ON THE ROAD AGAIN

After an hour or so of driving, Willie knew that he had to ditch the car as soon as possible. He simply couldn't stand it anymore. The car smelled like someone had set off a stink bomb in it. As awful as Leland had smelled during his lifetime, he paled in comparison to the stench of his butchered remains. What made matters worse was that every few minutes, a semi congealed blood clot plopped down from the ceiling. It was so vile that Willie knew he would never be able to clean it and he also knew that he was in no position to ask anyone else to do so either. All that blood would raise too many questions that he knew he wouldn't want to answer. Plus, the fact that the car belonged to an attorney who was about to be discovered among the missing didn't enhance anything. Oh, how he hated lawyers, especially this bitch lawyer of Leland's. He cursed Leland under his breath and spat on him. He was distraught at the idea of having lost not one, but two cars in less than twenty four hours. He had no idea how he would get back home to Moriah without a car. He figured he would just have to go on his luck until the answer revealed itself.

As he continued to drive northward on Route 684, he ran into rain. Visibility was poor, but the upside was that no one could see him either. When he pulled over to figure out which buttons controlled the windshield wipers, he spotted the sign for a reservoir. It's not Lake Champlain, but it would just have to do, he told himself, as he followed the sign. He noticed that the car behind him was following him too closely, which triggered his paranoia.

The reservoir turned out to be surprisingly accessible. He glimpsed in the rearview mirror. At least the car behind him was gone. He felt confident, since there were no signs of life and no cameras like the ones that had recently sprouted up all over New York City. He made his way past several canoes that had been chained to trees and a white sign whose forbidding black letters read "Do Not Trespass." He pulled all the way into the parking lot and backed the car as close to the reservoir as he could. He fumbled around with the buttons, until he figured out how to open the windows, the sunroof and the hatchback. Then he turned the motor off.

Grateful that it had finally stopped raining and that the reservoir had no lights, he left the key in the ignition, opened the door and peered out. He was alone, so he got out and stretched. Enduring the chill, he inhaled the fierce, crisp, fresh air. He loved the distinctively magical feeling that country air offered up in the fall and he didn't realize until this moment just how much he had missed it. It reminded him of how wonderful the earth smelled in Moriah right after a nice, long rain bath. He held the air down in his lungs for as long as he could.

He finally exhaled. Then he walked over to the embankment and looked into the watery depths. The reservoir was so black that he couldn't even see his reflection. He walked along the coping. After a few minutes, he stopped, removed his shoes and emptied his pockets. Keeping his clothes on, he stuffed Pattie's jewelry into his shoes and inched down the embankment until he reached the water. Then he took the plunge. Even though the water felt chilly to him, it was still warmer than the air.

He inhaled deeply, swam all the way to the bottom and forced himself to remain there for as long as he could, so that he could massage the blood, gore and traces of Leland's DNA out of his hair, face, clothes and body. A school of eels and elvers, slithered around him. The elvers were as clear as glass. When an eel bit his thumb, he panicked. His heart pounded as the eel continued to pull at his thumb. He struggled back up to the surface, dragging the eel with him. When his face hit the air, he exhaled with a violent force, raised his arm and shook the eel until it finally flew off of him and splashed back into the water. He fought to regain his breath as he did a slow breast stroke over to the edge of the reservoir. He clung to the coping for a few minutes before he climbed out. Then he carefully worked his way up the slippery embankment, shivering the entire time.

When he reached the top of the embankment, he peered around again to make sure that no one was watching him. Wishing he had a towel, he removed his wet socks, wrung them out and stuffed them into his pocket. He stuffed Pattie's jewelry into the other pocket, touched his earlobe to make sure that Justin's diamond was still in place and put his shoes on. His thumb continued to hurt, but since there was nothing he could do about it, he ignored it and went about covering his tracks. He picked up a tree branch that still had several dried leaves on it and he used it to sweep away his footprints as he walked backwards toward the car.

When he reached the car, he took a deep breath, glanced around to ensure that the coast was still clear and opened the door. Careful not to get any blood on him, he reached in, yanked the switchblade out of Leland's hand and wiped it clean on the back seat. Then he stuffed it in his pocket and started the engine. Annoyed by the slapping of the windshield wiper, he randomly pushed whatever buttons he thought would turn it off and inadvertently turned the headlights on instead. Leaving the motor running, he shifted the car into reverse, released the hand brake and closed the door. He used the outside mirror as leverage to help him push the car down the embankment. He watched it slide down the slippery slope, rear end first. The hatch back opened and Pattie tumbled out, with her maroon velvet dress billowing around her. It formed a parachute effect which kept her afloat. Her chin looked like a buoy, as it listlessly bobbed on the surface of the water. The rear end of the car jack knifed and slid past her right before it made contact with the water. Its nose stuck out of the water, as its rear end sank. Eventually, the nose descended and the headlights dimmed to a brown color. They sizzled, popped and burned out right before the nose sank completely.

Willie smiled. Getting these two pests to their final dumping grounds was an important accomplishment and the jewelry wasn't half bad either. Maybe now I can finally drown out my old man's voice when it keeps putting me down and telling me that I'll never amount to anything.

He wiped his hands on his pants, saluted the reservoir and turned toward the exit. He tucked his head down, so as not to be seen and without so much as a backward glance, he hurried out past the gate, onto the street. When he saw a sign that pointed to the nearby train station, he knew that he was destined to follow it.

When he arrived at the train station, the ticket office was closed, but he checked the map and train schedule to figure out the fastest route back to Moriah. He stood, rubbing his arms under the heat lamps on the platform and waited for the train that would take him home.

CHAPTER ONE HUNDRED TWENTY-TWO
ROCK BOTTOM

The cold air on Pattie's face and the pain from the bite on her left shoulder hurt her enough to blast through the depths of her concussion and force her to regain consciousness. She stirred, shook her head and blinked several times before coming to, completely. Her heart pounded and she could barely breathe. She gazed around in the pitch-black night, confused and clueless as to where she was and why she was surrounded by water. Listening to the void, she could never remember a time when the world had been this quiet.

Once her dress became waterlogged, its weight began to pull her down. She took a deep breath and pinched her nose right before the water swallowed her. The deeper she sank, the more she tried to struggle, but she was so exhausted, that she could no longer keep up the fight. She heard a thud, as a gigantic wall of water banged into her, propelling her body downwards, until her tailbone smashed onto the concrete floor of the reservoir. It hurt so much, that she actually saw stars for the second time that day. Her agony was compounded by the shock of watching a car just like hers land in the water right next to her.

Blood streamed from the windows, hatchback and sunroof and diffused into the water. Pattie felt a tickling sensation on her legs. She was afraid to turn around, yet she was more afraid not to. Once she did, she realized that a school of hungry trout was swimming past her to get to the blood. When she spotted Leland LeRoux's head floating past her, she wondered whether this was just another one of her nightmares. She gasped in horror when the trout zoomed in on it to devour it. As she did, she breathed in a mouthful of water. Mercifully, she blew it back out before she choked on it. She continued to hold her breath, as she watched a school of eels and elvers join the feeding frenzy. Like voracious monsters, the bigger members of the trout and eel communities surrounded their quarry. They cooperated with each other pulling and tearing, while at the same time blocking the elvers and smaller trout from getting anywhere near it.

How similar they are to humans, she thought, as she turned away from the macabre show.

She could no longer hold her breath, which caused her to panic. Fortunately, she realized that giving in to her terror would only lead to drowning, so she did her best to remain calm. She thought about everything she learned in judo class about holding one's breath and then she remembered a strange remark about hitting rock bottom and using it to propel herself upward from there. She tried it and when it worked, her head popped out of the water. She exhaled with a force so great, it felt as if her lungs were on fire. They ached even more when she inhaled her next supply of clean, cold air.

She did her best to stay afloat by forcing her tired, aching body to alternate between dog paddling and treading water. In spite of her efforts, she still felt as though something was pulling her down. She regretted that she never bothered to learn how to swim. A baseball cap floated past her, but she ignored it, because she was more concerned about finding a way out of the water. She dog paddled over to what she hoped was the water's edge and when she reached it, she clung to it for dear life with both hands, while she struggled to catch her breath.

Even after her breathing had stabilized, she could not stop wheezing. She used her upper body strength to pull herself up onto the coping and when she finally made it to solid ground, the frosty air laced into her chapped face, body and hair. She felt chilled right to her bone marrow. She shivered and her teeth chattered as she steeled herself against the cold, wishing she had a towel.

A sour taste filled her mouth and her skin felt clammy. In addition to her migraine headache, another agonizing wave of pain gripped her, zigzagging from the bump on her head, to her right ear drum, down to the bite on her left shoulder and to her tailbone. From there it radiated down the scratches on her thighs and it didn't stop until he reached the soles of her feet. She tried to shake it off by walking, but her legs were so wobbly that she stumbled. She winced when her tailbone hit the ground for the second time that day. Feeling defeated and too exhausted to fight her way back to her feet, she sat there and tried to find a position that did not trigger more pain in her tailbone. She glanced down at her torn bodice and sighed when she saw that her fishnet pantyhose and thong were slung around her knees. She realized they were what had been pulling her down in the water. She removed her wet boots and slowly traced her fingers over them. They were completely ruined.

Below the surface of her physical pain was a layer of mental anguish and emotional despair. A floodgate of tears formed in her puffy, red eyes. At first, she choked them back, but eventually they tumbled down her cheeks in black rivulets. She watched them drip down onto her chest, accompanied by deep sobs that shot forth from the bottom of her soul. They rang out into the empty air. Her entire body heaved and shook with each sob and splotches and welts popped up, covering her face, neck and chest. She continued to sob for several minutes until she wrung every tear from her body. She sat there drained and buried beneath layers of smeared lipstick, mascara and eye liner.

Eventually she galvanized herself into action. She removed her wet fish net panty hose and flung them to the ground in disgust. Leaving her sopping wet thong in place, she stuffed her wet, cold feet back into her soggy boots. Stubbornly ignoring the aches that scourged her body, she painstakingly laced them up.

She sighed, swallowed hard and cleared her throat. She fought her way up to a standing position. It felt like an eternity before she completed her struggle. When she did, she looked around in an attempt to get her bearings, but she still had no idea where she was. All vestiges of light were gone, leaving only a velvety night sky and one twinkling star to surround her. Once her eyes had adjusted to the darkness, she spotted what she hoped was an exit. Her tiny ankles wobbled in protest, as she forced herself to stagger toward it. Her boots squished with every painful baby step she took, but she continued to put one foot in front of the other, as she winced, trembled and shivered all the way. By the time she finally made it out onto the street, the only sign of life was the sound of a train whistle riding on the wind, as it left a nearby station.

CHAPTER ONE HUNDRED TWENTY-THREE
PATTIE'S BEST DEAL

Jordan drove through the rain at a snail's pace. Just as he reached the reservoir, the rain tapered off, only to be replaced by the fog that was settling in. A sign lay beyond the traffic light in the distance. He squinted and sighed with relief when he read that it was the sign for Route 684. The traffic light turned yellow, so he stopped and checked his messages. When there was still no word from Pattie, he began to worry. He glanced in the rearview mirror and frowned at the wild man with the bleary eyes who stared back at him. He could hardly believe that it was his own reflection. He raked his fingers through his hair in an attempt to tame it. When he realized that the damp weather had made that impossible, he shook his head and gave up.

He glanced out. The only other soul in sight was a frail look-ing waif who had just emerged from the pitch-black night into the glow of an overhanging street lamp. She slowly meandered through the mist like some tragic specter that had been sentenced to an afterlife of sleepwalking. With her petite frame and long, dark hair, she bore an uncanny resemblance to Pattie. At first Jordan's heart skipped a beat, but then he calmed himself, by reminding himself that it couldn't possibly be her. She had made it painstakingly clear that she wouldn't be caught dead this far away from New York City. On the other hand, she was soaked to the bone, just like Pattie and underdressed for the elements, just like Pattie. Whoever she was, she was a girl in trouble, so when the light turned green, he pulled the car over to the curb and inched alongside her.

Pattie's heart nearly stopped.

Someone wants me dead. First, they tried to drown me and when that didn't work, they followed me here to finish me off.

She stopped under the street light and used its pale sheen to help her memorize the license plate number, in case she somehow managed to survive. Although Jordan could scarcely believe his eyes, he recognized her the second it illuminated her face. He was upset, because her drenched condition and smeared makeup confirmed his suspicions that something was wrong. He slammed on the brakes, opened the door and bolted out of the car.

Pattie tried to jog away from him, but due to her weakened state and the condition of her boots, it didn't take Jordan very long to catch up with her. When he did, he jogged in front of her and stopped her. He gasped when he saw her dull, enormous pupils. There was no doubt about it. She was in a state of shock.

"Pattie?"

She nodded vaguely. She was shaking, her teeth were chattering and her pinched lips looked blue around the edges. Plus, her lungs rattled and wheezed every time she breathed.

"Jordan?" Her throat was so dry that her voice cracked. Even she couldn't believe how raspy she sounded.

He nodded.

"Yes, love."

"Please tell me that you weren't the one who tried to poison my mother's drinking water and then drown me in it."

He shook his head.

"Of course not, Pattie. You ought to know by now that I would never do such a thing.

"I know, but people on the lam often engage in acts of desperation."

He squinted at her and shook his head.

"I'm not on the lam. Are you?"

"Should I be? Someone is after me and they're trying to finish me off and if you're not in on it, they may be after us both, for all I know."

"Pattie, can I touch your forehead, to see whether you have a fever?"

She nodded.

"Sure, although I don't know how that could be possible, when I'm freezing to death."

He placed his hand on her forehead and checked her pulse.

"Pattie, you're in a state of shock. You may even be delirious. I've got to get you to a hospital," he said, as he took his jacket off and wrapped it around her.

She shook her head.

"Look, I'm not in a state of shock. It's just that an eagle swooped down on me from out of nowhere and bit my shoulder and then someone poisoned my mother's drinking water and tried to drown me in it. That's all I know."

He decided that it was useless to try to reason with her in her current condition, but he didn't want to patronize her either, so he simply nodded and ignored her remarks.

"Once we're in the car, I have another blanket I can wrap you in, plus I can crank up the heat."

"Thank you, Jordan," she said.

She showed him the bump on her head and the bite on her shoulder and he winced at the sight of them.

"Oh Pattie, I'm so sorry. You were right when you told me that I run away from everything unpleasant and I need you to know that you weren't the first one to tell me that. My father said it too."

She looked into his eyes.

"I know you didn't mean to hurt me, but running away every time you don't get your way is really just not cool, especially when I stand there pleading with you not to go."

"I did try to call you a number of times today, but you never picked up my calls."

"I couldn't, because the eagle made off with my cell phone and took it with him when he flew over a double rainbow."

He closed his eyes, stepped forward and pulled her toward him.

"Oh, Pattie, I love you so much."

"I love you too."

"Thank God, because I really don't want to lose you."

"If you really mean it, then promise me you'll never run away from me again, because I just don't think that I would ever be able to stand it."

He nodded.

"I promise you that I will never run away from you again. Do we have a Deal?"

She smiled and nodded.

"Yes, oh yes. The best deal ever."

He stroked the long strands of wet hair that hung like icicles down her back and then pointed to the sign for Route 684.

"I think that's the road that will lead us out of here. Somehow, we'll find a way to send for your car," he whispered.

She shook her head.

"No, We can't. It's back there, under a ton of water."

He nodded vaguely, kissed her cheek and ushered her out of the darkness.

THE END

BIOGRAPHY IN A NUTSHELL

Dawn Dittmar escaped from the law, but don't worry—she's not a fugitive. After seventeen years as an attorney, she changed careers to work as a writer, a teacher and a public speaker. Dawn currently teaches Astrology at Brookdale Community College's Life Long Learning Center and Ridgewood Community Schools. Dawn believes that when we tap into our creativity, it gives greater meaning to our lives. She currently lives on the Jersey Shore with her two cherished cats, Jasmine and Tajee. When she is not writing, you might find her on the beach, in a classroom or relaxing by her pool, (with a good book in hand, of course)! Pattie's Best Deal is Dawn's first novel in a series of four romantic legal thrillers. It means a great deal to her that you are reading it. Feel free to visit Dawn at Author Dawn Dittmar on Facebook or at www.Dawndittmar.com.

The cover photo for this book, "Leland's Door," was taken by John Salvi, an American artist, photographer, print maker and visionary. John has exhibited his highly imaginative and innovative art work across New York and New Jersey. Those who know John often describe him as soothing. For more information about John's heartfelt paintings and prints, please feel free to visit his website at www.Johnsalvi.net.

Bob Miller, CEO of Bob Digital, turned "Leland's Door" into a book cover. Please feel free to visit his website at Bobdigital.com.

Irene M. Zagorski took the cover photo of the author. Please feel free to visit her Facebook Page at Irene Zagorski.

CPSIA information can be obtained
at www.ICGtesting.com
Printed in the USA
FFOW02n2055040817
38338FF